THE
UNSEEN

ALSO BY ANIA AHLBORN

NOVELS

Seed

The Neighbors

The Shuddering

The Bird Eater

Within These Walls

Brother

The Devil Crept In

If You See Her

Dark Across the Bay

Good and Joyful Things

NOVELLAS

The Pretty Ones

I Call Upon Thee

Palmetto

SHORT STORIES

"The Governess" (from the collection *Other Voices, Other Tombs*)

"The Debt" (from the collection *Hex Life: Wicked New Tales of Witchery*)

COLLECTIONS

Apart in the Dark: Novellas

(featuring *The Pretty Ones* and *I Call Upon Thee*)

THE
UNSEEN

A NOVEL

ANIA AHLBORN

G

GALLERY BOOKS

New York   Amsterdam/Antwerp   London
Toronto   Sydney/Melbourne   New Delhi

G℡

Gallery Books
An Imprint of Simon & Schuster, LLC
1230 Avenue of the Americas
New York, NY 10020

This book is a work of fiction. Any references to historical events, real people, or real places are used fictitiously. Other names, characters, places, and events are products of the author's imagination, and any resemblance to actual events or places or persons, living or dead, is entirely coincidental.

First Gallery Books hardcover edition August 2025

GALLERY BOOKS and colophon are registered trademarks of Simon & Schuster, LLC

For information about special discounts for bulk purchases, please contact Simon & Schuster Special Sales at 1-866-506-1949 or business@simonandschuster.com.

The Simon & Schuster Speakers Bureau can bring authors to your live event. For more information or to book an event, contact the Simon & Schuster Speakers Bureau at 1-866-248-3049 or visit our website at www.simonspeakers.com.

Manufactured in the United States of America

10 9 8 7 6 5 4 3 2 1

Library of Congress Cataloging-in-Publication data is available.

ISBN 978-1-6680-5766-7
ISBN 978-1-6680-5768-1 (ebook)

For Marta
To our memories of youthful desert skies.

For Beebo
Your trust in the unseen shows just how brilliantly
smart you are, kid.

I knew nothing but shadows, and I thought them real.

—Oscar Wilde, *The Picture of Dorian Gray*

THE
UNSEEN

MISSING—JOHN LARUSSO

Golden, CO—A frantic search is underway for six-year-old John Larusso, a kindergarten student at Perry Elementary School, who mysteriously disappeared outside Golden.

John was last seen by his family early Monday morning when his mother, Emma, dropped him off at his bus stop on Iowa Street, blocks away from his home. Ms. Larusso watched as he boarded bus 237 at approximately 8:15 a.m. His teacher, Melissa Tiller, confirmed his presence in class, and he was later seen by the child's bus driver, Albert Finnegan, while boarding the bus after school.

Despite these confirmations, John never made it home. As John is the only student disembarking at the Iowa Street bus stop, Mr. Finnegan states he was "confused" as to why the child did not get off the bus that afternoon. "I didn't see him get off at any other stop," Mr. Finnegan recalled. "I would have noticed. John always said goodbye to me. I remember him getting on, but I have no idea where he could have gotten off."

John is described as a cheerful, energetic boy with brown hair and hazel eyes, standing about 3 feet, 9 inches tall. He was last seen wearing a blue Adidas windbreaker, a red backpack, and red-and-blue Nike Spider-Man sneakers.

The Larusso family is making a heartfelt appeal for anyone with information to come forward. "We are devastated and just want our little boy back home safely," said Ms. Larusso in a tearful plea to the Golden community.

Authorities, along with local volunteers, have launched an extensive search operation in the surrounding neighborhoods and wooded areas. They are seeking any witnesses who might have seen John after he left school along Perry Elementary School's bus route 9.

"We're doing everything we can to find John and bring him home safely," reassured Detective Mark Stevens of the Golden

Police Department. "We urge anyone with any information, no matter how small, to contact us immediately."

The community has come together in a show of unity, distributing flyers and organizing search parties to assist in the efforts to find John. Local businesses are also stepping up, offering rewards for any information leading to his safe return. "John is a great kid, and we want to see him back in our shop as soon as possible," stated Gavin McDaniels, owner of the local Mr. Frosty franchise—John's favorite ice cream spot. "Free ice cream for life goes to anyone who assists local authorities in locating our friend John."

Anyone with information about John's whereabouts is asked to contact the Golden Police Department or their local police station. The Larusso family and the entire community are hoping for a safe and swift resolution to this alarming situation.

Yolanda Evans for *The Golden Gazette*

1

ISLA

Six Weeks Before

Crouched in the garden with her hands in the soil, her head fuzzy and equilibrium a little off, Isla had escaped the house when the report had come on the TV—another missing child, this one in an adjacent county. Isla couldn't handle the news. Every newly vanished child was a reminder. Each urgent broadcast, a trigger. Another freshly pinned-up flyer, a jab at her heart. Children, missing. People's babies, possibly forever gone.

At least, she thought, *I know what happened to mine.*

I can't imagine the not knowing.

I can't imagine.

I simply can't.

Luke and August were arguing again. She could hear her husband and eldest—her only son—through the kitchen window. The breeze carried their angry voices across the backyard, into the garden, and past the insect-like buzzing in her ears. Buzzing, much like how every cell phone in the house had vibrated and chimed all at once only minutes before, a shrill alarm that never failed to stop her heart. Another Amber Alert. The third one that week. But it didn't matter how many there had been. Every single one wreaked havoc on Isla's nerves.

She glanced over her shoulder, her dark brown hair carried across her wide forehead by the wind. It was bucolic, really, that rural Colorado farmhouse she'd always wanted. It was a dream now tarnished by so much trag-edy and yelling. It seemed arguing was the only thing August knew how to do anymore, and Eden wasn't far behind. Neither of Isla's oldest children appeared to care about their freshly shattered family—the fact that she was out in the garden, yanking weeds out of the ground rather than holding a baby to her breast. She should have been sitting in a nursery, rocking back and forth the way she'd done for them all not so long ago.

Isla was usually good at handling the drama. She'd learned to tune it out. But she couldn't deal with August's theatrics since losing Adam nine months earlier, and the fresh wave of missing child alerts that seized their phones, televisions, and newspapers every other day only pushed her further into her sorrow.

Nine months. She'd been pregnant with grief for a full three trimes-ters. It felt both like forever ago and only yesterday. By now she should have started to feel better, should have started to find herself again the way she had after the others. And yet her wallow felt deeper by the day, refusing to lift. Unable to lift. As if waiting for something. But waiting for what?

Isla exhaled a breath toward the untended garden box before her. She could feel the whispered beginnings of another migraine, the kind that could take her out for days. She should have been upstairs, hiding from her thoughts, avoiding the news reports. She should have silenced her phone weeks ago when the reports had started pouring in. Or turned it off. Or given it to the dogs to destroy. She should have climbed into bed, shoved in her earplugs, and blotted out the world—the one happening both in and outside her home. But she'd fled into the sunshine instead, the garden calling to her. Because there was nothing better for a broken heart than distraction, or so she told herself.

So much to do out here.

She didn't give half a damn about the garden anymore, but it was something to do.

Isla had zeroed in on the weeds from the kitchen window while August yelled at his father to give him "a goddamn break!" Seventeen years old and already so obstinate. Him and his Punisher T-shirts, his steel-toed boots, and vintage punk noise. She had hardly recognized him when, months before, he had walked into the dining room with a shock of box-dyed black hair. Isla had cried while trying to hold a conversation with him, but he'd simply smirked at her and left the room. But two could play at that game, and as if to get back at him, Isla had pulled the same move on him only minutes before.

August and Luke had started their typical verbal jousting, and rather than standing there listening to them, Isla had pushed away from the kitchen counter and stepped out of the house. In her rush to escape, she'd left her phone, the screen door slapping the jamb behind her. *Let them fight,* she had thought. Because she didn't need to hear it. Not today. Not when every day she felt shattered, the memories eating her alive. When she felt so utterly alone.

The garden was at the far end of the property, surrounded by a picket fence. Luke had erected it when the garden had been nothing more than a fantasy—dirt and patches of crabgrass that Isla had yanked out of the ground during a sweltering week of July. Luke's fence had served as a promise that, yes, a garden would exist there one day, beautiful and vibrant, *alive,* if it was the last thing Isla achieved. August had only been three, then; wielding a huge paintbrush while donning his OshKosh B'gosh overalls and tiny toddler sandals, he made Isla laugh at how much he reminded her of Huckleberry Finn. She'd spent an entire week painting that damn thing white. Now the paint was peeling like a bad sunburn. It looked how she felt: cracked, exposed, struggling to hold on.

Eden had been two then, only a year behind August. Now, fourteen years later, the little girl who had helped Isla plant their first strawberry bushes often struck her as a stranger—another one under her roof, just like her brother. Eden, a once-sweet Peppa Pig–obsessed little girl, was now sixteen with flax-blond hair sweeping past her waist, her phone glued to the palm of her hand, and a perpetual look of irritation riding easy upon her lips. And August, the baby boy who had once hidden beneath her long skirt while she seeded carrots? He was now shouting loud enough for her to hear clear out by the tree line.

"You think you know so damn much, but you don't know a goddamn *thing*!"

She dug her fingers into the soil as if to root herself to the ground. The garden looked terrible this year. She'd once spent hours here every day, tending to herbs, tomatoes, and peas; battling aphids and beetles and an occasional outbreak of early blight. But the past nine months had been awful. Her migraines had returned. Fatigue had been a beast. The weird nightmares of her youth were worse than ever. All those ailments had left the garden a veritable weed field, wilting in the Colorado heat. The weeds swayed in the morning breeze, mocking her lack of motivation, daring her to let them continue to grow unrestrained.

We don't care what you're going through, they seemed to say. *Just give us time. A few more days . . .*

A few more days to choke the tomato plant she'd half-heartedly planted in early summer. It hadn't sprouted a single fruit all season. A few more days to snarl the strawberries that were too sour to be edible. Everything she'd sowed seemed poisoned, destined to die. The weeds would creep into the herbs, suck up their nutrients, and deprive them of sun. Finally, they'd simply grow unrestrained, choking everything out. She studied the tangle of dandelions, the curly dock and bindweed, idly wondering if she lay down between the raised beds, would the weeds slowly grow over her as well? Would their roots twist their way into her nostrils and down her throat? She pictured herself suffocating out there beyond the peeling paint of the fence, her eyes staring up past the clouds toward whatever was beyond. She imagined dying and caught herself wondering, *What would it feel like?* Had *Adam* sensed it? What about the babies before him? Had they known they would never be born?

Had Adam reached his due date, he would have been three months old this very day, just starting to babble, sucking on his tiny feet, and bursting into laughter at the most random things. August had thought the sound of tearing paper was hilarious. Eden had laughed herself into a fit while watching birds burst out of the trees. Olive laughed herself breathless at her father's singing—Raffi's "Baby Beluga" on repeat until Isla was sure her head would split. Willow had loved helium balloons tied to her ankle, and Sophie still cracked up when her dad chased her around the house with the kitchen tongs.

It was hard to think that five children were all there would be.

Five, she thought. *That's four more than most couples even want. Be grateful.*

But Isla and Luke were the kind of people who wanted a brood, never mind the impact on the cost of living, the endless diapers and whining and potty training and incessant *Bluey* episodes. They'd been over the moon when, only six months after August was born, they'd found themselves pregnant with Eden. Sweet Olive came nearly three years later with her sandy brown hair and wide smile. Then Willow three years after that: graceful, sophisticated, starkly serious. Sophie had taken them four summers more.

And after Sophie, shouldn't that have been enough? One more would have been another mouth to feed, another kid to battle at the kitchen table when they refused to do their math problems or read the book they'd been assigned. Except no . . . it hadn't been enough. It *wasn't* enough. Isla didn't feel finished. She longed for one more. But clearly some cosmic message had been received, and despite Isla's fertility, more children refused to come. And this time, after Adam, something seemed different. Final. Like it was the end.

You'd be over sixty by the time that baby graduated high school, she reminded herself, as though having a baby in her forties was the worst thing in the world. *You're done, then. It just isn't meant to be.* And yet she was ready to scream to the sky that she didn't want to give up.

God, why?!

As though he'd answer. As if he'd give her an acceptable reason for stealing her children away.

What is it about me? Is it a curse? Is it something I've done?

As if he'd finally open his arms to her and explain: *My child, let me tell you about the babies. About your mother. About Ruby Mae.*

These were the lingering thoughts that had led Isla to the medicine cabinet during a hopeless night. She could remember the sound of pills bouncing against the bathroom sink, the sound of Luke's panic-stricken cry, so different from yet simultaneously like her mother's scream so many years before. But the rest? A void. When she'd finally woken up, she'd found herself the proud recipient of an involuntary two-week vacation care of the local mental health facility. Luke begged for forgiveness as she lay there, peering at the fluorescent lights overhead, refusing to meet his gaze. *The loony bin,* as her mother would have put it. *I'd rather die of crazy than ever go to a place like that.*

"Why's it always about *your roof*?!" August boomed from inside the house. "What about the fact that it's *my life*?!"

Isla squinted at the pulled dandelion held tightly between her fingers. She couldn't recall whether she'd ever had such a typically teenage fight with her mother before things had fallen apart. Isla's most vivid memory was of Skye Berkley chasing her out the front door of their crappy little house on the outskirts of Golden, her long curly hair flying wildly behind her, like Medusa with her head of snakes. She'd screamed, *Get away from me!* Screamed, *Where's my daughter?!* Screamed like the lunatic she had inevitably become.

And what about you? Isla thought. *Missus Loony Bin.*

Luke yelled something unintelligible from inside the house.

"He's going to end up hating us," Isla whispered to the soon-to-be-wilting weed lying limp in her hand. "Won't that be ironic?"

If that happened, she'd be the estranged daughter that became the mother of an estranged son. The crazy daughter of the crazy mother.

I'd rather die of crazy than ever go to a place like that.

But Isla *had* gone to just such a place. She'd left there with a handful of prescriptions for depression, anxiety, stuff to help her sleep. But she was still spiraling, falling headlong into the depths of despair; and the idea of losing August to teenage angst, to vitriol and stupid callow fights? It made her skin grow cold. If August and Luke kept fighting, maybe August would finally be pushed too far. Hell, perhaps Luke would beat him to the punch and get to the point of shouting for their firstborn to get out.

Get out! Get the hell out!

Get away from me!

No. He'd never. Not in a million years.

But sometimes life didn't make a bit of sense, did it? People were unpredictable. She knew that for damn sure. So, why should that have excluded Luke?

"Then maybe I should *leave*!" August yelled from inside the house, and Isla's heart twisted into a hard knot within her chest. August, the "tough" kid who thought he could take on anything because he listened to the Misfits and owned a studded leather jacket, a shield of protection from the harsh realities of the world. She imagined him stomping out of the house, never looking back.

Or, maybe, Luke would finally lose it. *Good! Get out. Get out!*

The idea of history repeating itself . . . *impossible,* she thought Because despite their shortcomings, there was nothing August could do to push her or Luke to such reprehensible extremes. *Was there?* Isla would never abandon her kids like her own mother had. *Would she?* Not for anyone or anything. No. Not ever. Not on her life.

Except people were unpredictable.

Skye Berkley had at least taught her that.

A whip of wind dragged cool air across Isla's bare arms, drawing her attention to the swaying blue spruce and Douglas fir just beyond the property line.

It was then that she saw something out there. Maybe.

For a moment, her head throbbed in a painfully familiar way. The warning buzz of an incoming migraine crackled deep within her ears, angry and electric. Isla winced against the sunlight and looked away from the trees, dropping the dandelion and shielding her eyes from the morning's glare. When she could no longer hear her pulse whooshing through her skull, she looked up again, expecting to see nothing. Possibly a shadow, like the traces of darkness she'd experienced nearly all her life now. Except, no. This wasn't one of those peripheral mirages. This was ...

A child ...?

A boy, likely no more than five or six years old.

Isla's heart stopped, wound up, then slammed against her chest.

Adam?

Impossible, of course. Adam was dead.

But this boy ... she'd never seen him before. At least she didn't think so. He was no one recognizable. No friend of Sophie's or face on a billboard in town. And how would a local boy have gotten to her house anyway? They were nearly ten miles from town, over three miles from the nearest neighbor.

Yet, there he was, standing in the shade of the towering pines, dressed in a peculiar sort of linen jumper—sleeveless with short pants, once white but now filthy with God only knew how much time spent in the woods. A shock of fiery red hair was matted to the side of his head. His eyes—or what she could see of them—were wildly huge. Like a deer in headlights, a boy paralyzed by fear.

Missing, she thought. *He's one of the missing. Right?*

Not from one of the billboards, but that didn't matter. There were so many of them now.

But what shook Isla to her core were his feet—proof that this child was an unfathomable anomaly. Miles from the closest house, the kid was barefoot. No sneakers. No socks. Two words whispered within her head.

Nine months.

Hardly breathing and afraid to move, Isla gawked. She forced her mind back to the most likely scenario. This was one of the missing children, one of the Amber Alerts from the past few days. Of course he was. He had to be. But just as soon as the explanation presented itself—sound, logical, rooted in reality—Isla swatted it away.

Adam sent him. . . .

A wave of emotions swept over her as the child peered back. Shock. Surprise. A strange sort of hopeful joy, because while she knew it was a beyond-ridiculous notion, maybe her sweet Adam had somehow sensed her inexhaustible sadness. Perhaps, looking down at her from wherever he had gone, he knew how hollow she felt without him, how devastating his loss had been. Maybe this was his way of making things better. Maybe this was a gift. Nine months of carrying such an impossible burden of grief, now replaced by hope.

A sob wrenched itself from deep within her.

Oh, Adam . . .

Isla dared lift a dirty hand in silent greeting, her fingers unfurling in assurance that she meant no harm.

"H-hello," Isla said, her voice stuttering with emotion. She spoke loud enough for the child to hear but gently as to not startle him. It was the very same way she'd spoken to her own children any time they crossed paths with wildlife. A fox. A marmot. A fawn. *A boy.*

Don't be afraid.

The child furrowed his eyebrows at Isla's hand, as though not understanding such a universal salutation. He didn't move.

"My name is Isla," she said. "Are you lost, sweetheart?"

Say no, she thought, even though she knew it was impossible. *Say no. Say no.*

Again, nothing.

Isla dared to stand from her crouch, moving so slowly her legs trembled beneath her weight. Within her achingly slow motion, she became aware of just how hard her heart was pounding, just how erratic her breath was now that she wasn't holding it in. It was a sensation of complete alarm and absolute exhilaration, a feeling of both worry and bliss. Logic told her to run back to the house and retrieve her phone, to call the police. But her heart promised her that this child wasn't a face in any database. No, this child had been abandoned—*like me*—and however tragic that was, she yearned for it to be true.

She ached for Adam, desperate for a final child.

It's called post-traumatic stress disorder, they had told her. *You've likely had it for a very long time.*

Perhaps that's why she'd been so drawn to the garden that morning—not because of the weeds, but because something had called her out into the sunshine, wanting to show her what was awaiting her in the shadows. *Come,* the forest had called. *Come see what's hidden in our boughs. Come see who's waiting. . . .*

And here he was. A boy.

Extending a hand outward, she signaled that the child should move forward. *Come.* She expected him to remain motionless, or maybe to retreat. Instead, he took a single step in her direction, and Isla's hands flew to her mouth.

Is this what a miracle looks like? she wondered, her gaze fixed on the child.

"My God, where did you come from?" she asked.

Shooting a quick look behind her shoulder toward the house, she found Luke standing on the back porch steps, staring beyond her. His expression was something akin to fascination, as though unable to trust his own eyes.

It was August who threw her back into reality, his voice cutting through the surrealism of the moment from right behind her.

"Jesus," he remarked, unmoved by the wonder of it all. "Who the hell is *that?*"

EXCERPT FROM *THE HIDDEN MYSTERIES OF A FERAL CHILDHOOD*

Feral children are a truly rare phenomenon with only a handful of documented cases over the past century. Their scarcity adds to the intrigue of their stories. Both captivating and unsettling, these accounts reveal the depths of human resilience while highlighting the profound impact of social isolation.

Research has shown that feral children, despite their remarkable survival skills—like heightened senses and animal communication—face daunting challenges in integrating into civilized society. The lack of early social interaction leaves them with severe deficits that are extremely difficult if not altogether impossible to overcome.

The process of assimilating feral children into everyday family life is fraught with difficulties. Despite efforts by caregivers and specialists, these children often struggle with rudimentary social skills and fundamental emotional connections. In one notable case, a child found in the Ozark Mountains—the "Ozark Urchin"—exhibited behaviors more akin to animals rather than humans. Despite all exhibited kindness and patience by the caretaking family, placing the child in a home environment was met with resistance and distress and, ultimately, violence.

Experts unanimously agree that while feral cases are rare, they serve as a stark reminder of the crucial role of early human contact and socialization. The enigmatic circumstances of their discoveries often raise more questions than answers, fueling ongoing research into the causes and implications of these inscrutable and often unexplained lives.

Morgan, E. (1997). *The Hidden Mysteries of a Feral Childhood.*
Gate Falls University Press

DAY ONE

2

LUKE

Luke's eyes roved the walls of the social worker's office. It reminded him of elementary school, of the times he'd been sent to the principal's office for random infractions, like when he had climbed the outside of the tube slide or when he'd told a fellow classmate to *kiss my butt, jerkface*. With his eyes fixed on the classic kitten poster pinned behind the social worker's desk—HANG IN THERE!—Luke smirked at the onslaught of recollections he hadn't thought of in years.

"What?"

Isla's inquiry was lightning quick. She was nervous, tense as a wound-up spring, but she'd been that way for the past six weeks. Ever since the mystery kid had showed up, it seemed that he was all Isla thought about.

I know him, she had whispered. *I swear I've seen him somewhere before.*

Luke had been the one to call the police. Isla had acted as though she could have taken the authorities or left them. He chalked it up to her broken heart, her fractured state of mind, but he hadn't been able to help the words that had slipped past his lips.

He's one of the kids everyone's looking for, Isla. He's someone's baby. . . .

She had wept while the cops put the kid in the back of a cruiser, then wept again when the social worker she'd been in touch with finally confirmed what Isla had waited to hear: nobody had reported him missing. The state of Colorado had no idea who he was or where he'd come from, and from the sound of it, they wouldn't be finding out anytime soon because the kid didn't speak.

Despite this whole situation being Isla's idea, Luke had been watching her wring her hands in her lap for the past twenty minutes. Meanwhile, he had his own thoughts on the matter. Like, wasn't it crazy to bring a strange kid into their home? Forget the fact that they had no idea who he was or where he'd come from. Software engineering job or not, the recession had hit the Hansens just as hard as it had every other middle-class American family. Food was beyond expensive. They were already cutting corners, keeping their sacrifices quiet so the kids wouldn't worry. He'd been just about over the moon when Gus had spontaneously decided to quit guitar lessons. The fact that kids were buying all their clothes at thrift stores, looking like they stepped straight out of the nineties . . . that was a plus. At least Eden wasn't begging for Hollister money. And then there was the fact that the farmhouse didn't have the space for another dependent. They were full to the gills with five kids as it was.

That, and Luke still couldn't quite believe it. All those missing kids, but *this* kid shows up out of nowhere, and no one's searching for him? The police had put out a bulletin. There had even been a press conference on the local news. Luke was certain the authorities had reached out to all four corners in search of leads, in search of parents desperate to find their lost son. Sure, they hadn't located anyone yet, but the kid had a family, right? He had to have come from *somewhere*.

Secretly, that was the biggest reason Luke had agreed to foster the boy in the first place. After a handful of late-night battles and watching Isla crumble into a fit of sobs, he'd acquiesced. No one could locate the kid's family because the kid didn't speak, but his people *would* eventually turn up. When they did, Isla would be forced to surrender the child to his rightful parents. And that would become a whole other level of drama that he wasn't ready for.

But for now, at least she'll be distracted, he thought. *At least she'll be too busy to be sad.*

"What?" Isla asked again. "What is it?"

Luke simply gave her a shake of his head.

"Nothing," he said. "Just remembering how much of a little shit I used to be."

Despite her nerves, the corner of her mouth curved up in a subtle smile. "And we wonder where August gets it from," she said.

They both chuckled softly. It was anxious laughter that filled the quiet of that perfectly square office space. Four white walls. One lonely window looking out onto an even lonelier parking lot. A billboard in the distance, the word "missing" in red capitals next to a picture of a pretty little girl. Luke remembered getting an Amber Alert about that kid a few weeks ago. She was from a few towns over. Crested Butte, if he remembered correctly. He squinted at the headshot, half-obscured by the corner of a building.

He has *to come from somewhere,* he kept thinking. *How can all those others be missing, but nobody is looking for* him?

Diverting his eyes, he studied the linoleum. Eventually, the office door swung open, and the social worker stepped inside.

"Mr. and Mrs. Hansen, thanks for waiting," she told them.

She wasn't what Luke expected, though he wasn't sure *what* he had expected: maybe a beady-eyed old lady with Coke-bottle glasses, a woman who had worked for the state of Colorado for sixty-some-odd years. Instead, Helen Plummer was tall and elegant in a fashionable skirt suit and high heels. Shifting a manila file folder jammed full of paper in her arms, she lowered herself into her creaky desk chair, swept a flank of coily hair over her shoulder, and gave them both an imploring look.

"This is a difficult case," she told them, as though they'd forgotten. As though Luke hadn't spent the last few weeks conducting incognito Google searches about fostering kids . . . about how to get out of the situation if it all went south.

"We know," Isla said with a vehement nod. "Of course, yes. I mean . . ." She held her hands outward, palms up, asking for answers. *Fill us in. Please.*

Helen shifted in her seat, then glanced to the thick file in front of her.

"Honestly . . . I'm not sure we'd be here had this child not wandered onto your property," she explained. "This is such an extraordinary case. A *confusing* case. We have virtually nothing to go on. He's not on the radar—not for us, not for any other counties. We've checked Arizona, Utah, New Mexico . . ."

"Then what's all that?" Luke asked, motioning to the file beneath Helen's right hand. It sure looked like a lot more than nothing.

"Notes. Tests," Helen replied, glancing to what looked to be a fresh pink manicure.

"What kind of tests?" Isla asked.

Luke's gaze shifted to his wife. All at once he was overwhelmed with déjà vu. They'd been here before, just not in this office, not with Helen Plummer. He'd sat next to Isla in more than a few obstetricians examining rooms, his hands squeezing hers. The doctor would talk of tests and various possibilities.

There's nothing wrong with you, Mrs. Hansen. Not that we can tell.

Sometimes they'd just offer their condolences, give Isla's shoulder a tight squeeze, and excuse themselves, leaving the nurse to handle the fallout.

Watching Isla twist her hands in her lap, Luke could tell she was worried, scared that something would come up, something that would keep Social Services from releasing the kid and placing him with their family.

Sorry, this boy is much too complex. Sorry, you're out of your depth.

Right then, Luke would breathe out a sigh of relief. Because he'd seen the articles, cases of abandoned kids and how they were handled. Nothing he had come across sounded even vaguely similar to what they were dealing with here. He'd ended up searching terms that had made him uncomfortable. *Abandoned child syndrome. Severe neglect. Feral kids.* Everything he read on *those* subjects sounded more than terrifying, not something he wanted to voluntarily step into. And none of those cases had any information about how they were handled by Social Services, because those cases were so incredibly rare.

Had Helen come out and said the kid was too much of a challenge, Luke wouldn't have argued. He'd given in after the fights, sure, but secretly? He didn't want this. Not even a little bit. And yet here he was, holding his tongue, hoping to be denied . . . all the while knowing that despite his reluctance, Isla *needed* it.

"Psychological tests," Helen said, answering Isla's question. "We put all our charges through such basic testing before placing them in a foster home. But this case is much more complicated. Possibly the most complicated we've come across."

"Did he pass?" Isla asked, shifting her weight forward in her chair. The question struck Luke as rather weird. She sounded like a mother asking about an exam grade during a parent-teacher conference, not a hopeful foster parent asking about the psychological well-being of a kid nobody could make heads or tails of.

"Well . . . there's no passing or failing, Isla," Helen said. "But I'll be honest—if you folks decide to proceed, there absolutely will be challenges."

"Challenges," Isla repeated, giving Luke a quick look. "We can handle challenges," she said, then focused once again on Helen. "We have five kids," she went on, talking fast, likely afraid that Helen would lift a hand and stop her, maybe worried that Luke himself would beat Helen to the punch.

I love you, hon, but this is madness.

Luke reached out, placed a hand on his wife's arm, then turned his eyes to the woman behind the desk.

"I think what Isla's trying to ask is what *types* of challenges?" The words came out calm, collected—an Oscar-worthy performance if there ever was one. Because he couldn't have felt more on edge. He was keeping himself in his chair, but he wanted to get up and walk out, to get in the car, and blast down a lonely highway. Alone. Without Isla. Without the kids. Without any of them.

"Well, the child, he's—"

"I'm sorry, can we stop?" Isla cut in, blinking up at the caseworker. "Can we please give him a name? Him not having a name, it just . . . it's awful. Please."

"Within the system, we're currently calling him John," Helen said.

"John?" Isla leaned back, appalled. "Like *John Doe*?"

Luke squeezed her arm. *What does she expect an anonymous child to be called?* When she glanced his way, he gave her a look that said, *Easy.* If she didn't tone it down, she wouldn't be walking out with what she wanted . . . certainly what Luke knew *he* didn't want but would take on anyway, because that's what a good husband did. He'd been watching his wife's sadness grow by the day—a monster gorging itself on even the smallest joys of everyday life, swallowing all traces of Isla's optimism, leaving her hollow and weak. The idea of the monster becoming bigger than either of them could handle scared the hell out of him. Hell, it had grown big enough to nearly steal her away a few months before, and he'd been terrified, so scared that he'd refused to take her home. It was the main reason he was sitting beside her despite not wanting to be there now. It was why he was keeping his thoughts to himself, playing the supportive spouse—till death do us part and all that. He was frightened, scared that she'd try to take her life again, that this time she'd succeed and he'd be left on his own. And why? Because he had selfishly refused to ease her pain, not wanting some random kid in his house when, a year before, he had been happy with the idea of having another baby of their own.

"The name is standard procedure," Helen said, apologetic. "Not very elegant, I know."

"Helen," Luke said, drawing the social worker's attention. "Back to what you were saying a second ago. What types of challenges are we in for? Should we really be doing this?"

Isla nearly gasped, her expression both bewildered and betrayed. How could he say such a thing? Was he really voicing doubt? *Now?*

"What I mean is, is this best for *him*?" A quick backtrack, a sidestep away from what would have inevitably turned into a tearful screamfest of a fight.

"Well, the child—" Helen caught herself, self-corrected. "*John* . . . is nonverbal. That's going to be the biggest hurdle. Most nonverbal kids communicate on at least some level. Grunts. Pointing. Clapping. Stomping feet. John does none of that. At least, not from what we've seen."

"So, he's quiet," Isla said softly. "That might be a nice change of pace." She meant it to be funny, but her joke fell flat on the scuffed-up floor.

"It's beyond being just quiet," Helen said. "It's difficult to understand why John acts the way he does when he doesn't even communicate his basic needs, at least not in a way that we can understand. Even newborns cry if they're hungry or tired. But John . . . he gives zero cues. We suspect that may be due to the way he was raised."

"Raised," Luke echoed, lifting an eyebrow at the woman across the desk. "If he can't communicate, how can you guess at how he was raised? And if he was raised, why isn't his family looking for him?"

"We don't know," she said matter-of-factly. "But you're absolutely right; we're only guessing that he was raised at all. We're basing that on experience, on past cases. What I'm talking about is trauma. The least communicative children are typically the ones who experienced long-term abandonment. Spectrum kids pose unique challenges, and if they happen to find themselves in a non-nurturing environment, sadly, they're the children who suffer the most extreme abuse."

"Like what?" Isla asked. "You're saying these things, but you aren't giving us concrete examples."

Helen shifted her weight uncomfortably. "I can't give you concrete examples, Isla," she said. "All I can tell you is what we suspect, which is extreme neglect. In many of the cases I mentioned, we categorized the treatment as torture."

Isla's hands pressed over her mouth, and Luke cringed at the word. *Torture.* He'd read about more than a few of those types of cases. None had turned out well for anyone. Yet again, he had an almost undeniable urge to jump out of his chair and leave. Because this was a bad idea. Scratch that—why couldn't Isla see this was a *horrible* idea?

"Which is why I really need you both to be sure you want to take this on," Helen continued. "John will need constant supervision and care. He will demand more of you than you can imagine. I say this with the utmost respect for the both of you, because not many families would even consider taking on such a task. But"—she paused for emphasis—"I need you to be sure."

This was where Luke was supposed to speak up, to confess that he wasn't ready, he wasn't interested, he didn't want any of this. This was the part where he admitted he was only doing it for Isla, because he was worried that if he didn't, she'd end up in a mental ward again. He was supposed to say that, despite all that, he didn't understand why Social Services would even consider them as candidates. He'd argued that part with Isla more than a few times. *Why us? What makes us such a good fit?* Because from what he could gather, Helen Plummer was telling them this kid, John, was as good as feral. They didn't know the first thing about him. Yet Isla was still gung-ho about it, as though "feral" was something they could fix with some clean clothes, a bowl of spaghetti, and a cuddle session on the couch.

"But you said you're guessing," Isla reminded Helen, her hands dropping to her lap. "You aren't sure about any . . ." She hesitated, as though tasting the word. "Any . . . *torture*. You're just assuming. Maybe there was none of that, right?" She shot a glare toward Luke, looking for backup. When he didn't give her what she wanted, she faced Helen once again, even more determined. Luke knew that look. If he wasn't going to stand with her, she'd just get this thing done on her own.

"Yes, it's an assumption," Helen said. "But there are signs. That, and there's the issue of his physicality. We don't know how old he is. We're estimating perhaps seven. It's impossible to tell exactly because he's so small in stature. His muscles are underdeveloped. His bones . . ." Helen paused, as though not understanding it herself. "It's almost as though he'd been folded up? And left that way for a long period of time? His joints are malformed. Despite his age, on an X-ray, it looks as though he has arthritis. We're assuming chronic inflammation is why he walks the way he does—that lurching gait? He holds his hands up against his chest a lot of the time. We've concluded that he does this because it's how he's most comfortable, physically. Holding his arms at a different angle appears as though it could cause him severe pain. This could be—and its only speculation from me—because of the position he was forced to keep by whoever was tending to him. We've seen this sort of thing in kids before, but to a lesser degree. Kids that have been forced to live in cages, dog crates . . ."

"My God," Isla said into her hands. "Yet he managed to get away, walk through the woods, and find our house?"

"That's a big part of what we don't yet understand," Helen confessed. "The doctors that examined John aren't sure how he could have walked more than a mile in his current state. Your house is how far from the closest neighbor?"

"Nearly three miles to the west," Luke said. "Nine miles and some change from town. The woods north of us, the woods he came out of . . . they don't belong to us. It's just state land, as far as I can tell. We don't know how deep those go before hitting private property again."

"Authorities have canvassed most of the area around your home, regardless of whether John could have walked the distance or not," Helen told them. "Thus far, they've come up empty. There's nothing out there that they can find. No house. No campsite. No clue as to where he could have possibly come from, or whether someone had simply abandoned him where you found him. And as far as the rash of missing cases, well . . . still nobody has reported him. We have to assume that whoever was watching over him until now is either gone or has no interest in getting him back."

There was an energy coming off Isla. Luke could tell that the longer Helen spoke, the more agitated his wife became. He remembered what she'd whispered against his shoulder weeks before, the night after the boy had appeared just beyond their garden.

I feel like I already know him, she had told him. *The second I set eyes on him, it's like I'd met him before, like he'd come back to me from another life.*

Luke couldn't say he understood why his wife felt the connection she did—this boy was a kid, not a newborn, and a complete stranger. He belonged to someone else. *He had to come from somewhere, right?!* was his constant argument with himself. Why Isla was connecting with him the way she was after losing Adam . . . Luke just couldn't puzzle that one out.

But he also couldn't deny that the past five years had worn him down.

In the moment, while it was happening, it didn't really sink in, but those five years had passed with Isla growing increasingly forlorn about not being able to have another child. They'd both gone to doctors, had both gone through their own rigorous battery of tests—prodded with needles, lying on tables and wincing against the glare of fluorescent lights. In the end, Isla's doctor discovered scarring. Possible endometriosis was the conclusion, despite Isla having no symptoms to back up the diagnosis. *But otherwise, we don't see any reason why the babies continue to be lost.* They'd been left with zero answers and plenty of doctors' bills, and for what? Eventually, Luke and Isla's sex life—which hadn't been much to speak of after five kids—began to deteriorate even further. Part of him was tired of only making love in the hopes of creating a baby, a mechanical, almost obligatory process. He was tired of seeing negative pregnancy tests lying around the master bathroom. Sometimes he wondered if Isla deliberately left them behind to make him feel guilty, to remind him that they still had work to do.

When it had just been Gus, Luke and Isla had been over the moon. Then Eden had arrived, and it had been tougher to make ends meet, but they were still overjoyed. By the time Sophie had been born, they had suffered five miscarriages, all of them out of nowhere, each one hitting Isla harder than the one before, each one making Luke more reluctant to try again.

After Adam, their sixth loss, Isla's depression loomed like a shadow she couldn't quite outrun. And the worse her depression became, the more frequently she'd zone out, sit blank-faced and empty-eyed, sometimes for a few minutes, sometimes for half an hour or more. If they got pregnant and lost another baby, he was almost certain he'd lose her completely. And if they weren't able to take this boy home, this John . . . then what?

"What are we doing?" Isla asked, startling Luke back into the present. Her tone was edging toward impatience. "I mean, I'm sorry, Helen. I understand you're required to tell us all this, but are we being denied our request to foster this child? You said over the phone that due to the circumstances, it was better for him to be placed with a family than to stay at a state facility, so here we are. You've talked to me about after-care options, about socialization, occupational therapy, help with catching him up with schooling when he's ready. You *told* us to come. And yet, we're beating around the bush. So, is that what it boils down to? We're being denied? Please, just come out and say it if so, because I'm not understanding all this hesitation otherwise."

Helen grew quiet for a long while, taking both Isla and Luke in. It made him uncomfortable knowing that this woman was judging them so openly. On the other hand, he was more than happy to be assessed.

Please, he wanted to tell her, *explain to my wife how terrible of an idea this is. Remind her that this boy is nothing like the boy she thinks he'll be. Please, I'm begging you.*

"Okay," Helen finally said. "It's my job to make sure you understand this is a huge responsibility you're taking on, that's all. It's also my job to make sure you both understand John is far from neurotypical. He will be a challenge the likes of which you may not be ready for: his inability to speak, his physical appearance. Even if he does manage to assimilate into your family, he will have a difficult life. Children, including your own, may not accept him as he's growing up, and once he does become an adult, folks just won't—" She sighed, looking them both squarely in the eyes. "Of course, there's a chance that someone will come out of the woodwork and claim him, but if not, and if the court deems fit, he's a lifelong commitment, all right? I want you to understand that he will never be able to take care of himself. Forgive me for being so blunt, but I see it every day in this job—it's heartbreaking, and it angers me to no end, but most families simply wouldn't choose to take someone like him into their home."

When Isla straightened in her seat, a groan lingered deep within Luke's chest. Whether Helen had chosen her words carefully or had simply spoken off the cuff, Isla was triggered. He'd never seen his wife back down from a fight, heaven forbid with Luke, and Helen had just thrown down the gauntlet.

"Ms. Plummer—we *aren't* most families," Isla said. "And I'd like to petition to have his name changed to something less impersonal. Right away."

"So, am I to understand you're both on board with this, then?" Helen turned her focus to Luke, and for a split second he was sure he'd been found out. Helen could see right through him, couldn't she? She knew he didn't want this, knew he was simply buying in to appease his ailing wife, to save his waning marriage.

But God, what a hell of a buy-in. A lifelong commitment. And here was Isla, unable to see this decision for what it was: a choice that would ultimately change their family forever. Here she was, being guided by grief, blinded by a desperation to fill the void Adam had left.

"*Rowan*," Isla said, turning her eyes to Luke, saving him from Helen's heavy, knowing stare. "How about Rowan? It just feels right, don't you think? It's like, when I saw him, I heard it whispered it into my ear."

Nothing about this was hitting him in the right way, but Luke had to have faith that this was what would make things better. Otherwise, he had no idea what would become of Isla, and that possibility scared him a hell of a lot more than being stuck with this bizarre kid from God only knew where. If there was one unknown thrust upon his life, he'd rather it be the boy rather than the idea of finding Isla crumpled on the bathroom floor again, this time unresponsive, this time Luke too late to save her. Because, while he knew raising Rowan would be a monumental task, he also knew they could do it. Together. But if he stepped into their bathroom to find his wife soaking in a tub of crimson water, that would be the end of everything. With Rowan, life would be hard. But without Isla, it would become impossible.

And so, despite all his misgivings, he took a deep breath and gave Isla a nod.

"Yeah," he murmured, "Rowan. Rowan is nice." Because at least this whole thing would give her some hope for the future. It would give her something to focus on beyond her broken heart.

This is crazy, he thought. *This whole thing is fucking nuts.*

But it's what would root Isla to the earth, what would bring her back to the family.

And at least she didn't want to name the kid Adam.

At least there was that.

3

ISLA

The hallway was colder than a morgue, the opposite of what Isla thought a state-run children's home should have been. She pressed her palms between her knees to keep her hands from trembling, to keep her fingers warm. Her button-up blouse and linen capris were well-suited for the summer heat, but the ensemble did little to shelter her from the blasting air vent poised directly overhead.

"What's taking so long?" she asked quietly, partly because she was freezing, but mostly because they'd been sitting in the same stiff-backed chairs for the better part of an hour.

Luke shifted in his seat. He had hardly said a word after Helen had excused herself, only uttering a complaint about the chill before distracting himself with various news articles on his phone. When he looked up, it was as if he was finally realizing they were still in that same hall, still waiting, courting hypothermia.

"Why's it so cold in here?" he complained. "It feels like a goddamn Apple Store. Does the cold keep kids calm?"

Isla looked away from him, shivering at the idea of children being controlled by the harshness of their environment. Something about the situation made her think of *Lord of the Flies*. Once her favorite novel, she doubted she could ever read it again; it only made the images that had been tumbling through her head that much more gruesome. Rowan locked away in what she could only picture as a cell. Rowan lying on a bare mattress, his skinny arms wrapped around his trembling body, waiting to be saved. The ideas that Helen Plummer had put into her mind were ones Isla wouldn't able to shake anytime soon. Torture. Dog crates. All speculation, but still awful. It was enough to have an endless string of questions twisting through her brain. Had Rowan run away from someplace? Was he unable to speak because he'd never been spoken to? When she'd finally gathered up the nerve to approach him in the garden—while Luke had phoned the police—he had jerked away from being touched. Was that because he didn't understand physical contact? Affection? Anything beyond hands inflicting pain?

"This is the right thing to do," she said softly, a quiet reminder for the man sitting next to her, because Isla was no fool. She knew full well that Luke was in this not because he wanted it for himself, but because of her. He thought he could hide his true feelings, but she could see right through him, like flipping open one of Sophie's easy readers. *Here is Luke. Luke has doubts.*

"He came to us for a reason, you know," she assured him. "We lost Adam, but . . ."

Shoving strands of long brown hair behind her ears, she turned to face her husband, taking in his expression. Luke was handsome even in his mid-forties, but every time she looked at him for a little longer than usual, she could spot miniscule changes she hadn't seen before: the start of a new wrinkle, a glint of gray near his temples. They were the same subtle shifts she noticed in herself every day as she leaned in to the mirror to poke and stretch at her skin, to sigh at the stubborn dark circles beneath her blue eyes, the ones that refused to go away no matter how many miracle creams and celebrity-endorsed serums she tried. Every day she grew more annoyed by the three faint lines that were starting to form across her forehead, annoyed enough to keep her stylist from trimming her thick fringe too much at every haircut, as though bangs could teleport her back into her thirties. Within arm's reach, her daughters' youth only served as a constant reminder that the days were getting shorter and Isla was growing older. And with that, her chance of making an impact on the world was slipping away. Sure, she'd raised five amazing kids, but was that enough? Had she been born merely to be a mother, or was she meant for more?

"It doesn't matter where he came from," Isla said. It was a conversation they'd had at least a dozen times, but it bore repeating. "If we can make a difference in Rowan's life, if we could actually *give* him a life, wouldn't that stand for something?" If she couldn't have Adam, she could at least have Rowan, right? She could be a good mother to him—the opposite of what Rowan's mother undoubtedly was, the opposite of what her own mother had been. Nothing but a huge disappointment. A failure. A goddamn disaster. *Perhaps,* she thought, *this is the thing I'm meant to do. Maybe I lost them all for a reason. Maybe it's to help me embrace this moment, this special, helpless boy. . . .*

"Isla . . ." Luke sighed, then shifted his weight, reaching out to catch her hand in his own.

She stiffened despite herself, wondering if he'd choose this—the worst possible time—to tell her he'd changed his mind. There was still time for him to say this whole thing was a mistake. If he said it in front of Helen, it would be over, of course. Rowan would be forever lost to them. She wanted to pull her hand away but forced herself to sit with the contact. She'd hear him out one last time, if only to make him feel like he had a say. But the truth of the matter was, it didn't make a bit of difference what reason and logic he used. Isla's heart was set on this.

I know him . . .

"He doesn't talk," Luke reminded her. "If Helen is right, and he's coming from severe abuse—"

"She's guessing," Isla cut in. "She doesn't know."

"Okay," Luke said. "She doesn't know. But if someone *did* lock him up and denied him human contact, his brain . . ." He sighed. "Honey, I've read the studies. They all say the same thing. After a certain point, connections aren't made. Synapses don't form. It's brain damage. No matter how much we want to, we aren't going to be able to give him what you think we can."

"That doesn't matter," she insisted. "He came to us. To *us.* We have to try. How can we live with ourselves if we don't?"

Luke shut his eyes. When he did, her heart somersaulted within her chest. Here it came, the endless reasons as to why this was a terrible idea, the rationale that this was too big for them, that Rowan appearing on the fringes of their backyard exactly nine months after their baby had been lost was purely coincidence. He was going to launch into a diatribe about how nothing could replace Adam, how the children they had lost over the years were irreplicable, that it was a pain they were meant to bear—something that made them who they were. But after an extended pause, rather than arguing, Luke gave her a faint nod, then clenched her hand.

Able to see the doubt on his face, she turned away from him. When she did, her attention fell upon Helen Plummer in her professional skirt suit and heels. And there, to her right, was the boy.

Rowan.

He held his arms against his chest like an unnatural sort of rabbit. His slight frame was nearly swallowed whole by a plain white T-shirt and gray sweatpants two sizes too big. There he was, the boy who had been haunting Isla's every waking thought, the boy who felt like déjà vu.

She stood, hearing Luke do the same behind her, the legs of his chair scraping against the floor. Helen looked to Rowan, then leaned in to say something to him too quietly for Isla to make out. Rowan seemed to flinch at the sound of the social worker's voice, but a second later he began to hobble forward, each eerily awkward step bringing him closer to where Isla and Luke stood.

Abruptly Isla found herself reaching backward, searching for Luke's hand, seeking out his touch. She hadn't needed to think about it to know this was meant to be. But watching Rowan shuffle toward them, she was suddenly both captivated and afraid. It *felt* right, but the questions came rushing back all over again. Who was this child? Where had he come from? What awful experiences had made him the person he would inevitably become? Maybe Luke was right—maybe this whole thing was a huge mistake. Maybe she was crazy to think they could take this boy into their home.

She was suddenly overwhelmed with the weight of what they were doing. Helen's assessment was spot-on. Rowan was a special case. Rare. Once in a lifetime. If it wasn't the fact that he was mute and beyond neurodivergent, how would he navigate through life with those malformed limbs, with that unsettling, anomalous face? If they took him in, if no one showed up to claim him, he was theirs forever. Or, more accurately, they were *his*.

Luke caught her hand in his and gave it a pulsing squeeze. She imagined it to be Morse code. *Everything is okay. We're in this together. We'll make it right.*

Or was it more: *Well, this is what you wanted.*

The idea of that silent *told you so* had Isla straightening her shoulders. *You're right,* she wanted to say. *This is what I wanted. What I still want . . .*

. . . wasn't it?

Rowan continued to amble forward. The closer he came, the more Isla recognized the tension flowing from her shoulders. The sensation traveled down her torso and legs before melting into the floor beneath her. When the boy was a mere ten feet away, he stopped. Canting his head, his gaze zeroed in on her. She saw it in the odd contours of his face: he *recognized* her. That was something. *Perhaps,* she thought, *it's more than Helen expected. It's more than he's shown any of those doctors, more than anything he revealed during their endless tests.* Because, as she was so certain, as her gut instinct had told her, this was meant to be.

Rowan was meant for them.

This was the very definition of destiny.

Rowan had no family, no one looking for him, because he was meant for her.

Adam had sent him here.

Releasing Luke's hand, Isla took a slow forward step, then crouched down on the scuffed linoleum floor. She extended an arm, holding her palm up in offering.

"Remember me?" she asked, her voice but a breath above a whisper. "I'm Isla," she said, bringing her extended hand up against her chest.

"Rowan," she told him, allowing her arm to go out to him again. "Is it okay if I call you Rowan . . . ? We're going to take care of you, if that's all right," she said, pausing to give him a chance to respond despite knowing he wouldn't say a word.

He didn't speak, but he *did* reply. When Helen took a step toward him, making as though she was going to say something to him once again, Rowan took a few stuttering steps forward, making his choice clear. He wanted nothing to do with the social worker, nothing more to do with this cold, inhospitable place. Isla's glance jumped to Helen's face, quick enough to catch the surprise that lingered in the corners of the social worker's eyes. Helen gave her a faint smile.

"Well, all right, then," she said. "Congratulations, Mr. and Mrs. Hansen. It's a boy."

4

AUGUST

Gus was lying out on the roof of the house, headphones secured over his ears, the sun beating down on his face. The incline was comfortable, steep enough to keep him vertical but not severe enough to make him feel like he was going to slide down the shingles and into his mother's rhododendron. It was the only place he dared smoke the cigarettes he'd been mooching off Noah—cigs that his best friend was filching out of the open pack hidden in his older brother's dresser drawer. Lately, the roof was the only place Gus felt comfortable, the only spot where he could relax and not worry about getting into a verbal jousting match with his parents or one of his sisters. Sophie was okay—if not annoying in the way all five-year-olds probably were—but Willow was a know-it-all, Olive was infuriating with her golden-child act, and Eden was about as pent-up as their mom was. It was stupid, but he'd caught himself wondering at the very least if the wild kid from the woods might make things better. He didn't fully understand his mom's obsession with him, but at least there would be another guy in the house, right? Maybe it would chill his parents out. Perhaps, with the weird kid around, they'd shift their focus away from Gus and leave him the hell alone for once.

Hearing the pop of gravel during the lull of an old Killing Joke track, he mashed his cigarette against the roof's sandpaper-like surface, pocketed the butt, and yanked his headphones down around his neck. Once, there was no question his mother would have found the cigarette's remains amid the roots of her flowers. He doubted she'd bother looking these days—she hardly spent time out of the house, let alone outside doing yard work—but he didn't feel like taking the chance. Doubling up on breath mints would also seal the deal, if he couldn't completely get the smoky smell from his clothes.

He rolled onto his stomach, then belly-crawled up to the peak of the house. It was there that he peered over the pitch like a sniper scoping a battlefield, watching the family minivan ramble down the road. It was nearly dinnertime. His parents had been gone all day. Gus knew what that meant. If the people who'd been keeping the boy had said no, his parents would have been home hours ago. The wild kid was in the car, possibly strapped into Sophie's car seat.

If not a straitjacket, he crudely thought, *and let's maybe get a matching one for Mom while we're at it.*

Something about the idea of a freaky kid using his baby sister's booster made him uncomfortable, protective, maybe, which was both new and weird because his sisters didn't need his protection—their parents coddled them plenty. Meanwhile, Gus was expected to be the smart, responsible firstborn/only son, which was a major pain in his ass. Either way, his baby sister was the least offensive of all the girls. With her blond pigtails and squeaky kid voice, she certainly didn't deserve Gus's disdain, and she *really* didn't deserve to be displaced by some woodland creature their parents had decided to take in. Hell, Gus knew what it felt like to be invisible. And while he *wanted* to disappear—couldn't wait for the day, to be honest—if this kid made Sophie feel a certain way, Gus would single-handedly send the wild boy back to wherever the fuck he came from, be it the state-run orphanage or the forest behind their house. Was that callous? Sure. But who gave a shit? His own mother had essentially turned her back on them all nearly a year before, and if anyone asked him, that was pretty fucking callous too.

The sun glinted off the minivan's windshield as it came to a stop in its usual spot. Gus squinted as he watched the driver's-side door open and his dad step out. Studying him from a distance, Gus was surprised at how vulnerable his father looked. Gus was as tall as Dad now at five-foot-ten. The two of them would have looked a hell of a lot alike had Gus not dyed his hair from sandy brown to black. It was almost inevitable he'd eventually look just like Dad, with their matching brown eyes, their lanky stature, the way they both shoved their fingers through their hair when they were unsure or distressed. It was one of the reasons Gus was already planning out his first series of tattoos—Dad didn't have any. Gus intended to get as many as he could as soon as he turned eighteen.

Raising an eyebrow, he noticed Dad hesitate between crossing the front of the car to the passenger's side or staying where he was. Could it be possible that he was having second thoughts? Gus had already pled his case, relaying the inherent dangers of bringing a stranger into the house. He'd explained that allowing some out-of-nowhere mystery kid (and truly, what the fuck was that anyway?) into their lives sounded like a great horror movie opener. But all his warnings had achieved was serious-as-always Willow weeping at the dinner table and his parents' shooting daggers in his direction. So fine, whatever, right? If they wanted to chance it, he couldn't stop them. He didn't have too much longer with this shit, at which point six kids under one roof would drop back to five.

But right now, Gus couldn't remember ever seeing his dad looking so uncomfortable, so unsure.

His father pushed his hands down into the pockets of his kha-kis, pulled them out again, pushed them back in as though searching for courage the way he'd seek out loose change. He shoved his fingers through his hair, looked over his shoulder at the house, then back to the car. Ironic since, when Gus had voiced his opinion on this whole new-kid idea, nobody had given a shit.

You don't look so confident now, do you. . . .

After a long pause, the passenger door swung open, and his mother stepped into the sun. She winced at the glare, then sneezed, same as Gus always did. Gus's dad came around the van to meet her. They both stood there for a while, speaking to each other in hushed tones. For half a second, Gus wasn't sure whether the wild kid was with them after all. Something about the way his parents were behaving struck him as odd.

Then again, it wasn't every day that a nameless ghost of a kid joined a household of seven. If anything, the boy was about to get a crash course in big-family chaos.

Welcome to your new nightmare, asshole. You were better off out there chewing twigs.

His mom was the one to pull the handle and activate the minivan's sliding door—the "robot door," as Sophie liked to call it. *Our car is high-tech!* Mom partially disappeared inside the vehicle, confirming Gus's suspicion about Sophie's car seat. But rather than hopping out in a flurry of loud laughter or flying pigtails the way his baby sister always did, when Mom stepped away from the door, nobody surfaced.

Gus held his breath as he studied the side of the minivan, suddenly picturing the kid barreling out of the car, teeth bared, lunging at his mom. It had been the first argument he'd presented when the idea of Wild Boy residency had been floated.

Yeah, he had snorted, *great idea. Let's bring some feral kid into the house so he can rip our throats out while we sleep.*

It had been a dumb thing to say. It had certainly thrown Sophie into a confused tailspin. Meanwhile, Willow—forever the introspective analyst despite her age—peered at her plate of meatloaf and, out of nowhere, began to cry. It had gotten him grounded for a week, and yeah, it *had* been a shitty thing to say around a bunch of scaredy-cat babies, but his lack of finesse didn't render such a concern groundless, did it? They didn't know who the hell this kid was—nobody seemed to, for God's sake, not them, not the cops—which meant nobody knew what he was capable of. Mom appeared to be 1000 percent convinced that Wild Boy was some sort of gift or test or whatever. But all Gus was sure of was that they knew nothing about this new family member, which was a hell of a lot less than they had known about Maize and Buster when they had brought them home from the pound.

Of course, Wild Boy had been in the news. Gus had followed the story online, morbid curiosity egging him on. He'd read the comments beneath the police department's Facebook post. It looked as though every person in Colorado was having the same thought he was: *creepy.* For a minute, the kid was on the verge of becoming an internet meme (lucky for him, the internet had a hell of a short attention span). And yet, his parents were somehow completely fine with all of it, as though they were brainwashed or something. As though Wild Boy was at the helm of this entire bizarre situation.

"It's okay," Gus heard his mother say from below. "Come on out."

She was motioning with her hands, trying her best to be comforting, reassuring. It reminded Gus of all the times he'd been afraid to do something as a kid, like jump off the side of a pool into her arms or ride his bike without training wheels. As he hid here behind the roof's steep pitch, his heart tightened in his chest at the sight of her hair dancing in the wind, at the memories he hadn't thought of in so long—reminders that his parents weren't all bad, that he'd once been a scaredy-cat kid himself. Hell, even Noah had said it was cool of them to open their door to this kid.

My folks would never do something like that, Noah had said. *My parents are shitty people, man. You might fight with them now and again, but deep down your mom and dad are good.*

Gus squirmed against the rough shingles, the sun suddenly hotter than hellfire as it beat down on his back. He was fixated on the open minivan door, right along with his parents. Would the kid ever come out, or would they eventually give up and drive him back to the home? His mother continued to gesticulate with her hands, her gentle movements like fluttering sparrow wings. Gus decided the kid wasn't going to surface. He had to sneak back into his room before the sun baked him to a crisp.

But then there was movement below.

Something shifted inside the car. Eventually, one twisted leg spidered out of the vehicle, followed by another, both limbs bent at awkward angles. They were positions that legs weren't supposed to bend in, but somehow did anyway.

When the kid finally came into full view, Gus was startled by how small Wild Boy actually was. He swore, the morning the kid had appeared in the trees, he'd looked at least eight or nine years old, but now he was as petite as Sophie. That didn't strike him as right, but maybe he wasn't remembering correctly? Perhaps he had every bit of it wrong, because from what he *did* recall, the wild kid had looked relatively normal. But now, holy shit. He looked less like a child and more like disjointed origami. Every limb appeared to be placed on his body just slightly shy of where it should have been. Every joint bent in a weird, disconcerting way. Even his head seemed off.

Gus pulled himself up just enough to get a better look over the roofline. Was the kid's head way too big for his body, or was the heat finally making Gus hallucinate? And Jesus, his eyes . . . they were massive, like something out of a lousy anime film.

"What the fuck?" he said beneath his breath, because the kid didn't look much like a kid at all. He looked . . . unreal. A creature that didn't belong. Didn't his parents see that?

And then, just as it all crossed Gus's thoughts, the wild kid turned his head and looked up, directly into Gus's eyes.

"Shit!" Gus hissed, and ducked, his heart performing a metal drum solo against his ribs. Except . . . why? What was he getting so worked up about? This was some random boy who was going to live beneath their roof until Gus's parents got a clue and realized this whole thing was bullshit. Wasn't that how most foster cases went? And *this* case—the mindfuck case of the kid with no parents, no name, no anything—it was practically guaranteed to fail.

Yet, for some reason, Gus found himself now lying on those hot shingles staring up at the sky, his hands pressed hard against his Punisher T-shirt, struggling to breathe. He shut his eyes and tried to talk himself down.

"What's wrong with me?" he whispered, breathless. "Jesus, what's wrong with me?"

His heart continued to hammer away, as though trying to burst through his rib cage and out of his body. What the hell was this, a panic attack? He'd had them before, but why now?

"*Stop it*. It's just a fucking weird-ass *kid*," he reminded himself, trying to breathe around the viselike sensation clamped around his chest. But rather than calming down, he nearly jumped out of his skin when he heard Sophie scream "*Mama!*" from the front porch.

5

OLIVE

"**S**ophie, wait!"

Olive's feet skidded across the floor as she ran after her little sister, but despite the shortness of her legs, Sophie was somehow faster than any of the Hansen crew. Their mother had put Olive in charge of taking care of Sophie that day. It wasn't an *official* babysitting job. Official would have been looking after someone who wasn't related to her, who lived in a house not her own. Official would have been getting paid, but according to her parents, getting paid for babysitting was for the birds. Sometimes, Olive was convinced her folks were expecting her to watch both Sophie and Willow for the rest of her life, free of charge, but Olive had bigger plans. She was pinning her hopes on their closest neighbors, the Rodriguez family. They had three kids, ranging from seven to three, and they only lived about three miles away. She'd appeal to Mrs. Rodriguez for a chance in September, when Olive finally turned fourteen. And why not? She was responsible, good with kids. She was better than a mere sibling-sitter, stuck in her own house, underappreciated, making sure Sophie didn't slather homemade slime in her hair or paint a mural on the living room wall. At least, that had been the plan *before* Sophie had barreled through the living room like a tornado on the loose.

Mom and Dad were coming home with the boy from the woods. They'd told Olive to keep Sophie on a short leash upon their return. Mom didn't want Sophie running wild, scaring the kid before he had a chance to get settled in, and Sophie sure as heck could scare someone who wasn't used to her. Sophie could be a wild animal herself. And now the front door was swinging open, and the Hansens' original wild child was dashing outside into the sun.

"Sophie, stop!"

Olive's heart leaped into her throat while Sophie's mint-colored sundress fluttered around her knees, her bare feet stomping across the front porch and down the farmhouse steps. Meanwhile, Olive's dream of making fistfuls of cash at the Rodriguez place flashed before her very eyes.

"Stop!" Olive yelled again, running after her baby sister. She was ready to charge into the yard but stopped short of the porch steps when she heard the familiar sound of oncoming chaos.

"Oh no," she gasped, her dark eyes growing large behind the lenses of her wide-rimmed glasses.

Behind her, there was a cacophony of scrambling paws. She spun around at the clatter of nails on hardwood. Was there time to run back up the steps and slam the door shut before Buster and Maize made it into the foyer? *Maybe*, she thought. *Maybe*. Because between them both, the golden retrievers had a habit of taking the corners too fast and skidding into walls. Sometimes they took each other out like hairy bowling pins, one sliding into the other, both ending up on their backs, scrambling to get up again. Olive pirouetted where she stood, her long braid whipping across her back, but the dogs were already at the door, wild and crazed, their pink tongues lolling out the sides of their mouths as they rushed toward her like a pair of Spanish bulls.

"*No!*" The word tumbled uselessly from her mouth. Olive held up her hands, as though doing so would somehow stop the two animals from barreling past her skinny frame. Of course, they acted as though she was invisible. They bolted right by her and onto the front porch without so much as a sniff or whine, nearly taking out her legs on their way to the minivan.

"Crap!" Olive hissed beneath her breath, because just like that, the day had gone from good to terrible. She'd spent hours doing a great job with Sophie. She'd kept her little sister entertained with endless games of

Candyland and Don't Break the Ice. They had drawn a million princess pictures, read what had struck her as an entire library of books, spent a nominal amount of time in front of the television despite their parents being gone all day. All to fall apart at the last second.

Olive stood on the porch, and a pang of resentment sparked within the depths of her chest as she pushed her glasses up her nose. Why couldn't Sophie just listen for once? Why did she have to make Olive look incapable? Her mother would never let Olive ask Mrs. Rodriguez for that sitter job now. *You couldn't handle your own little sister,* she'd say. *How can you be trusted with other people's kids?*

"Goddamn it," she whispered beneath her breath, her fists tight at her sides. "Goddamn it all to *hell.*"

And then Mom's alarmed voice cut through Olive's discontent.

"Luke, the dogs!"

The words sounded absolutely panicked, which only made Olive feel worse. She watched her father scramble to grab both Buster and Maize by their collars, but it was impossible for one person to wrangle them both. They were uncontrollable, and that was a on a good day. But now? As soon as the dogs reached the van, their excitement took a turn.

Olive had never heard Maize make such an awful noise before. It sounded both angry and afraid, like something between a snarl and a yelp. Buster—typically the quiet one—began to bark at such a bizarre pitch; she couldn't help but press her hands over her ears. Sophie, who had run out to her parents with unfettered excitement, now looked frightened as the dogs she knew so intimately acted completely deranged.

Olive's mother cried out in a panic.

Her father yelled toward the front porch. "Olive, help us!"

Dad's strained request pushed Olive out of her stupor and down the front steps, her braid flying out behind her like a rope. Her bare feet stomped the patchy grass as she rushed toward the dogs and grabbed Maize by the collar.

Maize reeled back and bared her teeth. Startled, Olive cried out and let the dog go.

"Get him back!" Olive heard her dad shout.

When she turned to look, Mom was grabbing the new kid and lifting him back into the minivan. Olive held her breath and tried to catch Maize once again. She was scared to get bitten, but even more afraid to see Maize hurt the new arrival. If that happened, the social services people would find out and the kid would get taken away, but so would Maize, and Olive knew what that would mean.

"Maize, *stop it!*" she yelled, hoping her voice would snap the family dog out of it. Meanwhile, there was a dog whistle buried in one of the kitchen drawers. Olive had found it only days before while searching for an unused Post-it Note. When she'd blown into the thing, the dogs had all but peed themselves in alarm. Their heads had popped up so fast it had reminded her of a Whac-A-Mole game. If she only had that stupid whistle now. But she didn't, so she reached for Maize's yellow collar once more. But before she could slide her fingers beneath it, a hand fell onto her shoulder and gave her a quick backward pull.

Gus stepped in front of her, his dark hair and black T-shirt a moving shadow as he lunged forward and caught the dog himself. Maize tried to get away, her back legs scrambling, but Gus didn't relent. Rather than letting go, he gave Maize a stern pull toward the outbuilding they called the barn.

Sophie ran to Olive, crashed into her, and wrapped small arms around her elder sister's waist. Meanwhile, their father had managed to get Buster by the collar—green to Maize's yellow—and both he and Gus dragged the frenzied retrievers away from the van with stiff arms and determined steps.

Eventually the minivan's side door slid open. Mom and the new kid slowly stepped out onto the grass while Sophie cried into Olive's shirt. Olive was eventually able to push her away enough to hear, to finally able to make out what her little sister was saying.

"I'm scared," Sophie said, weeping behind strands of honey-blond hair. "I'm scared, I'm scared, I'm scared."

6

EDEN

Eden and Willow nearly crashed into each other as they rushed out of their rooms. The two girls stood motionless, Eden straining to listen over her pulse whooshing against her ears. For a split second she convinced herself that the yelling she'd heard had been nothing but her imagination, just static in her earbuds. Too many true crime podcasts. Too many documentaries about bad men she secretly found fascinating. But no, the yelling hadn't been a figment. Again, voices rose from outside.

"Get him back!"

"Was that Dad?" Willow asked.

Eden wasn't sure she'd ever seen her younger sister's eyes as large as they were just then, and she'd seen them plenty big before. She and Willow were total opposites. While sixteen-year-old Eden was hiding away in her room reading Ann Rule and googling death row inmates—a fact she was sure would horrify her mother had she known—Willow was into stuff like Jane Austen and doing her hair up into crown braids atop her head, somehow having mastered both classic literature and complicated hairstyles all by the age of ten. Eden listened to Billie Eilish and Lana Del Rey. Willow was a Swiftie with a mega-crush on Harry Styles. Willow was the perfect daughter, a parental favorite. Meanwhile, Eden was snapping at Gus's heels for the honor of worst kid in the Hansen household. She knew she annoyed her mother beyond words—maybe that's why Mom hardly spoke to her anymore. But even with all those complicated, resentful emotions, Eden felt her face flush hot at the strained cry coming from outside.

"What the hell?"

Scurrying past Willow's door, Eden took the stairs two by two. She could hear Willow behind her, and when the sisters finally found themselves on the front porch, Eden couldn't put together what she was seeing.

Gus and their dad were hauling the dogs to the barn, which was beyond weird. They had never put the dogs in there before. Dad had made it a point to tell them all to stay out of there. *It's dangerous. Rusty nails and stuff.*

By the van, Sophie was scream-crying into Olive's stomach, jumping up and down in tiny hops, same as she used to do when she was a toddler, desperately wanting to be picked up.

Eden squinted against the glare of the sun, shifting her attention to their mother. Mom's back was turned toward the house. She was crouching down, shielding something with her body. Despite the pandemonium, Eden couldn't help but call out.

"Mom . . . ?"

For an uncomfortable stretched-out moment, their mother didn't move. There was a second where Eden's heart skipped a beat, a familiar sense of ill ease falling over her like filmy, tattered gauze. Somehow she knew their mother had heard her loud and clear, but she was choosing not to acknowledge her. Mom's behavior had been weird for a while. It was something Dad blamed on her migraines, on the pain in her ears, on fatigue. But Mom's behavior had gone off the rails after Adam. There had been times when Eden had caught her completely zoned out, as though having an out-of-body experience. One such instance had occurred in the kitchen while Mom was preparing dinner. Eden had walked in on her standing at the kitchen counter, blank-faced, a giant kitchen knife gripped in her right hand. Eden hated to admit it, but it had scared the shit out of her. But this? Pretending not to hear her? It was creepy and gave her the sensation of being a player in one of the many dreadful podcasts she was so hopelessly addicted to—a bewildered girl unsure of where she was or what to do. The sensation of something being off, yet not being able to pinpoint exactly why.

Next to her, Willow caught her hand. When Eden glanced over, her little sister looked pale as a sheet. Willow's bottom lip was trembling. Her eyes were wavy behind a sheen of tears, like ancient glass.

"It's all wrong," Willow whispered. "Can't you feel it?"

Eden certainly sensed something, but she wouldn't go so far as to say it was *all wrong*. Gus had made his opinion on the matter plain. He'd scared the hell out of Willow and Sophie at the dinner table with stories of feral kids cannibalizing their hapless adoptive families. Personally, Eden had found her brother's dramatics beyond entertaining. She'd imagined the whole thing after he'd put the possibility in their heads—a child with knives for teeth and a taste for blood. A little bit of horror injected into their boring-as-hell daily lives? Sure, she was up for it. But Eden was no dummy, and she certainly wasn't one to slurp up her brother's histrionics the way Willow and Sophie did. She had conducted her own internet searches, and while she'd somewhat expected to feel the same as Gus— *the weird woods kid will kill us all*—she came away from the stories of abandoned kids with the opposite mindset. All the gruesome stories she listened to, day in and day out, had taught her that the world was cruel, but it also convinced her that kindness could save it. And what was taking in a kid with no family, no history, no identity, if anything but kind?

"It's going to be okay," she promised her sister, giving Willow's hand a squeeze. "Just a little weird at first, but we'll figure it all out."

Eden watched Willow attempt to swallow her tears, but the quiet gasp that tumbled from deep within her was less than encouraging. Eden turned back to their mother, and it was then that she could finally see the boy standing next to their mom.

Something within Eden's chest shifted at the sight of him. He looked different from what she remembered, all sharp angles, as though someone had carried him to the top of a building and dropped him to the ground. She could hear Willow crying softly next to her. Perhaps it was fear, or maybe her kid sister was mourning the life they'd all just lost, failing to acknowledge what they were gaining in return. Sure, the boy was hard to look at. There appeared to be something off about every bit of him, as though God (if there even was one) had put him together with his eyes closed. That, however, may have very well been why he'd been abandoned. Perhaps his original family couldn't see past all those flaws—the large head and wide-set eyes, the birdlike arms that were way too long for his frame. Even his red hair looked weird. Fake. Like something out of Jim Henson's brain. A Muppet. Maybe those very features were what had damned the kid in the first place.

Or maybe Willow was onto something here. Maybe something *was* wrong.

"Mom?" Eden called out again.

This time her mother met Eden's gaze. A moment of blankness passed between them, but Mom eventually smiled. That odd, empty-eyed smile pushed Eden into a tailspin of trying to convince herself that her own optimism was on point, that her dark side—the girl who relished all those serial killer documentaries—wasn't to be acknowledged here. Everything *would* be okay. Unusual at first. Mom was just overwhelmed, surprised by what she'd signed on for—a reality check, so to speak. But everything was fine, because their parents wouldn't have brought the boy back if there was something wrong with him, right? They wouldn't have put their five children in danger for the good of a stranger.

Or would they?

She pushed the thought away, then gave Willow's hand a tug.

"Come on. Sophie needs us," she said.

But rather than walking down the porch steps with her, Willow turned and stepped back inside the house. There was something about *that* action that made Eden uncomfortable, just as uncomfortable as their mother's vacant smile. Sophie was having a meltdown. Willow had chosen to avoid the situation entirely. Meanwhile, their mother continued to wear that unsettling expression, remaining eerily motionless where she stood.

Grinning. Frozen. As if unable to move. Unable to see.

7

LUKE

Luke couldn't think straight. With his fingers hooked beneath Buster's green collar, he marched the dog toward the barn, Gus not far behind him.

He'd never heard Buster bark aggressively at anything or anyone before, let alone pull the kind of bullshit he'd just witnessed by the minivan. Same for Maize, who was still snorting and trying to break free of Gus's grasp. Luke picked up the pace, imagining the retriever wriggling out of her collar the way she used to as a pup. Except this time, she wouldn't be leaping after butterflies and digging holes in the yard. This time, with teeth bared, she'd make a beeline back to the van and the kid inside it. Maize and Buster weighed at least seventy pounds apiece. Meanwhile, the boy Isla was choosing to call Rowan likely weighed forty, and that was soaking wet. Luke shuddered, his darkest thoughts tripping over the possibility. *Cujo,* he thought, then quickly threw open the barn's latch and escorted Buster inside. When he turned to look at Gus, his son wore a strained expression Luke wasn't sure he'd seen before.

"Gus . . . ?"

He and Isla used to call their only son Augie until one day at the ripe old age of five, August had screwed his face up in distaste and insisted Augie was a baby name. More than a decade later, his proper moniker wasn't acceptable either. He'd been Gus since thirteen, though Isla tended to "forget" more often than she remembered. Luke tried, however. Despite his and Gus's tendency to butt heads, he hated upsetting his kid. But at that instant, Gus looked less *I'm so pissed* and more *what the hell did I just see.*

"What's up?" Luke asked, realizing immediately how stupid of a question it was. The family dogs had nearly ripped their newest family member apart. Hell, his own nerves were live wires beneath his skin. But Gus? He wasn't the type to get shaken up easily. He'd always been the off-kilter kid, the one who liked Halloween more than Christmas, chose *Frankenweenie* over *Blue's Clues*, and favored punk rock by the time he was twelve. He'd always been stoic. Except, standing there with his fingers hooked firmly beneath Maize's collar, Gus appeared to have finally seen a ghost he didn't like.

"What's *up*?" Gus echoed, shaking his head in a not-so-subtle way. *Did you miss it?* his tone implied. *Were you asleep just now? Didn't you see what just went down?*

Luke motioned for him to close the door with a wave of his hand. Gus did as he was asked, releasing Maize as soon as the door was shut. Maize was immediately at the jamb, shoving her nose against the crack between the wall and the door, whining, instinctively pawing at the ground, blowing hot bursts of air through her nostrils like a bull ready to fight. How long would it take her to dig her way beneath the door? A few hours? All night?

"Have you ever seen them act this way before?" Gus asked, shooting Maize a look. "They don't get that worked up even when there are rabbits in the yard, and Buster nearly loses his mind then."

Remembering he was still holding Buster back, Luke let the dog go and exhaled. His fingers were sore from being yanked by the dog collar. "It's new" was all he could think to say.

"New? Dad." Gus was doing that thing he did, looking him squarely in the eyes, giving him a *don't kid yourself* face. It was an expression Luke wouldn't have dared give his own father. If he had, he'd have gotten the skin of his dad's knuckles stuck between his teeth. "It's *new*? Really?"

"What are you getting at?" Luke asked, sounding far more impatient than he intended. He wasn't about to deny that Rowan was the source of the dogs' strange behavior, but there was no telling as to why. They didn't know where Rowan came from, what kind of life he'd had before. Maybe he smelled in a way the dogs didn't like? Since he appeared from the woods, maybe he'd been raised by a pack of wolves, something he'd gone over in his head a million times. Who the hell knew?

"I don't know," Gus muttered. Having turned away from his father, he was kicking at the dirt floor like a kid being scolded. Luke was used to seeing him ornery. For Gus, that was par for the course. But the way he was holding his shoulders—tense and uncomfortable—the way he was flexing his fingers at his sides . . . it was clear that something was weighing heavy on his mind.

"Look," Luke said, trying to soothe a kid who wasn't the best at expressing himself. "I get it. That was . . . not what I expected."

Often, Luke felt responsible for Gus's emotional shortcomings. It was something he'd passed on to his son. After five kids, Luke had gotten much better at talking out his feelings, but back when Gus had been little, he hadn't been particularly "in touch" with his feelings. Now, whenever his son lashed out, he couldn't help but wonder if it was because of parenting issues. Could he have been more patient? More compassionate? Just plain lenient? Pretty soon, Gus would be a legal adult—a fact that made Luke's head spin, because where had the time gone? Time, that goddamn thief. Luke had no doubt his son would be out the door and on his own the first second he could manage it. The question was would he look back to his parents and see them as having done the best they could, or would he run away from them, having decided they hadn't done enough?

"And no," Luke continued, "I've never seen the dogs react this way. To anything. You're right. But we have to give this a chance, okay? It's been a whole twenty minutes, Gus."

"Yeah," Gus grumbled, his back still to Luke. "Just . . . never mind."

Luke frowned, then glanced to Maize. She was still whining and pawing at the door, her yellow collar quickly turning brown with kicked-up dirt.

"Maize, hey! Leave it!" Luke snapped, choosing to acknowledge the dog because it was easier than continuing to address his son. Maize gave another frustrated snort, then quickly wandered off in another direction, her nose sniffing the floor, determined to find some other way out.

"So, what, we're just going to leave them in here?" Gus asked of the dogs, deftly diverting the conversation to something less about him. He'd learned the art of deflection from a master, no doubt about that.

"Just until we're sure what just happened won't happen again," Luke said. "We'll ease them into it, start fresh tomorrow. Obviously, it's too much all at once."

"Too much," Gus scoffed, unconvinced. Frankly, Luke wasn't all that convinced either. Both Buster and Maize had dealt with plenty of guests before. In-laws. Various family members. Dinner guests. Babysitters. Even a homeschool playgroup of screaming, giggling, hyperactive children who had chased both dogs around the property like paparazzi pursuing two canine celebrities. Buster and Maize had always taken the appearance of any stranger in stride, and they'd always been considered sweet and friendly by everyone they met. Until now.

That, and Maize was Gus's dog. They'd adopted her as a puppy when Isla had been pregnant with Willow—a pregnancy that six-year-old August had had a particularly difficult time dealing with. Maize had been his reprieve from the thought of another baby in the house. Since then, the two had been inseparable. They had slept in the same bed until Maize had gotten so big she'd pushed Gus off his mattress. Luke and Isla had laughed about it, but Gus hadn't been happy at the thought of Maize sleeping next to his bed rather than in it. The kid may be nearing adulthood now, but he and that aging golden retriever were still thick as thieves. And compared to the bedroom rug, the barn was a world away.

"It won't be for long," Luke promised. "We'll make it comfortable. They'll be okay in here if they're together. It's only for tonight."

"Oh this is bullshit," Gus hissed beneath his breath. The curse twinged Luke's nerves; yet another act he wouldn't have dared perform around his dear old dad.

"Well, what else do you want me to do? It's better than letting them maul a kid, Gus!" he shot back, then shoved his fingers through his hair.

He hated how short his patience was these days, especially with his son. He'd been tense for what felt like a year. There had been Isla's pregnancy, then the loss of Adam. There was Isla's downward spiral, the hospitalization. And now there was this crazy Rowan situation. But this wasn't the time or the place for one of their epic father/son fights, no matter how stressed either of them were. Beyond the barn's closed door, Isla was still out by the minivan, or maybe she was trying to show the kid around their house. Sophie had been freaking out. Willow had looked shaken, and Luke needed to get out there, *now*.

"Keep them in here," he warned, giving Gus a serious look. "I'll bring out blankets and their food and water bowls. It's summer. They'll be fine."

"And what if they *don't* get used to the kid?" Gus asked, imploring his father for a genuine answer.

If the dogs didn't get used to Rowan, who would pay for the maladjustment? Would he and Isla have the stones to send a child back to the state orphanage, or would it be less of a moral burden to rehome a pair of senior golden retrievers in the name of giving someone a better life? It was a good question—one that Luke didn't have an immediate response to. Hell, what if the Hansens themselves didn't get used to the kid? What would happen then?

"They *will* get used to him," Luke said, a nonanswer if there ever was one. "I'm going to go check in with your mother, all right?"

Gus shrugged, brooding.

"You should come introduce yourself, maybe," Luke suggested.

"And if I don't?" Gus asked, sullen.

"Then you don't. But it would be better if you did."

"Better than what?"

It was Luke's turn to shrug. "Better than living in the barn, I guess," he replied, then turned to go, not sure where that answer had come from. He didn't like himself for saying it. Was he suggesting that his own son would be cast out if he didn't accept the stranger—the "stepbrother"—he and Isla had just brought in?

Letting it go, Luke exited the outbuilding and shut the door behind him, leaving Gus with the dogs . . . wondering if Rowan had been cast out as well. Wondering if, somehow, he was repeating a history that wasn't theirs to repeat.

8

ISLA

Isla's hands were quaking, but she was trying to keep it together. She didn't want her children to see her falter as she led Rowan up their farmhouse steps.

The act of it felt significant. It was a crucial point for both Rowan and the Hansens, a sea change that she wished Luke had been there for. But her husband was still in the outbuilding with August and the dogs, and that entire experience near the minivan had left Isla shaking. She couldn't believe Buster and Maize had come barreling out of the house the way they had. She couldn't wrap her mind around the fact that they'd been so aggressive, so unhinged. It was part of the reason why she ultimately refused to wait for Luke to come back. She was scared that, somehow, one of the dogs would find their way out of the barn and come rushing back toward Rowan, jaws snapping, hackles raised. In that instant, one thought repeated itself in her mind:

Protect him. No matter what.

Rowan ascended the front porch steps at a painfully slow pace, his awkwardly angled knees and ankles forcing Isla to clench her jaw. She was waiting for him to lose his footing and fall backward onto the front walkway. Something about the child made her feel as though any stumble would cause him to shatter, like a Swarovski figurine exploding into a million crystal shards. Part of her wanted to help him, to press her hand to his hunched back and push him along. She thought about stuffing her hands beneath his armpits and hoisting him up the steps—something she'd done a million times with her own children when they took too long and her patience wore thin. But the lizard part of her brain recoiled from the idea. There was a dark doubt twisted up within her that she refused to acknowledge, a doubt she was desperate to push down until she could catch it beneath her heel and snuff it out.

Teeth clamped tight, she forced herself to reach out, the palm of her hand just barely brushing the back of Rowan's shirt. The sensation of touch made Rowan pause and turn, his distractingly large eyes zeroing in on Isla's face. For the briefest of moments, she was sure she heard him purr deep in his throat. But before she could consider it further, she was distracted by a tingle in her palm—a sudden sensation of neuropathy, as though the second she'd touched him, her fingers had fallen asleep. It surprised her, proof that she was more nervous than she thought.

"It's okay," she said, forcing a wavering smile his way. "Home," she told him. "Do you know what 'home' means?"

Rowan didn't reply. He turned his attention back to the steps and continued his ascent, leaving Isla to wonder if this really was the right thing to do. Was bringing this mysterious child into their home a mistake?

Not just taking him in—fostering *him, for Christ's sake!* a small voice inside her head piped up.

Yet, just as her thoughts began to get away from her, she self-corrected and found the courage to press her hand firmly against Rowan's bumpy spine. Her palm prickled once more, but when she recognized the vertebral bulges beneath her palm, she was overwhelmed by a surreal sense of calm. It was as if the child had a power to him, an ability to quell her anxiety and give promise that all this was meant to be.

If she thought back, she was sure she'd experienced something similar when she had spotted him standing among the trees, her gloved hands holding fistfuls of weeds and dirt. Their eyes had met, and for just a second, a younger version of Isla was running through the prairie grass with a wilted dandelion bouquet held fast in her hand. She could smell the bright scent of clover, could feel the hot Colorado sun on her bare shoulders as she and her cousin, Ruby Mae, bolted through the fields behind Ruby's house. She was transported back to a time when things had been good, right before the world itself had wilted as quickly as those dandelions plucked from the ground.

It had been the summer before Isla's and Ruby Mae's lives were set to drastically change. Ruby Mae was going to be a veterinarian. She was off to California in the fall. Isla had dreamed of being a teacher and planned on working while getting herself through two years of community college.

That evening had been their last one. Walking in the prairie grass at dusk. Discussing the future. Discussing boys. Picking wildflowers and weaving crowns. There had been a storm in the distance, the scent of rain.

Then Isla found herself in a downpour on some random street in town.

There was the memory of Skye screaming at Isla when Isla arrived home. *Where's Ruby Mae?! Where is she? Where?!* Isla didn't understand. Because what did she mean? Ruby Mae was home, where she was supposed to be.

Except, after that night, Isla never saw her cousin again.

Isla gasped, pulling her hand away from Rowan's back, immediately returned to the here and now. It was so incredible, the way he could do that, just another affirmation (or was it a hallucination?) that there was something special about him. Isla felt a connection with this child—*I know him . . . I know him*—regardless of whether he'd ever speak a word. Every time she looked at his Picasso-like face, she was overwhelmed with a sense of the past, with the sense of a different time and place. Perhaps a different life, or the life she'd been denied when Adam had been stolen away. Or maybe it was the life that ended when her mother had slammed the door in Isla's face.

Get out!

Watching Rowan climb up the final step of the front porch, she wondered if that was possible—if, somehow, the two of them were kindred spirits. Connected. Bound by some inexplicable, undeniable thing. Or, perhaps, the therapist at the hospital was right, and the things she was feeling had nothing to do with Rowan at all.

Grief is a beast, she'd been told. *A monster. If you don't deal with it properly, it will destroy you. Eat you alive.*

But taking Rowan in was a way to deal with it, right? Of course it was. Yes, of course. It's why Isla was doing this, why she *had* to do it. Maybe the therapist was right. This had nothing to do with Rowan. This was a way to heal herself, a way to heal her family.

Rowan stopped when he reached the planks of the front porch. He stared down at his feet, though Isla couldn't place the expression on his face. Had he never seen such flooring before, or was it something else? Perhaps, somewhere within that nonverbal mind, he was processing the same feelings as Isla. Leaving old pain behind. Embracing change. Starting a new life, for better or worse.

Stepping around him, Isla motioned for Rowan to come forward, to move over the threshold and into his new home. She could hear a few of her children shuffling about behind her, their eyes no doubt glued to the mysterious new boy.

Again, Isla was hit with that familiar sense of dark doubt. Maybe this wasn't right. Maybe it was too much to ask of her family. Perhaps she'd gotten in over her head. Maybe she and Luke *could* have another baby if they just kept trying. After all, it wasn't that she couldn't get pregnant; it was keeping the baby that was the tricky part. But if they had Rowan, there would be no room for another. If they took this child on, that chapter of Isla's life, that hope, would be forever gone.

She looked down at her feet just like Rowan and clasped her hands together, shutting her eyes tight. She'd never been much for religion, but after pausing for a second of prayer to who knows what—*guide me; help me know what's best*—she opened her eyes to see Rowan standing in front of her. He was inside the house, the tips of his pigeon-toed sneakers touching hers. Before she knew it, she was back on the prairie. She and Ruby, laughing as they spun in circles, their arms held out propeller-straight.

They had spun until they'd both collapsed with laughter, hands catching hands, eyes looking up to clouds that, in the distance, were shifting from white to a deep, angry blue. Despite it having been over twenty-five years ago, Isla remembered that afternoon as vividly as if it had happened just a few hours before. It had been one of the last times she and Ruby Mae had been together, as close as sisters, as enmeshed as identical twins.

"Mom . . . ?"

Isla shuddered as the memory collapsed around her in a wash of red, Eden's voice cutting through the warm summer air that suddenly smelled faintly of ozone and rain.

"Are you okay?" Eden asked, her face a mask of concern.

"What? Yes, I'm fine," Isla said, rapidly blinking, as if to clear her vision, to shake off her reverie. "Why do you ask?"

"You're crying," Eden told her, surprised that Isla didn't know.

Isla reached up, her fingertips skimming her cheeks. Expecting to find a single tear, she discovered with mild alarm that her entire face was weeping wet.

"Oh," she said quietly, her focus rapt on her now-glistening fingers.

Finally looking up, Isla found herself staring into Rowan's face. He, too, was inspecting her fingers with fascination, as though never having seen a person cry before. And when their eyes met, he canted his head just slightly, then forced a chilling sort of smile. An imitator. An echo. A wavering expression reflected back at her, finding a home on a face other than her own.

9

WILLOW

Willow thought being good was super important. She was only ten—
still practically a baby, the way I see it, as her mom loved to remind
her—but that didn't mean anything. Willow had already figured out what
life was all about, and it wasn't about money or stuff or even about babies.
Mom was hung up on that part of it, especially after Adam disappeared,
poof, like a magic trick. But no, life wasn't about any of that stuff. It was
about being nice, sharing, and helping people. That's why nobody had had
to ask Willow to do what she'd done. She'd figured it out all by herself.

Willow had taken Mom's side before anyone else had. The family
meeting had been super tough. Gus had been really annoying that night,
and Eden hadn't been much help. Willow could tell even Dad had been
iffy on the whole idea, but she also saw how sad and tired Mom looked.
It was what had made Willow get up from the couch, walk across the
room, and sit right at Mom's feet. Eventually, Sophie had joined her, and
soon Olive did too. That was three against two, so Gus and Eden were
outnumbered. Mom had started crying, and after a while Dad came over,
making it all okay.

Willow knew her new brother would need a place to sleep, so a week
earlier, she had packed all her stuff into plastic bins and old cardboard
boxes she'd found up in the attic and moved it all into Sophie's room.
She'd only asked Dad for help when it came time to move her furniture.
She had tried moving that stuff on her own, but she gave up when she
got her dresser stuck against the door jamb. Surprisingly, Sophie hadn't

complained when Willow and Dad appeared at Sophie's bedroom door, pushing furniture into an already tiny room.

Their mother finally looked happy, and that made Willow happy too. Mom took both Willow and Sophie out on a fun mother-daughter date. Olive decided to stay home and watch Netflix, and Eden never went anywhere with them anyway. Willow was pretty sure Eden would have said no to anything unless it was a Billie Eilish or Lana Del Rey concert. But whatever. Her loss.

After Adam, Mom hardly went out at all. Sometimes she didn't even come downstairs. But *that* day Mom had been so happy, she'd taken the girls to Target and let them choose whatever they wanted, anything at all. Willow had gotten the final Miss Peregrine book while Sophie had chosen a really cute Squishmallow shaped like a unicorn. Mom had gotten some stuff for her new brother's room too. New sheets, a lamp shaped like a rocket ship, and a stuffed dinosaur. Then they'd stopped by Mr. Frosty's and gotten drippy waffle cones with sprinkles and gummy bears on top. It had all felt awesome, like Christmas or a birthday, and Willow had been proud of herself. It was proof that she'd done the right thing.

But now, a good half hour after Mom and Dad had come back from the children's home, Willow found herself watching the boy Mom called Rowan step into her old room, and she didn't feel quite so great about it anymore.

Sophie fidgeted next to Willow, maybe because she could tell Willow was feeling weird, or maybe Sophie felt that way too. Willow's old room had a new bed and dresser now. Mom—who had been nothing but sad for months—was super excited by the idea of having a new person in the house. She'd even painted a toy box to look like a robot's head, which sat in the corner now. A mobile of the solar system hung above it. Willow had put it together herself from a kit Olive had found on Amazon. It spun slowly, pushed by the breeze made by the ceiling fan. Rowan watched those rotating planets with a blank sort of stare, and Willow guessed he probably hated it. She had gotten mad with the paints the kit had provided, and the brushes had been awful. She could have done a better job putting it together, and she supposed he noticed. Or maybe he somehow knew that Willow had changed her mind about him. Perhaps she was giving off a "vibe," as Eden would have said. The fact of the matter was Willow had been okay with this idea a few days ago, but now? Now she kind of wanted her old room back. The new-brother idea no longer struck her as all that great.

Maybe, never mind. Maybe, let's move my stuff back the way it was.

Eventually, her mother nudged Willow's shoulder. *Go.* Willow didn't need to be told twice. She took Sophie by the hand and went back to their now-shared room, closing the door behind them.

Sophie climbed up onto her bed, pressed her back against the wall, and hugged her knees to her chest. With her chin hidden behind her knees, she curled into herself like a snail missing its shell. All Willow could see were her crooked pigtails poking up from atop her head.

"Are you still scared?" Willow asked.

Sophie had really freaked out outside, and Willow remembered how spooked she'd been when Gus had said all those awful things at the dinner table weeks before. It had been the night Mom told them she wanted to bring the boy from the woods home not as a visitor, but as a family member. Despite herself, Willow had burst into tears that evening. Their parents had blamed Gus and his dumb stories for Willow's meltdown—*you're terrifying your sister!*—but she hadn't believed any of the things her brother had said. Instead, she'd been overwhelmed by the idea of their family not quite being *their* family anymore. An outsider would come into their circle and things would change, and Willow hadn't wanted things to change. She liked things exactly the way they were.

But eventually, she forced herself to not only accept what was going to happen, but to be okay with it. It was why she'd sided with Mom when it came to the boy from the woods. It had been the right thing to do. And her bedroom? Well, Rowan was a boy. He'd need his own space. It wasn't as though Gus was going to share his room with an odd little kid. Willow thought offering her own room would help her get used to the new situation, and for a little while it had worked. But now, being in Sophie's room gave her an odd sort of feeling. Seeing her sister curled up that way, Willow knew something was off, something way beyond it all just feeling new and strange.

"What's wrong?" Willow asked from atop her own bed.

"My head hurts," Sophie said softly, as though not wanting to be heard.

"Hurts how?" Willow asked, pulling her legs up onto her mattress.

"My ears. A buzzing sound."

"Like a headache?" Willow asked. She wasn't sure whether Sophie had ever had a headache before. Did little kids get those, or was that only grown-ups and older kids?

"I don't know," Sophie said, her words so quiet Willow could hardly hear them. "I don't feel so good."

"You aren't going to throw up, are you?" Willow imagined her little sister puking all over the bedroom rug. If anything could make her regret giving up her room, it would be that.

Sophie didn't answer. She lay down on the bed, her body still curled into a ball, and hid her face in her pillow. From where Willow was sitting, it looked like Sophie was crying again.

"You got really scared downstairs when the dogs went nuts," Willow told her. "There are chemicals in your body that go into your blood when you're scared like that. I read about it in my science book just the other day. It's a fact."

Sophie peeked out from her pillow, listening.

"They can make you feel super sick if there's too much at once. But the feeling goes away. You just gotta wait it out, Soph." Willow gave her sister a smile, proud of herself for remembering at least some of the biology lesson she'd done as part of her science curriculum earlier that year. "Take down your pigtails," she told her. "Just close your eyes and try to take a nap."

Sophie did as she was told, yanking the pink elastic ties from her hair, then squeezing her eyes shut, willing herself to sleep with fists clenching her blanket tight. Willow lay down as well, trying to let her own worries about the kid now living in her old room go. Sure, he looked creepy, and yeah, it would be weird to have someone new at the dinner table, especially someone like him. But it would be okay. Right?

Willow closed her eyes the same as she'd told her little sister to do.

"Just take a nap, and when you wake up, it'll all feel more normal."

It's what Mom would have told them. *Take a step back. Relax. Let your mind settle.*

Except, just as Willow began to do those things, every muscle in her body went tight. A noise came from outside. Beyond the window, she could hear Buster and Maize going crazy again. She bolted upright, threw her legs over the edge of her mattress, and ran to the bedroom window to see what was up. She was just in time to catch Gus stepping out of the barn, struggling to close the door behind him without letting the dogs run back toward the house. Both retrievers were going bananas in there. Except they didn't sound angry—they sounded scared. And from the way Gus turned back to the barn and just stood there, staring at the door he'd shut, she could tell her big brother knew it too. Willow could feel how nervous he was. Anxiety was coming off him in giant, electrified waves, and seeing him so unsure made her chest feel tight.

She lifted her hand and pressed it against the window over where he stood, blotting him out. When she couldn't see him anymore, she took a deep breath and reminded herself that things were going to be okay. Everyone was just wound up. First-day jitters and all that stuff. They were all feeling out of step. It would be all right.

But for now, none of it struck her as right at all.

10

EDEN

Had the unease during that evening's dinner grown any more intense, Eden wouldn't have been able to help herself. She could feel a laugh sitting heavy at the pit of her stomach, the kind that was loud and sudden, untethered and inappropriate. Her blue eyes—exact replicas of her mother's—hidden behind the brooding veil of her flaxen hair, moved from face to face. Her family was sitting there, as silent as wax figures from Madame Tussauds. Meanwhile, the boy named Rowan occupied their mother's chair. Mom sitting to his right like a handmaid waiting to serve. *Under his eye.*

Eden watched Rowan from behind her lowered lashes, pretending to focus on her spinach salad and green beans. She found the kid both fascinating and horrible, the equivalent of an accident you'd catch just the slightest glimpse of while driving down the road. The kid looked like a creature who had crawled from the depths of the woods, but also just a boy who had come from God only knew where. A torture house? A middle-of-nowhere cannibal farm? A witch's hut with a monster in the basement? Terrible circumstances, no doubt. It was the type of thing she listened to on a loop, podcasts about shocking situations, about awful people stripping others of their innocence. It's the kind of stuff she loved to binge, the stuff Netflix Top Ten lists were made of. And here he was, sitting at the head of her family's dinner table.

She felt a confusing mix of sympathy and fright for him. She knew that beneath the surface, beneath his bizarre physical appearance,

Rowan shouldn't have been much different from five-year-old Sophie. Time was supposed to pass, leaving Rowan to grow up and hit his teens. He shouldn't have been much different from how Eden was now. But of course, Rowan would never grow up. His previous life had dealt him a bad hand. It had twisted him into something akin to Frankenstein's failed experiment, a monstrous Peter Pan.

Everyone picked at their food, seemingly distracted in their own way. Gus looked utterly livid as he poked a pile of mashed potatoes with the tines of his fork, stewing in silence, probably about to implode. Olive appeared to be praying over a bit of roasted chicken, her eyes narrowed behind her glasses in what Eden could only make out as frustrated disappointment. Meanwhile, Willow and Sophie sat so close to each other they may as well have been eating from the same plate. They both looked uncomfortable, like they could jump up and rush out of the dining room at a second's notice.

Rowan, on the other hand, simply sat there, not touching his fork, not even glancing at the food his foster mom had placed before him. Either he wasn't hungry, or—and this was a very real possibility—the food in front of him was so unfamiliar he didn't dare touch it. Again, Eden's thoughts tumbled to terrible scenarios. She pictured a dog's bowl, a few pieces of dry kibble lying at the bottom.

They think he may have been kept in a cage, her mother had whispered.

That image triggered an altogether different train of thought. Eden concentrated, listening through the dining room, through the walls of their house, stretching her ears all the way out to the barn, where she could faintly hear Buster and Maize whining to be let out.

She tried not to look directly at him, but Eden could see Rowan's eyes roving. His shock of red hair reminded her of cartoon fire, his wide-set eyes those of a fish. They all homeschooled now. The pandemic had taught them they liked learning at home far more than in a stick-up-the-ass stiff-backed classroom. Even Gus said it was better than getting up at the butt crack of dawn to sit beneath buzzing fluorescent tubes. But before COVID, they had all attended public school, and back then Eden had known a girl named Jessica with eyes just like Rowan's. *Hey, Fishface!* the boys had teased, sucking in their cheeks and pantomiming gills on the sides of their necks. It was the kind of cruelty Rowan would become familiar with, homeschool or not. During a trip to the movies or while on a quick grocery store run, there would always be someone ready to point with a mocking grin.

Rowan's focus shifted from Willow to Olive to Gus. Down the line he went, watching each person for a few eternity-feeling seconds before moving on to the next. Eventually, it was Eden's turn, and when Rowan's gaze moved to her, she was determined to meet his stare.

When the topic of "the wild boy" coming to live with them had come up, there was no consensus. Quite the opposite, really. Eden and Gus had remained on their own side of the living room while everyone else—even Dad—had congregated around Mom. Gus had muttered a *fuck this* beneath his breath, and Eden had agreed. This whole thing was beyond nuts. But their parents liked to pretend there was democracy here—pretend, because Mom almost always got what she wanted, Eden's sisters falling in line to appease her, Dad shortly following suit. They had given Gus and Eden a chance to change their minds, watching the two eldest children of the family with expectant eyes. Neither Eden nor Gus had budged on their decision, but it made no difference. Their mother could have gone to the foster home and chosen anyone, a sister Sophie's age who would play board games and draw unicorn pictures, dress up like a princess and watch endless Disney movies. But Mom wanted *him*—Rowan—because he had appeared out of thin air. In the middle of a missing-child epidemic, no less. And what was even weirder was that no one appeared to be looking for him.

Mom was convinced it was a sign, a gift from some higher plane. And so Gus and Eden had been outvoted, which was how Rowan came to be sitting at the head of the table like a little sultan—the mysterious prince of the coniferous Colorado forest.

Part of her wanted Rowan to know that he was seen, that she wasn't afraid to look him in the eyes, no matter how disconcerting that was.

Another part of her was determined to show him that she wasn't a push-over, that he may have scared her younger sisters, but she was prepared for whatever he was going to dish out. She wanted it to be a warning: *You aren't about to take over this place. This is* my *family.*

And yet she had no idea where that sense of Rowan wanting to *take over* was coming from, same as the thought she'd had about him never growing up. Nobody knew how old Rowan really was—seven, maybe? He was twig-skinny and looked like he weighed as much as Sophie, which wasn't a whole lot at all. But here was Eden, staring down a child nearly half her age, determined to remind him with her unwavering glance that regardless of how much Mom wanted him here, he was still a visitor. There was no guarantee he would be staying. He needed to watch his step.

Hey, Fishface!

She actually smirked behind her hair but immediately felt awful for doing it.

God, what's wrong with you? she thought. *How could you even think that?*

What, was she a bully now? She had told herself that despite her criticisms of this entire debacle, her parents were doing a kind thing. A good thing. The *right* thing. And yet here she was, thinking these bitter, resentful thoughts.

Shame forced her to look into Rowan's eyes. Out of nowhere, she yearned to convey what she *wanted* to feel: sympathy, some form of understanding, because all in all, she was a good person . . . or at least she hoped so. She sensed some aggression toward this kid, but he was a *kid,* wasn't he? It wasn't as though he had put himself out in those woods or purposefully sought out the Hansen farmhouse. But rather than compassion, the longer he held her stare, the more the dormant laughter at the pit of her stomach began to shift toward a garbled moan.

She caught her breath as she continued to eyeball him, each second revealing just how unnatural he really was. His features seemed to shift subtly, almost imperceptibly, as if they were rearranging themselves, trying to appear less unsettling, more ordinary. But it wasn't working. Rather, it was in that moment, when his face appeared to waver like disturbed water, that Eden knew she had to look away. He didn't look like someone who had wandered out of the woods; he looked like something that had clawed its way out of hell. How could no one else at the table see it?

With anxiety gripping her by the base of her spine, she was about to swivel around to face Gus. If anyone was as weirded out as she was, it would be him. *Jesus, do you see it?* But to her horror, she couldn't move, couldn't turn her head or even shift her eyes a fraction to the right or left. Her throat tightened. Those ugly words jumped back to the forefront of her mind.

Hey, Fishface!

She tried to suck in a breath but couldn't find air, transported to a memory she hadn't thought of in years. At eight years old, she'd been sitting in a McDonald's dining room with a couple of friends, a few of them those cruelty-spitting boys. She remembered taking a bite of her Big Mac, laughing at a stupid joke—shit, maybe it was a joke about Fishface Jessica—realizing that a poorly chewed bite had lodged itself in her windpipe. Her choking had likely lasted less than a few seconds, but it had seemed like eons. She'd sat there within reach of her closest friends, a few parents across the dining room gossiping about the school administration; none of her friends had noticed Eden couldn't breathe.

Fishface.

Doubled over with laughter.

Fishface!

Trying to suck in their own breaths.

Glub, glub, you goddamned freak.

Eden blinked past watering eyes.

Oh my God . . .

Paralyzed in her dining room chair, she couldn't call out for help.

Oh my GOD . . .

She couldn't even grasp at her neck to suggest she was in trouble.

All she could do was sit there in a silent panic, her windpipe spasming despite her mouth being empty. Her fingers went rigid against the table as she fought against the immediate thought that:

This is it. This is how I'm going to die.

And worse yet, that somehow she deserved it.

"Eden?" She heard her name but couldn't place the voice.

"Oh shit, *Eden!*"

Someone was grasping her shoulders.

The legs of her chair skipped against the floor.

There was a sensation of flying, of her arms opening up, rising and falling. Someone was yelling. What felt like a punch to her chest forced her eyes wide, a gasping breath finally, mercifully escaping her.

"Eden!" Her father's face appeared in front of her. Fear had made his eyes nearly as big as Rowan's. "Jesus, kid, are you okay?"

Her vision grew clearer. Her siblings came into view. Olive's hands were pressed over her mouth, her glasses shoved askew. Willow resembled a wide-eyed Renaissance princess with her hair piled atop her head, radiating pure fear. Even Gus looked shaken, as though he'd just had a close encounter with death. Sophie rushed forward and threw herself into Eden's chest, arms outstretched.

"You were choking!" Sophie bawled into her shoulder. "I thought you were gonna die!"

What the hell? She hadn't taken a bite of food in at least a few minutes, had she? No. She'd been far too busy watching Rowan scrutinize everyone else. How, then, could she have been choking? And yet her family was gathered around her the way people congregated around a late-stage hospice bed, all of them looking down at her while she sat on the floor, still recovering, still in shock. All of them save for Mom, who remained at the dining room table, not having moved an inch from her seat.

Mom was far away, lost somewhere in her thoughts.

And her hollow expression left Eden feeling nothing but a deep sense of dread.

11

LUKE

Luke sat at the edge of the bed, listening to the sound of Isla brushing her teeth. He was wondering if he should protest again, considered whether to bring up all the happenings of the day. He could present them as what Isla would have called *a sign*. The dogs behaving badly. Sophie weeping into her sister's chest. Eden choking at the dinner table. Gus's fearful expression in the dappled light of the barn. Christ, it had been a hell of a day. Anxiety was starting to uncoil in the pit of Luke's stomach, swelling like a snake after swallowing a mouse whole.

This kid. He was affectless, not the least bit moved by the goings-on of their family. Luke had been apprehensive from the start, but now? Now he was actually nervous.

Helen had warned them it would be tough. The boy had come from unknown circumstances, and there was no telling what trauma lay beneath the child's emotionless facade. And yet, while huddled over his eldest daughter, Luke had looked up to see Rowan watching with his head cocked sideways in a morbid sort of curiosity. Meanwhile, Isla sat statuesque next to him, as though not having noticed anything amiss. This whole scenario made Luke want to reach out, grab the kid, and push him out the door into the early evening. He wanted to watch Rowan— or whatever the hell his real name was—turn from the farmhouse and walk back into the trees. But the more he wanted to fight the whole situation . . .

This is stupid. Foolish.

... the more he worried he'd finally say something to send Isla tumbling over the edge.

The pills are out of the medicine cabinet, but what if . . .

. . . what if she has other meds hidden away?

The bathroom light clicked off.

Isla stepped into the room, barefoot and wearing a threadbare Portishead T-shirt. She shrugged her shoulders as if cold despite the summer heat, then crawled beneath the covers and pulled them up to her chest. Luke watched his wife as she went still, her eyes fixed on the wall opposite the bed. That wall housed two dozen framed photographs of their children at various points in time. He wondered which image she was studying. Was it the one where Gus and Eden were splashing in the ocean during a long-past trip to La Jolla, or the one where Olive—already wearing glasses by the age of six—was laughing open-mouthed with a missing front tooth?

"You know," Isla eventually said, turning away from the pictures to look at him. "I've been thinking about Ruby Mae a lot lately."

"You have?" Luke had heard Ruby Mae's story a thousand times, but to this day, he still didn't understand it.

Isla's cousin had gone missing when his wife was just sixteen. Eden's age. Sometimes Isla told it as though she and Ruby Mae had been together just before Ruby Mae vanished. Other times it seemed that Isla had been home with her crazy mother during Ruby's disappearance. Luke was convinced that whatever the circumstances, Isla was dealing to this day with a severe case of post-traumatic stress. He'd wanted to ask her to see someone about it on more than a few occasions, but it had always struck him as wrong to suggest it. He didn't want her to feel like she couldn't talk to *him* about it, and he certainly didn't want her to get the impression that he thought she was making it all up. But then they'd lost Adam, she'd hit rock bottom, and Luke had gotten so scared he had left her lying in a psych ward while figuring out how to explain to the kids that their mother had tried to end her own life. When Isla had finally come home two weeks later, it had been tempting to ask if she'd revealed the ghosts of her past to the therapist there, but he couldn't bring himself to do it. Even now it seemed intrusive, though he wasn't sure why.

Isla rubbed the bridge of her nose as though attempting to banish a headache. "I just keep *seeing* her. I keep seeing *us*. The last afternoon we spent together, back behind my aunt Sunny's place. On the prairie."

"Is that a happy memory?" Luke asked, unable to tell if remembering Ruby Mae in that context was good or bad, whether going back to that place of trauma was cathartic or simply ripping off a scab, tearing open a wound.

"I don't know." Isla laughed a little, as if flabbergasted with it all. "Sometimes I remember, and I feel at peace. Other times, it's like I'm going to fall apart. And then there are those blinks of time . . ." She paused, looking unsure whether she should continue the thought.

"Blinks . . . what?" he asked, urging her to finish.

"It's almost like . . . scary. I don't know." She squinted, not understanding her own words. Sitting there for a tick, she eventually gave up on figuring it out, slid down into bed, and sighed. It was her way of saying that the conversation was over. She was tired. It was late. Good night.

Luke was left to wrestle with the aftermath. *Scary.* Was that what it was? Adam had happened almost a year ago. They were coming up on the anniversary. Maybe this was all too much, too soon. His thoughts shifted back to the pills, which were in a lockbox high up in the pantry. Only he and Gus had the digital combination; Gus, because Luke felt as though he needed a fail-safe. The lockbox, though . . . *that* had been a hell of a fight, one of very few marital disagreements he'd absolutely refused to budge on.

"Eden scared the shit out of me tonight," he said, running a hand down his face, trying to physically wipe the memory of their daughter turning blue from his brain. "The dogs scared the shit out of me too." The memory of the afternoon came at him fast: Maize looking rabid, yet not striking when she had the chance. She'd been simultaneously vicious and prudent, like a dog getting too close to a rattlesnake.

"Yeah, it's been a strange day," Isla said softly. "We knew it would be."

But there was more to it than that. Luke could hear it in her tone. She knew it just as well as he did, but she was choosing to ignore it. The weird goings-on didn't fit her narrative. This whole fostering thing was supposed to be good for them, healing. What it *wasn't* supposed to be doing was throwing everything off-balance. But Luke could hardly get his footing since leaving Child Services that morning.

"Gus," he continued.

"Luke, can we talk more tomorrow, please? I'm exhausted. Truly."

"When we dragged the dogs to the barn, you should have seen his face."

It had been a haunted look, one that Luke hadn't been able to shake. And yet he'd gone cold and mean toward his son only seconds later, saying things that had come out of nowhere—suggesting Gus should stay in the barn if he didn't like what was going on in the house. It had been a cruel thing to utter, something Luke reminded himself he needed to apologize for. He cringed as he realized he'd sounded just like his own father, slipping into the role of a man he swore he'd never become. It was a grand transgression, something Luke had promised himself he would do everything to avoid. And yet . . .

"What about his face?" Isla finally asked, her words quiet, sounding nearly half-asleep.

"He just—he looked so young. So afraid."

"Afraid of what?"

"I don't know."

He looked to the wall across from them, his eyes settling upon a photo of his firstborn. In it, Luke was holding Gus (previously hailed as Augie during this brief, ecstatic era) up with one hand, the kid balancing atop his father's single palm while holding his own arms outstretched toward the sky. They looked like a father-son circus act—the Amazing Hansens. Luke vividly remembered it all. His only son had been two, and Eden had just turned one. Isla had packed a picnic, and they'd driven up to Aspen for the afternoon. Luke had thought it a good idea to try hiking a mountain trail. Isla had taken the picture of Luke and Gus less than a minute before Eden had succumbed to a shrieking fit, having been bitten by some sort of flying insect. She'd wailed for nearly an hour, the joy captured in that picture fading with every frantic cry. But still, Luke could transport himself anytime back to that Aspen hillside with nothing more than a steadying breath and a clear-minded thought.

"And Sophie," he said, now speaking more to himself. Even with the lamp on, he was pretty sure Isla wasn't listening anyway, drifting between consciousness and sleep.

"Sophie," Isla echoed.

"So afraid."

Just like the dogs.

They'd been terrified too, hadn't they?

But Isla was right—it was late. There was nothing left to do but close his eyes.

He rolled onto his side and reached for his charging cord, caught the end of the USB plug between his fingers, and pushed it into the bottom of his phone. But just before he slid his phone onto the side table, the screen lit up.

It was another Amber Alert.

Another kid was gone.

12

SOPHIE

Sophie was lying in bed, staring up at the star machine that sent dancing lights across the ceiling and walls. Her unicorn Squishmallow, appropriately named Unicorny, was lying halfway across her face. She couldn't sleep without hiding. The dark was scary. But Dad thought it was even worse when she'd pull the sheets tight over her head. He said, *You're going to suffocate, kiddo.* He said, *Leave yourself an air hole.* He said, *You're soaking through your pajamas with sweat.* So Unicorny would sit on her head instead, blocking out some of the dark.

The little motor that powered the night-light whirred behind her head. Usually she liked the noise, but tonight she couldn't sleep. She wanted to get up, to sneak out and knock on her parents' door. But their bedroom was at the end of the hall, and getting there would mean tiptoeing past Willow's old room. Except that wasn't Willow's room anymore. Willow was on the other side of Sophie's room, sleeping. That was creepy Rowan's room now, and the idea of Rowan yanking the door open as she ran by was enough to keep Sophie frozen where she was. Because he scared her. She told herself she was just being a baby, but he scared her just the same.

"Willow?" she loud-whispered, but her sister didn't respond.

Sophie swallowed against the lump in her throat, pushed Unicorny aside, and dared to sit up. She squinted at the darkened walls, shadowy despite the whirling rainbow stars. Her attention snagged on the closet door. She peered at it, as though narrowing her eyes would activate her super night vision. *Night mode, activate!* She often wondered if she'd end up with glasses like Olive, but she kept passing the eye chart test during her checkups, so maybe not. Either way, she could just make out the closet door across the room.

The door had been shut before Sophie crawled into bed. She was sure about that because it was a rule, *the* rule. *Close the closet door before turning out the lights.* Then again, Willow was new here and sometimes not a great listener. Maybe she had forgotten the rule or hadn't even heard it and had left the door cracked open.

Except, no.

I would have noticed, Sophie reassured herself. *I would have noticed because it would have been scary.*

She spoke up every time Dad forgot to shut the door, so why wouldn't she have done the same with Willow? That didn't make any sense.

Maybe if she left the bed to pull the door shut—she'd never be able to get back to sleep without doing so—it would be okay. But going anywhere near that door was about as scary as running past Rowan's door, even with her big sister only a little bit away.

She fell back onto her pillow with a loud sigh, hoping it would wake Willow, but it didn't.

"It's okay," she said in a quiet voice, then rolled onto her side with frustration. "Just shut your eyes. There's nothing in there. Just clothes and toys and Willow's junk." Because, as it turned out, her older sister had way more stuff than she thought, and a lot of it had to be shoved into a wobbly pile on top of the closet's high shelf.

It was only then—pulling Unicorny back over her head and focusing all her effort on drifting off—that Sophie realized there was a sound beneath the quiet whir of her star machine. She furrowed her eyebrows and curled up into herself, listening hard.

Was it a toy?

No, this didn't sound like a machine. It was a buzzing noise, like a big fat bug. Panic stirred in her belly. Something had gotten in from outside and was in their room. One of those huge, red-eyed cicadas. It was in the room, and it was going to land on her, maybe even crawl into her hair.

"*Willow!*" she yell-whispered, but still nothing from her sister. Imagining some nasty creepy-crawly skittering onto her covers, she did the only thing she could think to do to make the buzzing go away. She shoved her palms against her ears, but it only made the sound worse. Letting her hands fall to the sheets, she listened again. The buzzing went away a little. Again, she lifted her hands, pressed them against her head. The noise got bad once more.

Suddenly Sophie pictured insects crawling inside her head, laying eggs, dozens of tiny bug babies hatching inside her brain. Letting out a quiet whimper, she shoved Unicorny aside and kicked at her sheets. Unicorny fell to the floor and rolled halfway across the room. Now she'd *never* get to sleep. She had to wake up Mom and Dad. Her father would use the flashlight on his cell phone to look inside her ears. Mom would get the red-handled tweezers she kept in the bathroom for when someone got a splinter, and she'd use those to fish the bugs out of Sophie's skull one at a time. Maybe, after they got them all out, they'd let her sleep between them in their big, comfy bed. She'd cuddle up with Mom the way she used to, smelling a little bit of her perfume. Sophie loved the scent. Warm, spicy, like cookies baked in the fall. Or she'd stick like Velcro to her dad's side, breathing in his weird, Christmas-tree-scented soap. And if they *didn't* let her sleep in their room, Dad would at least check the closet. Whatever happened, it would be better than sitting here, scared, watching the cracked closet door, waiting for bugs to eat her brain.

"Okay," she whispered. "Okay, I gotta go get help." She was going to be brave and do it. But, ready to swing her legs over the mattress's edge, Sophie suddenly changed her mind.

Her star machine began to flicker, blinking and cycling through the night-light's various colors. Pink. Blue. Yellow. Green. The machine only had one speed, but somehow the constellations began to spin faster, twirling so rapidly they seemed to leave streaks of light across the walls. Sophie's eyes went big as she sat in the middle of a chaotic universe, stars whizzing by, the air in the room growing thick with the feeling of a staticky balloon. The tiny hairs on her arms stood on end, and the hair on top of her head started to lift the way it did on the playground slide. Up, up, up, as if reaching for the ceiling.

The bugs didn't like any of it. They were mad, and their buzzing grew louder, so loud Sophie could hardly hear anything but the bug noise anymore. She started to feel like she was coming off the bed, as though gravity was being sucked out of the room. She opened her mouth to yell, but the cry got stuck, silenced when, from the corner of her eye, she spotted something tall and dark shift, its movements quick and sharp.

A person. It was the shadow of a *person*!

Sophie gasped.

The star machine clicked off.

The room went dark. So scarily dark.

The fuzzy static left the room, and in the sudden gloom, her full weight fell onto her mattress. She exhaled an "oof" when she hit the springs.

Waiting for her eyes to adjust to the dark, she ended up peering at the skinny black line where the closet door wasn't closed all the way. Was it getting bigger? *That's dumb,* she thought. Except Dad had taught her that nothing was dumb. *Don't use that word,* he liked to say. *There's no such thing as a dumb question.* Which meant that, yes, maybe the crack *was* bigger. Maybe there *was* someone in her room. The shadow.

The person.

She held her breath, her eyes fixed on the closet door, her heart beating like crazy, because the more she watched that small crack, the more she was sure it was growing.

Little by little.

Bigger and bigger.

"Mom?"

"Sophie? What . . . ?" Willow sat up and rubbed her eyes, sleepy and annoyed. Finally awake. But Sophie had no time to say sorry for waking her sister. With her breaths coming in heaving gasps, she decided that she needed her mother, and she needed her now.

"Mom!" It was hard to see in the dark, but the inside of the closet was worse. And yes, it *was* getting bigger. She was sure it was. The air hitched in her lungs as she tried desperately to activate her night vision, sure that the door was creeping open. Something was definitely there, in that darkness. Something was watching her. Watching. Waiting.

A chill ran down her back.

One of the closet door hinges creaked.

The buzzing in her ears increased. She swore she could see the walls ripple with the scream that was suddenly tearing itself from deep within her chest.

A second later, the bedroom door flew open fast and wide, slamming hard against the wall behind it. Dad stumbled into the room, looking half-asleep, wobbly and scared.

"Sophie?!" He was sweeping her into his arms, squishing her to his chest. A few seconds later, the room exploded like a firework when Mom hit the light switch. Sophie turned her face into her dad's chest, cringing against the glare.

"What's happening?" Dad asked, his eyes darting from one corner of the room to the other, looking for answers.

Olive showed up in the doorway. She was fumbling with her glasses, looking worried. A second later, Eden appeared behind her, her face half-hidden behind her long hair. Only Gus was missing.

"It's fine," their mom said, waving the two girls away. "Just a nightmare. Back to bed."

"It wasn't a nightmare!" Sophie shouted, getting mad even though she was scared. Her mom never believed her. She never believed *anything*. "My star machine freaked out. And then I felt like I was floating. And my hair was standing up like this!" She drew her arms away from Dad, grabbed some of her hair, and pulled it up over her head.

Dad leaned away from her to get a look at her face. She could tell what he was thinking. *Sophie Ellery Hansen, are you kidding us?*

"I'm not lying!" Sophie swore. "And then I saw someone, but every-thing got dark and then the closet was open. Look!" She pointed to the closet door, proof that she wasn't telling stories. It was cracked open, same as she remembered. "Someone's in there!" she said, suddenly really not liking the scary pictures she was putting inside her own head. A dark shadow man, skinny as a pencil and tall as the ceiling, nothing but super-long arms and spiderlike legs. Sophie had heard about shadow people before. *They're there one second, gone the next,* Mom had once said.

"Go look," she whispered into her father's chest. "Something's in there, I know it. The door was closed, and now it's not."

Sophie peeked out to see her mother and father eyeing each other. They seemed nervous, but also kind of like they were maybe going to just tell her to go to sleep and leave her there. On the opposite side of the room, Willow sat on her bed, more than a little spooked; probably freaked out that she'd given up her room and was now stuck in a haunted one.

"Sophie, you *know* nobody is in there," Dad said. "The house alarm is on. The windows are shut tight. If someone had come in—"

"Dad?" Willow spoke up. "She's right. That door isn't supposed to be open." She looked from the closet door to their father's face. "After put-ting my clothes in the hamper, I shut it myself. Sophie can't sleep unless it's closed. It's one of her room rules. Closet door closed, no matter what."

"No matter what," Sophie echoed, watching Dad become a little un-sure. He peeked at the closet door again, and for a second she could swear she saw her daddy the way he must have been when little like her, scared but trying to be brave.

Eventually, Dad squared his shoulders, slowly breathed out, slid So-phie off his lap, and stood, walking to the closet door.

"See?" he said, pulling it open. "Nothing here. Just way too many toys that need to go into the donate pile."

Except, as soon as the door swung wide, Sophie saw her hung-up dresses move on their hangers. So did everyone else.

Sophie and Willow squealed as the hangers clattered against one another. Willow pulled her blanket up to her chin. With Unicorny still on the floor, Sophie grabbed a cow stuffy from the corner of her bed—Cowy, naturally—and hugged it to her chest, using it as a shield.

"Oh crap, Luke . . ." Sophie had only heard her mom use bad words a few times, but she supposed people said all sorts of things when they were totally creeped out. She'd heard all kinds of words from her brother and sisters, stuff she kept secret from her parents. Eden had once said "shit" under her breath when she'd spilled a box of Cheerios all over the kitchen floor. Sophie remembered that because she couldn't have Cheerios for breakfast after, and that's all she'd wanted to eat. She'd heard Olive mumble "goddamn it" over a math worksheet while Sophie sat next to her, decoding a BOB book. But Gus had been the baddest. He'd said the worst words ever, all together at once—"motherfucking goddamn bullshit"—right in front of her, then looked both scared and pleading when their eyes met. *Oh man, don't tell Mom.*

"What the hell?" Sophie's dad let his own bad word fly, but Mom didn't say anything because they were both scared, and when things were scary, grown-ups gave each other a free pass.

Dad fumbled for the closet light switch, afraid to stick his arm too far into the dark. She didn't blame him. Who knew what was in there? But after a while he did it anyway, because it was his job. Dads had to do the hard stuff, like kill bugs and look for ghosts. Sophie shut her eyes, not wanting to watch his hand get torn off his body by some horrible, hungry monster hiding in her fresh pile of laundry. Maybe the thing in the closet was what had laid its eggs inside Sophie's brain. Maybe it was a gigantic, man-sized cockroach. Olive had once talked about a book like that. It was a famous one she said Sophie would have to read one day, when she was old enough. But Sophie had already decided it sounded gross and would never read it, even if Mom tried to make her do it for school, because cockroaches gave her the heebie-jeebies. No way she was reading something like that.

Nothing happened to Dad's arm.

The light clicked on; he stepped inside and shoved Sophie's dresses aside.

He did this while looking at them, ready to say, *See? I told you there's nothing in here.* But before he could make some silly dad joke, Sophie and Willow shrieked.

There was Rowan, cowering away from the closet's interior light, away from Dad, trying to hide behind the frilly pink ribbons of one of Sophie's favorite dresses.

"Rowan?!" Mom dashed across the room and into the closet.

"Jesus!" Dad stepped back, though Sophie couldn't tell whether he was spooked by the screaming or because Rowan had been hiding in there like some boogeyman from one of Gus's movies.

"What are you doing in here?" Mom asked their newest family member, her tone soft and soothing, not mad at him at all. Something about that made Sophie's stomach instantly knot up inside, because shouldn't she have been at least a *little* bit upset? Rowan had broken the rules. He'd snuck into Sophie and Willow's room in the middle of the night. That was creepy and *definitely* not okay. Dad seemed annoyed, though he was trying to hide it. He had his arms crossed over his chest and was now far from the closet, as though wanting to get out of the room while Rowan was in it. Sophie looked to the bedroom door to see what her two older sisters thought, but they hadn't seen what happened. Mom had told them to go back to bed, and they had. It wasn't as though Sophie had never had a bad dream before. Her brother and sisters were used to the ruckus.

"Did you get lost?" Mom asked, and Sophie almost yelled, *Lost? How could he get lost?!* It was a bunch of baloney. If Rowan had gotten up to go to the bathroom, the bathroom light was on. He couldn't have missed it. Sophie's door had her name on it: SOPHIE'S PLACE. It was covered in glow-in-the-dark star stickers and paper flowers and a picture of a stick-figure Sophie standing next to Buster and Maize, which was taped right beside the door handle. And even if Rowan hadn't seen all that—*maybe his eyes don't work so well,* she thought, then immediately dismissed it given him staring at everyone over dinner—there was no space mobile, no robot toy box. Sophie's room still had Winnie-the-Pooh decals stuck to the walls, two beds crammed into a small space, and a curtain over the window dotted with prancing unicorns. The only way Rowan could have thought Sophie's room was his was if those huge eyes of his had gone blind, which was unlikely.

"Come on," Mom said, taking Rowan gently by the arm. "It's okay. Let's get you back to your room."

But Rowan didn't want to go. Sophie watched him pull away from Mom's touch. All of a sudden, Sophie wanted to yell at him to get out, get out, *get out!* But she didn't say anything, knowing it would only make Mom mad.

"What is he doing here in the girls' room anyway?" Dad asked, annoyed.

Sophie twisted her arms tighter around Cowy. A moment later, Willow leapfrogged out of bed and across the room. She crash-landed next to Sophie and pulled Sophie's unicorn blanket up to her chin, using it as protection from the intruder.

"He got lost," Mom repeated, her tone steady but stern.

"Really. Why was the bedroom door shut?" Dad asked. "He closed it behind him? And he didn't notice it was the wrong room as soon as he—"

"That's *enough*," Mom hissed through her teeth. It was what she did when she was super angry but didn't want to appear that way in front of anyone. It never worked, though. It only made Sophie imagine her as a snake. No matter how many times Sophie heard her mom talk that way, it always made her heart jump. At times like that, she didn't seem like Mom, but like someone else.

Dad lifted his hands as if to say *whatever.* It was something she'd seen Gus do in the very same way a million times. Then Dad stepped out of the room. That was what Dad did whenever Mom started the hissing; he'd sigh and turn away and leave, as if afraid of snakes. Sophie watched Dad disappear down the hall. She wanted to call after him. *Dad, don't go!* But she kept quiet, knowing it would make Mom just as mad as her yelling at Rowan to get out and never come back.

"Come on, Rowan," Mom said, patient as ever. "Come," she repeated, motioning for Rowan to step out of the closet. It took about a minute, but he finally crawled out of Sophie's dresses.

Sophie and Willow huddled together as their new "brother" limped across the room in that weird way of his, his gigantic eyes fixed on them both—nope, no sight problems there. When he stepped into the hallway, Mom looked back at them. "All done," she said, pulling the closet door closed. "Safe and sound. Go back to sleep." And just like that, she shut the bedroom door behind her, leaving them on their own.

The girls sat frozen and quiet for a long time, the ceiling light blazing as bright as ever. Sophie couldn't figure out what had happened. Both Mom and Dad had just . . . left? And Rowan hadn't gotten into *any* trouble? If Gus had pulled that kind of prank, he would have been grounded for life.

After a long while, Sophie decided to speak.

"That's wrong," she whispered. "Willow, it's wrong, isn't it?"

"What is?" Willow whispered back, her face still half-hidden by Sophie's unicorn blanket.

"I saw a shadow person," Sophie said. "But it wasn't Rowan. It was really tall and skinny and moved super fast. It wasn't *him*."

"Then who was it?" Willow asked, suddenly looking more scared than before.

"I don't know," Sophie said, abruptly realizing that she was frightened too.

"And where did it go, Sophie?" Willow asked. "If it was here, where the heck is it now?"

"I don't know," Sophie echoed, wondering if she'd be able to sleep. Wondering if she'd ever sleep again.

URGENT COMMUNITY ALERT: 9-YEAR-OLD RACHEL SMITHSON MISSING IN ASPEN AREA

Aspen, CO—The Aspen Police Department urgently requests the public's assistance in locating nine-year-old Rachel Smithson, who went missing late yesterday afternoon near Quaking Park. Rachel was last seen playing with her two older brothers in the park area, where they had been mushroom hunting following the recent rainstorm.

According to initial reports, it is believed that Rachel may have wandered off into the adjacent woods. She was last seen wearing a light blue Taylor Swift T-shirt, pink Crocs rain boots, and white shorts. Rachel is approximately 4 feet tall, weighs 60 pounds, and has long brown hair and hazel eyes. She does not have any belongings with her. Both her backpack and water bottle were found on top of a picnic table, where she had left them alongside her brothers' items. She does not own a cell phone.

Search and rescue operations commenced immediately after Rachel was reported missing, involving local police, volunteers, and drone surveillance to cover the wooded area and surrounding regions.

Police Chief Caleb Marx said in a statement, "We are doing everything we can to find Rachel and bring her safely back to her family. We ask anyone in the area who might have seen Rachel or has any information, no matter how insignificant, to come forward and help us in our search."

The community is urged to check their properties, sheds, barns, and outbuildings for any signs of Rachel. Residents with surveillance cameras are requested to review their footage and report any sightings or unusual activities.

The Smithson case is only one among a rash of child disappearances reported throughout the Four Corners region over the past three months.

A community command center has been set up at Quaking

Park Pavilion, where volunteers can receive information and join the ongoing search efforts. Anyone with information about Rachel Smithson or any missing child's whereabouts is encouraged to contact their local police department or call 911.

We thank the community for its cooperation and assistance and are committed to finding Rachel as quickly as possible.

DAY TWO

13

ISLA

Isla stood in the mouth of the dining room, watching her children attack the breakfast spread she'd set out only minutes before. Once, she'd had visions of beautiful settings—juices in glass carafes, matching plates, and gleaming silverware. Once, when the farmhouse was new and both August and Eden were still babies, she'd peruse catalogs from Crate & Barrel and Pottery Barn all while dreaming of an existence stylistically identical to that of Joanna Gaines.

But reality was much different from her once-imagined Instagram version of life. It was a plastic gallon of milk at one end of the table and a carton of orange juice at the other, leftover paper plates speckled with Fourth of July stars next to a pile of silverware beside boxes of Cap'n Crunch, Lucky Charms, and Cookie Crisp. It was heartening, however, to see her children gather like clockwork for the first meal of the day. Even August didn't miss breakfast, though this morning he looked like he might sleep through it, face down in his cereal bowl.

It had been a rough first night, but beyond a few of her kids looking exhausted, she told herself that all was well. Rowan hadn't tried to set the house on fire. He hadn't gone feral the way she was certain both August and Luke had hoped. And he hadn't escaped the house and run back into the woods, which, honestly, had been Isla's worst fear. She'd spent most of the night tossing and turning, imagining herself waking to Rowan's empty bedroom. Gone. *Just like Adam.* Hell, there had been a few minutes during the night when she was certain the whole thing was some grief-induced fever dream. Rowan wasn't real, was he? She'd imagined him. She was still in the hospital, wasn't she? Strapped to a bed. Drugged. *Keep her calm.*

Except, no, Rowan was still here, seated in Isla's spot at the far end of the table. That was the good news. The bad news was that he was motionless, not the least bit interested in the food Isla had arranged on a plate in the shape of a smiling face, just for him. Eggs for eyes. A bacon smile. A Belgian waffle hat dotted with blueberries and sliced banana. Sophie had eyeballed the funny breakfast face, her own plate left empty so she could fill it herself. Her youngest daughter's side-eye and crooked pigtails had left Isla overwhelmed by both annoyance and guilt. Why hadn't she made Sophie a plate just like Rowan's? How could she have forgotten about her youngest? And why hadn't Isla spared the few seconds it took to do her little girl's hair?

Because I've got a lot on my mind, she told herself. *Because I shouldn't have to be a super mom twenty-four hours a day, seven days a week, and I certainly shouldn't have to be one after losing a baby and taking in another child.*

Why couldn't Sophie understand that Rowan had to be given extra care?

Because she's still a baby. Your *baby, and you're neglecting her.*

Sophie was little, sure, but five was old enough to comprehend why Isla was going the extra mile, wasn't it?

Of course, she resolved, shaking off the mom guilt. *She needs to learn, and you need to learn to stop letting it get to you.*

Regardless of Rowan getting the VIP treatment, it was clear he wanted no part of breakfast, which stirred panic at the pit of her stomach. He hadn't eaten even a single bite of dinner, either. Sure, he'd only been with them for less than twenty-four hours, but what if she couldn't get him to eat anything at all? What if he began to waste away and she found him unresponsive in his room?

And there's always a chance he'll just disappear, remember?

It had happened before, so it could happen again.

A baby in her belly in the evening.

Blood-soaked sheets the next morning.

Don't be ridiculous, the voice of reason whispered. *That can happen with the unborn, but not with full-fledged children.*

Her heart tripped on that thought, instantly realizing how unhinged it truly was. If anyone knew about disappearances, it was Isla.

Have you forgotten Ruby Mae?

And what about all those children on the news reports? All those Amber Alerts? The brand-new one that had greeted her first thing that morning? Those kids had evaporated like ether. Where were *they*? Where was—

"Ruby . . ." she breathed.

"Isla?"

She jumped, her attention darting to Luke. He was standing at her elbow, looking as though he'd been there for a while. In one hand, he had a small tumbler of water. She could see a light blue pill pressed between the bottom of the glass and his palm. In the other, her favorite mug, handmade by a Navajo woman somewhere out in Santa Fe. It brimmed with steaming coffee, milky and sweet.

"Double cream, double sugar. Hardy coffee for the missus," he told her. Waiting for her to take the water first, he watched as she popped the tiny pill into her mouth and swallowed it down. Satisfied, he handed her the coffee and asked, "Everything okay?"

"Yeah, fine," she said, taking the mug with a murmured "Thanks."

She gave Luke a momentary once-over, trying to assess his mood. Not the one he wore on the outside, easy and casual like the Colorado Rockies T-shirt that hung limp and wrinkled from his shoulders. She was trying to make out the mood beneath the facade he was so damn good at putting in place—the mood she'd seen the night before, when she'd failed to scold Rowan for finding his way into Sophie and Willow's closet. Sure, she could have been stern. Yes, perhaps she absolutely should have told him the girls' room was off-limits, especially after lights-out, but what good would it have done? Would he have even understood her?

Besides, Luke knew what they had signed up for. Helen had said it would be a rough road, and here they were. How was it such a surprise?

She looked back to the boy. He was practically swimming in one of Willow's old Mickey Mouse T-shirts. She had expected the home to send him with some clothes, though she wasn't sure why. Either way, just that alone was proof that Isla had far more important things to think about than why Rowan was in the girls' closet last night; like what he was going to wear tomorrow, and when he would finally give in and eat something. She'd give him another day. If he still refused food by then, she'd contact Helen. She'd have some ideas on what to do. He must have been eating at the children's home, after all—he'd been there for weeks.

"Gus looks about ready to collapse," Luke observed, then took a sip of his own coffee, which he drank black—something Isla couldn't stomach. "Sophie and Willow aren't looking too excited either."

Isla narrowed her eyes at the comment because there it was. His subtle, passive-aggressive way of bringing up what they had left unresolved the night before.

She looked to her children. Eden and Olive were griping over the last half of grapefruit. August was slumped in his seat, looking miserable with one elbow propped atop the table. Willow and Sophie both appeared sleepy. They sat the farthest away from Rowan after what had happened last night. The family was all gathered around the table, but it was clear none of them wanted anything to do with the others. They were together, but they weren't a real family. It didn't feel cohesive. Rowan was the odd man out, and maybe that's why he wasn't eating. Perhaps he could feel the separation, and Isla knew firsthand how terrible of an experience that was. Isla's mother had made her feel that very same way.

"Hey," Luke said, gently touching Isla's elbow, bringing her back to the present. "You okay?"

"What? Yes, of course." She turned back to the kids and then spoke up to make an announcement. "I think we should do something fun today," she said, forcing the terrible memory of her mother's glowering face from her thoughts. Her suggestion drew her children's attention, or at least what there was to be had of it at eight-thirty in the morning. Before Rowan had arrived, she'd let the children know that there would be no "school" for a while—at least a week or two while Rowan got settled in, while Isla adjusted to the new routine herself. She hadn't made plans on how to fill that free time, but here was an idea.

"We should show Rowan around, maybe introduce him to a few of our friends to make him feel more at home. What do you think?"

Sophie and Willow looked down at their plates, as though considering whether the food their mother had set out that morning had been poisoned. August squinted at Rowan, seemingly sizing him up. Eden diverted her gaze in a confusing, self-conscious manner that didn't match her personality. Nobody spoke.

Finally, Olive came to the rescue: "I was going to ride my bike down and say hi to Mrs. Rodriguez. Maya and Sebastian are about Rowan's age, I think? And they've got that cool new clubhouse in the backyard. Sophie hasn't been there in a while." She pushed her glasses up her nose, forever wearing a look of approval-seeking anticipation.

Isla considered it. Dropping in was one thing, but an impromptu playdate was asking a lot. Perhaps it would be too much for Rowan, anyway. A leisurely walk along their town's lazy main street may be more his speed.

Walk? The quiet voice returned. *Are you kidding? Have you seen the way he moves?*

She looked down to her coffee with a frown, her reflection bending, rippling. Her head swimming as the medication began to kick in.

"I'll call Mrs. Rodriguez after breakfast," Olive said, noting Isla's silence. "I'll offer to take the kids off her hands for a little bit." She paused, then shrugged. "No charge, of course."

"Of course," Isla echoed, then gave her daughter a faint nod, deciding that keeping Rowan away from other children wasn't fair. Hell, maybe it was even detrimental. Sure, he might become overwhelmed, but she'd never know if they didn't try. "All right—go ahead and ask, as long as they aren't busy."

"Yeah, okay," Olive said, flashing her mother an eager smile.

Isla smirked to herself when her daughter turned away. Olive was tenacious, if anything, determined to get that babysitting gig. *Right, and perhaps she'll drop the ball again and one of the Rodriguez kids will get mauled by a dog.* But the playdate *was* a good idea.

Isla could only hope that a little time spent around kids his age would help open Rowan up and get Sophie and Willow to relax. After last night's incident, Isla was worried those two would never let their guard down, and that just wouldn't work. Not if Rowan was going to stay for good. And as far as she was concerned, she'd be damned if she gave him up for anything.

14

OLIVE

Olive loved the Rodriguez house. It wasn't anything super special in western Colorado, but she found it exotic anyway, the opposite of the boring Hansen farmhouse. The Rodriguez place had a flat roof and adobe walls, it had thick wooden beams and a lavishly manicured landscape. There were massive yucca plants standing tall and spiky, like sentries on either side of the front entry. Rivers of rocks in different shades of whites and browns and blacks created delicate weaving patterns along the walkway. And the backyard was a dream, dotted with ancient cottonwood trees. Mrs. Rodriguez had strung small globe lights from tree to tree, the lights hanging in gentle arcs above a roughly hewn farm table. That table was where Olive now sat, watching from afar as Willow and Sophie climbed up the slats of a custom-made playset. Maya and Sebastian Rodriguez clamored above them, stomping their feet and whooping in the clubhouse, which had a spyglass and a bucket-and-pulley system hanging off the side.

Rowan was taking no part in the children's imaginative game, of course. Rather than joining in, he stood far off from the swing set. Wildflowers bent in the breeze, brushing against his hand-me-down Velcro shoes. Olive watched him for a long while, wondering how he was able to get his feet into them in the first place. Sure, Mom had been the one to stuff his feet inside, but didn't that hurt? His legs were so twisted, she had to assume his feet were gnarled too.

The wind carried his red hair across his wide forehead. It reminded her of desert wildfires, of the fire that had cut through the prairie only a few years ago, less than a mile from home. The color of Rowan's hair was a perfect match to when the sun cut through the smoke at just the right angle, casting a hue of flaming brimstone across the sky.

There was something about Rowan that was drawing Olive in this morning, something that made her want to know him better. Her siblings were put off by him, but Olive didn't think Rowan deserved their disdain. She couldn't imagine how hurtful it must have been to come from isolation only to feel as though he didn't belong *here*, either. As he stood static and solitary out there in the yard, watching the kids play from a distance, Olive worried that even if he had wanted to, perhaps Rowan didn't know *how* to join in.

Olive pushed off the wooden bench seat of Mrs. Rodriguez's picnic table and let her Keds take her across the field. She stopped a few paces from the boy who was supposed to be her new brother, then crouched down, waiting for him to notice her. It took a few seconds, but Rowan finally looked away from the other children to meet her eyes.

"You can go play, you know," she told him. "They're nice. That's Maya, remember?" She pointed out the seven-year-old girl with long, dark hair. "Do you remember the name of that scrappy one in the baseball shirt?" She glanced back to Rowan, searching his unconventional face for some spark of understanding. "That's Sebastian. He's six. They're brother and sister. They have a baby sister too—Claudia—but she's napping. She's three. Maybe you'll get to meet her, too." Olive waited for some glimmer of recognition. *Brother. Sister. Baby.* Did he know those words? Did he have siblings too?

"That's their mom." Olive motioned to Mrs. Rodriguez, who had her back turned to the children. She was busy talking with Olive's mother. Both women were grasping sweaty glasses of iced tea, their faces drawn in stern, worried expressions. Olive didn't need to hear their conversation to know what they were talking about: the missing kids, the most recent news report. Another kid had vanished overnight, this one straight from their bed.

Looking back to Rowan, she forced a smile, pushing her own worries about current events aside.

"Mother," she said. *"Mama."* Maybe using a different word could unlock the puzzle that was Rowan's blank stare. But she saw nothing flicker across the boy's countenance. There was no spark or stirring in his unbelievably large eyes. Rather than nodding or trying to communicate, he looked away from her and back toward the other kids.

Willow and Sophie were now in the clubhouse. Maya was making a break for it down the slide, while Sebastian was climbing down a precarious-looking rope ladder.

"Do you want to go over there?" Olive asked. "I can go with you." No response. This time, Rowan didn't even bother looking at her as she spoke. He appeared to be deep in thought, watching the quartet as though never having seen children play together before. Perhaps he hadn't.

Olive wished her mom would tell her more about where she thought Rowan had come from—*thought*, because nobody *knew* much of anything about their new family member. But Mom and Dad were holding back a lot. Over the past six weeks, any time anyone asked a question of significance about him, they were quick to offer a canned answer.

We don't know that yet.

Maybe he'll eventually tell us.

We can only assume.

Then there was the fact that they both still considered her a little kid, and nothing of importance was discussed with a thirteen-year-old. Just that very morning, when she'd asked about the most recent Amber Alert, Dad had acted like it was no big deal. *Don't worry about it.* Meanwhile, both Eden and Gus were free to know all the details as long as they conducted their own investigations on their phones. Olive didn't get how that was fair. She felt like, some days, she was the most mature of her siblings. Certainly the most responsible.

Yeah, except for letting the dogs out, like an idiot. She doubted she'd ever forgive herself for *that* mistake, and maybe her parents wouldn't either. Rowan could have gotten really hurt. It would have been all her fault. Perhaps that's why Rowan's silence was suddenly upsetting to her, striking a nerve.

She turned back to Mom, who peered over Mrs. Rodriguez's shoulder, making eye contact with Olive. Mom flashed a small smile, and at first, Olive was sure the smile was meant for her.

You're doing a good job. I'm proud of you. Forget that mistake, Olive Evelyn Hansen.

A swell of pride filled up her chest . . . only to leave her deflated a second later. Following her mother's eyes more carefully, she realized that Mom wasn't looking at her at all, but at Rowan a few feet away.

All at once, she was overcome by a wave of sadness. Mom had been different for a long time. The time she'd spent in the hospital had seemed to have helped at first, but lately she appeared to be getting more distant, less interested in the happenings of the household. Olive had read so many articles and watched countless YouTube videos on the five stages of grief, desperate to discover whether a person could become perpetually moored in depression, never making it to acceptance, never making it out of the pit of sorrow her mother seemed to be drowning in. What she'd discovered hadn't been at all reassuring. She'd learned that some people never pulled themselves out from beneath that veil of grief. Olive wondered for a long time if that's what would become of Mom—perpetually woeful, forever distracted. Mom, but not Mom. Not loving them. Just going through the motions. But then Rowan had appeared, and Mom had changed. Olive had been so excited to see her face light up again, but before she knew it, Mom's newfound joy felt more hurtful than anything. Because it wasn't for them, the Hansen kids. It was for *him.*

Olive fixed her gaze on Rowan, wondering if her siblings were right in resenting him. A scream tore through the backyard, and Olive wasn't thinking about that anymore.

The gut-wrenching wail was unmistakably born of pain. With her melancholy derailed, Olive turned toward the outcry and found Sebastian writhing on the ground, his hand clamped against a shoulder.

"*Sebastian?!*" Mrs. Rodriguez's voice was even louder than her son's yell. And the way Mrs. Rodriguez took off across that field—had she not been a track star before, she could have been a gold medal Olympian right then. Two glasses of iced tea dropped to the grass, and Olive's mom was suddenly sprinting right behind her, soft linen pants and a breezy long-sleeved blouse catching the wind. Meanwhile, Maya was frozen stiff by the slide, her hands pressed over her mouth. Willow was rushing to get down the climbing wall to see if she could help. Sophie simply stood high up in the clubhouse, a stunned expression plastered across her face.

"His shoulder," Mom said when they reached the boy. "It's probably dislocated."

"What do I do?!" Mrs. Rodriguez asked, her voice edging toward panic. "Call an ambulance?!"

"Emergency room," Olive's mom replied. "He'll be okay, but we have to get him to the car. On the count of three . . ."

Realizing what was about to happen, Sebastian began to plead: "No, Mama, no! Don't pick me up! *¡Duele mucho! ¡Por favor!*"

Despite his begging, Mom and Mrs. Rodriguez hefted him off the ground. Olive winced at the yelping scream that came out of the kid. His injured arm hung limply at his side, looking longer than it should have. Olive turned away, not having the stomach for it. Once, Gus had described how he'd gotten a nasty cut down the side of his leg—something about climbing a chain-link fence and losing his footing. Olive had been seized by vertigo just hearing about it. When Gus had flashed the actual wound, she'd nearly passed out. It had become a big joke in the Hansen house for a few weeks. Nurturing or not, nursing was not in Olive's future. Medical school? No freakin' way.

"Olive!"

Her eyes snapped to her mother's face.

"Call your father! Don't take your eyes off these kids!"

Olive watched Mom and Mrs. Rodriguez struggle to keep Sebastian moving. He was weeping, shuffling toward his mother's car and the inevitable ER doctor that would make him cry even harder with various yanks and pulls.

"Crap," Olive whispered.

She'd once seen a kid fall from a park jungle gym. The kid had been snatched out of the air by his dad a split second before hitting the ground. She'd thought about that incident for days afterward, wondering about what the aftermath would have been had the dad not been in the right place at the right time. But this? Why did she feel responsible? Maybe because the playdate had been her idea, or perhaps because she had been hanging back, giving the kids space to play on their own.

You should have been closer. Olive, you moron!

But what was she expected to do, lord over them, remind them to be careful every thirty seconds until all the fun was sucked out of the day? *Killjoy. Buzzkill.* She'd been called those things by Gus and Eden since she could remember. She hated those nicknames and resented her siblings when they tossed the insults out like stray bullets. Because what her stupid family didn't understand was that if nobody was ever serious about anything, if nobody was ever cautious, the whole world would fall apart.

"Okay," she said to herself. "Okay, call Dad . . ."

Her hand-me-down phone was in her messenger bag, and her bag was back at the table where she'd been sitting minutes earlier. She turned to get it but then paused, reminded that her lack of attention was why Sebastian had been hurt in the first place.

She addressed her two sisters, no-nonsense: "Willow, get Sophie down from there before she . . ." She didn't finish her thought. Maya was right there, still reeling from her brother's accident, and Sebastian was scream-crying his way toward the driveway.

Olive turned away, then took off running to get her phone. She fumbled with her bag. Somehow it took twice as long to find the dumb thing as usual. Her hands trembled. Her blood was spiked with adrenaline. Finally finding what she was looking for, she scrolled to her dad's number and pressed connect.

"Dad, there's been an accident!" she told him. "Can you come right away?"

Her father began to ask a million questions, most of them regarding her sisters and whether they were okay.

"It was Sebastian," she said, focusing intently on Sophie and Willow. The two girls were climbing down from the clubhouse with an excessive amount of caution. "He fell from his swing set and hurt his shoulder. Mom and Mrs. Rodriguez are taking him to the hospital. There aren't any other adults here. . . ."

Out of nowhere, she was overwhelmed with the idea of being alone with four kids. As the oldest, she was responsible for everyone's safety, but she'd already messed up once . . . or was it twice? Why was her mother trusting her now? What if something else happened before Dad arrived? Why had she gone to the hospital with Mrs. Rodriguez instead of staying here with them?

Why does she do anything *these days?*

Tears sprang to her eyes, anxiety mounting within the cavern of her chest.

"Oh, Dad . . . please, just hurry, okay?" Olive said, her voice warbling with emotion. "I'm kind of freaking out."

Dad assured her everything would be fine. He'd be there just as soon as he could get out of the meeting he needed to attend. He'd tell his boss what was happening and jump in the car. "Fifteen minutes," he said. "Tops."

"Okay," Olive said. "Okay, okay, yeah . . . I'll be okay. Just hurry, please." She hung up with a shaky hand, then shut her eyes and took what she hoped would be a steadying breath.

When she opened them again, all three girls were standing in the wild grass, Sophie and Willow hand in hand. They were looking in a single direction, all eyes on Rowan. Rowan was still planted in the same spot Olive had left him. But now, rather than staring dead-eyed toward a group of playing children, his eyes were saucer-wide, his mouth a gaping maw. It was an awful, almost theatrical look of shock, his face stretched into an impossible mask of exaggerated horror. And yet, despite its extreme dramaticism, Olive recognized it.

It was the expression Sebastian's mother had worn the instant her son had hit the ground.

15

AUGUST

As soon as Mom pulled away from the house, three of his sisters and Rowan inside the van, Gus marched over to the barn and pulled open the door. Minus the occasional bathroom break, poor Buster and Maize had been stuck inside the outbuilding since the previous afternoon. Seeing them bolt out of their makeshift prison pissed him off, not because the dogs were still acting weird, but because this was their home. Yet somehow a stranger who couldn't even speak had forced them into captivity.

Gus had no idea when everyone would be back. All he knew was they were going to the neighbors' place, as though the neighbors were owed some Rowan-inflicted weirdness. Either way, there was no telling how long they'd be gone. It could be three hours or, if Rowan went super creepy, thirty minutes. Letting the dogs out was a risky move, but Gus would be damned if he'd leave them in there for any longer without a goddamn break. They'd been whining and yowling for the better part of the morning, it was hotter than hell outside, and it twisted him up to not give them at least a little relief. Gus couldn't bear to let them think they'd been forgotten, banished to some dusty outbuilding where they'd spend the rest of their lives.

He trailed the golden retrievers across the front yard as they frantically sniffed the ground. They were on high alert, sensing something. Gus stopped shy of the front porch and knitted his brow, suddenly remembering the summer before last when a family of field mice had built a nest just beneath the front porch steps. Buster and Maize had lost their minds, scratching at the steps with such crazed fervor they'd nearly made holes clean through the wood. It's how they were acting now. Agitated, despite the original source of their woe being miles down the road, and no mice to be seen.

Gus whistled, trying to get their attention, but it was no use. Both dogs were too wrapped up in their investigation, and he was too tired to drag them inside by their collars. He went in the house, leaving the front door open so he could keep an eye on them. But that took energy, and he'd had a hell of a night. First, there had been some sort of ruckus in Willow and Sophie's room—he'd avoided that nonsense, not interested in the drama he was sure Rowan had caused. He'd tried to get to sleep a little after one in the morning, but he could hear Buster and Maize yapping out there, sounding terrified. Then again, maybe it had just been his imagination. The barking hadn't seemed to annoy anyone else. Or maybe everyone in the house had finally gone crazy, and nobody gave a shit.

Real or not, Gus had attempted to drown out the dogs' cries by shoving in his AirPods and turning Nine Inch Nails up as loud as he could handle, but he couldn't stop picturing Buster and Maize out there in the dark, wondering why they were locked away in some scary building rather than sleeping in their rightful, cozy spots at home.

He hadn't been able to help himself. He'd grabbed an old sleeping bag out of the back of his closet and, a few minutes before two a.m., marched out of the house and across the property to where the dogs were trapped. They'd been happy to see him, but he'd hardly slept in there, either, and now he couldn't keep his eyes open. Collapsing onto the couch, he pressed his fingers against his eyelids with a groan.

"Just a few minutes," he murmured to himself.

A few seconds later, he was dead to the world.

He woke to the sound of popping gravel beneath the tires of an approaching vehicle. At first, he just lay there, discombobulated. It was déjà vu all over again, like the time he'd fallen asleep at four p.m., woken at six, and couldn't figure out if the darkness beyond his window was an early winter evening or still too early for the morning sun to have risen.

How long had he been sleeping? Was it the same day? Had it only been a day since Rowan had arrived, or was it now two? Gus searched the living room for clues, then fished his phone from his pocket. He'd fallen asleep, and nearly two hours had passed. And . . .

He gawked at the wide-open front door.

"Oh shit," he hissed, suddenly remembering the dogs.

Shoving himself off the couch, he paused when he spotted his father's sedan instead of the van. Thank God it was Dad rather than Mom and the girls. A relief. Except, why was his dad home in the middle of the day? With the car rolling closer to the house, Gus's heart tripped over itself when he saw Olive sitting in the front seat. If he squinted past the glare of the sun, he could make out three more heads in the back.

"Oh *shit!*"

Rowan was in the back seat, and the dogs were roaming free.

Gus pivoted on the soles of his worn-out Converse. He had no idea where Buster and Maize were. All he knew was they weren't where they were supposed to be. The only thought that whirled through his brain was *Find them, find them now.* Except seconds later he came to realize that he shouldn't have been so concerned with locating the family pets. What he *should* have been doing was warning his dad. *Keep the kid in the car.* But by the time it crossed his mind, he could already hear the barking—this time, absolutely without a doubt real. When he saw the retrievers making a beeline around the side of the house, everyone was already out of the car. He knew, then, it was too fucking late.

"Dad, the dogs!" he yelled.

Before his father could react, Buster and Maize were only a few paces away, teeth bared, jaws snapping, same as yesterday and completely unlike their docile, obedient selves.

This time, Buster slowed his approach, but Maize didn't hold back. She charged straight for Rowan. She'd played with the idea of maiming him the day before, but now, after so many hours out in the barn and away from her people, she was done. Judging from her approach, she never wanted to see him again. Not alive, at least.

Sophie and Willow squealed while Olive stepped forward, holding her hands up in a superhero sort of way: Iron Man trying to ward off a rabid dog, protecting the kid behind her by way of an invisible shield. Dad ran around the front of the car, his face twisted in alarm. But from where Gus stood, it all happened in cinematic slow motion. Maize leaped up and knocked Olive out of the way. Olive stumbled backward, her glasses skewed sideways across her face. She tripped over her little sisters behind her. The three went down like poorly positioned dominoes.

By the time their father made it to the other side of the sedan, Rowan was on the ground, his arms and legs jerking in a bizarre mechanical manner. He looked like an overturned automaton, like something that was running off pullies and gears, not a living, human being. He looked like a goddamn cockroach, spasming after having walked across a line of neurotoxin. Maize snarled, the noises coming from her throat raw and guttural. It was the sound of frantic defense. She was no longer Maize the family pet—she was now Maize the guard dog, prepared to kill.

Rowan's high-pitched cry cut through the yard. Confused, Gus stood momentarily stunned before shoving his hands against his ears. It was an impossibly loud screech, like metal screaming against metal or the tines of a fork scraping across a plate, so loud it could shake your teeth loose. Buster, having been only a few paces behind, now turned and ran in the opposite direction, terrified. The squeal had his sisters and Dad wincing and mimicking Gus's protective motion: hands slapped over ears, expressions pained. They all froze, stunned by the sheer volume coming from the kid on the ground.

Whether it was Maize's proximity or something else entirely, the attacking dog jumped back with a startled yap. She wavered for an instant, then crashed onto her side and into the dirt. Gus's heart stuttered at the sight of his best friend crumpled in a heap.

"Maize!" He bolted off the porch, skidded to a stop, and fell onto his hands and knees. By the time he was protectively folding his body over her, Maize was scrambling back onto her paws, spooked enough to not want anyone near her. He watched his dog run in the direction of her packmate, her gait not quite right. She moved as if hurt, but if she was injured, the pain wasn't enough to keep her anywhere near the house. Rowan, on the other hand, was still on the ground, eyes wide, gawking up at the sky.

"*What did you do to her?!*" The words tumbled from Gus's mouth, untethered and furious. He rushed to his feet, cutting the distance between Rowan and himself. "*What the fuck did you do?!*" His hands curled into fists, and for a split second he was sure he was going to reel back and punch the weird kid right in the teeth.

Before he dared to do it, a hand fell on his shoulder, pulling him away.

"Back up," his dad demanded. "*Now.*"

Glowering, Gus shrugged away from his father's touch and turned, still fighting his desire to grab Rowan by the back of the neck, heft him up, and march him across the property to the tree line beyond Mom's garden. Because if there was one thing he knew to be true, it was that dogs could sense danger. They could sniff out bad intentions. They knew who not to trust. It appeared, perhaps, that his father had gone completely blind to the fact that something was screwed up here, but Gus thought Maize had made herself perfectly clear: she hated this kid. She wanted him gone.

It seemed, however, that Maize and Gus were the only ones with decent heads on their shoulders, because Gus's father was now helping that little freak to his feet, ignoring both the question Gus had yelled in Rowan's face as well as the fact that Maize had been incapacitated by whatever the hell noise Rowan had made.

"You let them out?" Dad asked, his eyes finally meeting Gus's own. "What the hell is wrong with you?!"

The question stung. No matter what, Gus was always the fuckup. But another epic battle with his father would be nothing short of futile. He could have laid out the world's best explanation for why he'd opened the barn door and allowed the dogs to run free, but not a single word would have been heard.

"Do you realize what you've done?!" Dad's face was twisted with an overwhelmed sort of fury. Gus's heart hitched in his chest once again.

" . . . what?" He shook his head, not wanting to acknowledge what his father might have meant.

"God*damn* it," his father snarled beneath his breath, leaning into his son so the girls wouldn't hear. "Get them back in that barn *right now*." Then he turned away, leading a hobbling Rowan toward the house.

After the front door slammed shut and his family was gone, Gus stood motionless for a long while. He was busy concentrating on his halting, erratic breaths. He was distracted by the sun baking the top of his head, the back of his neck, his arms; distraught by the possible meaning of his father's furious words. But mostly, he was deafened by the sudden buzzing in his ears. Like a skull full of insects in a frenzy, determined to break free.

16

EDEN

Eden had watched the whole fiasco unfold from her upstairs bedroom window. She'd had an unobstructed view of the dogs running toward her father's Honda, of Maize lunging for Rowan, of Rowan collapsing on the ground and convulsing as though he was having an epileptic fit. When Rowan had started yelling, the noise had been loud enough to force Eden away from the glass. And while she knew it was impossible, she could swear she saw the window vibrate in its frame.

She'd almost cried out when Maize had fallen onto her side. But then the dog had somehow managed to get up and run away, and Eden had clasped her hand over her mouth, unable to tear her eyes from the scene. She was a bystander, rapt by an accident but distressed by the sight of blood.

About an hour later, Mom came home. That's when Eden finally heard her brother's heavy, plodding footsteps coming up the stairs. Gus shuffled past her door and into their parents' bedroom. She hadn't been able to turn away from the scene an hour prior, and there was no turning away now. She shoved her phone into the stash pocket of her yoga pants and followed her older brother into the master bedroom. When Gus saw her, he gave her an initial look of annoyance. *What the hell do you want?* But his expression softened fast. He knew he'd need backup. Their parents never listened to him. At least with Eden there, he stood half a chance.

Dad started in as soon as the door was shut.

"I don't even know what to say."

Mom hadn't been there to bear witness, but Dad had filled her in on the shit show that had gone down. And Mom being Mom, she immediately demanded a "family meeting," which was code for a lecture of a lifetime. Gus was going to get his ass handed to him this time. Eden could only hope Dad would reel their mother's ire in.

Taking a seat atop the storage bench close to her parents' bedroom door, Eden wanted to be a part of the conversation as much as she suddenly wanted to pull an Irish goodbye. Drawing her knees up to her chest, she shoved her long hair behind her ears and braced herself for the worst.

"How could you do that?!" their mother barked, finally speaking from her spot in the far corner of the room. Her tone was so clipped, so severe, it made Eden wince.

"Everyone was gone," Gus protested. He didn't miss a beat when it came to standing up for himself. He was used to getting the short end of the stick, always on the defense. It was something Eden admired about him, though she'd be damned if she ever admitted that to him. But no matter how many times their parents beat him down, Gus always came back swinging.

"You guys had just left," Gus continued. "It was just for a few minutes. Buster and Maize had been going nuts in the barn all morning. You heard them, right? And the heat—"

"And then everyone came home," their mother countered, interrupting.

"How was I supposed to know everyone would come back so fucking fast?" Gus demanded.

Eden's eyes widened. *Oh shit,* she thought. Their mother sucked in a sharp breath, as though Gus had physically slapped her with his profanity.

"Watch your language," Dad warned. "Or you'll be in a lot more trouble than you're already in."

Gus scoffed. "Is that even possible? This is so stupid."

"Stupid?" Mom's shoulders went stiff. She was still across the room, as though not wanting to be anywhere near her family despite being the one who had called the meeting. Dad would have let it go, would have dealt with this whole situation quietly, would have admonished Gus in private and tried to figure out what to do without all this bluster. This trial was their mother's doing. Her style. Had it been a few hundred years in the past, Eden was convinced Mom would have craved the gallows, a gleeful spectator clapping for the hangman's noose.

Gus looked at her mutely.

"No, please, enlighten us," Mom said, waving an arm around the room in a grand sort of way, motioning to Dad, then to Eden. "What's so stupid, August? The fact that you almost got a child killed today, or—"

"*Killed?*" Gus snorted. "Maize's lucky she was able to get up after whatever the hell it was that thing pulled out there!"

Eden grimaced.

"I—I'm sorry, what did you just say? That *thing*?" Mom stared at him, appalled by his word choice.

"Okay, whoa, hold on, pulled what?" Dad asked, wanting clarification, desperate to redirect. "I was there, Gus. What are you talking about?"

"What, you think that screeching noise was normal? It was like a million decibels."

"It was really loud, Dad," Eden quietly noted. "Like, even inside the house it was *loud*."

She considered telling them about how she could see the window quaking, how everything outside had blurred for a moment as if the glass was on the verge of shattering into a million glittering shards. But she knew how outlandish it would have sounded. Was that even possible?

"Of course it was loud," their mother cut in. "Rowan was about to be mauled to death. He was terrified! We brought him into this house to protect him, and he was suddenly under attack. And for a second time, no less! Let's see how loud either one of *you* would be if—"

"And then Maize *collapsed*," Gus interrupted. "Like, fell dead to the ground! How is that normal?!"

"Okay, all right!" Dad said, holding up his hands, attempting to keep the conversation on track. "It *was* loud. But Rowan was scared, like Mom said. And Maize did fall over, but she had stumbled over Rowan. Lucky she hadn't stepped on him. Either way, you realize we're in a bad place now, right?"

"A bad place," Gus echoed.

"With the dogs, Gus," Dad said.

Eden watched her brother's face flicker through a multitude of emotions. Her heart tightened within her chest as she recognized each one. Confusion. Realization. Panic. Disbelief. She twisted her fingers against her shins, pulling at the fabric of her leggings.

"What . . . what do you mean?" Gus finally asked, his expression making it clear that he wasn't ready for the answer, but he knew it was coming.

Dad sighed, looked down, then shoved a hand through his hair in exasperation. Mom stood statuesque in a far corner, waiting for him to drop the news like an air force pilot dropping an atomic bomb.

"We have to send Buster and Maize to Uncle Brian's place," Dad said. *Boom.*

"Wait, no! Buster and Maize don't even *know* Uncle Brian!" Gus shouted.

"It's an emergency move, kid. They've got to go. Right now. I've already made the call. Uncle Brian will be here first thing tomorrow morning to pick them up."

Eden's stomach lurched. It tightened even further at the sight of her brother's face, at the sound of his straining voice.

"For how long?"

Dad sucked air in through his teeth, stalling.

"For good." Mom didn't mince words.

Eden was surprised by how cold she sounded, how wooden she looked from across the room. Standing there with her arms across her chest and her face pulled into a scowl of disapproval, something about her posture struck Eden as peculiar. Familiar yet different. Something about her expression wasn't right. The longer Eden peered at her, the more she came to realize that what she was seeing wasn't her mother's run-of-the-mill disappointment. This wasn't Mom being annoyed by a missed curfew or an inappropriate movie choice or Gus going through an entire bag of Doritos fifteen minutes before dinner hit the table. This wasn't standard frustration. It was almost . . . a loathing. It was disgust.

"Wait—*what*?" Gus refused to accept their mother's response.

"Wait, Mom . . ." Eden jumped in, standing up from where she sat. "You guys, that's . . . that's crazy, right? Don't you think this is a bit much? Buster and Maize have never acted this way before. There's something going on. Maybe Maize is sick. I mean, that's possible, isn't it?" She shot a look over to her brother. "The way she fell onto her side . . . didn't that seem like some sort of a seizure? What if there's something going on and it's making her aggressive? We should take her to the vet. Maybe if we just—"

"There's nothing wrong with Maize," Mom said. "And your father and I are not overreacting." Eden could hear it in her voice. She was angry, her patience spent. Rowan—this kid from out of nowhere—was that important to her. More important than the family dogs or her children's broken hearts. "It's happened twice now. Not once, *twice*. There will be no third time. And Rowan aside," she said, "I'm not going to have aggressive dogs anywhere near Sophie. Imagine if she has friends over and Maize does the same thing."

"Sophie has had friends over dozens of times," Gus argued. "Maize always plays with the kids. She's never—"

"This isn't up for debate," Mom said, giving him a pointed look. "Uncle Brian takes them tomorrow, or we can drive them to the pound, where they'll sit in a cage for a few weeks before being put down. Which one is better?"

Gus pressed his mouth into a tight line, fighting to keep his composure.

"This conversation is over," Mom said.

Gus looked away from her and turned toward Eden instead, but it wasn't to ask for her help. It was to hide his twisting devastation from their parents, to give him a second to compose himself, to gather his thoughts. Maize was Gus's dog. He loved her intensely—enough to have slept in a spider-filled outbuilding all night so she wouldn't feel alone. Eden nervously coiled the hem of her oversized ABBA T-shirt around her fingers—one of her endless thrift-store finds. She wanted to take a forward step, to put her arms around her brother, but she knew he'd hate her for it. Comforting him would have been humiliating. It would have meant defeat.

"So, you're choosing some wild boy over them?" he asked, his back still turned to their parents. "Even though it'll hurt all of us? Your *actual* kids? The ones you birthed, not the one you found?"

For a long while, nobody spoke.

Eventually their mother turned and stepped into the bathroom, shutting the door behind her without a word. That left Eden and Gus staring at their father, but Dad looked as forlorn as Eden felt. It was clear he didn't know what to say. But he had to say something, so he finally exhaled a tired breath and spoke.

"This is important to your mother."

"Yeah, I can see that. More important than us," Gus murmured, eyes to the floor.

Something about those words twisted Eden's heart into a fist. Suddenly all she wanted to do was cry. Gus was right, their parents—no, their *mother*, was choosing Rowan over them. For that, Eden would have a tough time forgiving her. But she also understood the importance of sacrifice, of opting to do good in a dark and unforgiving world. Uncle Brian would take care of Buster and Maize. He lived in Denver, only a few hours away. And Mom was right; it was better than the alternative. Uncle Brian was a good guy with a nice, big house and a fenced-in yard. She and Gus could probably see the dogs whenever they pleased, time permitting. Hell, when Gus got his license, it would give them an excuse to get the hell out of town, far away from their parents. But Rowan? Who would take in a kid like him if it wasn't them? It was either save the kid or save the dogs.

And yet, there was that impossibly loud scream, that look Rowan had given her at the dinner table the previous night, only moments before she found herself unable to breathe. There was Rowan sneaking into Sophie and Willow's room, which had been beyond disturbing. If she found that kid in *her* room one night, she wasn't sure what the hell she would do. And, perhaps most obviously, there was what Buster and Maize were trying to tell them: *Something is wrong.* But rather than heeding their warning, their parents would simply pack up their toys and lumpy beds and send them away. A problem wasn't a problem if that problem was far away.

"This is bullshit," Gus finally said, breaking the heavy silence. "Mom is clinging to Rowan because she's using him as a surrogate for a dead baby."

Eden tensed at her brother's words. He was right, but his harshness cut through his honesty, tainting it with a cruelty. She could sense her father recoiling from Gus's brazen allegation.

"This new kid isn't going to bring anyone back, is he?" Gus met his father's eyes. "If anything, he's going to do the opposite."

"What do you mean?" Eden furrowed her brow, not understanding. "How will he do the opposite?"

Gus went silent for a long while, then eventually shrugged. "I don't know. Call it a hunch."

Eden's stomach somersaulted when he walked out of the room. Something about seeing him vanish down the hall after such a vague declaration scared her. Was he saying he would leave? Eden pictured him packing up a duffel bag and taking off. She imagined waking up one morning and him being gone. What if that's what this whole thing turned into?

"Dad." She gave her father a desperate look.

But when she caught his expression, Eden realized that her father was just as scared as she was. She was bearing witness to the fact that Dad was out of his depth. He had no idea how to navigate the scenario they now found themselves in. And that scared the hell out of her. Because if Dad didn't know what to do, then who did?

17

SOPHIE

Sophie sat frozen on one side of the playroom. Rowan was on the other, his legs spread out at weird angles. Sophie thought he looked like he'd fallen out of a tree. Mom had talked to her sisters about it when she thought Sophie hadn't been listening—something about Rowan not having grown right, or maybe something about a cage? She wasn't sure what any of that meant, since people didn't live in cages. All she knew was that Rowan's arms and legs were weird. They reminded her of when she'd tried to make a puppet out of Popsicle sticks and had glued the entire thing backward and upside down. Sophie wanted to ask Rowan if it hurt to have his limbs bend that way, but after the whole closet thing, she was too scared to talk to him at all.

Rather than talking, Sophie sat as far away from Rowan as she could, her own legs bent like the kind of pretzel you'd get at the mall. She knew staring was rude, but she couldn't help it. His eyes really bugged her. They were too big, like the huge eyes of those tiny monkeys she'd read about in her animal encyclopedia. Rowan's forehead went on forever. His red hair looked fake, like a crooked doll's wig. Like Elmo fur. Like . . .

Chucky.

The name suddenly bounced into her brain.

That doll's name was Chucky. But he was a good guy. At least that's what Gus had said. . . .

Surrounded by all the things she loved—toys every color of the rainbow; walls covered in cheerful homeschool lessons, with number lines and an uppercase alphabet—Sophie couldn't have felt less at home had she found herself on another planet. Rowan gave her a nervous feeling. Not nervous good, like the way she was sometimes nervous when Mom or Dad said they had a surprise for her. Nervous bad, like how her stomach would tangle up at the doctor's office right before the nurse came in with a giant needle on a silver plate. It was a feeling that, like at the doctor's office, made her want to jump up and run.

Mom had taught her to be kind, to be what she called "open-minded" and "accepting," but something about Rowan made Sophie's mind close up tight. She tried to picture him as part of the family, sitting next to her while they practiced their Ss and 8s and learned their math facts and phonograms. She tried to picture him becoming less weird and more like a regular kid, playing hide-and-go-seek inside the house when it got too hot to go outside in the summer, building Lego structures and messing with Gus's old Snap Circuits sets when the weather was cold enough to freeze the trees.

But she just couldn't do it. It was because of the night before, Rowan hiding in the closet like a creepy Halloween monster. *Like Chucky.* She'd seen that kind of stuff on TV, even though she wasn't supposed to, especially when Gus picked the movie. There had been a man in a white mask carrying a knife. He was quiet and moved on silent feet but breathed pretty loud. Still, nobody knew he was there until it was too late, just like Sophie and Willow not knowing Rowan had been in their room all that time. The memory of it made Sophie's heartbeat jump and her throat close up. It had been scary, but that hadn't been the only thing.

Willow hadn't said anything about the star machine freaking out, spinning at a hundred miles per hour. And she hadn't said anything about floating over *her* bed. That left Sophie wondering if maybe she'd imagined all those things. Maybe she had dreamed everything, and it had just seemed real. But Rowan *had* been in their room. And she was sure—totally one-hundred-million-percent, no-baloney *sure*—that the shadow figure she'd seen had really been there too.

It had only been there for an instant, but that shadow figure? *That* scared her a lot.

She'd heard her share of stories about sharp-toothed monsters and soul-sucking ghosts. She knew the white-masked man's name was Michael—a boring name, like Luke or Gus or even Rowan. Mostly she knew those bad guys, those monsters, hid in the darkest parts of houses. They became the inkiest shadows in night-filled rooms. Was there any place darker than a closet? She may have only been five—almost six, just a few more months—but she was no dummy. She knew a closet was a perfect hiding place for a goblin. So, was it an accident a closet was where Rowan was hiding? She didn't know, but something told her the answer was no.

He'd only been here less than two days, and Sophie already hated being alone with him. The rest of her family was in the house somewhere, busy, doing their stuff, but that didn't make her feel very safe. She imagined her family disappearing, pictured herself totally alone with this creepy, silent boy. What would she do if the thing she was most scared of really happened? She could run out the front door. Run for the road the way Mom and Dad told her to never do. Run across the highway and into the wheat field where Rowan could never find her because it was tall and went on forever.

But her family *was* there. Mom and Dad's room was right above the playroom. She could hear Gus upstairs through the floor. He was talking loudly, sounding upset. Mom was yelling at him. Gus was always in trouble, but this time the trouble was big.

Sophie looked away from Rowan, searching across the many shelves and cubbies of the playroom for something to keep her busy while Mom and Dad had a grown-up meeting with her brother. She tried to hear what Gus was saying, but it was all muffled, and she couldn't listen very well anyway because of the buzzing in her ears. That buzzing seemed to be getting louder, and that scared her too. She hadn't told Mom and Dad about the bugs living in her brain because she hadn't wanted her parents to take her to the hospital, but now she wondered if maybe she should have said something. Because what if the bugs had laid eggs? What if bug babies were hatching inside her head right that very second? She bet that would hurt a whole lot. She wondered if it would maybe even make her die.

But she couldn't tell them now, not when they were busy upstairs and she was down here with Rowan. Grabbing the nearest toy—a little talking oven—she pulled it into her lap, wondering why she'd been left with Rowan in the first place. Where were Willow and Olive, and why weren't they here with her, making sure Rowan's jaws didn't flop open like a trapdoor so he could swallow her whole?

"Ew," she whispered to herself, raising her shoulders to her ears. That had been a gross thought. A scary thought. She distracted herself by popping open the oven's small see-through door. The toy piped up as soon as the latch was disengaged.

"Time to bake! Let's cook and count!"

Mom said that when Sophie had been tiny, this had been her favorite toy. Mom said that Sophie would drag it around the house and demand that anyone she came across place an order at Sophie's Food Shop. Sophie's eyes flicked up to catch a glimpse of Rowan. He was still sitting there, his legs looking boneless, his giant eyes focused on her the way you'd look at someone during a staring contest: not blinking and super serious.

"Let's bake some cupcakes! Set the oven dial to three!"

Sophie looked away, fidgeting with a tray of miniature plastic pastries. She dropped a couple of them into the oven and shut the door, then pushed a small pink slider from one to three.

"Three!" the toy cheerfully announced.

Sophie cast another quick look toward the boy across the room. He finally blinked at her, and suddenly her stomach did a loop-de-loop. The hum in her ears got louder. All of a sudden she felt bad nervous even worse than before.

Maybe she was dreaming again? *I'm asleep,* she told herself. *Asleep.* Because last she checked, everyone she'd ever met blinked in a pretty normal way—a quick shutting and opening of the eyes. But from what she just saw, or *thought* she saw, Rowan had shut his eyes, and then shut them again a split second later, as though he had a second set of eyelids hidden beneath the ones she could see. Not one pair, but two.

"*Three! It's ready!*" She nearly jumped when the happy voice of the toy shouted into her lap. "*You're a great counter, and a great chef!*"

Overhead, she could make out another muffled yell.

Where were her sisters? Why weren't they checking in on her? Weren't they wondering where she was?

Her bottom lip began to tremble. She sucked it into her mouth and bit down, trying to imagine what levelheaded Olive would have told her had she been here, watching Sophie fight a meltdown.

He's just a kid. Just a kid. Just a kid like you.

Except Gus would have said something different.

Chucky.

And Dad had taught her to follow her instincts.

If something doesn't feel right, it's probably not.

So, which was it? Was Rowan just a kid, or was he not right? Was she supposed to sit there and try to be nice to him, or was she supposed to run away?

"*Let's play again! Open my door and we'll bake something tasty!*"

Sophie pried the toy's door open with quaking fingers, if only to keep herself from crying. She tried to ignore the noise in her ears, loud and distracting. She fumbled with the cupcakes inside, and they tumbled out of the oven. One fell between her legs and landed on the carpet. The other rolled down her leg, hit the rainbow-colored rug, and continued along until it tapped one of Rowan's Velcroed shoes—the same pair he'd shown up in, scuffed and dirty, like some other kid had worn them down before Rowan had gotten them. Sophie stared at the plastic cupcake near his foot for a long time, then slowly inched her gaze up his sweatpants, up the front of his way-too-big Mickey Mouse shirt, and eventually stopped on his face. His expression felt different. *Felt,* because she wasn't sure. *Felt,* because she thought he was smiling, but his mouth wasn't smiling at all.

"Let's cook and count! Set the oven dial to five!"

Rowan slowly canted his head.

Sophie sat frozen, suddenly unable to look away.

"Five!" The oven singsonged without her touching it. *"One, two, three, four, five! It's ready!"*

Rowan's focus flicked to the toy.

"Let's bake some cupcakes! Set the oven dial to two!"

She watched him blink again, and this time she was a billion percent sure. There *was* a blink before the blink, a transparent scrim sliding over his eyes a split second before his eyelids followed.

"Two!" the toy screeched without the slider being engaged. *"One. Two! Great job! Let's do it again!"*

Sophie's breaths came faster. She could feel that weird, fuzzy sensation again. The hairs on her arms were perking up, standing at attention—like when Gus rubbed a balloon on her head to make her hair point up toward space. She gulped, feeling like she really, really needed to find her big brother, to duck behind him and hide there forever.

Rowan's expression started to change. He began to look frightened. Meanwhile, Sophie sensed herself growing lighter, like someone was tying helium balloons to her back, adding one after another until she'd find herself floating off the ground, like that house from *Up*.

Except, when she looked down, she was still sitting on the floor. Maybe it was how astronauts felt, weightless but strapped into the seats of their rocket ships, floating like angels, gazing out toward planet Earth. Reaching out to touch the floor, she let her fingertips sweep the soft carpet beneath her—it was proof that her bottom was still firmly on the floor. It was also proof that she wasn't sleeping, that Rowan was there with her, that what she was feeling was real.

"Let's bake some cupcakes! Set the oven dial to four!"

The sound shocked Sophie into motion. She jerked away, scurrying a few inches back until her shoulder blades hit the wall behind her.

"One, two, three, four!"

She turned to Rowan. It was then that Sophie noticed that he looked as scared as she felt. He was wearing the same expression that was probably pulled tight across her own face.

She opened her mouth to scream for her mother. Rowan did the same.

Before she could yell, the room exploded into nothing but noise. Every battery-operated toy burst to life. The remote-controlled robot unicorn she'd gotten for Christmas began to freak out, its legs moving back and forth in jerky motions as it lay on the floor. Her mini karaoke machine lit up with rainbow lights. It screeched the way it did when she put the microphone too close to the speaker. Her talking baby doll began to giggle. Frozen in both surprise and fear, Sophie struggled to pull in air.

And then, nothing.

Total silence.

The quiet lasted long enough for Sophie to exhale.

Another blast of noise filled the room, this time so loud it made her gasp. She slapped her hands over her ears. This time, she really sensed that she was starting to float, the carpet seeming farther away. Rowan's face continued to twist, growing more terrified by the second. He sat among th. flashing, booming toys, but his eyes didn't look afraid. Instead of real feelings, he was wearing a mask. It reminded her of the awful costume Gus had picked last Halloween. A blank face. White with no nose. Just two gaping holes for eyes and a matching black hole for a wailing mouth.

The memory of that awful face pushed her over the edge.

Sophie screamed, and then Rowan did too.

The shriek he released was as booming as the one Sophie had heard outside, when Maize had knocked him down into the dirt. It was so loud it made the buzzing in her ears feel as though something was digging deeper into her skull—those bugs waking up, using their pinchy mouthparts to chew their way deep into her brain. It *hurt*, and she imagined the worst—her head swelling up and bursting like a water balloon, but instead of water inside, there were eggs. Millions of tiny, transparent eggs like swollen water beads, spilling out across the floor.

Sophie slapped her hands over her ears and cried out again, not because she was scared, but because it hurt really, *really* bad. The pain was coming from deep within her head, from somewhere behind her eyes. The bugs had found their way inside. Now they'd eat her up, eat her alive.

Finally, she could feel someone stomping upstairs, rushing down the hall toward the stairs. Before she could scream again, whatever had lifted her up suddenly vanished, and she fell to the floor hard, her legs crumpling in a heap beneath her.

"Ow!" she cried out. Coiled with her hands pressed against her ears, Sophie began to weep. She hardly heard her parents when they burst into the room, but she recognized arms circling her in a hug. Their voices were muffled beneath the buzzing of a thousand bees building a hive between her ears.

Someone started to pull at her hands, and when she finally looked up, Dad was there, studying his own fingers with a confused sort of look. Sophie glanced to his hands. They were streaked with red. Was that . . . blood?

Before she could ask anything, Dad was grabbing a box of tissues off the top of her cubby shelf and pushing wads of soft paper against the sides of her head. He looked totally freaked out. But what scared her the most was that when she watched her parents' mouths, she couldn't hear the sounds she was sure should have been there.

Sophie.

She read her name on their lips.

Sophie. Sophie!

Over and over.

Dad lifted a hand and snapped his fingers. She imagined the sound they made, so familiar but missing, like the television on mute.

She shook her head at them, confused.

I can't hear you.

She knew she said the words, but she couldn't hear herself say them. And as her parents continued to lose it, Sophie looked back to where Rowan sat. He was no longer wearing that awful expression of phony distress. Instead, his face was blank. His eyes were empty. He was watching Mom and Dad scramble, studying the way they were reacting, his eyes darting between them. Yet, for some reason, neither one of her parents stopped to look at him, to ask what had happened or to point a finger at him the way they always did with Gus. *What did you do?!*

It was as though Rowan had done a magic trick and made himself invisible. Like a monster that didn't want to be seen; some dangerous thing that hid in the dark when kids were sleeping.

Like something that was waiting. Waiting. Waiting to strike.

18

ISLA

Sitting in the emergency room for a second time in a matter of a few hours, Isla couldn't believe the disaster that had become her day. It was as though the world had come unglued, as though there had been some shift in reality, and now everything was falling apart.

The look the ER nurse gave her upon recognizing her from earlier turned Isla's stomach. The glance wasn't only brimming with judgment, but carried an edge of suspicion. How did a woman end up in the ER twice in one day with two different kids? First, a boy falls from a playset and dislocates his shoulder. Now, a little girl comes in bleeding from the ears.

Two serious injuries with one common thread: the adult.

Isla was waiting for Child Protective Services to arrive and demand answers. The mere thought of it made her shake, because she didn't know what the hell she would tell them, especially when they discovered she'd just started fostering a child, a vulnerable, nonverbal boy who wouldn't have been able to tell anyone what exactly was going on in his new home.

Why is he so skinny? When was the last time he ate?

Oh God.

All at once, Isla resented Luke for yelling at her to get in the car when she had wanted to stay with Rowan. She should have put her foot down, should have insisted that she needed to make him some toast. Or maybe he'd be okay with warm milk. Christ, what was she supposed to do here at the hospital that one capable adult couldn't have done themselves? She should have been back home, making sure Rowan was all right.

Then she reeled at her own audacity.

What is wrong with you? How could you even think to be anywhere but here with Sophie?

But the guilt was fleeting. Before she knew it, her thoughts were back to Rowan, worrying about him, wondering if he was okay. Her mind spiraled, snagging on the "missing" billboards they'd passed to get to the hospital, her brain replacing those children's smiling faces with Rowan's startled, wide-eyed stare. She imagined the internet articles she actively avoided, the social media Reels both August and Eden were addicted to. Imagined them shifting from the topic of random missing kids to *her*, forty-something Isla Ann Hansen, a mom from rural Colorado who just so happened to "find" a kid after losing yet another baby . . . now accused of abusing her own five-year-old daughter. Christ, she'd be crucified. They'd lock her up forever. They'd send her back to the hospital. . . .

She nearly jumped when the privacy curtain's metal rings clattered along the overhead rail. Luke's hand fell to her knee. *Steady.* His touch repulsed her. She was about to shove him away but stopped herself when the ER doctor, Dr. Devi, stepped into their makeshift cubicle. He was young. Handsome. That annoyed her. Isla was sure she was old enough to be his mother, so how medically proficient could this "kid" really be?

The space was claustrophobic. There were various medical machines, two hard-backed chairs, and a motorized bed where Sophie was currently sleeping. Isla considered getting up and leaving. She wondered if there were cabs outside or if she'd need to book an Uber. She'd remember where those billboards were and keep her head down as they passed. *And if the driver wants to talk about the missing kids?* She'd demand they pull over. She'd get out and walk for miles if she had to. Anything to not think about Ruby Mae. To not think of the babies. To not think of any of it ever again.

And if someone comes for him? The question plagued her. *If someone finally comes because he's one of them?*

No. Goddamn it, *no*. She refused to replace those random missing children with Rowan's face. She pressed her fingers hard against her eyes, blocking out the fluorescent lighting of the ER. She should be home.

Should be home.

Should be home . . . ! Now!

"So . . ."

Isla's heart hitched.

"As far as our tests go, we can't find the source of your daughter's injury," Dr. Devi explained. He looked South Asian with his dark eyes and inky black hair, but he had no accent. Like his youth, that annoyed her too. At least an accent would have helped her place where he was from. Not that it mattered, but it would have given her something to think about.

Dr. Devi cradled a laptop in the crook of his left arm.

"Honestly, we can't see any injury at all." He tapped a key repeatedly, scrolling through Sophie's charts. "Physically, the internal structure of Sophie's ears looks fine." He frowned, as if unsure of how else to put it: *I don't know what this is. I don't know why it's occurred. Because I'm young and stupid, too young to be doing this job. I don't know anything. I'm a fraud.*

"But her ears *aren't* fine," Luke said. "She can't hear us."

His words pulled Isla out of her tailspin. She looked up, searching the young doctor's face. He was likely fresh out of med school. Dr. Devi's eyes flicked between her and Luke. Without any proof, she decided he was in his early twenties, *too* damn young. How long could he have possibly been practicing medicine? Two weeks?

"Was Sophie exposed to any extraordinarily loud sounds?" Dr. Devi asked. "Fireworks or yard tools or anything of that nature?"

Isla shook her head. *No.*

But Luke contradicted her.

"Screaming," he said. "We had a few instances of screaming today, so there was definitely loud noise."

Her chest tightened at the recollection of the sound. So awful. So desperate. So in need of protection. And what had she been able to do?

How had she been able to help? Isla was abruptly overcome by a wave of defeat, her thoughts spiraling to the babies she hadn't been able to save, that her body hadn't been able to hold on to. She swallowed against a squirming sense of guilt, wondering if she should come out and say it, admit it to Dr. Devi and the entire ER: *I'm a bad mother! I'm trying, but I fail every time!*

"Screaming." The doctor squinted at his computer screen, considering it, then looked to Luke. "Sophie was screaming?"

Isla shuddered. *What?* She shot a glance at Luke. Had Sophie been screaming? She didn't remember that at all.

"No. Another pers—" Luke paused, corrected himself. "Another one of our kids."

Isla's eyes darted to the doctor, then back to her husband. She searched Luke's face. Did he mean that? Was he identifying Rowan as one of their own? Except, no. The second their eyes met, she found the lie. He'd only said it to avoid an awkward explanation. She marked the stiffness of his shoulders, the discomfort it brought him to call Rowan anything but a stranger.

"Screaming directly into her ears?" Dr. Devi didn't seem convinced. If it was just a kid screaming, it would have been one ear affected, not both. And could a scream of any sort be loud enough to rob a child of their hearing? No way. Because this wasn't Rowan's fault. If anything, it was hers, right? She was the one who kept fucking things up.

"No, but . . . it was loud. Like, *really* loud."

And there it was, Luke placing blame, and not even on her but on an innocent child. Isla looked away from him, disgusted. If she *did* just get up and walk out, what could he do? If she decided to get the hell out of that emergency room and find a way home herself, then what?

Do you really care?

"It's highly unlikely that a scream would be at a high enough decibel level to do something like this, but . . . well, nothing is impossible," Dr. Devi said. "Maybe Sophie has been having some auditory issues that she hasn't mentioned, either because she thought they were normal or because they weren't that bothersome. A loud enough noise could trigger something like this. Though that's not a diagnosis I can give. Your daughter needs to see a specialist as soon as possible." He reached out, handing Isla a business card. She took it, looked down. Scribbled on Dr. Devi's card was an unfamiliar name: Dr. Alexander Gerber, ENT. "Dr. Gerber is one of the best otolaryngologists in the state. If anyone can figure out what's happening here, it's him."

There was a long silence. Eventually, Isla spoke.

"So, we're just supposed to take her home?" she asked, her tone clipped. Sophie had lost one of her five senses for no explainable reason. Not explainable, and not blamable. Regardless of how it had occurred, how could they just take Sophie home as though everything was fine? What were they supposed to do for her when they got there? How was Sophie supposed to function? And what the hell was Isla supposed to do other than look like the incompetent mother she was? She was right, Dr. Devi didn't know a damn thing. *Nothing but a toddler,* she thought. *A fetus.*

That word made her stomach lurch. Suddenly she was sure she was about to be sick.

"All I can say is call Dr. Gerber as soon as you can," Dr. Devi replied. "His practice makes room for emergency cases, and this certainly qualifies. I'll call ahead, leave a message, make sure you get in as soon as possible."

Isla looked back down at the card between her fingers, her annoyance shifting to confusion. This was all wrong. Her being in the hospital for the second time today, wanting to go home without her husband and youngest child. Her being beyond distracted, unable to pull her thoughts away from Rowan—not once thinking of her other children, hardly thinking of Sophie at all. *A bad mother raised by a bad mother.*

Isla shut her eyes, forcing herself to conjure the thoughts she knew were right. Should Sophie even go home? What if her ears started to bleed again? What if she started screaming and they found her curled up in a ball like they had a few hours before? What if Rowan saw it take place, and it triggered something in him—a memory, a past trauma? Would he be taken away then?

What about Rowan?

Would Helen Plummer want him back for more of her tests?

What about Rowan?

Would he . . . oh God. Would he run away?

What about Rowan?

What about Rowan?

What about him?

"Yes, that would be great," she heard Luke say. "Thank you, Doc."

She glanced to her daughter. Sophie was still dozing on the hospital bed. She looked so small—more like three years old rather than five. Her hair was a tangled mess, her pigtails so skewed they appeared more like matted dog ears than anything else. Her T-shirt, dotted with little flowers, was crumpled and soiled with small spots of blood. And what if her hearing loss was permanent? What then? What if she and Rowan couldn't be in the same house together? Was she supposed to choose? The mere idea of it gripped her by the base of the throat, and before she knew it, she was weeping into the palms of her hands, because where would Sophie go? Who would take her? How would she survive?

"My God," she whispered. "What's happening?"

Luke's hand found the curve of her back.

"Mrs. Hansen . . . I realize this is all incredibly frightening," Dr. Devi said. "But for Sophie's benefit, it's best to not let her see you panic. Again, there doesn't seem to be anything physically wrong with her. And even if there is a genuine issue, the technology in this field has made incredible advancements, especially in the case of children. I'm sure Dr. Gerber will help you out." The reassuring smile from the doctor made Isla feel both thankful and stupid—thankful that he was so kind, stupid because he was a know-nothing kid talking her off a ledge.

"Don't panic?" she asked bitterly, looking back down to the business card held between her fingers. "Clearly, you don't have children of your own." She paused, then murmured, "Doogie Howser to the rescue."

Luke's hand increased pressure, shifting down between her shoulder blades.

She didn't look up, but she could sense Dr. Devi seeing himself out in silence, ducking through the privacy curtain that did nothing to shield them from the noise of a busy ER. Somewhere not too far away, a woman was crying. Down farther, a person was retching into what she imagined was a steel, kidney-shaped pan. Farther still, a man moaned, *"Where's the doctor? I need the doctor!"*

"Jesus," Luke said softly. "Let's get the hell out of here."

He rose from his seat, moved toward the bed, and began to gather the things they had brought with them into Isla's oversized purse. Isla remained motionless, but her husband's voice swirled in her ears, a record on repeat.

Jesus, Isla. Jesus.

Suddenly she was overwhelmed with both hope and anger. Hope because *of course*, how could she have forgotten that this wasn't in her control? Here she was, trying to figure out a mystery that wasn't ready to be solved. Anger because this was a test, one of those tests her mother had spoken of but Isla had rejected as nonsense. Isla's mother was a nutcase, but suddenly it made some sense. Somehow, sitting next to Sophie, staring at the blood that had dried rust red in her daughter's blond hair, blood that had streaked down the sides of her neck, giving up control and putting her faith in God had slipped Isla's mind.

So was that it, then? This was God testing a life-long agnostic, promising her that things would become more difficult before they became easy? Isla already knew the conversation she and Luke would be having behind their closed bedroom door. He'd bring up Rowan, bring up the fact that misfortune had suddenly chosen their family. He wouldn't outright say it, but everything would point to sending Rowan back from where he came. As though Rowan was responsible. As if he had brought with him some unspeakable curse. As though sending him away would somehow shift their destinies. But that was the thing about destiny. It was preordained, right? Whatever was going to transpire would have taken place regardless of whether Rowan had ever stepped out of the trees. Whatever had been set in motion would come to pass whether Rowan stayed with them or not.

"He's right," she finally whispered. "We just have to trust it'll all work out."

Leaning over the bed and readying himself to lift their daughter up in his arms, Luke paused to look at his wife. His gaze lingered on Isla's face for a long while, as though trying to decipher exactly what she meant by that. There was something in his eyes that Isla didn't like, something that made her feel edgy, made her want to recoil. Was that suspicion? Mistrust? Exasperation? *Did you take your meds today?*

She was shocked when she finally placed it. Her mother had given Isla that same look. And then she had torn Isla's world apart. But if that's what Luke was planning, he had another thing coming. No, she wouldn't let him. He could try, but Rowan wasn't going anywhere. This was a trial. *Her* trial. A way to prove that she *was* a good mother. Rowan had appeared for a reason; she just knew it. It was fated.

Destiny, she thought. *Fate.*

Preordained.

Written in the stars.

19

LUKE

Luke knew it was unfair, but he couldn't help but think it anyway: this was all Rowan's fault. The kid had only been in the Hansen house for a single night—this was evening number two—but it had been nearly two months since he'd come out of the trees behind their home, and that's when the shift had come to pass.

It had been overwhelming how quickly Isla had become obsessed with Rowan's case. Before Luke knew it, it was all his wife talked about. Six weeks ago, kids had started disappearing. Before Rowan had materialized, they'd been bombarded with Amber Alerts and news reports about children from all Four Corners states vanishing without so much as a trace. At first, Isla had been both horrified and overwhelmed. The missing children had opened up the floodgates to something beyond Luke's understanding. With each new missing person case, he could see Isla coil more and more into herself, like a nautilus retreating into its shell.

Before the loss of Adam, Isla spent her good days working on lessons with their kids, teaching them English and history, googling solutions to impossible math problems, watching YouTube videos about foreign countries, making a bucket list of places they had to visit before the offspring grew up and scattered to the wind. They'd do art projects that Luke would find hanging on random walls—pictures made from pompoms and pipe cleaners, three-dimensional masterpieces of twigs and leaves hot-glued into place. All of it was both inspired and instigated by Isla. She was the conductor, and the children were her orchestra.

After Adam, Isla struggled—an understatement, to be sure—and things had gotten progressively worse. But she had done her damnedest to try at the beginning. Try to keep things normal. Try for her kids. After Rowan appeared, though? Isla's attentiveness went out the window. From where Luke had been sitting, it appeared that she wasn't able to focus on anything. She was constantly on edge, chewing her fingernails, calling Child Protective Services to get updates about the mysterious boy who had blinked into existence out of the shadows of *their* forest. The attention she usually gave their own children was without warning completely wrapped up in her obsession over that still-nameless child. She started complaining that her migraines were worse. *Of course they are,* Luke had thought. *You're completely consumed.*

Whatever art the kids ended up doing, they now did alone. They'd hang their pictures up on the walls, same as always, but Isla no longer admired them. She either didn't notice, or didn't care, or both. She'd made Sophie and Willow cry with her absent-minded negligence. She hadn't noticed *that*, either.

But there was more to it than headaches, strange boys, and overlooked kids. Luke had caught Isla standing in the kitchen a few times, looking ahead, blank-faced and empty-eyed. She'd been zoned out like a corpse bride, like something out of *Night of the Living Dead.* And *that* had scared the shit out of him, because he'd seen it before.

Ever since they'd met—more than twenty years now—Luke had caught his wife gasping, turning every now and again as though sensing someone behind her, someone who wasn't there. He'd asked about it, of course, but Isla had shrugged it off every time. *Just jumpy, I guess.* After Rowan, that jumpiness grew exponentially worse. Even her sleeping habits changed—always a light sleeper, now she slept like the dead. That, however, wasn't exactly new. She conked out the same way every time she'd been pregnant, which Luke had consistently found confusing. Didn't pregnant women sleep worse than before conception? Not Isla. She was comatose, out so deeply it seemed like nothing could rouse her. Now, weeks after Rowan had stepped out of the pines, Isla moved so little in her sleep that only a week ago, Luke had caught himself making sure she was breathing by leaning in and listening. His mind had dared wander to the morbid parlor trick of putting a mirror to a dead person's nose. Spooked by her stillness, he'd gone close to her, then nearly screamed when he found her eyes wide-open. He'd almost called 911, but before he could grab his phone, she'd come out of it, confused and hardly able to place where she was, as though she'd been somewhere else.

The logical part of his brain assured him that Rowan had nothing to do with any of the things going on with his wife. No, all of it was medication and trauma. Isla had suffered from depression and anxiety since the day Luke had met her at the shitty little diner where she'd been working. Times had been tough after every lost baby, but it had all spiraled out of control over the past year. So much so that, out of desperation, Isla had swallowed a handful of pills. Because there was only so much one person could take.

Then there was the sudden uptick of missing kids. The Amber Alerts, the billboards, the flyers stuck to telephone poles throughout town. *That* couldn't have been easy after losing a baby. Shit, Luke hadn't even factored in Ruby Mae until Isla had brought her up.

I can't stop thinking about her, Isla had said. *I feel her all the time now.* Meanwhile, Luke hadn't thought of Ruby Mae in years.

So, no, Rowan wasn't doing anything. And even if it had been him and they did end up sending him back to the children's home, it wasn't as though Luke could wipe Isla's mind of the boy who had somehow found his way to them, right? Suggesting that they send Rowan back wouldn't change anything but Isla's opinion of Luke. She'd forever see him as a callous, uncaring, small-minded asshole with an ugly black heart.

But the dogs . . .

They had run right at the kid. Gus had said it himself: they'd never acted that way before. Sending Maize and Buster away was eating at Luke—of course it didn't feel right. It wasn't fair to the kids. But Isla wouldn't let that go either. If Luke argued, he'd be the guy who was fine with a foster kid getting mauled. He'd be the guy putting his own family in jeopardy, because clearly the dogs were more important than the safety of a child.

He couldn't win.

And Sophie was in the playroom, alone with him. . . .

Except assuming a kid could make another one's ears bleed was ridiculous. How the hell could that happen unless it had been physical assault?

What if it was?

No. Sophie would have told them.

Unless she was in too much pain. Unless she was too scared.

As Luke sat on the edge of the bed, his thoughts were mired in chaos. He pushed his fingers through his hair and let out an exhausted sigh, then drew his hands down his face and stood. Moving to the master bathroom, he joined Isla at the double sink, where she was brushing her teeth. He watched her reflection. When their eyes met, he looked down at his own toothbrush, grabbed the Colgate, and turned on the tap.

Isla leaned forward, spit foam into the basin, and frowned. She was waiting for him to speak.

"It's just weird," he told her, the topic needing no introduction.

"Maybe it's supposed to be weird," she replied, rinsing off her toothbrush.

"How's that?" he asked, unsure whether he was prepared to have an in-depth conversation about anything while feeling as bone-tired as he did. It had been another day from hell. He just wanted to fall into bed and forget he existed for a handful of hours, though he'd be lucky if he could sleep at all.

"Maybe it's supposed to be weird, because if it wasn't, it would be easy," Isla said.

Luke shut his eyes, the steam from his tap rising, streaking the mirror in front of him. "Please, Isla, no riddles, okay?" If she threw a brainteaser at him in his current state, his brain might just tease its way right out of his fucking skull.

"It's *not* a riddle," she muttered, dropping her rinsed-off toothbrush into the cup near her sink. "It's a test of faith." Clearly aggravated with his lack of understanding, she stepped out of the bathroom, leaving Luke to glower at his steam-stained reflection.

Luke peered at himself in the mirror, all thoughts but one suddenly wiped from his mind: *What did she just say?*

Luke had been brought up in a religious family. He had been expected to warm a pew every Sunday, come hell or high water. When he and Isla had first met, Luke had been the one to bring up God this and God that. Having been raised by a crystal-worshipping hippie from whom she was now estranged, Isla couldn't have cared less about God or Jesus or anything faith-based. She had been the one who had given Luke permission to stop being duped.

He'd gone along with the idea of God because it was what had been expected of a boy raised by a nice, Christian family. But nowadays? Luke didn't believe in any of it. God. Jesus. Angels. Demons. He'd grown up, met Isla, and, with her help, had finally seen through the ruse. God didn't save people. People saved themselves. And God certainly wasn't taking their babies through miscarriages to test them as a couple, just like he wasn't making kids vanish from local townships, from adjacent counties, from neighboring states, to make people question their faith.

But now Isla was telling him it *was* a test. Brushing his molars, he wondered what the fuck she was talking about. God? Since when did she *ever* believe in that?

When he stepped into the bedroom, Isla was already under the sheets. Propped against the headboard with a pillow behind her back, her eyes were shut and her hands were clasped in silent prayer. He paused to study her intensity. He knew she could feel him watching, but she didn't open her eyes to regard him. Instead, she continued to pray.

He slipped under the covers and examined the blank screen of his phone while she finished imploring the Almighty for . . . whatever. Finally, when she glanced over to him, he spoke: "I'm calling Dr. Gerber first thing in the morning."

She said nothing.

Luke took a breath, then sighed. He knew she'd turn it into an issue, but he'd held his tongue about everything else. He had to speak his mind about this. "Will you do me a favor?"

"Sure," she said. "What is it?"

"Keep Rowan in sight from now on. Don't let him be alone with the kids."

Isla's expression shifted from pacifying to incredulous. He waited for her to smirk at him, but she frowned instead, as though appalled.

"Okay," she finally said, "but I think you're being ridiculous." She paused, glowered at her hands, then spoke beneath her breath. "Fucking *ridiculous*."

And what about you? he wanted to ask. *What about taking this kid in isn't ridiculous? What about you praying before bed isn't completely unlike you? What the hell is even going on?*

But before Luke could dig himself into an even deeper hole, Isla turned away, adjusted her pillow, and lay down, her back to him. Conversation over.

Just like that, despite Luke's best efforts, a wall materialized between them, stone by invisible stone. And while he couldn't blame Rowan for much, he could certainly condemn him for that.

20

AUGUST

Gus couldn't sleep, and he wasn't sure how anyone else could. The dogs were whining inside the barn. Couldn't anyone else hear them?

The sound of Maize's and Buster's cries was starting to drive him crazy, slowly boring into the soft tissue of his brain. The more he lay in the darkness of his room, the less he could tell if what he was hearing was an auditory hallucination or real. So, rather than simply lying there glaring at his wall, he shoved the blankets off his legs, slid his feet into a pair of ratty Adidas sandals, and padded as silently as he could down the stairs.

He wasn't sure what it was about being alone outside in the dark that made him uncomfortable. Perhaps it was the fact that their farmhouse was a few miles from their closest neighbor. Maybe it was that the moon was missing, offering nothing in terms of light. Hell, it might have been a stupid childhood fear rearing its ugly head. He'd been afraid of closets when he was a kid, just like Sophie was now. His best friend, Noah, would have laughed his ass off had he found out Gus slept with a night-light until only a few years ago. August Emory Hansen, the guy who listened to the Misfits and the Ramones, afraid of the dark? No way in hell he'd ever live *that* one down.

Unlocking the front door and stepping onto the front porch, Gus snorted at the butterflies fluttering at the pit of his stomach. "Dumb," he told himself. And yet the instant the word slipped past his lips, the dogs began to howl. It sent a chill so intense down his spine, he physically shuddered. What the hell was up with them? If they were just pissed off at Rowan, well, the weirdo kid was inside, hopefully asleep. Gus needed to shut them up before Mom threw open the window and yelled down at him like some sort of angry Dickensian character. *Those wild animals will never be allowed back here, Gus! Do you hear me? Never!*

He squared his shoulders and forced himself down the front porch steps, but the closer he got to the barn, the slower his steps became. Moving away from the house caused his anxiety to spike, sending it clawing up his windpipe. Before he knew it, he was standing motionless in the middle of the front yard, equidistant from the house and the barn. Frozen in the darkness, he felt torn—part of him wanted to bolt for where the dogs were now yelping in fear, while another part urged him to turn around and run like hell back to his room. Because what *was* this? What had them so freaked out? Curling his fingers into fists, he couldn't help the whimper that escaped him. The dogs were practically braying now, though he couldn't figure out whether it was to get him to come to them faster or to scare him away.

"Maize . . . ?" The name escaped him in a strained sort of croak. His throat felt parched, too tight for his vocal cords to work the way they were supposed to. "Buster . . . ?" Hearing the tremor in his own voice was unnerving. Standing there with no light, he told himself there was nothing to be afraid of. He was just being stupid. Yet he was more terrified than he could remember ever being.

"Oh my god," he whispered, "Just move your fucking feet, idiot!"

He sucked in a sharp breath and forced his body to comply. The action of walking was enough to dispel some of his fear. The dogs' yowling was suddenly far more concerning than scary. They needed Gus's help. The rest of the family didn't seem to give a damn, so they were relying on him. He quickened his pace.

When he reached the barn door, he yanked on the Master Lock. He'd left it hanging open on the latch earlier that day, but it looked like Dad had secured it before everyone had turned in for the night. The key to the lock was in the kitchen junk drawer.

"Ah shit," Gus hissed through his teeth, then spoke loud enough for the dogs to hear. "I'll be right back, you guys. Just sit tight."

He pivoted on the soles of his flip-flops, took a single forward step, and froze dead in his tracks.

There was someone there, close to the tree line in what appeared to be the exact spot where Rowan had appeared weeks before.

Dark. Bone-skinny. Impossibly tall. It was a person whose silhouette didn't look like a person at all, their arms bent at awkward angles, legs looking more like that of an animal. A centaur. A monster. A ghoul.

"Oh fuck."

Gus's mind reeled. He wasn't sure whether to play dead, pretend to be invisible, or to take off at full speed. There were only two outcomes if he made a run for it. He'd either make it . . . or he wouldn't. And what then, about that latter choice?

Before he could decide, he saw something move just beyond the pines. There was another figure out there, this one hiding, though not very well, waiting in the dark of the woods.

Waiting.

Waiting for what?

"Oh fuck, oh fuck, oh fuck."

If he *did* run, if he *did* make it back to the house, wouldn't those things just follow him inside and slaughter everyone? What if, by trying to save himself, he ended up sealing his family's fate and bringing about their untimely end?

Behind him, the dogs were losing their minds. They were scratching wildly at the door, their yapping and snarls like nothing Gus had ever heard. They were so beside themselves with primal instinct it would have been surprising if their paws weren't bleeding, claws broken and torn. God, what he wouldn't have done to be able to release Maize and Buster and sic them on whatever the hell was standing out there, watching him from a distance. But he was forced to remain motionless, waiting for the figures to make the first move. If they retreated, Gus could run back to the house. But if they advanced, what then? His mind reeled at the thought of it. An eternity passed—or what seemed like one—leaving Gus to wonder how long he could stay in one spot. How many minutes could he manage before his limbs began to ache and cramp, before he started to hear his own blood flowing through his veins?

A train whistle cried out in the distance, jarring Gus out of his terrified stupor.

"You can't just stand here forever," he whispered to himself, trying to psych himself up. But if he moved, they'd break into a run. Their legs looked daddy-longlegs long, undoubtedly fast. They'd be on him in seconds. They'd crack open their jaws and—

There was a flash; the world's biggest camera igniting the earth in cold white light. Gus winced and instinctively shielded his eyes with an arm. He could hardly see when, less than a second later, darkness fell like a veil once more.

The train whistle blasted again. Maybe it was a coincidence, but it struck him as a warning.

When he looked up, he could make out the ghost of a lightning streak across the sky, thin and delicate, like a webbing of veins. His breath hitched as the frightening phenomenon faded. The sight left him breathless. It was both beautiful and terrifying all at once. His eyes may have been playing tricks on him, but he could swear the afterglow wasn't a fading electric white like that of a lightning strike. Rather, it was a red so deep it reminded him of blood. The sky was veined with it, like the wall of a beating heart.

He shot another look toward his mother's garden.

The figures were gone.

Where did they go?

He couldn't see them, but he was sure they were out there somewhere. They'd moved while he was distracted by the sudden light. For all he knew, they'd sprinted at him while he'd been rendered blind, and now they were behind him, hidden in darkness but so close. *So* close . . .

Gus was suddenly overwhelmed with the need to scream. He willed himself to open his mouth, to shout for his parents, for his siblings, hell, for the dogs. It didn't matter for whom. He just wanted to make noise. Because maybe if he was loud enough, he'd scare off whatever was huddling out there among the trees, or behind the barn, or wherever the fuck they were now. The thought of them lingering behind him sent his blood pressure thundering against his ears. And yet, even with the sudden whine of tinnitus deep inside his head, he still managed to notice the all-consuming silence that surrounded him.

Not a breath of wind.

Not a cricket's chirp.

Not a single bark or whine from the dogs.

How is this possible?

Gus's scream was swelling, threatening to choke him if it didn't escape soon.

How is this fucking possible?

Finally, he lurched forward, falling into a sort of stumbling run as he tripped his way back toward the house. But rather than finding comfort inside the safe space of home, the moment he stepped into the foyer, the hairs on the back of his neck stood on end.

The air here tasted metallic. He could feel it swirling across his skin. Heavy with static, it crawled over him like an army of millipedes, eventually settling in his hair and sending an almost seizure-like shudder down his spine. He forced himself farther inside, desperate to retrieve the Master Lock key, though no longer understanding his own compulsion. He'd just seen creatures standing in the yard—Jesus, is *that* what they were? *Creatures?* He'd watched the sky light up as intense as an atom bomb. Surely there were more pressing things to do than find a missing key. Yet his body pushed forward, moving through the living room and toward the kitchen as if directed by a puppeteer, pulled by invisible strings.

Reaching the kitchen, he stopped in front of the junk drawer just shy of the stainless-steel refrigerator. It's where Dad stashed the barn key. Gus would find it attached to a dirty, rubberized key ring shaped like Mickey Mouse's guffawing face. He squinted in the dimness of the sensored night-light plugged into one of the kitchen outlets. It had winked on soundlessly as soon as he had entered the room. Pulling open the drawer, he peered at the piles of Post-it Notes, receipts, and pens. Mickey Mouse lay dead center in the middle of the pile, waiting to be retrieved. *Hiya, pal!* As though having been left where Gus wouldn't be able to miss it. He squinted at it, his mind flashing back to when his dad had grabbed it off a rotating display next to the register on Main Street, U.S.A. Reaching out to hook a finger through the loop, only then did he notice that the piles of papers jammed into that drawer were all blank. Not a single phone number or random recipe of his mother's. Not a doodle from Sophie or a stray home improvement receipt from his dad. Gus swallowed the spit that was gathering in his mouth, trying like hell to reason out what it was he was looking at, standing so still that, a second later, the night-light decided that Gus had left the room and blinked off.

Click.

Gus's breath stuck in his throat.

He was about to move, to wildly wave an arm to trigger the light again, but the heaviness of the room told him to be still.

He sensed something shift behind him.

Click.

The night-light sensor tripped.

A tense stillness fell over the room, the kind that manifests during a game of statue; a breathless sort of horror movie silence, when the victim waits out the axe murderer behind nothing but a slatted closet door.

Gus clenched his teeth as that unsettling electric charge crossed his skin for a second time, his tinnitus amping up a notch. Amid the faint glow of the night-light, he could make out a shadow undulating in the stainless-steel surface of the fridge.

Something was standing behind him.

The night-light turned off again.

Click.

He could hear it—a muffled sort of clacking. An oscillation. Or was it a purr? Seized by a tremor, the shudder that started at the root of his soul forced his hand into a fist, squeezing Mickey Mouse's laughing face, the key chain pressing hard against his palm.

Again, that nonsensical determination skirted his mind.

Get to the barn.

He had no idea why he had to go back there, only that if it didn't happen, he would likely die standing where he was.

Swallowing down the whimper that was trying to uproot itself from the pit of his stomach, he decided: *On the count of three.*

One.

The electric charge in the air intensified. He could smell it, like ozone after a spark.

Two.

Perhaps that tingling sensation was growing because the thing from outside was drawing nearer, closing in, reaching for Gus while his feet were rooted to the kitchen floor. He imagined it—whatever *it* was— sliding its bony fingers over the slope of his shoulder, leaning forward, that throaty chittering caressing his ear.

Three!

He yelled. It was a garbled sound born of terror and adrenaline, noise to help him steel his nerves. Bolting through the house, he cut through the air, his arms and legs pumping like a quartet of pistons. When he hit the foyer, he felt unstoppably speedy even in his clumsy flip-flops. By the time he ran down the front porch steps, he could swear he was floating, running so fast his feet hardly touched the ground.

He crashed into the barn door, his free hand shrieking against the half dozen splinters that jabbed hard into his palm. The faster he could get inside, the quicker he could get away from whatever was behind him. Somehow, without any logic or reason, he was sure that, whatever that thing was, the shoddy barn door would keep it out. Somehow he'd be protected. He had to be. Otherwise he was as good as dead.

Fumbling with the key, he jammed it into the bottom of the Master Lock and yanked the padlock open. He jerked the lock out of the latch, tossed it aside, threw open the door, and barred himself inside. With his breath coming in heaving gulps, his palms and forehead pressed hard against the back of the rough planks. What he hardly noticed was that, while he may have escaped whatever was tracking him out there, he hadn't outrun the quiet.

By the time he got used to the ringing in his ears, it was too late. The stillness of the barn had wrapped itself around him. His eyes darted across the interior of the outbuilding as he struggled to see.

The dogs were gone.

The entire barn was empty.

All his dad's tools, missing.

Gus's road bike, nowhere to be found.

Old baby furniture, dusty boxes of toys that kid after kid had refused to donate—all of it had vanished.

There was, however, one thing in the barn with him.

A shadow. Tall and impossibly thin, moving toward him.

A bony arm reaching out.

FIFTEEN-YEAR-OLD MYSTERIOUSLY DISAPPEARS IN GOLDEN, COLORADO

Golden, CO—Authorities are seeking the public's assistance in locating 15-year-old Steven Schneider.

The teen was last seen by his family on the evening of Thursday, July 20, at approximately 8:00 p.m. in the family's quiet Golden, Colorado, neighborhood near the foothills of the Rocky Mountains. According to his parents, Steven had been in his room, finishing homework and listening to music. When his mother checked on him approximately thirty minutes later, he was reportedly missing from the home.

What has authorities particularly baffled is the complete lack of evidence or indication as to where Steven might have gone. There are no signs of forced entry, no suspicious activity captured by neighbors or nearby surveillance cameras, and no witnesses who saw him leave.

"Steven didn't take any personal belongings with him," said Detective Michael Lang of the Golden Police Department. "His bed was left unmade, his room exactly as you'd expect it to be. There's no indication that anyone entered the home or that Steven was planning to leave. It's as if he just ceased to exist."

Steven is described as a quiet but well-liked teenager known for his love of music and the outdoors. He is 5 feet, 8 inches tall, with light brown hair and hazel eyes, and was last seen wearing a black T-shirt depicting the rock band Smashing Pumpkins, as well as dark jeans and white Converse sneakers.

As the search intensifies, the community is on edge, grappling with the unsettling nature of Steven's disappearance. Golden Police and local search and rescue teams have scoured the surrounding area, including nearby trails and parks, but have yet to uncover any clues that might lead them to the missing teen.

"We are so scared," said neighbor Julie Dawson. "This isn't supposed to happen here. People don't just disappear, you know?

We moved here because we thought it was safe. I've got kids, and now I'm dead-bolting my doors."

Authorities are urging anyone with information, no matter how seemingly insignificant, to come forward. The Golden Police Department has set up a dedicated tip line and is working closely with state and federal agencies to follow every lead.

"Our top priority is bringing Steven home safely," added Detective Lang. "We are asking the public to remain vigilant and to report any unusual activity."

The Schneider family has requested privacy during this difficult time but expressed their hope that Steven will be found safe. They have been fully cooperative with investigators and are desperate for any news regarding their son's whereabouts.

If you have any information, please contact the Golden Police Department or the Colorado Bureau of Investigation.

Good morning, Grand Junction. Molly Moss here. We're starting the day with a breaking story that's as unsettling as it is
heartbreaking, and it's one that has left this quiet town reeling.
Imagine this: a sunny afternoon, kids playing at the park, families enjoying the day—and then, out of nowhere, a little girl dis-
appears. That's exactly what Grand Junction Police are reporting
occurred yesterday to five-year-old Shiloh Morris, and authorities are desperately searching for answers.

Shiloh was at Edelweiss Park yesterday with her grandparents,
Claudia and Peter Morris. You know the place—the one with the
big playground structure shaped like a wooden castle. Shiloh,
with her bright red hair done up in pigtails, was wearing a yellow
Bluey T-shirt, pink shorts, and those ever-popular pink Crocs.
She was just another happy kid enjoying a summer morning at
the park. But here's where it gets downright eerie: one minute
she's there, the next she's gone—without a trace.

Now, this isn't some sprawling forest or open field we're
talking about. You all know Edelweiss Park is fenced in, with
only one way in and out. You'd think it would be impossible for
a child to just disappear in broad daylight, but somehow, that's
precisely what took place.

The police have been all over this since yesterday afternoon,
combing through the park, talking to everyone who was there,
knocking on doors. But so far? Nothing. Nada. Zilch. It's like
Shiloh just up and vanished, leaving behind devastated parents,
grandparents, and a community that's now on high alert.

Sergeant Emily Parker from the Grand Junction Police Department summed it up: "This kind of thing doesn't happen
here. We're doing everything we can to find Shiloh, but we need
the public's help. If you saw anything, we need to know, and we
need to know now."

Claudia and Peter Morris, Shiloh's grandparents, are beside themselves with worry. Claudia shared with us, "We never took our eyes off her. At least not really. The castle has closed spots, and that's where she went, into one of the towers where you can climb up. But we knew exactly where she was. There was only one way in and out of there. We're so confused. We feel so guilty. How could this happen?"

So, folks, here's what we need from you. Keep your eyes peeled. Talk to your neighbors. And if you were at Edelweiss Park yesterday morning between the hours of nine and eleven a.m. and saw anything suspicious, call the Grand Junction Police Department immediately.

We're a tight-knit community here in the Junction, and we know you'll step up. Whether it's sharing this story, keeping an eye out, or just offering a prayer for Shiloh's safe return, every little bit helps.

How about some music to help you through the morning traffic. Here's "Too Sweet" by Hozier.

DAY THREE

21

EDEN

Lying in bed, Eden kept the covers pulled up to her chin. It was an act of rebellion against the slash of sunlight cutting across her face. She had slept terribly, tossing and turning the entire night. At one point she'd gotten up, grabbed her AirPods, and jammed them into her ears, hoping music would stop her from thinking about her baby sister and the awful outcome of the previous day. She had had her eyes shut when she saw the flash through her eyelids—a single bolt of lightning, hauntingly silent without any rain. She'd eventually drifted off while wondering where that mysterious storm had landed. Close? Hopelessly far away? Lightning storms were one of Eden's favorite natural phenomena, but that night she'd been thankful it had passed them by without a show.

She didn't hear the popping crunch of gravel over Billie Eilish's latest album, only the slam of a vehicle door when the music paused on a downbeat. Pulling her earbuds out, she sat up, then drew her window curtain aside to see her uncle Brian standing in the front yard. He was looking up at the house as though he'd never seen it before, gazing at it the way people in movies check out haunted houses before buying them for suspiciously small down payments. *This place is a steal!*

For a handful of seconds, Eden was beyond confused. What was her uncle doing here, hours from Denver? And then the previous day's conversation hit her like a runaway truck. Gus had practically pleaded for their parents to reconsider. Their dad had looked sympathetic. Meanwhile, Mom wore her uncompromising expression. *And that's final.* And so it was.

Kicking her blanket away from her legs, Eden yanked on an unwashed pair of shorts and pulled a wrinkled sweatshirt over her bedheaded hair. When she stepped barefoot onto the front porch, Dad and Uncle Brian paused their long-overdue reunion to look her way.

"Eden?" Uncle Brian's face blossomed into a smile. "My God, girl. Look at you!"

It had been a few years since Uncle Brian had visited; two Christmases, if she was remembering right. Eden offered her uncle a faint smile and a little wave before glancing to her father.

"Dad?" She gave him an imploring look.

Maybe if it was just them, one-on-one, she could talk him out of this. Maybe, if Mom wasn't there to intervene, he'd listen to reason and realize that Gus was right: this was a terrible idea. There was nothing fair about it. If anything, it was a cruelty against them all. Maize and Buster were family.

"Is Gus awake?" Dad asked.

Eden shrugged. *I don't know.*

"So, you never said exactly what was up with the dogs," Uncle Brian said, raising an eyebrow at his older brother. "They're okay, right?"

Eden considered blurting out something stupid. *They're rabid and will tear your throat out as soon as you get them home.* Maybe it would be enough to scare him off, have him skip the good-brother bit and bail the hell out of there. But she just stood there, staring at her uncle's unnecessarily oversized Dodge pickup, wondering how it had come to this, wondering how it had all transpired so quickly.

"They're fine," Dad murmured. "There's just something about Rowan they can't handle right now, and he can't exactly tell us what it might be, so . . ."

Uncle Brian furrowed his brow and glanced back to Eden, as if assessing the situation via his niece rather than taking it at his big brother's word. Dad and Uncle Brian were two years apart, but they could have been twins. The sandy brown hair, the brown eyes, and slender physique. The only difference was the clothing. Dad was more nondescript—band T-shirts and jeans when he wasn't working, button-downs and cargos when he was. Uncle Brian had always had a penchant for flannel and hiking boots.

"It's either this or the animal shelter," Dad murmured. "Thanks for coming down so damn fast, Bri."

"What do you think, Eden?" Uncle Brian asked.

She lifted her shoulders in a weak sort of gesture. "I think this is all a bunch of bullshit," she said, blinking at her own profanity a second after it had drifted past her lips. Her dad's expression was just as surprised, but he said nothing. It was then that she realized he agreed with her. This was Mom's idea, not his.

Pivoting on the soles of her bare feet, Eden tromped back into the house with a newfound sense of determination. "Mom?!" Where was she? She was the one ordering the dogs to be taken away. Eden wasn't about to let her get away with missing Buster and Maize's goodbye.

She checked the kitchen, but only found Olive—her long braid ratted against her back, her skinny frame draped in a mint-green pajama set—pouring herself a bowl of Cheerios with one hand and holding open a copy of *Little Women* with the other. Their eyes met.

"He's here, isn't he?" Olive asked, solemn. A rhetorical question.

"Where the hell is Mom?" Eden asked, then turned away from her, not waiting for a reply.

She checked the laundry room before jogging back up the steps to the second floor. The master bedroom was vacant, though the bed had been left unmade. Pausing in front of Sophie and Willow's door, she could hear Mom talking. But rather than barging in and announcing that it was time for Mom to take responsibility for her heartless decision, something made Eden pause. Her focus shifted from her younger sisters' door to her big brother's at the end of the hall.

She peered at the bright red Killing Joke poster that hung crooked on Gus's door. Black-and-white faces of a woman and child smiled up at the sky. TURN TO RED was printed in bold white font so large it took up half the picture. She moved down the hall, stopped there, lifted her right hand, and rapped her knuckles against the wood.

"Gus . . . ?"

She waited, assuring herself that he was still out cold. It was early, and Gus was the type to sleep in past noon if nobody woke him. When no reply came, she knocked again, louder this time.

"Gus, Uncle Brian is here. . . ."

The announcement would get her brother onto his feet. Inevitably, he'd put in one last fight and try like hell to get their parents to relent.

But still, no reply at the door.

"August Emory Hansen, pull your pants up. I'm coming in."

She tried the knob. The door swung open, revealing walls so crammed with posters that they were effectively wallpaper. There was Gus's messy bed, the blankets thrown aside. The thought was immediate. *The barn.* He'd slept out there with the dogs again.

She pivoted on the balls of her bare feet, then stopped at Sophie and Willow's door. Swallowing hard, she pushed it open but paused in surprise, because there, sitting on Sophie's bed, was not only her mother, but Rowan as well.

Eden hesitated upon seeing the kid, her train of thought suddenly gone. Her attention snagged on Sophie—hair a mess, unicorn pj's wrinkled and twisted. She was coiled up as though trying to keep as much distance between herself and Rowan as she could, but their mother either didn't notice or care. Rather than comforting Sophie, she was holding Rowan's hand instead.

Eden's eyes fixed on the kid's long, spindly fingers resting against her mother's palm. The way she held his hand reminded Eden of the way someone would hold a tarantula—careful not to make a sudden move, hand flat as to not receive a long-fanged bite. A flash of anger ignited within the cage of Eden's chest. Their mother had been less and less of a parent over the past few years, but Eden had swallowed down her agitation. She'd forced herself to be understanding while Dad repeatedly explained the situation.

Mom doesn't feel well today.

Mom has another migraine.

Mom has cramps.

Mom's ears are bothering her.

Not today, kids; Mom is thinking about the baby.

The baby.

Mom is thinking about the baby.

Mom. Mom. Mom.

But now, seeing her holding Rowan's hand while Sophie cowered, Eden wanted to scream, *What's wrong with you?! Who the hell do you think you—*

"Eden?"

Eden's gaze jerked away from their hands. Her mother canted her head ever so slightly, a curious, nearly dog-stupid look having crossed her face. Eden glowered at the expression. Maybe it was her mother's eyes, which looked slightly glazed over. Or perhaps it was that weirdly faint smile, hanging on her face as though it was pinned there, just slightly askew. Whatever it was, there was something about it that gave her the creeps.

"Uh . . . Uncle Brian is here," Eden spit out.

Her mother's face remained static in its inquisitiveness, as though she couldn't remember why Uncle Brian was there, or who he even was.

"And Gus is missing," she added, "if you could be bothered to care."

Eden was compelled to force a reaction out of her, worried that if Mom failed to respond this time, reality would finally split, fracture, and fall apart.

Mom's smile quivered, flickering like static on an old TV.

"What? Missing? What do you mean?"

Eden let out a breath she didn't realize she was holding, but she also didn't wait for Mom to make a move. Instead, Eden tore her eyes away from Rowan's own blank stare and marched across the hall, jogged down the stairs, and hurried through the front door again, bare feet be damned. Dad and Uncle Brian were still talking. Dad had his hands shoved deep in the pockets of his lounge pants, kicking at the dirt like a kid. She could read his body language. Everything about the scenario upset him, but as she passed him on the way to the barn, she couldn't help but feel just as pissed at him as she did at her mother. Maybe if he grew a pair and dared to stand up for himself and his kids, Uncle Brian wouldn't have needed to make the drive down from Denver. If Dad sucked it up and told Mom that her oddball indulgence of Rowan was hurting their own children, she'd snap out of it. Or maybe she and Rowan would simply run away together—*hooray!*—and the whole family could finally stop pretending that everything was a-oh-fucking-kay. Because the real truth was nothing was okay. Nothing would *ever* be okay. Not after Adam. Not after the hospital. Not after the way Mom had been acting. Not after this.

"Eden?" Dad called out to her when he realized where she was going, but she refused to stall her search. "Hey—the key's inside," he told her.

Eden paused her approach, but it wasn't to turn back for the key. It was, instead, to narrow her eyes at the Master Lock lying in the wildflowers, yards from the barn door. It wasn't even that Gus had dropped it—this had been tossed aside. Thrown. What had been determination to find her brother seconds earlier shifted to hesitation.

"Gus?" She peered toward the closed door.

Yesterday's conversation suddenly spiraled through her head, Gus suggesting that Rowan living with them would end in loss. Maybe he was just being dramatic—it was Gus, after all—but it *had* sounded like a threat. *Keep Rowan, lose someone else.* And now with the dogs, with Uncle Brian here for Buster and Maize . . .

"Wait." It was only then that she realized, what the hell? She didn't even *hear* the dogs. "Gus . . . ?!"

Eden fell into a run, the ground biting at the soles of her feet, the quiet of the barn promising that she was too late. In her heart, she knew her brother was gone. He'd packed up a few things, grabbed the retrievers, and taken off, because at the end of the day he was the only smart one in this unraveling shit show of a family. She pictured him hitchhiking along a lonely highway (did people even do that anymore?), his floppy black hair mussed by the wind, his thumb jutting out, the dogs at his side, pleading with every passing semitruck to pull over and give him a ride, to not murder him before he arrived at whatever destination he was aiming for.

Eden fumbled with the barn door, every awful podcast she'd ever listened to ramming its dark ending into the hard muscle of her thudding heart. Every disastrous documentary whispering against the shell of her ear.

Imagine how awful having a dead brother will be.

How tragic. How sad.

Imagine how awful.

So young. A waste.

She yanked open the door. Before her eyes had time to adjust, something moved in the dim dust-speckled glow.

Two pairs of eyes flashed, bolting toward her.

Eden yelped as Buster and Maize fled the shadows, escaping through the open door behind her, inexplicably silent as they raced toward someplace other than where they'd been locked up all night.

Her heart jumped into her mouth. She squeezed her eyes shut to regain her bearings, then remembered why she was in there in the first place.

"Gus?"

She searched the shadows, her breath catching when she finally saw him.

There, at the farthest end of the outbuilding, Gus stood facing the corner, so still it forced a kitten-like mew from deep within Eden's chest.

" . . . Gus?"

The name left her in a whimper. Yet, somehow, despite her sudden fear, she began to move farther into the mottled shadows. Her mind reeled as she put one bare foot in front of the other, everything about the situation screaming that she needed to stop, to turn, to go the other way and get help. Get help *right now*. But she kept on until she was mere steps away from him, unmoving.

She lifted her right arm, her fingers extended to brush the curve of his shoulder with her fingertips. And it was then, as if her touch had broken some sort of spell, that Gus spun around, looked into her eyes, and opened his mouth to cry out. But no sound came.

It was a silent scream.

As silent as the barn was still.

As silent as a black hole devouring the universe.

22

WILLOW

The moment Mom left the room to follow Eden, Willow's body went stiff. She almost rushed after her eldest sister but stopped herself. If she did that, Sophie would be alone with . . . him. And after whatever had happened the day before, there was no way she was ditching Sophie with Rowan, no matter how bad her heebie-jeebies got.

Willow had tried to talk to Sophie the night before, after they had been tucked into their beds—Willow beneath her flower blanket, Sophie under her unicorn sheets.

Sophie, she had loud-whispered across the bedroom, her voice tripping over a spiral of colorful, orbiting stars. *Tell me what happened. What did he do?*

But Sophie couldn't hear her, and she'd turned her back to Willow anyway. It didn't matter, though. Her little sister didn't have to explain for Willow to know: whatever had taken place last night, Rowan was to blame.

Willow had tried to think of Rowan as just another kid. A creepy-looking boy from some scary place in the woods, sure. But still, just a boy who had been given a second chance. But now, the more time she spent around him, the more he made her nervous. Both Eden and Gus often talked about how certain people "give off a vibe," but they meant an aura, an ambience. Rowan, though? He had a literal vibe, as in *vibration*, like the low and constant hum of a tuning fork—and the longer Rowan spent at the house, the more distinct that resonance became.

Now, with their mother making a quick exit, Willow and Sophie were left on their own with creepy Rowan. He shouldn't have been in their room. Not after the closet thing, and not after whatever the heck had happened to Sophie's ears, but Mom had brought him in anyway. She hadn't explained it, just led Rowan in by the hand before sitting him down on Sophie's bed. Sophie had still been asleep. She'd rolled over, opened her eyes, and Rowan had been the first thing she saw. Willow tried to imagine it—those weird eyes and hollow cheeks greeting her good morning. As soon as Sophie had realized it was him, she'd shrunk away, nearly disappearing back into her comforter. Mom had said nothing of it, hardly reacting at all. And now Mom was gone, having ditched them with the wild boy of the woods.

Willow was pretty sure Mom was trying to salvage things, trying to maintain a sense of everything being okay, but they all knew okay was far from what it was. Rowan had quickly racked up a questionable track record, and being alone with him put Willow on edge. That, and she found it increasingly strange that Mom was forcing Sophie and Rowan into the same space. Wasn't she even the slightest bit suspicious about what had happened in the playroom yesterday? Didn't she get that Sophie suddenly not being able to hear was beyond completely weird? Heck, Willow didn't know a thing about ears or hearing or anything, but even *she* knew that a kid going deaf was totally bizarre.

But Willow wasn't given much time to consider her shifting feelings toward her new foster sibling because, from out in the yard, there was a high-pitched scream. There seemed to be a lot of that going around since Rowan's arrival. Squinting at Sophie, she almost believed that she was hearing things. Her little sister wasn't responding to what was certainly Eden hollering at the top of her lungs. It was only after a beat of confusion that she recalled: *Of course—Sophie can't hear it.* Rowan hadn't responded either, but that was just normal at this point.

Willow jumped off the bed, rushed to the window, and looked out across the front yard. She was in time to catch her dad and Uncle Brian running to the barn.

"What's happening now?" Willow asked no one in particular, her eyes fixed on the open outbuilding's door. She willed herself to see through the shoddy, wooden walls. Maybe Eden had gone in there to check on the dogs and ended up hurting herself. Dad had always told them not to play in there. There was a bunch of rusty nails sticking out of the walls that he needed to take care of, not to mention a collection of tools with sharp edges that could cut off their limbs. He'd even told them an awful story about an old friend of his—Colin.

Colin had been running around barefoot in his driveway when he had impaled his foot on an old screw. From how Dad told it, Colin had bragged about his injury to their fourth-grade class for nearly a week before he came down with a stiff jaw and sudden stomach cramps. Dad said he was a classic *boy who cried wolf* type, so nobody really believed him when he said he couldn't swallow. When the belly spasms hit, their teacher was convinced he was faking it. She even threatened to send him to the principal's office, but by the time the teacher's doubt started to waver, Colin couldn't even walk. The school nurse was brought in, but she was slow getting to the class. When she finally arrived, Colin was having a full-on seizure. The nurse called 911. Dad recalled the class watching the whole thing. While waiting for paramedics, Colin looked like he was dying. *We got to see it all,* Dad had said, *and let me tell you, it wasn't pretty.*

The moral was: don't play in the barn or you might die in front of all your friends. But it seemed Eden hadn't heard that story. Maybe she'd stepped on a nail or caught her arm on an errant blade, because why else would she have shrieked like that?

Maybe it was too hot at night. A stray thought drifted across Willow's brain. *Maybe one of the dogs has—*

"Oh no." A hand flitted to her mouth. "Sophie, we should go down there to see what's—" Willow's words trailed to nothing when she turned to look back at her little sister's bed.

Her eyes went wide, her jaw tightening like Colin's must have during his fit of spasms. She gawked, wanting to scream bloody murder as Rowan stood on top of Sophie's bed, crouching like a gargoyle over her huddled little body. Balancing atop the bed with those awful, wrong angles of his, Rowan reached down and pressed one of his palms against the side of Sophie's blond head. For a heart-stopping moment, Willow was sure he was going to push down, push so hard that Sophie's neck would snap. She was about to witness a wild boy kill her little sister right there in her bed.

Willow should have done something—rushed at him, yelled for help, but all she could manage was to stand as still as a store mannequin, each breath an audible gasp. Rowan slowly turned his head to look her way. She wanted to cry out *Stop! Get away from her!* But her throat was so tight, too closed up to shout.

Rowan watched her intently for a long while. He tilted his chin just so, as if to get a better look at her dread. A second later, he was jumping off the bed and scrambling out of the room, moving faster than she thought was physically possible for him. Willow continued to stand there, frozen and freaked out, trying to absorb exactly what it was she had just seen. Then she remembered that Sophie was still hidden beneath her unicorn sheets.

"Sophie!" Willow sprang across the room, leaped onto her little sister's bed, and tore the blanket away. "Are you okay?!" She scanned Sophie's pink pj's, and her eyes fell upon the large wet spot that had bloomed beneath her baby sister's waist.

"Oh man. That's okay, Soph. It's fine. We'll get you changed. I just . . . What was he doing?!"

Willow reached forward to push a strand of Sophie's long blond hair out of her face. It had come loose from one of her pigtails. Her little sister's head looked like a golden rat's nest. She'd be surprised if they didn't have to cut the hair ties out.

"What the heck was he doing?!" she repeated, unable to shake the sight of Rowan from her mind. Something about the way he had been perched above Sophie reminded her of an animal—a predator stooping over a fresh kill. It made her think of vultures. Vampires. Mouths smeared with blood.

Unable to get a reaction out of her sister, Willow clambered off the bed, ready to run downstairs and seek out her dad or one of her siblings. She had to find help. She had to tell someone about what had just occurred. But just as she reached the open bedroom door, Sophie's small voice stopped her from dashing down the hall.

"Willow . . . ?" she said, her face half-concealed behind a tangle of flaxen hair.

"Yeah?" Willow said.

"I—I can hear you again," Sophie said softly. "I think my ears are fixed."

23

ISLA

sla had prayed all night and into the morning, collecting her fear and putting it into what she assumed was faith. And while she never in her wildest dreams would have guessed God was likely to respond so quickly, here it was, prayers answered less than a few hours after she had decided to put it in his hands.

It was a miracle, plain and simple.

From a distance, she watched Luke and Sophie sitting on the couch, a father subjecting his youngest daughter to an amateur hearing test with snaps and claps and whispers. Willow sat not too far away, her arms coiled around her legs, her face pulled into a forlorn sort of countenance, her hair a ratty, braided crown atop her head. Meanwhile, August and Eden occupied the kitchen. August was mimicking Willow's posture after whatever incident had taken place in the barn, heels hooked on the edge of the chair, arms tight around his knees. Everyone had asked him what had gone on, but he refused to explain. Well, everyone except for Isla. If he didn't want to tell Luke or even Eden, there wasn't a snowball's chance he'd consider telling her.

Olive drifted between the living room and the kitchen, silent as a barefooted phantom, seemingly unsure of where she belonged or what was needed most. Eventually, she settled next to Isla, pulled her long braid over her shoulder, and began to suck on the end of her ponytail—a habit she'd had from the time her hair was long enough to reach her mouth, a habit that drove Isla crazy, one she'd pressed her daughter to break since the age of four.

"Mom?" she said, pushing her glasses up the bridge of her nose.

"Please get that out of your mouth," Isla requested, unable to help herself.

Olive sighed and tossed her braid aside, then spoke again. "Doesn't all of this feel, like . . . off?"

Isla furrowed her eyebrows at her daughter's question. These were certainly odd events, but she supposed that's what the hand of God felt like. Otherworldly. Inexplicable. A little frightening but somehow reassuring. She'd prayed for an answer and her daughter had regained her hearing, and thank the Lord for that. Between their already stacked curriculum and taking care of Rowan, working sign language into the homeschool lessons would have been next to impossible.

And beyond that miracle—because let's face it, that's exactly what it was, praise God and get the Vatican on the phone—she couldn't remember the last time she'd felt as good as she did that morning. No migraine. No muscle aches or lingering cramps. Her vision even seemed clearer than before, not mottled by ghostly auras or unsettling, floating shadows. Somehow, despite the billboards of missing children, the news reels and endless calls to action—*if you have any information, call your local police department immediately*—Isla actually felt . . . hopeful?

"I guess it is a little odd," she admitted, "but it also feels like everything is going to be okay, doesn't it?"

Olive paused to consider it, then lifted her shoulders to her ears in a typical teen shrug. "Gus doesn't seem okay," she said softly, glancing toward the kitchen. "He seems really scared, and he's not scared of anything."

Isla nearly smirked at that. August, not afraid of anything? She'd beg to differ. She had left the hallway light on for him until he was nine. Before then, Luke had checked his room for monsters every evening. He'd even bought a spray bottle, which he filled up with lavender-scented Febreze, and taped a label across the front that read MONSTER REPELLENT, written in bold. And now, beneath that hard punk rock facade, Isla was certain that August was still the same anxious little boy, jumping at the slightest shifting of shadow, all those horror movies and skull-and-crossbones T-shirts be damned. The tough guy act was nothing but a ruse to fool the world. But no child could ever truly fool their mother.

"What happened to him?" Olive asked, and Isla found herself blinking at the question. In her mind's eye, Olive was suddenly replaced by Isla's own mom, clear as day in front of her.

What happened to her?!

Yelling over and over.

Where's Ruby Mae, Isla? What happened to her?!

All at once Isla was back in the house where she'd grown up, her mother advancing toward her, fists clenched as if ready to strike. Her mom's face held a peculiar mix of fury and heartbreak—a look of devastated rage. Despite the anger, Isla reached out, desperate to embrace her, to reassure her that whatever had transpired could be fixed. She was sure she could make things right if only given the chance. But as soon as she touched her mom's shoulders, Skye screamed.

Get your hands off me! Get out of my house! You're not welcome! You've never been welcome! Why won't you just leave me alone?!

"Mom?"

Isla's vision came clear. Before her, Olive was waiting for a reply.

"August . . . ?" Isla said, shaking off the memory. "He's just upset. He knew Uncle Brian was coming to take the dogs. He's been working himself up since yesterday afternoon."

"But wouldn't he just be mad?" Olive asked, somehow skeptical. "Why would he seem so . . . afraid?"

"He's had panic attacks before," Isla murmured, reaching out to give her daughter's arm a squeeze. "He'll be fine. He just needs some time."

"Is that what happened with Sophie?" Olive asked, turning her gaze back to her dad and youngest sister. "Is that how her hearing came back? She just needed time too?"

Isla didn't respond to that. The comparison was utterly ludicrous. The simplicity of a child's logic when faced with a true miracle struck her as borderline insulting. Sophie and August were nothing alike.

August was just being dramatic. Sophie's situation had been a test of faith.

Faith was what she'd been missing all along.

The visions she'd been having should have been proof enough—the memories of Ruby Mae looking over her shoulder, her long hair and dress hem whipping in the wind. Ruby smiling as a towering cumulonimbus swept across the Colorado prairie, as if descending onto Ruby herself. Isla now understood that the storm was Rowan. Ruby Mae's smile was a promise: Isla had to roll with the punches, wait it out, see where the journey took her, and good things would come. Such things were never easy, of course. The journey had been painful, and now it needed to be taken *with* Rowan, not without.

Isla had to believe that. She *had* to.

Because if she didn't, none of this made any sense. . . .

Squaring her shoulders, Isla gave Olive a faint smile.

"We should celebrate," she said.

Olive looked confused.

"Sophie's recovery," Isla clarified. "Let's take everyone into town to get ice cream at Sophie's favorite place."

It would get Rowan out of the house, at least, get him out among society. She was determined to make him feel like part of the family, especially now, after receiving proof from above that everything unfolding within their family was happening for a reason.

"I'm not sure ice cream will make Gus feel better," Olive mused, more concerned for her big brother's well-being than her little sister's miraculous healing.

Something about that agitated Isla to no end. The family should have been focusing on helping Rowan assimilate. August's histrionics were little more than a distraction. She swore, from the instant August had entered the world, he had wanted to be the center of attention. *Of course* he was having a panic attack—it was a great way to pull the focus from Rowan, just another test, another reason Isla had to push even harder to get through.

"I'll go get Rowan," she said, taking a few steps toward the stairs. "Why don't you tell everyone the plan? Ice cream and the park. We'll make an afternoon of it." Olive hesitated, and Isla canted her head, giving her middle child a curt smile. "Olive . . . ?" Really? *Olive* was going to fight her on this now?

"Yeah." Olive said with a nod, but she was doing a terrible job of not looking worried.

Isla assumed she was remembering the incident at the Rodriguez place. Like everyone else, she'd found blame in a boy who couldn't possibly have been at fault. Pausing at the foot of the stairs, Isla considered scolding her daughter, maybe snapping at the entire family. Just who the hell did they think they were, anyway? Had they no heart? Somehow, in the two short days Rowan had been with them, every single one of them had found a reason as to why he shouldn't stay. And *she* had been the one left at the hospital, right? When all of *them* had lost their damn minds. Perhaps it would have been easier for her to pack up some of her things and—

"Mom . . . ? Did you hear what I said?" Olive asked, but Isla had no idea what she meant. Had she said something?

I zoned out again, didn't I?

She winced, reaching up to tug on her right earlobe—a habit whenever she began to feel the needling of what could only be described as chronically stopped-up ears. Sometimes there was a loud whine, like tinnitus. Other times there was just pain. She sighed as she yanked on her ear. Silly of her to have thought her own physical maladies were gone, that God had not only blessed Sophie but also chosen to show Isla such mercy as well. She could already hear it—the buzzing. It was coming back. Or maybe it had never left. Maybe she'd just blocked it out. Maybe . . .

"I said gather everyone up," Isla repeated, her tone more clipped than before. But she wasn't about to apologize.

I'm angry, and why shouldn't I be? Not a single one of them is making this any easier.

She turned away to climb the stairs, then paused when she saw a shadow shift along the upstairs wall. She didn't even flinch when she noticed it this time, because how many times did she have to see it before it became familiar? A thousand? A hundred thousand?

At least that many times. Isla figured it was what, about thirty years of seeing it now?

Like the ringing in Isla's ears, it was perpetual, never really gone. Like an uncurable malady. One that seemed like it had been there all her life.

24

OLIVE

"**F**ucking *ice cream*?"

Gus hissed the words from between his teeth, setting Olive's already frazzled nerves on edge. She looked to her big sister for backup, but Eden remained silent as she sat across the breakfast table. Her brow was furrowed, her face half-hidden behind her hair, eyes focused on her phone.

"I'm just doing what Mom told me to do," Olive said. This wasn't Olive's idea. She thought ice cream was dumb too. But Gus either didn't buy it or didn't care.

"Yeah," he snorted, shooting her a glare. "What the fuck *else* is new?"

Olive looked away from him, giving Eden another beat to come to her rescue. When that didn't happen, she fled her brother's sneer, escaping into the safety of the hall.

Sometimes she hated him for making her feel so small. He thought she was stupid—Olive could tell by the way he looked at her in that certain way of his. Gus, always the brightest one in the room. That was funny, since she suspected she was far smarter than him by a long shot. Olive read books while he sat locked away in his bedroom like some jail-house prisoner, listening to his dumb noise-music. Olive studied and wrote in her journal, helped around the house, and took care of Sophie. Meanwhile, Gus vanished behind his locked door sometimes for days at a time, only coming out to eat, watch Netflix, or fight with Mom and Dad. Sometimes, Olive was sure Gus hated all of them, even Sophie, and she couldn't for the life of her figure out why. Surely there were worse families to be a part of. But what bugged her the most was when she was tasked with something simple, like gathering the family for an afternoon outing, and being met not only with fierce resistance, but with open disdain. Glares and jeers, bared teeth like that boy from *Where the Wild Things Are.* How hard was it to go with the flow, to get himself ready, climb in the car, and shut the hell up for once? It was no wonder Mom was so on edge all the time.

"Get your shit together, Gus," she whispered to herself, the curse word tasting both sharp and sweet atop her tongue. Olive never swore. She was the good one. The responsible one. The middle child who was still too young for rebellion. But maybe bending to the pressure of the Goody Two-shoes act was her problem. Perhaps if she started sputtering fucking profanities left and right the way her asshole brother did, she could get out from beneath her mother's thumb, goddamn it. She cracked a grin at that idea, her anger wavering. But then she remembered that Mom would probably blame her if Gus didn't go with them into town. Clenching her jaw at the thought, Olive stepped into the living room to tell Dad and Sophie the plan.

Of course Sophie's face lit up at the mention of ice cream. Before Olive could say anything else, Sophie was dashing up the stairs to change out of her pajamas. The promise of sugar erased every trace of apprehension that may have been festering in the pit of her kid sister's stomach. So easy. But not for Olive.

She sat down on the couch opposite her dad, pressed her hands between her knees, and gave him a faint smile. She and her father had never been close, though she never quite understood why. It always struck her as awkward, their conversations always stilted, too difficult to achieve. Dad was annoyed a lot, though he tried to hide it. Possibly because it was only him and Gus in the house, outnumbered by a bunch of girls. Except now Rowan was there, if Rowan even counted.

Olive peered at her father's wrinkled T-shirt, NIRVANA written across his chest, a white silhouette of an angel beneath it, palms up. Olive wondered if that angel was offering something or waiting to take what belonged to her.

"How's it going, kiddo?" Dad finally asked. He sounded tired. Worried. "A little crazy around here these days, right? And the dogs . . ." His words faded, as if reliving the awful moment when Uncle Brian had driven away with Buster and Maize in the back of his truck, reliving the second Gus had turned to face him only to spit *"I fucking* hate *you"* into the space between them, that awful curse word having felt like a slap across the face.

Olive frowned at the questions. Did Dad want her to talk about how awful it had been to hear Gus cry as he stomped back into the house? Or how heartbreaking it had been to watch Maize absolutely refuse to be shoved into a crate she'd never minded before, as though knowing she and Gus were being separated forever? Was Olive supposed to say she was fine with everything that had happened over the past few days, or was now the time to fess up and drop a curse word? *This is all so fucked up, Dad.* Was he looking for reassurance that everything was going to be all right, or was he searching for someone to share in what she assumed was his overwhelming doubt?

"I'm okay, I guess," she lied, immediately hating herself for being such a coward. "How about you?"

Dad looked surprised. He hadn't expected the question to be turned on him.

She recalibrated, changed course.

"Do you know what happened with Gus in the barn?"

He shook his head that he didn't.

"Mom said he had a panic attack," she told him. "Because he knew the dogs were being taken away."

Dad looked away. The mention of Maize and Buster pained him. She could see his guilt and wondered, *If he feels so terrible about it, why did he go through with giving them up? Shouldn't he have fought against Mom's demands? Is that how it had been with bringing Rowan home too?*

Suddenly she could see it—her parents at the foster care place, Mom all in while her dad vacillated between admitting he thought it was a bad idea or keeping his mouth shut. Except Olive knew as well as anyone else that Dad *always* kept his mouth shut. In that way, she felt terrible for him. How much did he sacrifice of himself every day? How much of himself had he lost since the first time he stopped speaking his mind? And then, within the same thought, she realized Dad was why she didn't speak her mind either. Olive was just like him, always keeping her thoughts to herself. What a terrible trait to share.

"If it was a panic attack, I think it was because of something else," she said, pushing herself to say something of significance for once. "He was scared of something." If she spoke her mind, maybe he'd finally speak his.

"Scared," her father repeated, then glanced in her direction. "Scared of what, Olive?"

She shrugged. All she knew was what she'd had witnessed—the unsettling, strained expression on her brother's face as though he'd seen a ghost, one he hadn't liked one bit, though. She'd spotted the same frightened look settle into the soft corners of Eden's face after she'd choked at the dinner table. She'd most certainly seen fear in Sophie's and Willow's eyes after they'd discovered Rowan in their closet. It seemed that every one of her siblings had, at one point, sensed the same thing she was sure Gus was experiencing now: apprehension, unease, doubt.

It had been the same when Sebastian had fallen in the Rodriguez's backyard; the exact emotion when, watching her mother and Mrs. Rodriguez help the hobbling kid to the car, Olive had turned to see Rowan's gaping, horror-stricken face. Logic convinced her that there was no way Rowan had had anything to do with Sebastian's accident—it was impossible because he'd been standing yards away, never leaving Olive's sight. When Sebastian fell, Olive had been speaking to Rowan, encouraging him to go play. She'd been less than three feet from him, yet somehow she'd been struck with the suspicion that maybe, somehow, he *did* have something to do with it after all.

She couldn't know whether it was the same thing Gus and the others were feeling. But had they all sat down together and talked like grown-ups, Olive had a hunch they'd confess to the same sense of disquiet. If she asked Dad right now if it's how he was feeling, would he finally have the courage to spill his guts?

"Olive?" Dad's voice pulled her out of her thoughts. "Hello? Scared of what, kiddo?"

What was she supposed to say? *Scared of Rowan?* But why?

Beyond the obvious, Olive knew there was something deeply wrong with the boy who her parents—or probably it was just Mom—had invited into their home, but there was no proof, nothing to link back to him. Rowan hadn't touched Sebastian before he fell. He hadn't been anywhere near the barn when Gus was found inside. Sophie's hearing had miraculously returned, and Eden had been eating dinner when she'd stopped breathing on her own. All of it was easily explained away. And yet the second Mom suggested they all go to town, Olive pictured it unfolding all over again. Maybe this time there would be an accident right in front of them. Perhaps a kid would be mowed down while crossing the street. And if something *did* happen, would *that* be proof enough? Of course not. Of course . . .

"Earth to Olive." Dad gave her an unsure smile. "You all right?"

"Yeah . . . yeah, sorry. I'm spacey today, I guess."

"Want to tell me what you meant by scared?" he asked, not letting it go.

"I don't know what I meant," she lied, crawling back into her cowardly shell. "I mean . . ." She shrugged again, her go-to motion. "Gus isn't afraid of anything, so . . . I guess I'm just being dumb."

She could tell by the look on Dad's face that he wasn't buying it, but she wasn't going to give him a chance to push it further. She forced another smile, one that was tinged with apology.

"I gotta go get ready, Dad. Mom said she wanted to leave soon." Olive popped up off the couch and moved toward the stairs. "You should probably get ready too."

"Yeah," he said, as if only then remembering they were going out. "Right."

"It'll be fun, I guess," she said, then paused at a passing thought. "Do you think Rowan has ever had ice cream before?"

Dad tilted his head, appearing both uneasy and curious. "You know, I have no idea." As she watched him, she could tell that not knowing such a simple detail about the boy upstairs bothered him. She knew right then and there that he, too, just confirmed feeling that odd uncertainty.

Every single person in the house felt it.

Everyone except for Mom.

25

LUKE

They took two cars into town. There were officially too many Hansens to fit in the van. Secretly, Luke had been relieved when the group was split in half. He needed some distance, some time to process and think, which was why he grabbed his two eldest kids and climbed into his sedan.

The drive was silent. He tried to find something on the radio that they could all agree upon, but it was either country, gospel, or static-muddled pop. He struggled to get his phone to connect to the stereo, but he had yet to replace the glitchy USB cable and his phone refused to cooperate. Eventually, he simply shut off the stereo. Eden had her earbuds in anyway. He could make out the faint drone of a female's voice: another podcast. Meanwhile, Gus was in the front seat, turned almost completely away from Luke, staring out the window as the trees rolled by.

"Want to talk about what happened in the barn?" Luke asked after a while. "You slept out there again, right?"

Gus didn't respond, and Luke wasn't surprised. Why would he answer? Luke was the one responsible for Buster and Maize being taken away, so why bother treating enemy number one with any kind of dignity or grace?

"Gus, look . . . I'm sorry about the dogs, okay?" he began, unsure of how he could ever make something so unforgivable up to his kid. He tried to put himself in his son's shoes, tried to imagine how furious he would have been with his old man had it been *his* dogs. Forgiveness? Fat chance. Luke's dad had been a real bastard, a man who thought empathy was for sissies. Perhaps that's how Luke would turn out in the end, a shitty father, the apple not falling far from the tree. Forcing his kids to give up the family dogs made him Father of the Year, that was for damn sure.

"Yeah, you're sorry," Gus practically sneered the words. "Whatever."

Luke sighed and considered pushing the topic, but quickly decided against it. He was already tempting fate by talking at all. Bringing up the dogs wasn't a cruelty he wanted to bestow upon his son so early in the afternoon.

"I'd still like to know what happened back there," he said, giving his kid a quick glance. "Olive said you looked scared, and I've seen that look on your face before." He waited a beat, then decided to risk saying more. "It was the morning Rowan stepped out of those trees." Still nothing from Gus. "Come on, it's just us here. Don't you think we should at least talk about it?"

"I think we should talk about not talking," Gus said flatly. "Maybe both of us shut up and enjoy the silence for a while."

Luke pressed his lips together in a tight line, sucked in a breath, and closed his eyes for half a second. He was trying to keep his cool, but his agitation was taking a hit. Sometimes it seemed impossible to have a conversation with his firstborn. He was losing him. It didn't matter how much he tried to fight against it, Gus was pulling away a little more every day. Luke wasn't sure how he was supposed to win. Forget that—how the hell was he supposed to engage at all?

"I wish you'd tell me how I could make things better," Luke said. "That's all I want, okay? We don't have to talk, but just know that fixing things between us is all I want. All right? I'm here, and I mean it when I tell you I'm sorry." They were words Luke's father wouldn't have been caught dead saying, a conscious attempt at breaking generational cycles, of being a better parent than he had ended up with.

There was another minute of silence before Gus sat up in his seat, turned to glare at Luke, and gave him a mocking look of enlightenment.

"Oh, I know what'll help!" he said, his tone dripping with sarcasm. "Ice cream!"

Eden choked out a laugh from the back seat. For trying to stay out of it, she was doing a lousy job.

"This wasn't my idea," Luke said, his tone sharp, his patience wearing thin.

"Yeah? Is it *ever* your idea?" Gus fired back, his words dripping with disdain.

Luke's grip increased on the steering wheel. The ache in his joints flared as he wrung his hands hard—a reminder that he wasn't getting any younger, that his body was starting to slip. That's what they meant when they said "over the hill," wasn't it? You start to lose your footing, begin to stumble and slide. And once inertia takes hold, it's all over. He'd be fifty before he knew it. Seventy a year later. Ninety-five and blowing out a single candle on a sad birthday cupcake, wondering if that was it, the end of all birthdays, the final year of his life. And then he'd shit himself and get wheeled off to his suite in the old folks' home, if he could even afford it at that point. Perhaps that's where he'd spend his remaining days, either thinking fondly of his early years as a father or about how much Gus pissed him off at times like these.

With Isla driving the van ahead of them, Luke hit the brakes and veered the sedan onto the shoulder. The right wheels of the car struck prairie grass and both kids perked up. They shot him unsure glances, then looked to each other in unspoken communication. He paid them no mind. Rather, he shoved the sedan into park, took his foot off the brake, let his hands fall to his lap. Eventually, he looked to his son.

"Why don't you just get whatever you want to say off your chest, Gus?" Luke said. "Go ahead. Say what you need to say."

Gus glowered, then rolled his eyes and looked out the window again, arms crossed over his chest.

"That wasn't a suggestion," Luke told him. "I mean it. Out with it. Lay it on me. Or lay into me. Whatever it takes. Just do it."

Gus smirked.

"*Say it!*" Luke snapped, his hands slamming against the steering wheel. Both of his children jumped at his sudden bellow, startled because when it came down to it, Dad never yelled. Those emotions were usually bottled up inside, nice and tight.

"I'm fucking *tired* of it, August," he said, his tone on a more even keel now. "Either say what you want to say or—" He didn't know where that train of thought was going. Or what? Or never speak again? Or get out of the house? Or go live in— "The barn. What the hell happened in the barn? I *want to know*," he demanded, but his kid wasn't even looking at him anymore, so Luke reached out and grabbed Gus by the arm. "Gus, fucking *tell me*! *Now!*"

"Get off me—I don't know!" Gus yelled, jerking his arm out of Luke's grasp. "I can't remember, all right?"

"You can't remember," Luke echoed.

"No, I can't fucking remember! Want to drive me to an institution and hook me up to some electrodes or something? Maybe *that'll* jog my memory. Jesus *Christ*, Dad."

"An institution . . ." Luke was faltering. "Gus, what—"

"Sure, maybe Mom can come too," Gus muttered. "Two-for-one special. She fucking needs it all over again, right? You should have left her there—"

"*Hey!*" Luke couldn't help the shout that clamored up his throat. "Enough of that shit, August! That's your *mother* you're talking about."

"Then *remind* her!" Gus hissed back. "*Remind* her she's our *mother!*"

Luke furrowed his brow, then went quiet. He understood what Gus was saying. It was a bizarre sort of slipping. They were losing her. Him. The kids. Isla was fading, and it scared the shit out of him to think that one day she would just altogether vanish. But he couldn't confess that to his kid, couldn't talk about his failing marriage or Isla's fractured state of mind with his children. It wasn't right to do so. It wasn't the responsible thing. He pushed those thoughts down and veered back to the point.

"You don't remember . . . anything?"

"I remember not hearing the dogs," Gus said. "I remember wondering if they'd gotten out, or if someone had *let* them out. I remember running."

"Running," Luke said.

"Running from what?" Eden asked. She'd since pulled her earbuds out and was now leaning forward, her torso square between the driver and passenger seats, her effort to stay out of the conversation abandoned.

"I don't remember," Gus mumbled.

"But you found the dogs," Eden told him. "That's why you stayed in the barn, right? They were in there and you stayed with them. So where were they? Just sleeping?"

Gus shook his head ever so faintly, and while he wasn't facing his father, Luke could still read his kid's expression. Gus was baffled, unsure of what was real or imagined. Luke had felt that way only once in his life, but the incident was crystalized in his brain.

A truck had T-boned his vehicle while he and Isla had been driving home from a movie—the Rob Zombie *Halloween* remake. He and Isla had sat on the curb together, covered in blankets given to them by the paramedics, and Luke had stared in disbelief at the mangled wreck that had once been his car. It was a miracle either one of them had survived. Isla hadn't had a single scratch on her despite the pickup having crashed straight into the passenger door. The accident had practically decimated that side of the car. It had left him confounded, because Isla should have been dead. It was actually terrifying despite Luke not knowing why, and for a long while he went back and forth trying to decide if that crumpled passenger door was an actual memory or just a story he'd made up in his head. Yeah, he could relate to his son on this particular playing field any day of the week.

"Gus," Luke said, frowning as he dared to reach out to him again. "Please. What the hell happened in the barn?" Maybe Gus genuinely couldn't recall, but Luke could read his posture. Whatever it was had shaken his kid to the core.

"I told you," Gus said, "I can't remember."

"You don't even remember staying out there?" Eden questioned. "You were standing in the corner. . . . Why were you standing there like that?"

Gus raised his hands, pressing them to his face.

"Gus. You don't know how scary the whole thing was. I was completely freaked out. And then I had to walk all the way in there to make sure you were okay, you know? It was like that movie, remember? The one you made me watch with you last summer? What was it—"

Gus exploded, his hands flying forward, fists hitting the sedan's dashboard hard enough to jolt Luke's nerves. "I told you, I don't fucking *remember*! You're just as bad as *he* is! Christ, what the fuck does it matter anyway?!" Reaching for the handle, he shoved the passenger door open while unbuckling his seat belt.

"Hey, where are you going?" Luke asked, startled that his kid was getting out of the car. This was a highway, for Christ's sake. Home was miles behind them, and town was still miles ahead. If Gus got out, he'd be walking for a few hours, and Isla would be livid. But before Luke could further protest, Gus slammed the door shut, shoved his hands into the pockets of his jeans, and started his march forward along the road's soft shoulder.

" . . . what?" Luke could sense Eden starting to lose it in the back seat. Gus's reaction felt heavy. This was serious, far beyond the usual arguments and tension of too many people living under one roof. He watched his boy, now yards away from them, his dark hair a mess atop his head, his faded black hoodie way too warm for the weather. He saw himself in Gus's position, brooding and angry, a high school teen pissed off at the world. Storming out of his own house, beating asphalt beneath a pair of worn-out Vans. Right then, Luke fully understood why he and Gus fought as much as they did. They were exactly alike. Identical twins.

"*The Blair Witch Project*, that was it," Eden whispered to herself. "It was so freaky, Dad. Gus looked just like the guy at the end of that film."

Luke remembered that theater experience well from years ago. Everyone had been terrified to see it. They'd handed out vomit bags before each showing in case people got motion sickness from the jerky footage, a frequent complaint. The whole thing had been wild. But Luke had left the movie feeling duped by all the hype. What was so scary about a few friends getting lost in the woods, screaming at each other about sticks and maps? It was only *after* he'd gotten home and turned off the lights that the overall vibe of the film hit him—the crescendo, the panic, the big question mark at the end. Luke hadn't really thought much of that movie in over two decades, but now he was picturing Gus down in the basement of that forested house, unmoving, facing the wall. *Jesus . . .*

"Dad . . . ?"

Eden startled him. An involuntary spasm of his shoulders ran right through his entire body.

"Please, Dad, do something."

So he did the only thing he could think of—he shifted the car out of park and cruised up to his son, rolled down the window, and spoke, clearly and calmly: "Please get back in the car, Gus."

No response.

"What, you *want* me to leave you out here?"

"Dad!" Eden leaned forward, her eyes wide. *Don't give him that option!*

Luke tried again. "Come on, Gus. I'll drive you back home, all right? You don't have to come with us. I'm sorry we roped you into this to begin with."

Gus slowed his steps, as though contemplating Luke's words, but after a moment's consideration, decided to refuse the offer: "Just leave me alone, all of you."

"What the hell does he want, then?" Luke asked himself softly.

"Dad," Eden said, quieter, so Gus wouldn't hear. "Don't you get it? He's walking toward town. He doesn't *want* to go home. He doesn't want to be by himself."

God, that bothered Luke. It made his skin crawl, as a matter of fact, his thoughts tumbling back to that damn movie, to the way people were frantically asking themselves if it had been a documentary or a hoax. *Did that really take place? Holy shit, was all of that real?* A lot like how Luke was asking himself about certain points during the past few days—the dogs losing their minds, Rowan screeching like an animal being torn apart, Luke coming away from Sophie with blood-smeared palms.

"Tell him we'll take him to Noah's," Eden suggested.

"Gus?" Luke rolled up a little closer. "How about Noah's place, then? You okay with that instead? A compromise?"

Again, hesitation, but a beat later Gus walked over and jerked open the door, Luke tapping the brake as his son climbed back inside.

"Fine," Gus said grudgingly. He snapped his seat belt into place and crossed his arms over his chest. "Noah. But no more goddamn talking."

As they drove in silence, Luke couldn't shake what Eden had said. The person who thrived on being locked in his room suddenly wanted no part of his solitary routine. Regardless of whether his son could recall what had transpired the night before, one thing was clear: Gus—who lived off a steady diet of horror movies and punk rock music—was suddenly afraid to be alone. It only made Luke wonder even more: What the hell had *really* taken place out there in the barn?

26

AUGUST

When Gus spotted Noah's house in the distance, he was overwhelmed with a sense of relief. Finally, he could get out of this damn car.

His father rolled up to a stop sign, and Gus shoved open the door, got out, and slammed it behind him before anyone could think twice. His ratty Converse sneakers stomping the pavement, he hopped onto the curb and began to stalk down the sidewalk. He was waiting for either Dad or Eden to yell at him: *Hey! Stop! Come back!* But they didn't. And while his father's Honda idled at the stop sign for a good fifteen seconds, the vehicle eventually turned left instead of following him straight down the road.

He gave a sigh of relief as soon as they were gone. *Thank God.* Because Jesus Christ, he couldn't deal with much more of that third degree.

But when Noah's mother answered the door, Gus was struck with an overwhelming sense of awkwardness. Why hadn't he thought to text Noah that he was coming? His mind had been elsewhere, sure, but texting was ingrained in his everyday life; it was reflexive, like breathing. He and Noah went back and forth dozens of times per day. Yet somehow, pulling out his phone and shooting his best friend a quick note to prep him for a spontaneous drop-in hadn't even blipped on Gus's radar, and that was weird. It left him feeling unmoored, like he'd been so far away from his thoughts that he'd somehow disconnected from his own body.

Not that Mrs. Richland made a big deal out of the spontaneous visit.

"He's in his room," she told him, then turned away from the front door and left him standing at the threshold as though he lived there, because he may as well have.

Gus shut the door behind him and went upstairs.

"Astral projection," Noah concluded.

His room was an amalgam of Doritos, art supplies, dirty clothes, and lavender Febreze; that last element was a byproduct of the battle between Noah's pervasive funk and his mother's desperate attempt to mask it, but clearly the funk was winning.

"I've read about that stuff," Noah said from his collapsed state on his bed. Lying on his back and propped up on his elbows, he shrugged at Gus from across the room. "Or maybe I saw it on TV or something. I don't know, man. Probably Netflix?"

Gus peered at Noah's T-shirt as he listened to his best friend talk. Maybe discussing bizarre shit with a guy who had a penchant for shirts with comic werewolves howling at the moon wasn't the wisest move. In a lot of ways, Noah was a real-life personification of Shaggy from *Scooby-Doo*. But who else was Gus supposed to confide in?

"Yeah no, it wasn't astral projection," Gus murmured, looking away from Noah and his werewolf shirt. He let his eyes roam the walls instead. "That's like floating over your body and being able to see what's going on, like watching a movie. If that had happened, I would be able to remember *something*, and I don't remember shit."

"Maybe you had a stroke." A stupid grin crossed Noah's face. "Though, that's not really funny," he said a second later, suddenly frowning. "My grandpa died of a stroke, like, less than a year ago. Why would I joke about something like that?" He grimaced, then gave Gus an apologetic expression. "I don't know why I'm such a dick, man. Sorry. Not funny. Not even a little bit."

Gus focused on the bedroom rug. He wondered how many heart attacks Noah's mother had over the countless shades of acrylic paint splattered across the area rug. Much like in his own room, Noah's walls were plastered with paper, but instead of band posters and random crap torn out of magazines, this was a veritable art gallery. There were completed drawings and delicate sketches, as well as paintings in various stages of completion. A drafting table took up half the room. Noah's cramped twin bed ate up the remaining square footage. He had a postage stamp of space to move around in, which was why the boys spent a nominal amount of time inside when they were hanging out together. Most days they opted to wander the streets surrounding Noah's house, making the neighbors nervous. Or, at least Gus did—he was the one with the dyed hair and Misfits logo painted onto the back of his sweatshirt. Noah, on the other hand, had adopted more of a stoner vibe despite never touching anything beyond a cigarette in his life. Still, they somehow managed to match each other, Gus's yin to Noah's yang, and people didn't like that. Two somewhat disheveled older teens walking in lockstep down an upscale suburban street? Most times it was fine. But occasionally it didn't go over well.

Once, while they were making suicide slushies at the corner 7-Eleven, some lady had loud-whispered to her friend, *My god, it's Columbine,* beneath her breath. Gus had no idea what the hell that meant, and, while sucking down his extra-large Slurpee and walking back to Noah's, he googled the reference on his phone. The smiling faces of twelve murdered kids filled his iPhone screen. It had left Gus feeling sick and angry. Some stranger who didn't know a damn thing about them was assuming they were unhinged mass murderers, all on account of his penchant for black clothing and Noah's paint-splattered Docs.

"Anyway, whatever it was, it sounds creepy, dude," Noah said, trying to keep their stalling conversation afloat. "And it sucks about your dogs. I don't know what I'd do if I lost Boomer like that. Stress, you know? *Trauma.* Maybe nothing happened in the barn and you're just majorly freaking out."

"Yeah. Stress." Gus had considered that could have been the culprit, but it didn't fit the whole picture.

Sure, he'd been beyond upset about his uncle Brian taking the dogs away and up to Denver, and that could have triggered some sort of anxiety-induced state of hypnosis or something. Who the hell knew? But that didn't explain why the dogs were being taken in the first place.

"Buster and Maize *weren't* stressed, though," Gus said. "Not until what's-his-face entered stage right."

Noah narrowed his eyes, then nodded, agreeing. "I wish you had gotten that whole thing on video. It sounds nuts."

"It *was* nuts. But now they're gone, so what does it matter? My goddamn asshole parents . . ."

Noah frowned. "How's your kid sister, by the way? Her ears . . ."

"Miraculously cured. Hallelujah, she can hear again."

"Wait, what? *Seriously?*"

"Seriously. None of it makes sense. The whole family is in town right now, getting celebratory ice cream as though she was brave enough to get a vaccine or something. Except she'd gone fucking *deaf*, Noah. I was there. And now she can suddenly hear again. My mom is acting like, *Oh, it's a miracle!*" He scoffed, rolled his eyes. "*God* is testing us. It's so fucked up."

"Dude, I had *no* idea your mom was religious."

"She's not!" Gus fired back. "She's always been a little weird about that stuff, but this is beyond her regular bullshit."

Noah sat silent for a long time, his hands folded in his lap, the beds of his nails packed with rainbow colors of paint or chalk or pastel. Eventually, he exhaled and slapped his knees in a conclusive sort of way. "Well, it's the kid," he said. "What's-his-face. Obviously."

"Oh, *obviously?*" Gus nearly laughed. "You don't think I've been thinking it's been him this entire time?"

"Well, how are your parents not figuring it out, then? They can't be that stupid."

"Want to bet?"

"Then why don't you just tell them?"

"Tell them what? I've already suggested it with the dogs. Dogs know when shit is off, right? It's the only reason Maize would have acted so bizarre. She was the best fucking dog, Noe. But instead of listening to reason, my mom doubles down and gets rid of both of them because now they're *violent* and *unpredictable* and God is testing us, a-fucking-men."

"And your dad? He was just . . . cool with it?" Noah quirked an eyebrow. "Seriously? That's weird, right?"

Gus smirked. "Not since my mom laid eyes on this kid," he recalled. "The second he showed up, she's been fighting tooth and nail to get her way. And I just don't understand it."

"Get her way with what, though?"

"Everything," Gus said. "But especially anything that she thinks could harm or upset Rowan." He paused to fully appreciate the sudden tightness in his chest. "It's like we've all disappeared, and he's the only one left. She doesn't give a shit about anyone else. Just him."

"Yeah, but your sister . . ." Noah began.

"But my sister lost her hearing and . . . got it back? How does a kid make another kid go deaf?"

Noah thought for a beat, trying to piece together the mystery. "Maybe he jabbed something in her ears," he suggested, snatching a drawing pencil off his side table, pretending to stab himself in the head. "Maybe he used his secret mind powers. Maybe he knows black magic. Hey! Maybe, when no one was paying attention, he played really awful music and Sophie's ears were like, nope! Sometimes my dad makes me go deaf when he plays fucking Smash Mouth downstairs. Have you ever watched your patriarch jump up and down with one arm over his head like he's reliving some sort of core concert memory? It's terrifying." Noah's eyes momentarily glazed over. "A goddamn nightmare."

"It doesn't make sense," Gus said to himself.

"That's what I keep telling him," Noah said. "But he's like, *You don't know what's good, kid.* It's ridiculous. Like, taste is subjective, Dad. Get a grip."

"They think he's this helpless kid from the woods," Gus continued.

"But the truth of the matter is, we don't know a single thing about him. Neither do the state people. Nobody knows anything."

"Right. And he was on the news?" Noah asked.

"And on the internet," Gus said. "He was the creepy-ass woodland creature kid for a little while, but that got drowned out by all the other missing kid stuff. Conspiracies. That sort of stuff. Either way, the cops were hoping to figure out where he came from, maybe find someone who had seen him before or who knew his family, but nothing. Hell, I was sure someone would claim him before all the foster stuff went through and we had to let him live at the house. No dice there, either. But that's the only thing that makes sense, right?" Gus asked. "He's one of the missing kids. Who the hell *else* would he be? Except—"

"Nobody's looking for him." Noah sucked in a breath. "Ugh, that's really creepy, dude. And he doesn't talk?"

"He hardly even moves," Gus said. "Doesn't talk. Shit, he barely blinks. I don't think I've seen him eat since he came to live with us."

"And that was what . . . ?" Noah asked.

"Like three days ago, I think. I don't know."

"You should have gone to get ice cream with your family, then," Noah countered. "At least you'd be able to see whether he eats it or not. If he doesn't, he's not human. No kid can resist ice cream, right?"

But Gus would bet real money Noah was wrong about that. If anyone could resist, it would be weirdo Rowan.

"So, what is he, then? Some *Omen* kid come to haunt your family? That makes as much sense as believing God's pulling strings, right? I mean, it's cool if you do believe that. No offense to your mom or anything. I'm just saying, it would be freaky . . . right?"

Gus balled his hands into fists. "You're going to think I'm crazy, Noe," he whispered.

"Why? Are you about to say some crazy shit?"

"I'm about to ask you a question, and I want you to give me a real answer."

"Uh, okay?" Noah shifted his weight on his mattress, looking as uneasy as a kid suddenly remembering a quiz he'd forgotten to study for.

Gus hesitated. He was nervous. He loved Noah like a brother but knew that as soon as he dropped his suspicion, there was no way of taking it back. Regardless of what Noah said, his opinion of Gus would be forever altered. But he wasn't sure that mattered anymore. Gus could feel something changing, something shifting. He could sense the energy that surrounded him distorting.

For the life of him, and no matter how much his dad needled him with endless interrogation, Gus couldn't remember what had gone down in the barn. He'd forgotten to text Noah before dropping by. He didn't feel like himself, and he suspected it was all interconnected. So, what if Noah thought him stupid? Would it really make a difference? His gut told him it wouldn't. Instinct was screaming it was already too late.

"Hey," Noah said. "Don't leave me hanging, dude. Are you going to ask me or what?"

Gus swallowed against the sudden lump in his throat, then looked up at his best friend and spoke: "How many galaxies do you think there are in the universe?"

Noah canted his head, giving Gus an inquisitive glance.

"Billions," Gus answered for him. "And what's the chance of us being alone in a number that big?"

Noah squinted, surprised but undeterred. "Like, less than zero. Obviously."

"Yeah. Obviously." It was then that the subdued dread Gus had been carrying with him began to bloom. "Oh God, obviously," he whispered. "Oh man. Oh holy shit."

27

WILLOW

Mr. Frosty's was less a shop and more a stand, just a little trailer painted mint green and pastel pink with a giant wooden cutout of a drippy cone tacked to the side. But it was always crowded. Sometimes, during the hottest parts of summer, the line appeared to snake around all of Green Pines Park. There was a big playground there and lots of picnic tables in the shade. It was one of the most popular spots in town this time of year. It struck Willow as a little unusual to bring Rowan here, but she wasn't about to say anything. She didn't really feel like having ice cream, or hanging out at the park, either. She just wanted to get this odd family outing over with. Eventually, Mom would realize this was a bad idea, they'd all pile back into the car, and this whole mess would be done . . . at least for today.

It seemed to Willow that nobody noticed the missing person billboard peeking out from behind a tree across the street. A set of giant eyes stared right at her, imploring someone to *find me*. Willow frowned at the obscured picture of a girl about her age. She didn't need to see the letters to know her name. Rachel Smithson. She had vanished from a few towns over, but her Taylor Swift T-shirt told Willow all she needed to know: she and Rachel weren't much different from each another, and if Rachel could go missing, well . . .

"Oh, Rowan!" Mom gasped, drawing Willow's focus back to her family.

The kid was standing stock-still in the sun, his nothing-but-bone fingers awkwardly gripping a waffle cone. Vanilla ice cream was melting down his skinny arm and dripping a sticky lake onto the toe of his right sneaker. Mom came at him with a fistful of brown napkins. Willow frowned as she watched them both—Mom ignoring Rowan shrinking away from her, Mom's approach swift and no-nonsense.

"Sweetheart, you're making a mess. Here."

Mom took the cone from him, licked around it to clean up the drips, and held it out to him again, waiting for him to stick out his own tongue and have a taste. Rowan gawked at her, and for a second Willow thought, *Here it comes, he's finally going to be a real kid. He's going to wail about how she's just infected his perfectly good ice cream with her germs.*

"It's good," Mom told him. "So sweet. Try some." She made a second attempt, holding the tall tower of soft serve toward him, the ice cream starting to drip again. "Oh my—Willow, here." Willow suddenly found herself holding Rowan's cone while her mother grabbed more napkins off the table.

"Mom, eww!" Willow wrinkled her nose as her left hand was almost immediately covered in vanilla. "It's getting everywhere!"

"Just hold it," Mom insisted, clearly having forgotten that getting dirty was one of Willow's least favorite things.

Sophie loved stuff like making mud pies and playing in the dirt, smearing finger paints onto big sheets of paper and cardboard, and had no issue with licking handfuls of Nutella off her fingers at the breakfast table. In that way, she was Willow's opposite. Willow had an aversion to all things grimy or unhygienic. Her parents often joked that she'd started running her own baths at four years old, that she hardly ever went outside during the summer because it meant getting slathered in sunscreen and bug spray—something she'd had to endure only a half hour before, which had been completely gross. And now she was being forced to hold a disgusting ice cream cone while it melted all over her fingers. With vanilla streaking the back of her hand, her aversion took hold. Willow couldn't take it anymore. She dropped Rowan's cone onto the dirt with a squelch, the soft serve splattering the leaves of a dandelion close by.

"*Willow!*" Mom wasn't happy. In fact, she sounded downright furious. "Why would you do that?!" she insisted, clearly not remembering her daughter being the "clean kid" of the family.

But Mom wasn't remembering much of anything today—Willow's antipathy, Rowan's skittishness, the fact that Sophie was out on the playground by herself, unsupervised despite all the kids and strangers milling about. Mom used to freak out about Green Pines Park because it wasn't fenced. There were main roads on all sides, tons of trees for bad guys to hide behind. *All it takes is an instant,* she used to say. But now, rather than worrying about safety, she was fuming over—

Willow was seized by the arm and yanked forward, her mother's eyes hard as polished river stones. "What's *wrong* with you?!" she snarled through her teeth, as though Willow had done way more than drop a stupid ice cream cone into the dirt.

"Mom, *ow*! It was dripping all over me!" Willow whined, then held up her sticky left hand, still gripping her own chocolate cone in her right. It was only then that she realized her chocolate ice cream was about to pull a repeat performance. Drips were already making a slow crawl toward her palm. She gasped and began to work at the runnels with her tongue. But a moment later, her own ice cream flew out of her hand, splatting on the ground just shy of her shoe. Her eyes darted to her mother, whose arm was still extended from taking a swing.

"That was *Rowan's* ice cream." Mom scowled. Willow gawked back at her ruined cone on the ground, hardly able to believe that it had just been rudely slapped out of her hand. She could feel eyes on them. A couple of families, occupying picnic tables close by, were now deeply invested in what should have been a private Hansen family meltdown. "If Rowan can't have his," Mom continued, "then *you* can't have yours."

As if suddenly sensing the concern of strangers, Olive spoke over the cheerful squeals of kids climbing monkey bars and playing tag. "Jeez, Mom, take it easy—it's not like he was going to eat it."

Olive was sitting on top of a nearby table, spooning raspberry sorbet into her mouth. Her pale pink lips were stained a jarring, gaudy red. It was as if she was a girl playing dress-up, unsettling, like an accidental clown.

Willow found herself searching the park for her father, Eden, and Gus. Where the heck were they? This was getting way too tense to handle without Dad's help.

"That makes no difference," their mother said, her voice now harder. "It was *his*. What is wrong with you two?!"

"Were you going to eat it or just stand there and make a mess?" Olive asked, adjusting her glasses. Bolder than usual, she looked straight at Rowan, as though she genuinely expected an answer.

Rowan continued to fixate on Mom as she did her best to clean up his shoe. Of course, he didn't acknowledge the question, and it was no wonder. Even if he'd heard it, the playground was full of kids. The noise was next level. Meanwhile, Mom was practically snarling.

"See?" Olive said, shrugging her shoulders.

Shrugging was Olive's new thing. That, and rolling her eyes behind the black rims of her glasses. But Olive still somehow remained the golden child of the household. She was Mom's number one, but was also becoming more like Eden every day: *a teenage disaster,* as she'd heard Mom once mumble beneath her breath.

"What's gotten into you?" Mom asked, clearly annoyed by Olive's attitude. "Why aren't you helping me?"

Olive frowned, then gave a soft sigh and murmured "sorry." That was when she abandoned her cup of sorbet and pulled napkins out of the holder next to her. "I'll go wet these at the fountain," she said, holding up the napkins, falling into her standard role. "Be right back."

Willow watched her sister go but turned toward the playground when she heard a few boys laughing. They were closer than the kids enjoying the jungle gym and slides, standing only a few yards away. She blinked at the trio. They were gawking at Rowan. One of them was pointing a finger right at their family's newest member.

"Look at *that*!" the pointing one cackled.

"Dang, dude!" a boy in a Minecraft T-shirt said. "What happened to his face?" He noticed Willow looking at them and fixed his eyes on her. "He with you? Was he hit by a truck?"

The third boy, wearing a Denver Broncos baseball cap, said nothing. He was too busy guffawing thanks to his friends' comments, taking gulps of air between hysterical belly laughs.

Something in the pit of Willow's stomach stirred. She was officially out of the Rowan fan club, but seeing kids being so openly cruel painted a harsh look on her face, and one of the idiot boys noticed the change.

"Red alert!" he bellowed, elbowing Minecraft Boy to draw his attention. "We're making Pretty Pretty Princess mad."

The moniker confused her. *Pretty Pretty Princess?* She looked down at her outfit—a simple T-shirt dress with short sleeves and a polo collar. Then she remembered her favored hairstyle. Most girls didn't wear their hair up in braided crowns, but it was Willow's signature, her absolute favorite thing. Furrowing her brow, she scowled at the pink and white stripes of her dress. This was one of her favorite outfits, too. It was comfortable in the summer heat. And it *did* make her feel pretty and a little more grown-up, because it wasn't the baby-blue PEACE, LOVE, AND SUNSHINE Old Navy tee she'd put on at first. But here were these stupid boys, these *morons* making fun of her for being herself, being cruel to Rowan for things that weren't his fault or any of their business in the first place.

"Hey," Minecraft Boy said, nodding at her. For a second, Willow's annoyance was replaced with a nervous tingle. These boys were about her age, the three of them looking right at her with their ugly eyes, sizing her up. If she was still attending public school, they might have even been in her class. Without warning, she felt as though she was beneath a microscope—the first uncomfortable twinges of womanhood, of being watched while wishing their stares away. "Are you with this freak?"

Willow looked to Rowan, whose wide-set eyes were now giving the boys their full attention. She looked back to the trio. Two of them were still laughing, their faces twisted with gross amusement. The third—Broncos Kid—had paused his hysterical cackle to swat at a dive-bombing wasp.

The insects, especially those with stingers, loved the surrounding picnic tables with their sticky spatters courtesy of Mr. Frosty. They congregated around the trash cans overflowing with cups, napkins, and spoons. There was no doubt the park had more than a few of their nests hidden in the sagging branches of the ancient cottonwood trees. Unless they were yellow jackets—those nasty bugs were hiding underground. Either way, Sophie had nearly gotten stung once. Last summer, one of the trash cans had been roped off like a crime scene, warning people to not get too close.

Willow looked back at Rowan. She watched him while he studied the taunting boys. But unlike her, Rowan was doing it without so much as a twinge of emotion. His rapt concentration was what finally tipped Mom off. It appeared that she hadn't heard any of the exchange—or at least hadn't realized Rowan was the target of the bullying. But now, noticing the boys' jeers, she stood up straight, balled the sticky napkins in her right hand, and hissed.

"Get out of here!" She glared at them. "You nasty little rats! Leave him alone!"

Willow was startled by both her words and tone. This wasn't the mother Willow knew. Not even a little bit. The more she watched her, the more Mom even *looked* different, like her face was rearranging itself to match her new personality. Her eyes appeared a little larger, but not in a good way. More like a sick way. And speaking of sick, her cheeks were oddly hollow, too . . . or was it just the light?

A chill crawled down Willow's spine as her mother's top lip curled up. The almost rabid expression reminded Willow of Buster and Maize rushing the van the afternoon Rowan came home, which now seemed so long ago.

Pointing Kid was now just as distracted as Broncos Boy. He was frantically waving his arms at wasps.

Minecraft Boy's grin was replaced by an equally ugly frown. "Come on," he said, motioning for Pointing Kid to follow. "Who cares about that freak and his freaky family, anyway?"

"Crap, this bee!" Pointing Kid bellowed, ducking and dodging like a boxer avoiding hits.

"That's a wasp, dude. Just walk away from it," Minecraft Boy told him. "They don't follow you."

As if in response, the wasp darted at him in a challenge. A squeal erupted from Minecraft Boy's lips. "Ugh, let's go!" The two boys shuffled backward, tripping over each other's feet.

Broncos Kid didn't notice his friends retreating. He was too busy fighting off not one wasp, but a few.

"Hey, come on!" Minecraft Boy yelled at Broncos Kid. "Stop swatting at them! That's just gonna make them mad!"

But Broncos Kid appeared to have a fear of stinging insects. Despite his friend's sound warning, he couldn't help but wave his skinny arms around each time they flew in his direction. The wasps now seemed to be circling him, and Willow watched in wonder as a fourth and a fifth joined in.

Again, Willow's eyes darted to Rowan. He seemed fixated on Broncos Kid as well. Before she could look away, a sixth insect buzzed past Rowan's ear and made a beeline for the boy yards away.

Willow gawked, both understanding and not believing what she was seeing. Was Rowan really making this happen? No, that was impossible. People couldn't just control such things . . . right? Unless Rowan had some sort of mind powers? She was pretty sure that stuff only existed in movies, but what if?

Mind powers. Maybe that's why Mom had appeared so zoned out when she'd come into their room that morning, Rowan in tow. She hadn't said a word as she shuffled in, his hand in her own. It was almost as though Rowan *knew* he'd get in trouble if he entered Sophie and Willow's room by himself, so he'd found himself a grown-up. Using her. Like one of the puppets in the toy box.

He needed to get in so he could do whatever he did to Sophie, Willow thought. *He needed to get to her so he could push his hands against her head.*

"Where have you been?!" Mom's loud, aggravated question made Willow jump. It drew her gaze to Dad and Eden, who had just arrived at the park. "I needed you here. These damn kids . . ." She motioned to the three boys, ready to tell Dad about how awful they were being to Rowan, how mad she was at Dad for not having been here when the bullying had occurred. But before that argument could get started, Broncos Kid began to scream.

"*Get them off me!*" he cried, his arms now flapping wildly about his face and chest.

The wasps were full-on attacking, circling and striking, then making their retreat. What Willow knew from one of her nature studies that perhaps others didn't was that wasps weren't anything like bees. Where bees could only sting once, like a kamikaze pilot sacrificing itself for the hive, wasps could attack over and over. Wasps were relentless.

"They're biting me!" the kid caterwauled, which got a few adults to rush over, but they were unsure of what to do. *Stinging,* Willow absently thought. *They're injecting you with venom. They don't bite at all.*

Alarmed by the yelling, Sophie abandoned the playground equipment and ran over to Willow, wrapping her arms around her sister. Meanwhile, someone's dad flapped a picnic blanket around like a bullfighter waving a cape, trying to shoo the insects away from the panic-stricken idiot boy.

But the wasps weren't dispersing. Instead, even more were coming to the aid of the others.

Helpless, the adults yelled at one another, trying to figure out the best course of action. Broncos Kid was now screeching, a horrific sound. It was as though he'd been set on fire. He spun around, his hat knocked off and lying in the grass.

"Run, Aiden!" Minecraft Boy yelled. "They'll stop if you run!"

In the distance, a woman cried out. "Aiden? Oh my god, Aiden?!"

"Mom! *Help!*" Broncos Kid shouted, then began to run as suggested, only to collapse onto the grass a few feet away. He twisted, his hands pressing hard against the sides of his head. When he turned his face toward Willow, she gasped and clutched Sophie tight against her chest. Broncos Kid was swelling up, his face bloating before her eyes, his skin matching the bright pink of her shirtdress. It reminded her of Willy Wonka and Violet Beauregarde. *Holy Toledo, what's happening to your face?!*

"He's allergic!" the boy's mother cried. "Aiden! Oh my God, someone help him!"

Broncos Kid began to heave, his hands falling from his temples to bat at his neck. Before his mother was able to reach him, he tipped over, his body stiff as a board. *Rigor mortis,* Willow thought. She'd read about that, too. Biology. *An involuntary tightening of muscles that happens after death.* She imagined this is what it was like. It was terrifying, and yet she couldn't look away.

"Shit," Willow's dad said from over her shoulder. "He's going into shock." Before she knew it, he was running toward the kid, now convulsing, his body spasming as though he'd grabbed a live wire, a fatal electric current scorching his every nerve.

"Stop," Willow whispered, shooting Rowan a beseeching look. Her heart thumped hard when he turned his head to look at her. "Please," she said softly. "He's gonna die. You have to stop."

Rowan glared at her for an instant, long enough to make her wonder if he understood the words being spoken. Oh. Maybe he'd been playing deaf and mute at the expense of everyone around him this entire time. He peered at Willow for long enough to remind her that no matter what she thought she was seeing, nobody could control wasps the way she was imagining. Nobody could make them swarm and attack. Rowan wasn't some magical entity. He hadn't come from Hogwarts, regardless of what she thought.

And yet.

Willow continued to search his face with a sort of desperation, waiting for him to respond, to assure her that he wasn't doing anything. He was an innocent bystander, just like her.

But instead, Rowan turned his head back to the frightening scene before them. Broncos Kid was still convulsing. Willow's dad was there along with a handful of other parents, trying to assist while the shouting mom swept in with something that looked like a bright green highlighter in her hand. She uncapped it with her teeth, reeled back, and stabbed the end into the meat of the kid's upper thigh. Willow cringed. Broncos Kid let out a gasp, reminding her of how Eden had gulped air after choking at the table.

Willow shut her eyes as Dad headed back toward their table, waving at the air, ducking a couple of dive-bombing wasps himself.

"My God," he said, clearly shaken by the incident.

But rather than regard the kid with sympathy, Mom hissed beneath her breath, "Good. Serves him right." She then turned her back on the scenario and marched toward the closest trash can, still holding a wad of sticky napkins in her hand.

Willow glanced back to Rowan. It was only then that she noticed the wasp resting on the tip of his shoe where his ice cream had dripped. Rather than threatening him, it appeared as if it was waiting, wondering when it would be told to strike again.

28

SOPHIE

The ride home was long and annoying. Sophie squirmed in her car seat. She could hear again, but the buzzing hadn't gone away. If anything, it had grown louder, and the wasps at the park had only made the sound that much worse.

After seeing those awful stinging insects, she was sure they were living inside her skull, building a nest out of the soft stuff that made up her brain. Soon everything there would be nothing but honeycomb, if wasps even made honey. She guessed it didn't matter. Wasps weren't supposed to live inside heads, either, but her wasps didn't care about that. She'd ooze honey out her eyes, her nose. They'd make so much of it, it would fill her up. She'd drown in it while she slept.

"What does everyone want for dinner?" Mom asked from behind the wheel.

Sophie shrank away from the sound of her voice. Ever since her hearing had come back, things sounded different, staticky, like a radio station that wasn't coming in clear. Perhaps her ears were getting used to sound again, or it could have been the constant hum inside her head. Sophie didn't know why everything sounded weird, only that the closer Rowan was, the louder the crackly noise became. And Mom's voice was especially bad. It wasn't that she *sounded* different, it's that the tone *felt* different. Something about it was wrong, like someone was talking through her instead of Mom saying the words herself. An echo, or a magician making one of those wooden dummy puppets talk.

And then there was the shadow.

Sophie was now seeing it often, a sudden escalation in its appearance. Just that morning, she'd spotted it in her room out of the corner of her eye. She'd noticed it while swinging at the playground. It had been hiding behind a tree and had scared her enough to send her running through the swarm of wasps. She was sure it was the same shadow from the night Dad had found Rowan hiding in the closet. But then again, maybe she'd dreamed that part. Heck, she couldn't even remember what had happened before her parents had run into the playroom yesterday, only that they were there and that there was blood on the sides of her face and that her head felt like someone had hit her with something really hard. She couldn't remember if she'd been in the playroom by herself when that horrible pain took over, or with someone else. Had she been playing? Reading? Coloring pictures with her new crayons, so fresh that they were still sharp?

Her dad had asked her, his voice soft and sweet. *Do you remember what happened, Sophie? Can you tell me what went on?* He had watched her with worried eyes as she shook her head no. Dad had looked scared and asked questions, but Mom hadn't done any of that. Part of Sophie was glad for it. If she couldn't remember anything, what was the point of saying *I don't know* over and over? But another part of her knew it wasn't right. Mom *should* have wanted to know what happened. Even if she didn't really care, she should have at least pretended. But Mom seemed like she was okay with everything, like she just wanted to move on, forget. The same kind of wrong as when she asked *What does everyone want for dinner?* as though they hadn't all just seen a kid get stung like crazy in the park. It even *sounded* wrong. *WhAt dOes evEryoNe waNt fooor diNner?* Her voice was off. It had a robot sound to it, hollow and flat.

Nobody responded to the question, and Sophie wondered if anyone could tell that Mom wasn't Mom anymore.

Olive was glaring out the car window. Her face was turned away, but Sophie knew she was chewing on the end of her ponytail. Willow was pulling at the edge of her dress as though trying to rip it apart. Rowan was unchanged, staring straight ahead, studying the fabric pattern on the back of the driver's seat. And Sophie sat stiff as a Barbie doll in her car seat, still strapped into that dumb five-point harness even though she was big enough to touch the car's ceiling.

"How about tacos?" Mom asked. "Everyone likes tacos."

Sophie winced at the buzz coming from deep inside her head, pretty sure it would never go away. But despite the pain, she knew that Mom wasn't thinking right. Rowan wouldn't like tacos because Rowan didn't like food. It had only been what, two days, but she'd never seen him eat anything. And now that she really thought about it, she was pretty sure she'd never seen him drink, either. But that was impossible. Living things *had* to eat and drink. She and Olive had talked about it in the spring when they'd planted some seeds in the garden. They'd even done a science unit on it, so Sophie was aware living things needed air and sunlight and food and water and all that stuff. She'd known that since she was a baby, helping Dad scoop kibble into Buster's and Maize's bowls.

Remembering the dogs made her heart feel tangled. She hadn't had time to think about them a whole lot, between her ears not working and Mom taking them into town. It was only now, stuck in the back seat while heading home, that the overwhelming sadness of it hit her. When they got home, Buster and Maize wouldn't be there to greet them, happily barking and wagging their tails as they pulled up the driveway. They wouldn't be there to chase Sophie through the grass right before bedtime, her favorite time to hunt crickets and grasshoppers. Buster wouldn't be there to drop his gross, Frito-scented squeaky duck at her feet when he wanted to play. Maize wouldn't be there to sleep in the middle of the living room rug, blocking half the room, all four legs sticking up like crooked, hairy flagpoles. *Bottoms up!* as Dad liked to say.

Tears welled in Sophie's eyes. She tried to hold her breath, to push them down and be a big girl. But as soon as her eyes met Willow's, the floodgates gave way and Sophie began to cry.

Olive twisted in her seat to look back. Her eyes looked worried, but her entire face appeared to understand. Willow took Sophie's hand and squeezed, but she didn't say anything. She only looked through the window and breathed out what sounded like a tired sigh. Mom kept driving even though Sophie was sobbing, almost as though she couldn't hear it. Or chose not to.

Everything about that struck Sophie as bad and wrong, not like her mother at all. It seemed like only a few days ago she worried too much. Even Dad had said that sometimes she was too "hands-on." Sophie wasn't sure what that meant but was pretty certain it was no longer the case, simply because she couldn't feel the love radiating from Mom anymore. Even when Mom had her migraines, even when she had awful days because her stomach hurt, there had always been room for Sophie to climb into Mom and Dad's big bed and snuggle. But then Adam died and Mom went away for what had felt like forever. Sophie had been over the moon when Mom returned, but then Rowan showed up. Ever since then, Mom struck her as colder. Emptier. Like she was being hollowed out. And the idea of *that* only made Sophie cry harder. But the van continued to roll down the road. Mom didn't look back. She didn't even bother to check Sophie out in the rearview mirror.

And to make matters worse, Rowan wasn't peering at the back of the driver's seat anymore. Instead, he was watching Sophie wide-eyed and blank-faced as she wept. He'd leaned forward, nearly resting his chin on the edge of the car seat, as though wanting to be as close to her emotions as he could, to absorb them somehow.

It was only then, with him so close to her, that the memory suddenly came clear.

Rowan had been in the playroom. She couldn't remember why she'd screamed, only that she had, and when he'd responded in kind, the noise from his throat had made her head feel as though it was going to explode.

Sophie gasped. She reeled away from him to get some distance, scared that it would happen again. But no. She was in a car with her family. If he did it right now, they'd see it. They'd *know* it was him. So instead of trying to make herself smaller, Sophie peered at him and leaned forward. If he wanted emotion, she'd give him emotion.

She was nearly nose to nose with the strange boy, and her ears were buzzing loud enough to hurt, which was good. It made it all the more genuine when she opened her mouth, sucked in a breath, and hollered as loud as she could. Right in his stupid face.

29

EDEN

"What the—"

Dad didn't need to finish his sentence—Eden saw it too. The family van was parked on the soft shoulder of the highway a good quarter mile down the road, though "parked" was being generous. It looked as though the vehicle had veered off the highway. It was halfway in the ravine that ran along the road, almost directly in front of one of the many missing person billboards scattered across the county. As they got closer, Eden could see that the van was stuck, both right tires trapped in the runoff. The left tires looked as though they were ready to lift off the asphalt.

"Oh, what the *hell*?" Dad groaned. "That does *not* look good."

It was only when they pulled up farther that they could see the girls sitting in the wild grass, surrounded by dandelions and lupine. Rowan and Mom were nowhere to be found. Unless they had wandered off into the endless horizon, Eden assumed they were holed up inside the car.

Dad guided his sedan onto the shoulder and slid it into park. Meanwhile, Eden's eyes drifted upward, settling into the corners of a little girl's smile. Shiloh Morris was five, just like Sophie. She had freckles and wore her red hair in crooked pigtails and had been missing for the past three weeks. Eden couldn't help but replace the little girl's face on the billboard with one of her sisters'. Sophie. Willow. Hell, even Olive. She'd listened to countless podcasts about abductions. Not a single one had a happy end.

Eden and her father exchanged a wary glance.

"Maybe you should stay here," he suggested, but there was no way Eden was doing that. She grabbed for her door handle same as he did, and he didn't protest. Neither one of them knew what to expect, but they would stick together, and hopefully that would make it all right.

Simultaneously pushing open their doors, they stepped into the brush. Eden's sisters squinted up at her, all three of them seemingly dazed by whatever had occurred.

"What's going on?" she asked them. "Where's Mom?"

"Inside," Olive said, nodding toward the van.

"What happened?" Eden shot a look over her shoulder, noting that her father was pulling open the driver's door to get a look for himself. She was almost tempted to tell him to stop, to yell for him not to do it. *We don't want to see what's inside, do we, Dad? I mean, do we really?*

"Sophie was crying and Rowan got in her face," Willow said, jumping into the conversation.

"What do you mean, got in her face?"

"Like this," Willow said, lifting her hand so her palm was less than an inch from her nose. "Just staring like some . . . some . . ." She tightened her hand into a fist, clenched her jaw, and let her arm fall to her side. *Freak,* Eden finished inside her own head, knowing it was a word they'd never utter out loud, not even to each other. It was a dirty word. An awful thing to call anyone. Even someone like Rowan, who as much as she hated to admit it, fit the bill in every sense.

"So Sophie screamed," Olive continued. "And then Rowan screamed right back."

"And then Mom started driving crazy," Willow added.

"Wait, what do you mean?" Eden asked. "Like swerving, or . . . ?"

"Like, the car was out of control or something," Olive explained. "At first I thought she'd just gotten freaked out by all the screaming, but she was zoned out again."

"The radio went nuts too," Willow said. "Maybe nobody else heard it because it was so noisy, but *I* did. We were listening to Harry Styles and the song started going all staticky and then we were suddenly off the road. I thought we were gonna flip over."

Eden tried to picture it. Sophie screaming. Rowan shrieking. Their mother pulling her zombie act. The van careening madly down the road while Harry Styles's smooth vocals accompanied the madness.

"Jesus," she whispered, because what if there had been another car on the highway? What if instead of veering onto the shoulder she had plowed into oncoming traffic? "She could have killed you. . . ."

"She won't come out," Olive said after a beat. "She's just sitting in there with him. She hasn't even asked if Sophie's okay."

"Well, are you?" Eden gave Sophie a pointed look. "You can hear me, right?"

Puffy-eyed, Sophie nodded, then swiped at her nose with a reluctant sniff.

"Okay, good," Eden whispered to herself. "Good."

As she pressed her fingers into her eye sockets, that now all-too-familiar flame of resentment ignited deep in the pit of Eden's stomach. She was unsure of what to say to comfort her sisters, unsure of what to do, of how to act. She was the one they looked up to, who they relied on if their parents weren't pulling their weight. Nobody in their right mind was going to see Gus as a caretaker. Eden was the unofficial backup parent, and right now, Mom was the opposite of doing her part. The more time that went by with Rowan in the house, the less of a mother she seemed to be.

"Okay," Eden said again, giving the girls a stern look. "You guys, get in Dad's car." She didn't know what the hell was going on right now, but it was enough to understand that Sophie absolutely wasn't going home in the same vehicle as Rowan. As far as Eden was concerned, nobody was going to be riding with either Rowan or their mother ever again, not until they were certain Mom wasn't going catatonic behind the wheel.

She was suddenly wishing Gus was with them instead of at Noah's. Dad had given him the occasional driving lesson, finally prepping him for the learner's permit he'd been begging for all summer. Hell, Eden didn't have her permit yet either but was pretty confident she'd do fine driving back to the house herself. It was a straight shot down the road with two right-hand turns. Easy peasy. But Dad would never go for it. Gus, however, would have permission.

She watched her three siblings get to their feet and shuffle to Dad's Honda. After they were all safely in the back seat with the door shut, Eden marched to the van, imagining herself letting open the floodgates and telling Mom exactly what she thought of how she'd been treating them all. She wanted to hiss at her about how she'd forgotten her priorities, spit barbs about how the family was being replaced with someone else: a damn *stranger*, let's face it.

Reaching the open side door, Eden stuck her head inside. She found Dad sitting in the second row while Mom was in the open trunk area, Rowan next to her. His oversized eyes locked almost immediately onto Eden. When they did, she was hit with a wave of anxiety. All at once, she was recalling the dinner table, the moment she hadn't been able to breathe. It was a similar feeling now, though she could catch her breath just fine. She couldn't help but think it was a warning. *Get involved and see what happens. See if you don't choke to death* this *time.*

Her gaze jumped to her father, imploring. Her dad shook his head faintly as her mother sat silent and motionless beside the boy who didn't belong. It was only when Mom finally turned her head and noticed her daughter that Eden's stomach sank to her feet. Mom's expression brightened, which seemed hopeful at first. But then she spoke.

"Hi, honey," she said. "What would you like for dinner tonight?"

30

ISLA

After Luke shut the door and left Isla lying on the bed, she knew something was beyond wrong. It was the way he did it that made her draw into herself. He'd crept out, silent, holding his breath the way a parent does while sneaking out of a sick child's bedroom. So, it was official. The entire family suspected that Isla was irrevocably broken inside. Something had finally slipped within her mind.

But that wasn't anything new, she supposed. She'd been locked up after her grief had gotten the best of her, after all. That, however, had been a big to-do. The pills. The collapse. Luke finding her on the bathroom floor. Ambulances and emergency rooms. Eventually, a cold room with mint-green walls and a windowless door. No, this quiet creeping around felt different, more ominous. The way Luke had slunk out of the room assured her that something was beyond just wrong with her mental state. This was a bigger sort of wrong. Wrong, down to her very existence. Wrong to her core.

But she'd known something was out of sorts for many years now.

That "wrong" was what had been too much for her own mother to bear. After the police had dropped Isla off at her childhood home, rather than being greeted by a hysterical hug and a weeping mother—*oh thank God. Thank God you're okay!*—Skye Berkley had raged at her daughter instead. *Where is she?! Where's Ruby Mae?!* As though Isla had left her cousin somewhere, forgotten like a set of keys. Isla had been in the dark. Hell, before her mother had keened at her about it, she hadn't known Ruby Mae was even gone.

Except, no . . .

Her thoughts kept spiraling back to that final afternoon on the prairie, watching that foreboding storm roll in. She kept reliving that striking, beautiful snapshot. Just two teenage girls breathing in the summer air, fingertips holding tiny pappus bouquets. The storm wind sent dandelion seeds adrift like miniature parachutes, destined to reseed the Colorado landscape behind Aunt Sunny's home where Isla and Ruby had played since they could walk.

They'd spent entire summers out there, running into the tall grass just after breakfast, only abandoning the field when they were hungry or wanted to watch an episode of *The Mickey Mouse Club*. Endless hours. Endless days. Solid months turned their skin a deep shade of bronze, their blond hair lightening to a flaxen white. They chased horned lizards to keep as pets, marking their backs with bright splotches of tempera paint: red, yellow, blue to deem the lizards theirs.

Except, no . . .

The shadows had been there even before then. The shadows that lingered, sometimes in broad daylight. The figures Isla could never quite see, like ghosts in her periphery. She'd catch one just outside her field of vision, turn to spot it, but it would be gone. Figments of her overactive imagination.

The shadows had especially dallied years before Ruby Mae had vanished. Isla could remember the very first time she'd noticed one. She'd gone downstairs for a drink of water; the house had been dark, just faintly lit by the glow of the moon. Coming back from the kitchen with her cup, she saw it at the end of the downstairs hall. Frighteningly tall. Rail thin. Isla had spent the entirety of her childhood watching her mom shoot distressed looks over her shoulder. She'd heard Mom quietly gasp when she thought no one was around. Was this the thing her mother had been catching glimpses of as well?

She came to a dead stop, her heart thudding hard enough to make her cheeks flush. A ten-year-old Isla stood motionless and frightened in a night-swallowed house, wondering whether she should take a back-

ward step and see if the silhouette was still there, or whether she should
bolt as fast as lightning up to her room. She had chosen the latter, terrified of what might be right behind her; even more afraid of feeling long,
bony fingers snatching her by an ankle and yanking her back down the
stairs.

That had been the first time she knew things weren't quite right.
She'd been so young, and yet she'd still managed to explain it all away.

The figure, just her imagination.

Her mother, jumpy and irrational.

Lying on the bed, Isla stared at the master bedroom wall, her fingers crumpling the sheets against her palms. She could recall the way the
prairie had smelled—bright green but somehow simultaneously parched.
She remembered looking out across wide open vistas, of picking rocks
out of her shoes. She recalled the storms, wild and electric, lightning
slashing the sky with blinding cracks of white. The clouds, so heavy with
pent-up rain they appeared blue black like a deep, poignant bruise. Cool
air rolling across the flat plain. Wind rising from a whisper to a roar.
They had been far from Ruby's house that evening—farther than they'd
ever walked before. Ruby Mae had just turned sixteen, Isla a few months
older. Earlier that afternoon, Aunt Sunny had dropped them off in downtown Golden, and the girls had spent hours buying pretty blouses and
books and ice cream. It had been a perfect day marred only by countless
sheets of paper taped to shop windows and stapled to electrical poles.
That evening, walking through the prairie grass, they talked about the
fliers they'd seen, a girl's face plastered onto every available surface. *It
must have been a guy,* Ruby had assessed. *The next Ted Bundy or Zodiac.*
Lightning sparked, illuminating their faces as they witnessed the incoming clouds. Ruby grabbed Isla's hand, then yelled toward the sky. *There's
something up there! Do you see it?* But whatever Ruby Mae spotted, Isla
couldn't discern at all.

Wind whipped their faces as they both squinted into the gale, fat
drops of rain beginning to fall. Lightning bolts ignited the sky one after
the other, nary a breath between them, like God's anger made electric.

The grass bent, thrashing their bare legs hard enough to sting. Isla tried to pull Ruby Mae back in the direction of the house, her fear eventually overwhelming her awe. But Ruby fought, her feet planted solidly in the dirt. She stood rigid and determined, her face pointed upward, her eyes fixed on the undulating clouds, their movement so fluid the storm almost appeared to breathe. Isla strained to view whatever held Ruby's concentration so thoroughly. But she saw nothing.

There was nothing.

Nothing.

Except, no . . .

Where's Ruby?! Isla's mother had demanded, not touching her, not offering comfort or a single word of relief. *Ruby Mae is missing and your aunt Sunny is losing her mind!* There were more accusations, more rambling anger. Something about the police, about a search party, about how Isla's mother wanted Aunt Sunny to stay with them, but Aunt Sunny wouldn't leave the house in case Ruby came back. But came back from where? *Where is she, Isla?!* she had bellowed. *Where the hell is she?! What have you done with Ruby Mae?!*

Isla cringed at the memory of her mother's ceaseless fury. Had her anger been born of her fragile mental state? Had Skye Berkley looked both livid and afraid because of some beyond-crazy story she'd made up in her head? Or was there something more to it, something more to the memories that were haunting Isla now?

Rowan had appeared out of the woods, and at that very same instant Ruby Mae had rushed back into Isla's heart, a ghost finally finding her home. Surely that wasn't a coincidence. Rowan, Ruby Mae, all part of a destiny Isla didn't yet comprehend. If there was a God, this was him trying to speak. She just needed to decipher what he was trying to say. His message was still a mystery, but if she kept trying, if she kept chipping away at it, it would eventually come clear.

All she knew was she could *feel* Ruby Mae whenever Rowan was near, could practically hear her laughter, could smell the fields once more. She could see her spinning, head thrown back, could feel her tugging against Isla's hand, trying to keep her from running away from the storm.

There's something up there! Do you see it?

Pulling at Isla's hand, keeping her in place—*that's* what Rowan brought out of her long-forgotten memory. A connection. A weightless pull. After Rowan had appeared at the edge of their property, all those recollections became a tsunami. Except they were no longer just memories. They were *moments*, swallowing her whole. She'd recognized the sensation of crossing over when she'd walked Rowan up their home's front steps, her hand pressing against the knobs and ridges of his spine, urging him on. She'd experienced it that afternoon, her thoughts now firmly over two decades in the past. The cries of a terrified child being attacked by wasps turned the park into a prairie, and the prairie a frightening shade of red. She'd lost herself while driving her children home. Sophie screeched, but Isla had been too far inside her own head to react, the road now a field, Isla standing there with Ruby, the storm rolling forward. The cry had belonged to Sophie, but it had come out of Ruby's mouth . . . cracked open the sky with a fissure of white-hot electric current. And as Isla had gaped up at the churning clouds—her hands gripping the van's steering wheel—she watched with wide eyes as something pulsed red and ominous overhead in a different place. In an altogether different plain.

Do you see it?

No, she hadn't. Not then . . . but she thought she could see it now.

Lying in bed alone in her room, Isla drew the sheets up to her mouth as the memory flashed across the backs of her eyelids. Pulsing scarlet lightning. Veins spidering across the sky like arteries of blood. Anxiety crawled up her throat, tasting of metal, reminding her that she'd felt this way before.

So many times, she'd felt this way.

She'd go to bed on the precipice of something, like falling. Then she'd wake up among bloodstained sheets. Another baby gone. All those kids from various towns, gone. Ruby Mae, especially gone. But Rowan? Here. Still here.

Do you see it?

"Yes," Isla whispered to herself, to Ruby, "I think I see it."

Something was in the clouds, so faint it was both seen and unseen.

"I think I see it," Isla repeated. "Oh my God, I think I see it . . ."

The faintest ghost of a shape.

31

LUKE

Isla was on the brink of madness. He'd seen it when he'd climbed into the van an hour before. It had been the way his wife had stared at him, as though she didn't recognize who he was.

Luke kept himself busy by looking up countless articles on past trauma, about how big events could unlock memories suppressed for an entire lifetime. Losing Adam had clearly been a trigger, and Rowan's sudden appearance behind their house certainly counted as a big event. There was no denying it was what had sent Isla into yet another downward spiral. But what Luke had seen in the van today was way different. This hadn't been his wife working through a new stage of grief or navigating the uncharted waters of foster care. It hadn't been pills or hopelessness. What was worrying him was that it hadn't seemed like his wife at all.

Sitting out on their wraparound porch, Luke peered at the outbuilding where Buster and Maize had slept, where Gus had been found just that morning by a visibly shaken Eden. Rowan had only been with them proper for about three days, but ever since he'd come into their lives, everything had turned to shit. First, Isla hadn't stopped obsessing over him since his first appearance, they jumped through hoops to adopt him at her relentless insistence, and then came the mess when they finally got him back here. The dogs had gone nuts. Both Gus and Eden had given the family a scare. Christ, Sophie went deaf under inexplicable circumstances. These terrible, awful things all had to be connected somehow.

At least that's what Luke's heart was saying. His brain? It asserted that blaming Rowan was illogical, irresponsible. Rowan was a child, a *child*. So these events were coincidences, then. Bad luck. Shit, maybe it was a goddamn curse. But nothing to do with Rowan? No. That, he promised himself, was beyond impossible.

But none of that mattered anymore, because it was clear now that he needed help. Things were getting out of hand. He thought about calling Brian again, but it wasn't as though his kid brother could provide aid and comfort beyond the huge ask of taking the dogs in as his own. He considered reaching out to Helen Plummer at the children's home, but that only circled back to blaming Rowan for things beyond anyone's control. Helen would immediately pull Rowan out of their home, and then what? The kid would continue to live out his life in a broken system that could hardly manage to serve perfectly typical kids. And if Helen appeared, what the hell would he tell Isla while the caseworker packed up Rowan's things? That he was sorry? She'd never forgive him for placing a call like that without talking to her first, and certainly not for setting something in motion that would impact both their lives, *all* their lives. Forever.

It was then that Luke was struck with a terrible idea. He knew Isla would resent him for it, but he had to believe it was a step above bringing Helen Plummer into the fold. Reaching into his pocket, he drew out his phone, scrolled through his contacts, and stopped when he came to a name he hadn't uttered in a good handful of years.

Skye Berkley.

He paused to reconsider, trying to weigh a million impossible pros and cons within the span of a few seconds. He'd spent countless evenings listening to Isla go off on tangents, hissing through her teeth at the selfishness of the woman Luke had only met a few times in his life. He recalled the fights Isla had on the phone, the way she paced, her hands in her hair. He'd often worry that she'd rip out fistfuls of chestnut brown in a blind rage with how furious conversations with her mother left her— anger and frustration that lasted for days. Isla had cried so many times over the years, reciting hitching diatribes about how she didn't understand, how she would never forgive her mom for abandoning her. Isla hated Skye Berkley for not caring about her when she was a girl, then hated her fifteen times as much for not putting in a single effort after Gus had been born. Despite Isla being Skye's only child, rather than trying to reconnect, to right her wrongs and become "grandma," Skye had embraced a nomadic lifestyle and doubled down on bizarre conspiracy theories. According to his mother-in-law, the United States never put a man on the moon, the CIA killed JFK, the Denver International Airport was headquarters for the Illuminati, and Bigfoot was real. If anyone had a reason to despise Skye Berkley, it was his poor wife.

It was why he hadn't called Skye when he'd had Isla committed. Skye would have been the last person Isla would have wanted to see. But at the hospital, there had been doctors to help. Now, Luke felt more alone by the minute. And calling Skye actually made sense. Isla was talking about Ruby Mae, and Skye had been there when that lifelong trauma had occurred. Regardless of Isla's feelings for her mother, Skye had been present when something within his wife had fractured and snapped.

He went back and forth for a few minutes. Yes, he should call her. No, he absolutely should not. Yes, just do it. No, Isla would annihilate him.

He winced as he jammed his fingers against the call button and waited for the line to pick up. Either that or go to some likely oddball hippie voicemail.

Six rings in and Luke was ready to hang up. *For the better,* he thought, almost relieved. Because what would he have said to her after all this time, anyway? How could he even begin to explain without sounding just as out there as his mother-in-law? He pulled his phone away from his ear, ready to hit the red button marked END. That was when he heard the voice on the line. Not a recording.

"Luke . . . ? Is that you?"

He hesitated, staring at the phone screen that displayed an image he'd set as a contact photo so long ago, a snapshot from when he and Isla had gotten engaged. Skye and Isla together, both with strained smiles, trying to look happy, but Luke knew better. Happiness had never been a factor in the Berkley household. It was all for the camera. For the appearance of being normal, of being real.

"Hello?"

"Skye," he eventually said. "Yeah, hi. It's me."

There was a long silence. It was Skye's turn to weigh the situation, to decide whether she wanted to speak or hang up. She didn't owe Luke anything. He'd never gone to bat for her, always a die-hard Isla supporter. He'd even supported his wife when Isla had decided Skye was too batshit insane to have anything to do with their family. *Good riddance!* Isla had cried. *She'd have been a shitty grandma anyway!* But finally, Skye spoke, asking the question he knew was coming.

"Is Isla all right?"

He didn't know how to answer that, vacillating between the truth and playing it off as no big deal. But he knew the latter wouldn't fly. Isla and Skye had gone through numerous spans of no contact. This current stint had been going strong for at least what, fourteen years? He was pretty sure Skye wasn't aware of Olive's existence, or that Isla had been pregnant at all beyond Eden. Certainly Skye had no idea about Willow or Sophie. But Luke wasn't about to bring up the kids. The news wasn't his to tell, and this definitely wasn't that kind of call.

"Luke?" She sounded surprisingly concerned. "Is she . . . is she gone?"

He furrowed his eyebrows at that. *Gone?* Whatever did that mean? Skye didn't know about the initial suicide attempt, so she couldn't have meant that. So where would Isla have—

"Luke—you called me. What's wrong?" she asked. Finally a question he could handle, one he could understand.

"Hey, Skye. I . . . I don't know," he eventually said, deciding on a half-truth. Isla wasn't okay, but that was where any understanding of the situation stopped. All he knew was that Isla seemed completely lost, as though stuck in a memory. She was haunted by Ruby Mae, and nobody knew more about what had happened to Isla's cousin than Skye.

"What do you mean, you don't know? Luke—what's going on? Why are you calling me? What do you want?" Skye asked, her patience short.

Luke was the annoying son-in-law, the kind who dragged his feet and never quite knew much of anything, too busy keeping fantasy sports scores tallied in his head. The useless type who would call his wife's mother when things got too complicated, when he couldn't figure out his ass from a hole in the ground because of his own emotionally stunted upbringing. Except Luke wasn't any of those things. Right now it fell along the lines of utterly desperate.

Instantly he knew calling Skye was a mistake, already racked with guilt, like he'd betrayed his wife in the worst possible way. Isla certainly didn't want to see her—she'd been wounded enough to commit one of the most unnatural acts a child could toward a parent: she'd turned her back on her mom and chosen to live life as a voluntary orphan. As Isla had put it, *What's the difference if I cut her off? She's not here. But when has she ever been? When was the last time she gave half a shit about anyone other than herself?*

That thought gave him pause, and he wished he had come to his senses sooner. Because, really, why *was* he calling this woman? Would she even care?

Too late now, I guess.

"Jesus, Luke, are you going to tell me what's going on or not?" Skye asked, her husky voice reminding him of Stevie Nicks, rumbling with aggravation.

"Yeah, uh . . ." He shut his eyes to clear his thoughts, to get on with it, come what may. "I can't really explain it, I guess. Isla's been having some recurring memories lately, and I think they're getting worse."

"Recurring memories. About what?"

"About Ruby Mae and her aunt Sunny," Luke clarified.

The line went silent. For a second, he was sure Skye had hung up, but when he pulled the phone from his ear, the line was still connected.

"Are you still there?" he asked, knowing she was but uncertain of what else to say.

"Yeah. I'm here," she replied, her aggravation now replaced with what sounded like unease.

"So, I obviously don't know what exactly went on with Ruby or Sunny. I know what Isla has told me, but it's always been muddled."

Again, a long silence, then a quiet "Oh yes, it has."

"I figured the shortest distance between gaming out what's going on with Isla and those memories would be to reach out to someone who knew them, who was there," Luke explained. "I'm sorry to spring this on you out of the blue. I'm sure I'm the last person you expected to hear from today, and I'm sure these aren't things you want to relive yourself. But I honestly don't know who else to turn to, and Isla, she's . . ." He paused, confused as to where he was going with this rambling, uncomfortable with how many words he was stringing together while concurrently feeling like he wasn't saying enough. He wanted to tell his mother-in-law everything, but he also wanted to hang up and delete her number, never speak to her again, just like his wife. He wanted to be guaranteed that all would be well but also silently gave her permission to tell him to fuck off and never call again.

"She's what . . . scaring you?"

Luke's spiraling thoughts abruptly stopped mid-spin. He was thrown back into the moment, forced back into the conversation.

"Yeah," he confessed. "Yeah, a little." He hated admitting it, but Skye had hit the nail right on the head.

"And you want *my* help now . . . after all these years." He could hear the bitterness in her voice, could pick up on the slightest wisp of pain. "You want help from the crazy old lady, is that it? Because that's exactly what my daughter thinks of me, but I'm sure you're well aware of that."

Luke frowned down at the worn wooden planks of the porch. He'd been meaning to repaint them for over two years now. Isla had asked him to do it about a million times. Yet here he was, shoes on peeling paint. Maybe he was kidding himself. Perhaps he really was one of those oblivious, useless husbands who couldn't navigate an emotional pitfall to save his life. Was that why he was calling Skye, seeking refuge with a person whom Isla had completely cut out of her life? The instant shit got tough, Luke caved, even if that meant running into the arms of the enemy?

"I—I just don't know what to do, okay?" he murmured more to himself than to the woman on the phone. "It's just the worst possible timing, and I have no idea how to take care of Rowan. She's good with him, but I'm just—" *Go ahead, say it. Useless. Oblivious.*

"Who's Rowan?"

Luke cringed. *Aw shit.*

"Did . . . did you all have another baby? Didn't bother to tell the grandmother?" The aggravation was back, as was the egocentricity that made Isla climb the walls. He forced himself to ignore it.

"No," he said. "No. Not a baby." *More like* babies, *Skye. We have five of them. How about them apples?* "A boy. We're fostering him."

The silence returned. This time it was heavier than before.

"Listen, I'm sorry I called," Luke said. This whole idea was a colossal blunder. What the hell had he'd been thinking? Just as all the events of the past few days had nothing to do with Rowan, Isla's memories of Ruby and Sunny had nothing to do with Skye. Calling her had been a stupid, knee-jerk move. "I should go. Please, don't—"

"Wait," she said. "Wait a second. You're right. I *was* there."

It was Luke's turn to go silent.

"I'll come," she finally said. "Just need to get myself together here."

"No—it's—" Luke stammered. Skye . . . coming to the house? Oh God. Never. Isla would flip the fuck out. He couldn't imagine it, couldn't possibly allow it to unfold.

"I'm not asking. You called me, and now I'm coming."

Luke pressed a hand to his face. *Oh, shit.*

"I'm just outside of Boulder, anyway," she said. "Not too far."

Oh shit. Oh shit. Oh shit.

"I'll be there in the morning."

And when the line went dead, all he could wonder was, *What the hell have I just done?*

32

OLIVE

The more time that passed since Rowan had moved in—it had only been a few days, though it somehow felt like forever—the faster things were moving from normal and boring to beyond bizarre. The incident in the van where Sophie and Rowan had screamed at each other like a pair of banshees had left Olive beyond confused. All the electronics had gone haywire. The radio, which had been playing Harry Styles, had disconnected from Willow's phone and started flipping through regular stations. The air conditioner had been on at nearly full blast, but abruptly turned off, then blew a torrent of heat into the car. The moonroof slid open all on its own. The sun that had beamed down from overhead had blinded Olive as she tried to navigate the chaos, but before she could figure out what the heck was happening, Mom jerked the steering wheel to the right toward that missing kid billboard, and the van's front wheels hit the ravine. Hard.

When Mom had veered off the road, the swerve had struck Olive as both purposeful and accidental, if those two possibilities could even coexist. Olive was more anxious with each passing hour, and the more she thought about her own trepidation, the more she realized she wasn't waiting for something "big" to happen. After that afternoon, even the most mundane situation like driving into town to get ice cream felt hazardous, riddled with an almost unavoidable sort of peril.

The girls had eventually gotten home by way of Dad. When he'd come back with Mom and Rowan, the family had immediately scattered to different corners of the house, clearly avoiding the situation that had just occurred. Because what the hell had that been, anyway? Olive didn't know anything about cars, but all the electronics going crazy at the same time was . . . unlikely. Freaky odd. Like someone had done something to the car while they had been at the park. A possibility? She doubted it. But what other explanation was there?

When they'd arrived home, Mom and Dad had gone upstairs. A few minutes later, Dad had gone out onto the porch. Olive had heard him talking on the phone. Eden had locked herself in her room. Sophie was with Willow, likely playing in their bedroom or hanging out in the playroom downstairs. Gus had yet to show his face since that morning. Now that she thought about it, she was certain she hadn't seen him at the park, which was also odd. He'd given her shit about the ice cream thing that morning (like it had been *her* idea), but Gus knew better than anyone that skipping out on a family function led to way more drama than it was worth. And yet, no matter how hard she tried to place him at the park, she couldn't. Had he been at another picnic table? Maybe he'd hung back by Dad's car? But if that was the case, why hadn't he come home with them?

And then there was the case of Rowan. With everyone in all corners of the house, who'd been watching him? Where had he gone? And where the heck was he now?

Standing in the kitchen, Olive suddenly found herself looking around, squinting at her surroundings before removing her glasses and wiping at a smudge with the hem of her shirt. She loved being alone, but this solitude struck her as heavy. Almost spooky. Save for Gus, everyone was home, yet the house gave the impression of being beyond deserted. *And where the heck is Rowan?*

The fact that she didn't know sent a chill up her spine. Again, she found herself pining for her brother. Gus would have made her feel better in that stupid way of his, blaming it on curses or killers or ancient burial grounds. He'd have convinced her Mom was turning into a zombie, hungry for brains.

Olive Evelyn Hansen, don't be a dolt, she thought. *Mom zoned out and nearly crashed the car. There's nothing spooky about that. If anything, the whole thing is completely predictable.*

"Predictable," she said to herself. Maybe that was it; Mom needed to go back to the hospital. More time spent where she'd been or different medication or *something.* Pulling open both doors of the refrigerator, Olive stared inside the unit if only to give herself something to do. She grabbed a package of sliced turkey and cheddar cheese off a shelf and found bread in the pantry and a tomato in a basket on the counter by the stove. She wasn't hungry, merely bored and nervous and just about crawling out of her skin. She placed a cutting board onto the marble countertop, then headed to the magnetic strip on the wall to grab a knife . . . but stopped short of pulling down a blade. If there was a day she'd accidentally cut off a finger, this would be it. But that was ridiculous, right?

"Right," she whispered. She was just being paranoid. And yet she turned away from the knife strip and pulled open the utensil drawer instead. A butter knife would do just as well. She wasn't sure how she was going to cut the tomato—probably make an absolute mess with juice and seeds everywhere—but it was better than eating a severed-finger sandwich.

She rolled her eyes at that and stepped up to the cutting board, placing the butter knife down. Honestly, she was just freaking herself out. Her mother had veered off the road, and okay, maybe she *had* zoned out again. But it could have also been all that screaming. That had been just awful and earsplitting—it was no wonder Sophie had lost her hearing; Mom jerking the wheel sideways, pulling off the road—anyone would have done the same thing. The van just got away from her.

But what about the radio and the van going haywire?

The car could have been acting weird before this afternoon. Possibly a solar flare, a shift in the earth's magnetic field. Why not a full moon, and that's why both Sophie and Rowan had gone temporarily insane. Olive frowned as she made an honest attempt at explaining it all away.

But logic wasn't working. She was still on edge, waiting for something else to drop on top of the quickly growing pile of what-the-heck-just-happened plaguing her family. She glowered at the cutting board, racking her brain for other explanations. Finally, she looked up from the loaf of bread between her hands and realized she wasn't alone.

She yelped when she saw Rowan, her hand flying to her mouth in both embarrassment and surprise. He was standing in the opening between the living room and kitchen, his almond-shaped eyes boring into her. Allowing her hand to drop to her chest, Olive tried to play it off with a laugh and a forced smile.

"You scared me," she scolded him, but unlike her sisters, who would have laughed along with her—*oh, Olive, you're so jumpy!*—Rowan said nothing. He just scrutinized her in that disconcerting way. Blank. Emotionless.

. . . dead?

Again, Olive spoke to soothe her own nerves. "Do you want a sandwich or something?"

Nothing.

Adjusting her glasses, she looked away from him, unable to maintain eye contact. She looked down at her gathered sandwich supplies and wondered whether Rowan's silence was purposeful, or if he wasn't reacting because he couldn't comprehend what the words being spoken to him even meant.

All at once, a part of her felt awful for him. Her family had dispersed, and Rowan had been left alone. It was a lot like how everyone relied on Olive to be responsible, but when things went sideways, she had the wherewithal to be on her own. *Perhaps we aren't so different after all,* she thought. Maybe, if the world flipped inside out, Olive would be the one who would end up alone in the woods, forgotten.

"Sandwich," she repeated, peeking up from the cutting board to see if it elicited any sort of a response. "See—bread," she said, waiting for a glimmer of recognition, a spark of understanding. "Cheese." She continued with the list, waiting, assessing, wondering if this was the kind of test they put him through at the children's home. Her mother had mentioned there had been a battery of them. Pop quizzes. Examinations to make certain he wasn't homicidal, she hoped. Surely they'd check that he wasn't dangerous before placing him with a family. They had to do that, right? Had to make sure he wasn't going to kill his new family while they slept?

Olive swallowed against a sudden, acrid lump in her throat.

"Uh, knife." She spit out the word, immediately regretting it. What if that single syllable finally elicited a response? What if it was the only word he knew? What if, upon hearing it, it threw him into some sort of crazed, uncontrollable bloodlust?

It didn't. She let out a long, relieved breath, grabbed the loaf of bread, opened the twist tie, and selected two middle slices from inside the bag.

"Dumb," she muttered to herself, uncertain of what she expected. *I've watched one too many of Gus's stupid movies.*

Did she really think motionless, blank-faced Rowan was going to spring into action, teeth bared, cackling like a maniac? Like that little kid from the old movie Gus loved, the one about the adopted boy who was the devil's son. That kid had made the nanny jump off the roof of a fancy house. Recalling that cinematic scene made Olive think of yesterday morning at the Rodriguez place, the way everything had been so pretty, so perfect, until Sebastian's shrieking wail had cut through the calm. If the kid in the movie had the power to make the nanny kill herself, was it possible that Rowan could coerce Olive's mother to do something as equally gruesome? Olive shuddered at the idea of it, suddenly remembering the whirling lights of the ambulance when, months ago, it had taken Mom away.

"Well, anyway, Rowan, it's rude to just stand there like that—" she began, distracting herself with talk, but when she looked up, he was gone. She shot a glance around the kitchen, then looked back to the spot where he'd had been.

"Rowan?" Abandoning her still-disassembled snack, she stepped away from the kitchen island and slowly approached the threshold.

She peeked around the door frame and into the living room, but he wasn't there, either, which made no sense. With his legs and arms at such bizarre angles, he dragged his feet and stumbled more than he walked. Which was why, when she spotted him staring down at her from the top of the stairs a second later, her heart sputtered in her chest. She'd seen him go up and down those stairs more than a few times, and he could hardly get up a single step without Mom holding his elbow and pushing him along. There wasn't any possible way he could have gotten up there so quickly, let alone by himself. Yet there he was, plain as day.

" . . . how?" She took a few backward steps, eventually finding herself in the kitchen once more, out of Rowan's view. Was it possible that he'd been upstairs the entire time, and she'd imagined him standing there, watching her? Or maybe it was the opposite, and she'd just hallucinated he was upstairs when he was still somewhere downstairs. Either scenario left her feeling unsteady, calling into question her own mental health.

"What the heck?" she whispered to herself, unable to shake the unease. "God, what the *heck*?"

She pivoted away from the threshold and walked back to the kitchen island, her heart still somersaulting. *Sandwich,* she thought, desperate to focus on something normal, something so mundane it couldn't possibly be upsetting. She looked at her supplies, realized she was missing mayonnaise, and began to turn to the fridge.

Something dark shifted just beyond her peripheral vision.

Olive froze, her breath hitching.

The shadow—while she hadn't quite seen it—hadn't struck her as small like Rowan. It had loomed large, like an adult. When it passed, her skin tingled. Every hair on her arms stood on end, as if electrified. She swallowed hard, forcing herself to look in the direction it had appeared. The doors of Mom's double oven winked at her, its dark glass freshly polished, her own startled reflection looking back at her, distorted and monstrous like Rowan's face.

"Get it together, Olive," she whispered, breathing out a soft laugh at how completely wound up the afternoon had left her. She was being ridiculous. Every thought, absurd. But that chuckle died out when her eyes stopped on the butter knife she'd left lying on the cutting board.

A chill grabbed her by the base of her skull. A shuddering breath quaked from between her lips as she stood fixed in place, unable to look away, her eyes wide and disbelieving. A soft mew left her, quiet in its startled terror. Because there, as if being moved by a phantom hand, the butter knife first spun left, then spun right, then rotated a few times around in a circle.

Like a broken compass.

Like something in a haunted house.

33

WILLOW

Willow eyeballed the threads of the bedroom rug while Sophie tried to shuffle the Candyland cards.

"Just one more game," Sophie swore. She'd said that the game before last, but Willow wasn't going to fight about it. Her thoughts were still in town with the idiot boys. She was still thinking about the wasps.

She could hear the kid in the Broncos baseball cap screaming, could see his arms flailing about his shoulders and head. It was like he'd been set on fire, those wasps dive-bombing him—flying away, then back again with a doubled ferocity. She couldn't remember if she'd simply thought the words or had actually spoken them: *He's gonna die. You have to stop.* The "you" meaning Rowan. Because no matter how impossible it seemed, she was sure he had somehow orchestrated that bizarre attack. She *knew* it was him.

"Wanna be the same color?" Sophie asked, holding up a plastic gingerbread man. "I'm gonna switch to blue."

Willow grabbed her green game piece and placed it on the starting line while Sophie drew the first card.

"Double red," Sophie announced, then moved her token down the board. "Your turn."

Willow picked a card off the pile and flipped it over, but she was hardly paying attention. Her eyes kept drifting to the bedroom window. There was nothing there, yet her gaze kept going back to the glass.

"Yellow," Sophie told her, then paused. "Willow, are you gonna move?"

"Sorry," Willow said, then advanced her little green man. But after she did so, she rose from her place on the floor. Rather than just looking at it from across the room, she stepped to the window. Maybe if she got closer, an answer would appear.

"Ha!" Sophie clapped her hands behind her. "Peppermint!"

Willow peered across the sloped roof toward both her parents' cars. Her dad's sedan was parked in its usual spot. Mom's van was off to the side, left there by a rusty red truck that had towed it onto their property. The van was sitting crooked, like it had a twisted ankle.

"Wiiiil-low."

Her little sister's whine forced a sigh out of Willow. She wasn't in the mood for any of this—for games or babysitting or playing nice and not bringing up the fact that what had happened at the park had been beyond creepy. And forget the incident with the van, how completely haunted their mother's appearance had been when the vehicle finally came to a jarring stop. There was no way Willow could bring *that* up with a five-year-old, but she also couldn't handle another round of Candyland.

"Hey, why did you scream?" Willow asked, turning to her kid sister.

Sophie looked up from the game board, giving Willow a puzzled look. "Willow," she said, startlingly serious for her age. "You're cuckoo bananas. I didn't scream anything. I said *peppermint*."

"Not just now. In the van, earlier. Why did you scream?"

Sophie still had a baby face. Her cheeks were full, her nose nothing but a button. She still had an innocent, cherubic baby look, especially with those silly pigtails on top of her head. Sometimes it was fun to watch her features shift, to see her go from calm to beyond excited in the blink of an eye. But those sudden shifts could also be off-putting, like now, as her expression changed from confused to frightened, from *what are you talking about* to *let's please not talk about that* within the blink of an eye.

"You aren't going to tell me?" Willow asked, frowning.

Sophie looked away, scowled at the game board, and then swept both gingerbread pieces off their rightful spots with a huff. "Forget it," she muttered beneath her breath, folding up the board and dropping it into the box. All it took was a few seconds for Sophie's eyes to shimmer behind a sheen of tears. "I don't want to play anymore. I would have won anyway. I was way ahead."

"Why won't you tell me?" Willow pressed, not understanding her little sister's reaction. "What was Rowan doing to you this morning when he was standing on top of your bed?"

Her lip quivering, Sophie grabbed the box off the floor and walked it over to the closet. They had a whole shelf full of board games in there, but Candyland remained Sophie's personal favorite. Before Willow could toss another question at her baby sister, Sophie stepped out of the closet, climbed onto her bed, and pulled her sheets over her head.

"What's your problem?" Willow asked.

"I'm taking a nap," Sophie announced from beneath cheerful unicorns. There was a pause before a little arm shot out from beneath the sheets, grabbed Unicorny by its squishy body, and pulled it under.

"Pretending to take a nap so you don't have to talk to me," Willow said. "That's basically lying, you know."

"My ears hurt again!" Sophie yelled from inside her makeshift tent, clearly crying now. "I'm gonna sleep it off! Just go away!"

Any other time, Willow would have choked out a laugh. *Sleep it off* was their dad's way of fixing anything. Headache? Sleep it off. Bad day? Stain on your favorite shirt? Sleep it off. Busted front tire on the van? Let the car sit there for a while and sleep it off. But this time, Sophie's response felt less like a joke and more a desperate attempt at isolation, her tears a punctuation mark to some unspoken fear. So Willow turned back to the window.

She nearly missed the figure quickly ducking behind the barn.

It was likely that their father would be out there, looking around, trying to piece together their own personal family mystery of what had happened to Gus and why Eden had been so completely freaked out when she'd discovered him. But before Willow was able to write it off, Dad wandered onto the prairie grass they all called the front lawn. He was just below her window, burying his hands in his hair the way actors did when they were pretending to be super upset . . . or when the world was falling apart.

Willow watched him for a while before looking back to the outbuilding, like maybe Dad had seen that figure too—was that why he was out there?—but he wasn't making a move to check it out. Dad turned back to the house and disappeared beneath the porch's slanted roof instead, going back inside.

Didn't he see that person? she wondered. *Maybe it was Gus.*

Willow turned, the carpet plush against her bare feet. She took a single forward step when, from behind her shoulder, something cut across the window, momentarily blocking out the light. It was quick, less than a second of temporary dimness, like when the total eclipse had blotted out the sun. Willow froze.

What the heck was that?!

A cloud. Just a cloud. Just a shadow . . .

She whipped back toward the window, looking for the source . . . but there was nothing. What's more, when she looked up, she was startled that there were no clouds in the sky at all.

Her eyes darted back to the barn. She couldn't see anyone there, but something told her that they *were* there, hiding. And the darkness that had dashed across the bedroom window? If it wasn't the sun being blotted out, it meant it was a person. A person . . . on the roof.

Willow bolted from the room, leaving Sophie behind to yell, "Hey! Where are you going?!"

Down the hall, down the stairs, and into the living room, Willow found Dad standing with his hands still stuck atop his head. He looked like he'd made some sort of huge mistake. But there was no time for questions.

"Dad, there's someone outside!"

Dad nearly jumped when she spoke, then finally let his hands drop to his sides as he took her in with a cautious glance. "Outside . . . ?" he asked, as if having forgotten what the word meant.

"I saw from my window. It was a person. They went behind the barn." A beat later, she offered: "Yes, I'm sure!" The guarantee was a reflex. She hated being questioned, but it seemed that every claim she made was challenged. Often she doubted herself, but this time she knew what she'd seen. "And I think they might be on the roof."

Dad frowned, tossing a glance toward the front door. She knew what he was thinking: he'd just been outside. And he would have seen them, would have noticed someone prowling on top of the house. Except he hadn't had the luxury of Willow's vantage point—high up, like a crow's nest—and he'd been beneath the porch awning when the shadow had streaked across the upstairs window.

"Dad, I mean it. Can you go check?"

"Wait," her father said, dubious. "Were they on the roof or behind the barn?"

"Both!"

"Kid, how could a person be in two places at once?" he asked.

"Because maybe there were two of them?" Willow huffed, annoyed that it was happening again. Nobody ever believed her about anything. "I don't know, Dad! Can you just go out there and *check*?"

"Willow, I'm sorry—there's nobody out there. How would they have even gotten here?"

Yes, their house was a few miles from their closest neighbor. But Rowan had managed to find his way onto their property, so why couldn't someone else?

Only then was Willow struck by a jarring thought.

"Oh my gosh, Dad, what if it's—" She hesitated, iffy on whether she should say what she was thinking.

Dad wasn't waiting for her to finish. He was already moving to the front door, making as though he was going to verify her claim, just in case. Normally she would have been glad. *Finally, someone's listening . . .* But this time she rushed after him, grabbing his arm.

"Wait, Dad. Dad. *Dad.* What if it's them?"

Her father furrowed his brow at her. "Who's *them*, Willow?"

Again she caught herself wavering. She wasn't certain why, but she was scared to voice the possibility that had popped into her head. Dad gave her a reassuring smile, then gently pulled her hand from around his wrist. "I'm going to go check," he said. "Okay?"

Finally, just before he reached the door, she managed to spit it out.

"Rowan's family," she said, stopping Dad in his tracks. "What if they're looking for him? What if they live in the woods too?"

She watched Dad's face as he processed her suggestion. They'd all considered it before: Rowan's family showing up at some point, taking him back to wherever the kid had come from. But that idea had never been scary. Rowan's family would contact the children's home, Mom and Dad would get a phone call, there'd be another dramatic family meeting, and Rowan would be gone the next morning, just like Buster and Maize. But this? The idea of people coming *out of the woods*? Dad's look of reassurance was gone, erased by startled apprehension. Willow had never seen that look on his face before, but it was undeniable. His expression was one of dread.

"Dad . . . ?"

He shook himself out of something—a trance, or the spiral of his own thoughts. Eventually, he met her eyes and forced another smile onto his face. It made her heart hurt because she knew it was fake. He was terrified, but he was pushing through it to make her feel safe.

"Um . . . I'll be right back, kiddo," he told her.

Then he pulled open the door.

But before he could step outside, they both yelped in surprise. Gus was standing there, his right hand extended as if reaching for the knob, his expression no doubt matching theirs. Nothing but anxiety and surprise.

34

AUGUST

"Jesus!" Gus took a backward step. He hadn't expected to find himself chest to chest with his father and sister at the door. "Are you *trying* to give me a heart attack?"

As he looked from Dad to Willow, he watched both their faces shift in mystifying ways. Dad's surprise morphed into a peculiar sort of relief, while Willow's alarm changed to what could only be described as annoyed resignation.

"What . . . ?" Gus asked, giving them both a weary look. He hadn't had a chance to set foot inside the house and was already being assaulted by weird glances and beneath-the-breath sighs.

But judgment was the least of his worries. The mere act of standing on his own front porch was triggering a panic attack. He honestly didn't want to be anywhere near home right now. Noah's brother had been nice enough to give Gus a lift in his hatchback lemon, but the plan was to simply grab some of his shit and get the hell out of there for a while, maybe camp out at Noah's for a few days. Hell, he didn't know. But there was no way he could stay under this roof. Not now. Not yet. Not until he was sure.

"Never mind," Willow muttered, then rolled her eyes and did an about-face toward the stairs.

"What's up with her?" Gus asked his dad, then shot a look over his shoulder. "What's wrong with the van?" And where the hell was Rowan? It made him immediately uncomfortable not knowing the kid's exact lo-

cation. He could have been upstairs, hanging from one of the attic rafters, wrapped in a silk spider cocoon. Or he could come crab-walking
down one of the walls, his head spinning around a full hundred and
eighty degrees.

"Mom had an accident," Dad told him. "It's fine. Nobody was hurt."

His father turned away, preoccupied with his own thoughts.

"Wait—she's all right?"

Gus stood in the open doorway, his ratty All Stars on the porch
planks, feet refusing to move. He looked toward the back of the house
and the bay of windows on the opposite living room wall. The curtains
were wide-open, allowing the sun to shine in. Gus could see all the way
through their home and into the backyard from where he stood. It was an
odd sensation, being able to feel the warm summer breeze whisper across
his arms while staring through the heart of where he lived, his line of
sight cutting straight into the safety and security that home once offered
only to be thrown back out into the wild beyond. Something about being
able to have a complete perspective of his house—like looking through
the lens of a telescope—left him feeling vulnerable.

The view was of the exact spot beyond the garden where Rowan
had first appeared, so perfectly placed it struck him as beyond coincidental. It reminded him of the night before, of when he'd run through
that very door and into the kitchen in search of the barn key. Everything
had looked the same but had felt different, alien. All the little taken-for-
granted familiars that made his home feel safe were missing . . . which
made him wonder, *was* this home, or could it be something else?

Before he knew it, he was pushing past his trepidation and forcing
himself to move forward, leaving the door wide-open in his wake. He
took a sharp left and stepped into the kitchen, then paused when he spotted Olive sitting at the kitchen table. She had her bare feet up on the
chair while her arms circled her knees. She was gnawing at the end of
her trademark ponytail, blinking past the lenses of her glasses when she
saw him, but didn't speak. Brother and sister exchanged a silent glance
before Gus moved to the drawer where he'd found the barn key the eve-

ning before. Pausing to take a steadying breath, he yanked it open, half expecting to see what was there last night: blank Post-it Notes, misplaced receipts, his mother's scribbled writing on recipe cards, gone. But it was all there, now joined by a yellow copy of an invoice from a place called Big Chief Towing.

Mom had an accident.

It didn't sit right. Not even a little bit. Because if anyone was an over-cautious driver, it was Isla Hansen. He couldn't count the times she'd boasted about never having gotten so much as a speeding ticket. Accidents happened, but something about this situation hit like an alternate reality. Real, but not real. Home, but not home.

The idea of it made his skin ripple. That all-too-familiar chill crawled up his back and settled atop his skull, the sensation of a thousand spiders skittering through his hair. Pressure filled his ears, then popped, then rang. He cringed against the onset of tinnitus, pivoted on the soles of his sneakers to face his sister, but Olive was gone. Vanished. As though she hadn't been sitting at the kitchen table at all.

Gus squinted at her empty chair, ready to call after her. Why was everyone being so fucking weird? But then he noticed the loaf of bread and turkey sandwich fixings on the island, and his stomach clenched, a reminder that he hadn't eaten anything all day. Screw it—he'd grab a bite, pack some of his stuff, and get the hell out of this insane asylum. He let Olive's disappearance go and stepped up to the cutting board, unscrewed the mayonnaise cap, and grabbed the butter knife lying next to his right hand.

There was a whisper, like the rumpling of fabric. He glanced up, and rather than it being Olive, he caught glimpse of something just beyond the kitchen's threshold. Not his sister.

Out of the blue, he was overwhelmed by the sensation that home was the last place he should be. What the hell had he been thinking coming back here? There was something *bad* here, and yet here he was, making a sandwich like it was no big deal. He forced his attention away from the doorway and down to the loaf of bread between his hands, but the bread, the cutting board, the butter knife were gone. He shoved away from the island, a reflexive move, like yanking a limb away from fire.

"What the fuck?"

Gus could feel the panic coming, preparing to seize him at the worst possible time. Remaining where he stood was an awful idea, so he rushed across the kitchen, ready to flee the room, but he stopped short when he came across the junk drawer he'd pulled open only a minute before. He studied the handle, his breaths coming way too quick now. If he kept it up, he'd hyperventilate, pass out, and wake up to . . . what? Wake up where? He reached out, yanked the drawer open while resisting the urge to scream. The Post-it Notes were blank. The crumpled receipts were gone. Recipe cards were missing, as was the yellow invoice from Big Chief Towing. And yet he'd witnessed their existence with his own eyes. He'd verified that they had been there. But now, standing at that same drawer, he found himself peering down at something that didn't make any fucking sense.

Before he could spiral into a full-blown meltdown, his eyes snapped upward. Again, something was definitely there, and a feeling deep in his gut promised him that it wasn't Olive. Gus hadn't seen more than a wisp of it out of his peripheral vision, but he'd *heard* it. Skittering past the doorway and down the hall.

A flash of memory rushed in, hitting him head-on like a wrecking ball of recollection.

The things from outside. The ones he'd seen last night in the dark.

Oh my God, he thought. *Oh holy shit, they're in the house. . . .*

Wanting to escape but too afraid to move, Gus couldn't decide whether to wait and see what may have been coming, or risk running into whatever it was that awaited him in the yard. Because there had been more than one of them yesterday. Two, maybe three, probably more hiding where he hadn't been able to see them. A couple of them may have been inside, but there was no doubt the others were waiting out in the woods. This was a fucking ambush. A trap.

His eyes jumped across the kitchen counter to the magnetic knife strip mounted to the backsplash. His mother's knives winked at him, glinting in light that had been bright as day when he'd stepped into the room but now looked far ruddier than before. Somehow the light resembled a sunset. Or an oncoming storm.

Again he sensed a figure in the hall just beyond the kitchen door. Quick. Rustling. Lingering. Biding its time. Gus forced himself to move, practically falling forward, propelling himself toward his mother's knives, as if that would save him. The first step felt natural, but the one that followed was heavy, as if his sneakers were filled with sand. The third was even slower, dragging feet through mud. Meanwhile, every inch of him was crawling with the same sensation from the night before. Electricity. Waves of it pulsing across his skin.

He groaned as he tried to push forward, his legs nearly cemented in place. Gus was too far away but reached for the knife strip anyway. And, as if responding to his movement, that invisible current of electricity amped up in intensity. The sudden shock forced a gasp out of Gus. His eyes widened, confused as to what he was feeling. Was the air going out of the room? Was he getting lighter?

The knife strip lost its magnetism, the blades clattering against the marble countertop in a cacophony of razored steel.

Gus wanted to turn, to get the fuck out of there, but no matter how much he struggled, he remained frozen in place. It was only then, as he searched the room for some way of flight, that he noticed a familiar face.

Rowan was standing in the far corner of the kitchen, watching Gus struggle.

Gus swallowed against the cry that was strangling him from the inside out, unable to get his throat to work. One second, he was winded, like he'd run a mile and a half without warming up. The next second, he was certain he was suffocating. *Like Eden,* he thought. *Like Eden that night at dinner.* He tried to reach for his neck, but the air had become impossibly heavy. He could no longer lift the weight of his arms.

All the while, Rowan stood staring. Watching. Studying.

He canted his head to one side as if to get a better look at Gus's strained expression, to fully see his fear. When Gus couldn't meet Rowan's insectoid eyes any longer, he looked back to the pile of knives on the counter. Rather than seeing a clutter of metal and wood, each blade was balancing on its tip unassisted, as if held by a phantom hand. They were spinning, completing slow revolutions, throwing slashes of red light across the room.

He couldn't pull his eyes away from those blades as they rotated like freakish versions of a child's top, even when he sensed something slither up behind him, the energy shifting from a pulsing static to a steady electric hum. There was a sensation of his sneakers lifting off the floor, but Gus couldn't look down to see whether it was really happening. Inside his head, he was screaming, but on the outside, his throat refused to work. There was no air to suck in, no way to make a sound. His eyes darted back to where Rowan had been, but the corner of the kitchen was empty. He was gone, just like Olive.

Just like everyone. The thought squirmed into his brain. They're all gone. Everyone is dead. Rowan killed them all.

Except, no. This was a nightmare, right? He was asleep?

Fuck! Wake up, Gus! Wake the fuck up!

But the more he resisted, the further the electric pulse developed along his arms and down his back. The weight of his limbs became impossibly ponderous, unmovable despite his body feeling buoyant and weightless. There was still the distinct sensation of someone standing behind him, so close he could feel them about a foot away.

Finally, he caught sight of the thing behind him in the knives' now rapidly spinning reflection.

What he saw was impossible. Emaciated. Blurry like an overexposed photograph, yet sharp enough to make out a few terrifying details. A pair of massive wide-set eyes took him in. He could make out limbs that didn't bend the way they were supposed to. Behind him, Gus imagined an exact replica of the wild boy living in his house, except six or seven feet tall. Having shed the disguise of human skin.

A shadow of a hand came forward, long sinewy fingers reaching out toward Gus's shoulder.

Simultaneously the memory of what happened in the barn came rushing back. The tall figures. Gus frozen in place. One of those things lifting its hand, its thin fingers curling outward toward him as he felt himself rise up off the ground. Drifting up. Up. Up so high he could smell the mold growing on the rafters. A million cicadas buzzing inside his skull, the noise so loud he'd been certain he was about to go deaf. *Like Sophie. Just like her.* A squeezing sensation, an invisible hand reaching through his rib cage and strangling his heart. He struggled for control, his vision beginning to blur. *I'm going blind!* The noise inside his head seizing an altogether different bodily sense. The throbbing synced with bleary flashes of bright light against the backs of his eyes. Suddenly overwhelmed with the sensation of shaking—no, *vibrating.* The trembling movement was so quick, so deeply oscillating, that he briefly wondered: Could human cells resonate fast enough to tear themselves apart? The barn, filling with that blinding white light. Instead of shouting for help, he felt his lungs suddenly empty, as though they'd collapsed within his chest.

Gus remembered all of it, the recollection giving him a momentary push toward free will. He took advantage of that fleeting determination, spun himself around, and looked forward, despite his fear.

His eyes were wide-open, but he couldn't comprehend what he was seeing.

His home was gone.

He was now surrounded by walls made of metal. No hard corners. No windows. No doors. A pale blue glow filled the cold space, but there was no discernible light source. Hundreds of panels lined the chasm, but there were no buttons, no screens. And at the far end, bizarre, streamlined pods lined the walls. Faces were visible beneath the curved, cloudy glass. Small faces. Children.

Gus began to shake—tiny, rapid movements, as though his muscles had lost their original function. The shock-like motion continued as his breath, having finally returned, came in small, sharp gasps. His chest rose and fell, quaking. Tears streaked his cheeks. Because what was this? What the fuck *was* this?

He didn't dare move closer to the pods, but he didn't have to.

He recognized some of them. It would have been hard not to after seeing their photos blown up two stories tall. Giant billboard photos flashed through Gus's head.

The missing kids. They were here, wherever the hell Gus was. Whatever the fuck this was supposed to be.

He didn't understand what this was. Couldn't comprehend how he'd gotten there. Terror speared his heart, because nobody would find them, would they? Not the kids. Not Gus. Somehow he was sure that they could look until the earth stopped turning, and still, there would be no trace.

That fear—no, that *realization*—gave birth to a deep, bone-rattling breath, and finally, *finally,* Gus found his voice.

And screamed.

35

EDEN

Eden was concerned about her brother. During dinner, both Willow and their father said they'd seen Gus on the front porch. He'd shown up out of nowhere, asked about the damage to the van. Olive mentioned that he'd walked into the kitchen and was grabbing a sandwich, but she'd looked away for half a second, and when she glanced up again, he was gone. That was where the August Hansen sightings stopped. Eden had checked the house, his room, the barn.

"Nobody's worried?" she asked at dinner, her eyes darting from Dad to Mom. The general consensus was Gus was at Noah's, because life wasn't a true crime podcast. There was no suspicious evidence, nothing pointing to foul play. But that made no difference to Eden's gut instinct. Everything about the situation telegraphed *weird, not right, unsettling, strange*.

Eden had tried Gus's cell earlier that afternoon probably a dozen times, but it went directly to voicemail. His phone must be off, except Gus never did that. He didn't even put his phone on do not disturb when he slept. With little more than a thin wall between their bedrooms, she'd spent countless nights listening to her brother's various chimes alert him about new emails, TikTok posts, Reddit replies, and whatever else he did on his device—all those dings and dongs and whistles and blips going off at all hours because it was Gus's lifeline. Phone off? Not a chance.

That had been hours ago.

Now, at dinnertime, Eden waited for a reply about Gus's whereabouts from her parents. Dad looked plenty stressed. His lips were drawn tight and his knee was bobbing beneath the table, but something about his demeanor told her that his anxiety wasn't coming from Gus going AWOL. She frowned as she watched him. His mac and cheese—which Olive had made because Mom had forgotten about dinner—was growing cold, congealing on his plate.

Eden shifted her focus to Mom, sitting mute and motionless next to Rowan. Meanwhile, the kid continued to occupy the head of the table despite not having eaten anything in front of anyone since he'd arrived. Of course, Eden knew better. Willow had been picky as a toddler. Mom and Dad even considered taking her to an occupational therapist. They'd been beyond worried, but even at her pickiest, Willow still ate chicken fingers and blueberry waffles. Rowan, though? Not a bite. But he had to have been eating *something.* Maybe he simply refused to eat in front of others. It could have been part of his trauma, right? Whatever crazy people had put him in a cage could have force-fed him and made him fear food. That had to be it, because kids *had* to eat. All kids. Even those like Rowan.

Eden scowled, then looked down to her own plate, taking a bite of her dinner.

"This is good, Olive," she said, prompting a weary smile from her younger sibling.

There was a beat of silence, then Olive spoke.

"He probably went back to Noah's," Olive concluded, but would Gus have just left without saying a word to anyone? Unlikely, but not impossible after the morning they had had. He'd been acting so oddly after the incident in the barn, and he'd thoroughly freaked Eden out when he practically leaped from Dad's car on the way into town. But none of that changed the fact that Gus wasn't answering his phone, and *that* was what Eden found scariest of all.

After dinner, she found herself loitering around Olive's bedroom door.

"His phone probably just died," Olive said with a shrug. "He's got that wonky outlet in his room."

"Oh yeah." Eden recalled her brother hissing through his teeth about *the stupidest outlet in the entire universe*. It was the one between his bed and nightstand. The bottom socket worked, no problem. The top one was on a light switch, and that switch was always off. If Gus accidentally plugged his charger into the wrong socket, his phone wouldn't power up. Eden had an exact replica of that same wall plug, but unlike her brother, she'd had the novel idea of plugging a lamp into it, as intended.

"This is Gus we're talking about," Olive said. "I'm positive he's fine."

"Unlike some people in this house," Eden replied beneath her breath.

"What, you mean Mom?" Olive asked softly. Eden said nothing, then looked over her shoulder toward her parents' bedroom. The last thing she needed was those two overhearing gossip. "Or do you mean Rowan?"

Eden looked back to her sister.

"Rowan is the reason Mom is the way she is, you know," Olive said, lowering her voice further. "He's got a hold on her. I don't know what it is, but it's creeping me out."

Eden frowned, thinking how Mom had acted that very afternoon: zoned out, far away, her face blank save for a dead-eyed stare.

"I think she's just tired, maybe? Or freaked out by what happened earlier?" Eden suggested. It was easier to make up excuses than accept the alternative. Except what *was* the alternative? What were they talking about here? That Rowan had somehow brainwashed their mother? The kid couldn't even seem to talk. . . .

"Earlier, like the accident?" Olive asked. Eden couldn't imagine how frightening it must have been inside the van as it careened off the road. It was lucky the airbags hadn't deployed. They could have hit that damn billboard. Or flipped over.

Eden leveled her gaze on her sibling. "Or maybe it's just Adam. You know . . . I didn't even ask you if you were okay after the van thing."

"You did, actually," Olive said, adjusting her glasses. "As soon as you and Dad got there. And anyway, I'm fine. We all are. Except for Mom . . . who isn't."

"You really think her acting weird has something to do with the accident?" Eden asked. "Did she hit her head or something? I mean, it wasn't that big of a deal, but maybe it triggered something?"

"Maybe," Olive said. An awkward sort of pause fell between them, as though neither girl knew how to tackle the topic of their mother's growing madness. "Anyway," Olive said after a beat—her way of bringing the conversation to a close. "Gus is definitely at Noah's. It's not like he hangs out with anyone else. His phone didn't charge, and now he's off the grid. Not like anyone would blame him for staying far away from here right now. I mean, wouldn't *you*?"

Eden nodded. "You're probably right."

"I'm always right," Olive whispered to herself, pushing long hair behind her ears.

Eden laughed a little, rolled her eyes at her sister, then went to her room and got ready for bed. But her brother's absence still nagged at her. For one, it was way past curfew. Typically, their parents would have hit the roof had he stayed out so long. If he was planning on crashing at Noah's, he would have at least sent a text. And of course, had Gus's phone really been dead, Noah had a charger, duh. Gus would have taken care of his phone there, or just used Noah's phone to call home.

Pulling a Kate Bush T-shirt over her head—vintage, stolen from her mother—she stepped out of her room and paused at Gus's door. Waiting a beat as if to reconsider breaching her older brother's privacy, she eventually turned the knob and quietly slipped inside his room. Eden's intention wasn't to snoop, but to ease her own worry. She walked across the room to the stupidest outlet in the goddamn universe and, as she suspected, there it was: August's charger, plugged in to the bottom socket, not the top. His phone should have been fine.

A shudder racked her from the top of her skull to the base of her spine. It was like something she'd hear on one of her podcasts, or maybe a tagline from a new horror movie. *His phone wasn't dead, but he was.*

Eden shook it off and rushed out of his room, shut her own door behind her, and climbed into bed. She knew she wouldn't sleep. She'd likely hold her breath all night, waiting to hear the soft click of Gus's bedroom door . . . waiting to hear those annoying but somehow comforting blips come from his phone. Because something about this entire affair didn't sit right at all. What was even more unsettling was that nobody appeared to be bothered that Gus was missing. And he *was* missing. She was sure of it. Every fiber of her soul said so. Her brother was gone.

36

SOPHIE

Sophie woke to buzzing in her ears so loud it made her teeth hurt. Sitting up in bed, she winced and pressed the heels of her hands to the sides of her head, but it didn't help. The noise was worse than ever, bad enough to make her wonder whether she could still hear, or if that loud buggy sound would be the only thing she'd experience for rest of her life.

She thought about crawling out of bed and running down the hall to her parents' room, but a few things kept her in place.

Firstly, her and Willow's bedroom was super dark. There was usually a night-light that glowed a soft green behind the big reading chair, but that green glow wasn't there now. Plus, Sophie's star machine was off. She had no idea why either one of those things wouldn't be working. They were like a security blanket. Without them, the room was way too scary to cross.

Second, getting to her parents' room would mean going into the hall, and Sophie hated doing that at night. If her room was dark, the hall was darker. There were no windows to let in moonlight and no outlets to plug in a night-light. Mom had solved the issue by hanging a small string of Christmas lights around the edge of the bathroom mirror, but those were faint, and sometimes that yellow glow was more spooky than comforting. Not that it mattered. Mom and Dad's room was way past the bathroom, all the way back where Willow's old room used to be.

Which brought her to the third reason she was too scared to make the trek. To get to Mom and Dad's room, she had to go past Rowan's door, and something about the idea of doing that in the middle of night made her skin crawl. After what had happened in the car—Rowan staring, Rowan screaming, the van crashing—she wanted nothing to do with him ever again. Not to be mean, but as soon as Mom was ready to listen, Sophie was going to ask for Rowan to go back to the kid's place where he came from. Not to be mean, but he had to go.

She thought all of that within the span of seconds, all the while trying to hush the noise inside her head and decide whether the scary journey to her parents' room was worth it. But before she could make her choice, she found herself squinting at the window across the room. It was covered by a blackout curtain, but light could still sneak in from around the sides. And right then, it was allowing in a creepy kind of light Sophie didn't recognize. A red, flashing glow. It was like the night the ambulance came. *Oh no, Mom!* she thought, but no, that couldn't be it. Those flashes had been steady. The light coming into the room now was random—pulses coming super fast, but then slowing down. Was it a strobe light, or maybe the flash of a camera?

"No, lightning," she said. Spurred on by the desire to see if she was right, Sophie pushed her unicorn comforter away from her legs, hugged Unicorny to her chest, and dashed across the dark distance to the window.

When she pushed the curtain aside, her eyes went wide.

The sky was bright red. She could see storm clouds, their edges looking as though they were burning, glowing like embers, red orange and hot. Another flash lit up the night, and Sophie had her answer; it *was* lightning . . . but it was unlike anything she'd ever seen. It wasn't the normal bright white she was used to, but a deep red splitting the darkness into a thousand blackened shards. Veins of red stretched down to the earth, then spidered across the prairie grass, as if alive. That electric webbing traveled across the ground toward the house. Sophie gave a startled cry when she saw it bolt up the outside wall next to the window. Stumbling backward in the dark, she stepped on a toy that suddenly lit up the room in a carnival of colors, its calliope music sounding far more sinister than it should have.

She spun around. Hiding behind her unicorn, she recognized the toy as her own. It was a little electronic keyboard she'd had since she was a toddler. *Not scary*, she told herself. But that didn't make her feel better, and Sophie's heart beat harder when that cheerful music began to slow, began to melt, began to sound like something that could only come from a dark and wicked place.

Ready to cry out for her parents, she was shocked into another yelp. Every toy came to life. Anything with a battery lit up and began to make noise or sing, spin, or cycle through a rainbow of colors. Dropping Unicorny to her feet, Sophie slapped her hands over her ears, wincing against the cacophony over the buggy buzzing inside her head. She squealed and ran for Willow's bed, certain to find her big sister sitting there, her eyes round as dinner plates, her mouth an O of fear. But the bed was empty. Willow was . . . gone.

"*Willow!*" Sophie shrieked. "*Willow, where are you?!*"

Now too scared *not* to run to the door, Sophie yanked it open, ready to bolt to her parents' room, come what may. But she stopped short at what she faced.

Beyond the door, there was nothing.

No hallway.

No pictures hanging on the wall.

No carpet, because there was no floor.

Beyond the door, there was emptiness.

Absolute black.

A cry wrenched itself out of her, barely audible over the noise. She slammed the door shut, afraid of what might be hiding in the nothing beyond. Pivoting on the balls of her bare feet, she ran past the menagerie of blaring, blinking toys and back to the window. Dad always said, *If there's ever an emergency, get out of the house however you can.*

There was a wooden toy box to the right of the window. It was heavy, but Sophie gave it her all, breathing out a scream as she shoved it closer to the glass. She hopped on top of it, then fought with the window latches. When she finally got them to pop open, she pushed up on the bottom sash, preparing herself for a fight. The window never wanted to open. Dad called it "sticky" and always told her to leave it, he'd fix it later, but he hadn't gotten around to it yet. At least she was pretty sure he hadn't. But now the window slid upward smooth and quick, as though someone was helping Sophie. Maybe Dad *had* fixed it? Catching her breath, she leaned forward and crawled out the window onto the roof.

Sophie hadn't felt wind when she'd first thrown the window open, but now that she was outside, it whipped her hair back. A storm was coming. The tangle of clouds overhead convinced her of that. She stumbled, her feet slipping against the steep pitch of the roofline. There was no way off unless she jumped, and that would break bones from this height.

"Be careful," she whispered, breathless and tearful. "Be careful, be careful."

Having reached the end of her escape plan, she sat down, hugged her knees tightly to her chest, and began to cry as the clouds pulsed overhead.

"What do I do?" she asked herself, her mouth pressed hard against her knees.

There was another electric flash, that ghostly red lightning coursing downward, then across the ground—tendrils of currents mapping the terrain. The lightning traveled up the sides of the house just as it had before, but now Sophie was out on the roof, exposed and unsafe. She shrieked as the current jumped onto the rooftop and coursed toward her. Sophie expected to burst into flame, burn, and turn to ash. She was instead enveloped in a wave of static electricity so intense it made her feel like she was floating. Like a small lady she'd seen on the computer once—a part of a wonderful circus act, the lady, attached to six massive helium balloons, floating up, up, up as she gleefully kicked her feet. *Bon voyage!*

Then, as though the lightning strike had located exactly what it had been looking for, the red light overhead began to grow an eye of pale white. It started out faint, brightening as it widened. It reminded Sophie of the way car headlights looked in the fog—hauntingly pretty, brighter than usual, the light dispersing in fuzzy halos. With her neck craned back, she couldn't bring herself to look away as that point of radiance grew wider, clearer. Finally, she realized that it wasn't one light but many. Hundreds of them, small, round, spiraling about what looked to be a black disc completing a lazy spin.

The disc soundlessly lowered through the clouds. There was a seam in the shape of a circle in the center. Seams everywhere, as though the whole thing could blossom like a flower if provoked. Just as the thought crossed Sophie's mind, the disc chose to show her that she was right. The center began to bloom, splitting into petal-like sections that retracted into its base. Inside the opening, Sophie could see other lights. Long ones, like the tubes Dad used in the garage. But rather than being a cold white, these lights gave off a warm red-orange hue.

Sophie was so distracted by the lights that she hardly noticed how low the disc thing had come, how huge it really was. She only realized she couldn't see the sky anymore when, as abruptly as it had come, the buzzing in her ears stopped and she couldn't hear anything anymore. No crickets. No nightingales. Not the train whistle that occasionally cut through the night. With her breath heaving in her chest, she dared to whisper into the wind whipping hair across her face.

"Hello?" Relief washed over her. Yes, she *could* hear! She hadn't gone deaf again. But her excitement didn't last long. Her greeting had provoked something overhead.

The lights inside the disc grew brighter as though having heard her, as if responding. Sophie gaped at the gigantic structure floating above her.

"Hello . . . ?" she tried again, her curiosity getting the best of her, overpowering her fear.

The light inside the disc responded with a faint shimmer.

It can hear me.

For a split second, Sophie was delighted. Despite how little she was, it *saw* her. It was listening. And then, just as quickly as excitement had come, the opposite gripped her.

It can hear me.

Except that was wrong, wasn't it? The thing she was looking at wasn't alive. She was just a kid, but the craft overhead couldn't answer—not really, right? What could answer, however, was whoever may have been inside.

"Oh no." The words slipped past her lips. The disc shimmered, hearing *that* as well. "No," she said a bit louder. "No. Get out of here!" She twisted to climb back to her open bedroom window, but would she really risk the emptiness, the void? "Oh no," she whispered again. "Oh no, oh no, oh no . . ." How was she supposed to get out of her room if there was nothing beyond the door? How was she supposed to escape if—

With her hands and knees raw against the roof tiles, she suddenly understood. The blackness in the hallway had been on purpose. Willow being gone and Sophie crawling out onto the roof, it was all part of a plan. This whole thing was what Gus would have called a setup. She'd been tricked. And usually, when someone played a trick, there was a reason. Like how Willow sometimes scared her to be funny, or when Gus hid her fruit snacks so he could eat them himself. Or hey, how about Rowan making Sebastian fall off the playground equipment to see what would unfold? Or what about the wasps stinging those boys so he could watch them panic? Or how he'd made Sophie go deaf with some sort of magic trick to see how she'd react, to see how afraid the grown-ups would be?

Rowan.

He'd been playing tricks on the whole family since he'd shown up.

All at once, Sophie put it together. This nasty trick was one of his too. And that soundless, hovering machine? He was up there, *inside* it. She didn't have any proof, but it didn't matter. She *knew* it.

And right then the disc's ethereal glow disappeared, swallowed by light so bright it made her cry out again. She shut her eyes against the sudden glare, but she'd already gone blind. And when that electric current seized her by the chest, she could feel herself turn toward heaven, could feel the roughness of the shingles vanish from against her palms and knees. Her back arched, her arms and legs as heavy as stones. Her shins dragged against the roof. The tops of her feet. The tips of her toes. Yes, she could feel it.

Somehow she was flying.

Going up into the sky.

SEVEN-YEAR-OLD GIRL MISSING FROM GOLDEN, COLORADO, HOME

Golden, CO—The quiet suburb of Denver has been shaken by the sudden disappearance of Abigail Steeple, a seven-year-old girl last seen by her mother, Marilyn Steeple, late Tuesday night. The search for Abigail began early Wednesday morning when her mother discovered she was missing from her bedroom.

According to *The Mile High Herald,* Marilyn Steeple reported that Abigail was tucked into bed around 10:45 p.m. in their Golden home, part of a peaceful neighborhood just west of Denver. At some point during the night, Marilyn reported hearing a faint thump, which she initially thought might be Abigail getting up to use the bathroom. "I listened for a few minutes, expecting her to come to my room, but when she didn't, I just assumed she went back to bed," Marilyn stated.

It wasn't until 7 a.m. the next morning, when Marilyn went to wake her daughter for school, that she realized something was terribly wrong. Abigail, typically reliable about waking up with her alarm, wasn't in her bed. Marilyn checked the house but could find no trace of her only child.

Panicked, she immediately called the authorities. Golden Police officers arrived on the scene and conducted a thorough investigation. All windows and doors appeared secure, with no signs of forced entry or any indication that someone had entered or exited the home during the night.

Abigail was last seen wearing a My Little Pony pajama set. She is described as approximately 4 feet tall, weighing around 55 pounds, with shoulder-length chestnut hair and brown eyes.

Her father, Allen Steeple, works as a night watchman for a local security company and was not home at the time of Abigail's disappearance. Authorities are interviewing neighbors, combing through security footage, and have enlisted the help of search and rescue teams to assist in the search.

The Golden Police Department is urging anyone with information to come forward. "We're pursuing every lead we can and are hopeful that the community can assist in bringing Abigail home safely," said Detective John Emerson, the lead investigator on the case.

As the search intensifies, residents of the normally tranquil suburb are left anxious and fearful for the little girl's safety. Family and friends have gathered in support of the Steeple family, praying for her safe return.

DAY FOUR

37

OLIVE

Olive didn't recognize the vehicle now rambling down the gravel driveway. It was an old RV, sun-faded and ugly beige. It sported a crunched-in front bumper and a windshield had a crack as big as the San Andreas Fault. Something large and round hung from the rear-view mirror—on closer inspection, it was a dreamcatcher with feathers hanging low; crystals shimmered with light. When the RV came to a stop next to their damaged van, Olive's knee-jerk reaction was to call out to her parents, but she waited. It was early. The house was still asleep. Even Sophie wasn't up yet. Sucking on the end of her ponytail, Olive watched the dust billow around the funky vehicle from behind her glasses, squinting to see through the flying grit as the door of the RV swung wide.

"Who the hell is that?"

Olive jumped at Eden's question, her hand flying to her chest as if fending off a heart attack.

"Jeez!" Olive hissed.

Eden held up her hands. *Don't shoot.* "Sorry, sorry," she said, giving Olive a look. "Didn't mean to give you an aneurysm."

"You're up?" Olive asked, surprised to see her eldest sister next to her. Eden sometimes slept till noon.

"I couldn't sleep. And I was checking on Gus," Eden confessed.

"He's back?"

"No."

Olive sighed and looked to the RV, which both she and Eden peered at through the dining room window. It was then, just as Olive was about to answer her sister's original question with an *I don't know who that is*, that a woman came ambling out of the vehicle, swatting at the dust. She was tall—almost regally so. Bohemian. Her head of wild curly hair glinted gray in the morning sun. It was long, voluminous. *Gorgeous*, Olive thought. A perfect pairing with the broomstick skirt and ultra-bright fuchsia shawl tied covering her shoulders. *Who the hell is that?* was the question of the morning, and Olive couldn't wait to discover the answer. Lucky for her, it didn't take long.

"Oh *shit*," Eden hissed through her teeth.

"What?"

"I've seen her before," Eden said, watching the woman slam the RV door shut. "Mostly in old photographs, but I recognize her. She looks exactly the same."

"Who is she?" Olive asked as the curly-haired stranger approached their front steps. She could already hear the half dozen bracelets circling the woman's wrists jangle like bells on Santa's sleigh. Or, depending on who she was, like the bells on a leper's shoes.

"That's Mom's mom," Eden muttered. "Grandma." The word was both thick and ominous on her tongue. "Why the hell would *she* be here?"

The sound of footsteps shuffled up the front stairs. Then came the inevitable knock at the door. Eden suddenly fell into motion, moving in the opposite direction, as though running from fire. Olive blinked.

"Wait, where are you going?" she asked, panicked. Eden was really going to leave her there? Olive had never met this woman before. She'd only made out smatterings of her mother's long-festering bitterness and angst. It was clear, if the woman on the other side of the door was indeed Grandma, she was not welcome here. And now Olive was expected to greet her on her own?

"Eden!" Olive loud-whispered at her sister's back. "What am I supposed to say?"

"I don't know!" Eden aggressively hissed in response, then pivoted and ran up the stairs.

Another knock shook Olive out of her stupor. She assumed Eden had gone upstairs to alert their parents, but how long would it take for them to come down? It would be rude to just let a family member stand out on the front porch waiting. *Technically* a family member, anyway. There was the mug Willow had given Dad the previous Father's Day—ANYONE CAN BE A FATHER. IT TAKES SOMEONE SPECIAL TO BE A DAD.—and she wondered, did it really matter that this woman was her mom's mother? Olive had never met her, so could this stranger really be considered her grandma, blood relation be damned?

"Hello?" A voice sounded through the door, startling Olive out of her thoughts. Another knock followed. It sounded impatient, insistent. *Little pig, little pig* . . . Olive frowned at the rapping of knuckles against the wood. She didn't want to answer it, and yet she couldn't help but reach out, flip the dead bolt, and turn the knob.

When the door swung inward, Olive was immediately assaulted by the scent of patchouli: earthy, spicy, completely overwhelming. Her maternal grandmother stood lean and beautiful, like something out of a fairy tale.

"Oh!" the woman said, gasping as though seeing a specter. "Why, hello."

"Um, hi." Olive shifted her weight from one bare foot to the other, tugging on her long ponytail out of nervous habit. "May I help you?"

"Oh, well . . ." The older woman hesitated, then forced what looked to be an oddly uncomfortable smile. "Sure. Your father called me, said your mama isn't feeling well?" She paused, then gave a quiet laugh. "Goodness, you just have no idea who I am, do you?"

"No, ma'am," Olive lied, glancing down to Grandmother's jangly bracelets. She recognized one as being made of amber. Another looked like milky green jade. The rest were elaborate silver cuffs. One had a large slice of white agate at the center; another, a huge turquoise stone.

"I'm your grandma," she said, her awkward smile growing a little warmer around the edges. "My name is Skye. Your mama, Isla, is my baby girl. Though, judging by the look of you, she's not quite a baby any longer, is she? How old are you, darlin'?"

"Thirteen," Olive said. "Fourteen in September. I'm Olive."

Grandma Skye gasped, flabbergasted. "My God," she said softly, and then, almost bashfully, "Olive. Such a beautiful name for such a pretty girl. Do you have any brothers or sisters?"

"Four," Olive told her only to watch her grandmother's face grow nearly ashen at the reply. Clearly it was news she hadn't been prepared for. A grandmother of five, but only just learning that fact? Yikes.

"Skye?"

Olive veered around, relief washing over her as Dad jogged down the stairs, still in his pajamas.

"Luke," Grandma Skye replied, though she didn't sound quite so friendly anymore. "Just as I remember you."

"Thanks for coming," Dad said. "I know this is . . . awkward."

"Glad to," Grandma Skye said, lowering her eyes.

Olive swallowed, her gaze darting between the two adults. She didn't know much about Grandma Skye other than that she and Mom had a strained, unhealthy relationship, if it could be called that at all. Mom didn't like talking about it, but she occasionally made little comments here and there, and Olive had picked up on them over the years. Every Mother's Day, Mom would look sad despite all the gifts she'd get from the kids. Sometimes, during outings, she'd murmur about how nice it was to spend time with everyone, how not all children got to make such wonderful memories with their parents, how not all parents cared to create such lovely moments for their children. When Olive grew perceptive enough, she recognized the loneliness—it radiated from Mom like an aura. But that sort of thing was easy to write off as depression, especially when one minute, Olive was expecting a new sibling, and the next, that child was dead. She'd seen the medications in her parents' bathroom. She'd spent her entire life watching her mom gasp at nothing. *I thought I saw something. I'm just jumping at my own shadow today.* Honestly, it hadn't been all that surprising when Dad had sat them down and explained that Mom had gone away for a while, that she needed help from actual doctors to cope with Adam's loss.

But now, watching Dad and Grandma greet each other, Olive started to pick the mystery woman apart. The clothes, the RV, the clanging bracelets and suffocating patchouli—it was a romantic nomad stereotype from another time in American history. Hippies, they used to be called, and not so nicely. The problem with people like that was they were always somewhere far away. Even on Mother's Day. Even when grandchildren were born. Olive was a little fascinated, part of her thirsty to know more about this odd person who hadn't been allowed into her life. But she was also smart enough to understand that Mom wouldn't have kept Grandma Skye out of their family without an especially good reason. Something lingered beneath the surface here.

Olive shot a look toward Dad, suddenly curious about his nervous posture, about how he'd greeted this woman with hushed tones. That was it, then, wasn't it?

Mom doesn't even know Grandma Skye is here.

The idea of that turned Olive's stomach, because Mom had made it crystal clear that this woman was an adversary. A perpetrator. A source of pain. And now here was her father, inviting that hurt right in.

38

LUKE

The way Olive bolted up the stairs made Luke nervous. His kids were both whip-smart and perceptive. No doubt his girls were putting two and two together, figuring out that Skye shouldn't have been anywhere near the house, let alone inside it.

"Let's talk outside," Luke suggested, motioning for Skye to step onto the front porch.

"Your daughter, Olive?" Skye said, moving outside as she spoke. "She said she has four siblings?" She paused as if in disbelief, giving Luke a pleading look. "So, I have *five* grandchildren?"

Luke hesitated, then gave her a faint smile. "Yeah. One boy and four girls."

Skye's hands lifted in a clamor of metal and stone, her fingers hiding her mouth. It was an attempt to hold back emotion, but the despair was impossible to miss. Luke's heart twisted at the sight of it. Despite all Isla had told him about Skye, it was impossible to not feel for her, if only for the split second before he remembered everything else Isla had ever said.

"Plus, um, one more now," Luke said, drawing Skye's focus back to the conversation, away from the thoughts of how much she'd missed out over the years. "The one we're fostering. Rowan."

"Rowan," she echoed quietly, her brows knitting together. Luke could see shadows of Isla in her mother's face: the way Skye's mouth turned down at the corners, the faint frown lines along the bridge of her nose. She was a pretty woman—one who was wearing a look of discomfort, as though she'd also known a Rowan once . . . a not-so-pleasant one, maybe.

There was a beat of silence; then Skye squared her shoulders and gave Luke a pointed look.

"Well, where's Isla anyway?" she asked.

Luke floundered about. He wasn't sure why it hadn't crossed his mind that Skye would actually want to *see* her daughter, but here it was; an awkward situation getting worse by the second.

"Um, she's . . ." *Upstairs. Asleep. Losing her mind. Going to kill me if she finds out you're here.*

"Ah." Skye smirked, glancing down to the tips of her cowboy boots. "I see. Well . . ." She lifted her chin, looking Luke square in the eyes. "Let's get on with it, then. Why did you call me? Why am I here?"

Again, the awkwardness of the entire situation was making him want to crawl out of his skin. Him and his brilliant fucking ideas.

"Isla's always had some, um . . ." He stalled, not knowing how to put it without sounding like he was talking badly about his wife.

"Issues?" Skye finished for him, terse.

He gave a tight smile but let it lie between them, unspoken. "Yeah, you could say that. Some depression. She's battled it since I met her, since she was young. But things have gotten worse since Rowan appeared, and exponentially so since he's come to live with us." There was no way in hell he was going to bring up Isla's recent stay at a mental health facility. God, what was he thinking—if Isla found out Skye was here, she'd have his head to begin with. If she found out that he'd told Skye details about her current mental state . . . she just might douse the entire house in gasoline.

"What do you mean *appeared*?" Skye asked, suddenly suspicious.

"Like, literally appeared," Luke said, unable to help the little laugh of exasperation that escaped him. It was ridiculous when he thought of it, really: a child materializing out of the ether while others were going missing. "Isla was out in the garden one morning a while back, and this kid just . . . stepped out of the woods. The authorities couldn't piece it together. Nobody knows who he is, no family, nothing. It's deserted back there—nothing but trees for thousands of acres, as far as I know."

Skye stood silent for a long time, then crossed her arms over her chest in a protective sort of embrace. With her gaze turned down to the front porch's peeling planks, she waited for Luke to continue.

"Isla had already been on edge." Again, he stopped short of details. He wasn't going to bring up Adam. Absolutely not. "But that's when she really started acting differently. Everything changed, and I mean *every-thing*. Her sleep habits. Her routine. The way she interacts with the kids." The problem had started with Rowan, and no matter how irrational, Rowan's appearance and Isla's problems were too much of a coincidence to not be linked. It made him feel stupid to point the finger at a child—a kid who was likely not much older than Sophie—and blame him for all the troubles Isla had been having for the past couple of months. Yet he was back to that same thought process, unable to accept that it was illog-ical and absurd. Because, was it really? It wasn't as though Rowan was a normal little boy. Blaming these things on a kid who laughed and played and actually spoke, emoted, *ate . . .*

"What are you thinking?" Skye asked, shaking Luke out of his thoughts, forcing him back into their conversation. "It's like that movie," she said, lifting a hand, flitting it above her head with a jingle. "*A Beau-tiful Mind*, I think it was. I can practically see the thoughts unspooling above your head."

Luke didn't respond. He'd never seen that film, and what could he say anyway? Was he supposed to confess he thought it was Rowan? That would make Luke look like a lunatic.

"You think it's the boy," she said after a while, the statement so matter-of-fact it nearly made him laugh.

"Would that make me crazy?"

"No," she said, perhaps a little too quickly. "When you mentioned him on the phone, I knew I had to come."

Luke didn't follow. Was Skye saying she thought it was Rowan too? How was that possible? He'd barely told his mother-in-law anything. Yet he could see it in her face. He recognized the worry in her eyes. It was as though she knew the entire situation without being told.

"I doubt Isla's told you exactly why we aren't close," Skye began. "Not because she's keeping things from you, but because she doesn't know the whole story herself."

"What story? The thing she keeps talking about with Ruby Mae?"

Hearing the name spoken aloud seemed to throw Skye for a loop. Her expression faltered from stoic to shattered, but she appeared to pull herself together with astonishing speed.

"For the longest time, I thought she was lying to me, telling me she didn't remember what had happened to Ruby Mae. But the fact that she hasn't told *you* makes me think that maybe she really doesn't recall what occurred . . . even though they were together."

"Wait, what?" Luke stared at her, his brain tripping over new information. "What do you mean? Who was together?"

Skye shifted her weight upon the porch planks. It appeared that it was her turn to withhold information. But after a moment of squared shoulders and pursed lips, she sighed—a breath seemingly held for ages, perhaps since the time Isla had left home.

"Isla and Ruby Mae," Skye said, hesitant. "My sister, Sunny, she said they had gone out into the field the way they always had. They'd been going out there since they were small. It was safe. Open. There wasn't a thing out there that could have caused them harm."

Luke swallowed against the acrid taste that was slowly filling his mouth.

"The only reason Sunny looked out there was because she saw a lightning flash. She said a storm was coming. So she went out on the back porch to call them in, but they were gone."

This was the part where, at any other time, he would have invited his guest to come inside, to sit at the kitchen table with a cup of coffee and lay out the whole, wild, complicated story in comfort. But it seemed to him that Skye understood that wasn't an option. He hadn't said as much, but she knew if Isla happened to come downstairs, there would be hell to pay. Aware that Isla didn't know she was there, Skye seemed as though she didn't *want* to come in, didn't even want to chance it for the sake of her grandkids.

Why? The question was on the tip of Luke's tongue. *What's so scary about this? It's just Isla.* But there was no time for that. He had to stay the course.

"Gone," Luke echoed, not quite remembering the meaning of the word. "Gone . . . how?"

"Just gone," Skye said, meeting his eyes.

"So, they ran off, right?" From what Luke understood, Isla and Skye had more problems than a single person could count. Would Isla taking off back then have been so surprising? Perhaps Ruby Mae had had a fight with her own mother and the girls had gone out into the field to talk. Maybe they had whipped themselves up into a frenzy. *I hate my mom! I hate my life!* He could see Gus doing the very same thing—raging, talking himself up, blowing things out of proportion, turning regular teenage angst into something big enough to merit the end of the world.

"Ran off," Skye said. "No. They didn't *run off.* That field was endless. It was flat. No trees. No place to hide. Sunny said she looked out there and saw the biggest raincloud she'd ever set eyes on, like something out of a nightmare. The girls were *gone,* Luke. Both of them."

"I don't . . . I don't understand," he confessed. "No. I mean . . ." He shoved his fingers into his hair. "If Isla was gone, that means she was what . . . found?"

"The police brought her home," Skye said.

"From where, though? Where was she?"

Skye gave him a peculiar look, then. The expression struck him as apologetic. *I'm sorry,* it appeared to say, *but I don't know any more than you do. I'm sorry. I'm her mother. I should have these answers, but I don't. . . .*

"I don't understand," Luke said again. "Did she, like, escape something . . . ? Or was she just lost? I don't . . ." Isla had never mentioned anything that even remotely suggested she'd vanished along with Ruby

Mae. All she'd ever said was that Ruby Mae had disappeared from the prairie behind her aunt Sunny's house. She'd been there one minute and was gone the next.

"Isla had been gone for three days," Skye told him. "A grocery boy noticed her out in the alley in the rain while he was closing up for the night. He said she was clutching her stomach, screaming at the sky." A sad smile crossed Skye's face. "She wasn't the same Isla afterward, I can at least tell you that. Isla had been—" Skye's words came to an abrupt stop. Her eyes darted away from Luke's face.

The front door flew open. Isla stood in the doorway, her hair wild with all the tossing and turning she'd done in bed the night before. She was still donning Luke's Stone Temple Pilots T-shirt and a pair of pajama pants, her toes poking out from beneath too-long hems.

Luke took a few steps away from Skye, his thoughts immediately tumbling headlong into a stream of expletives. *Oh shit, fuck, goddamn it, CHRIST!*

"*What* are you doing here?!" Isla barked, gaping at her mom. But it shifted just as quickly, and suddenly Luke was in her crosshairs. "Oh my God. *You* invited her here?! After everything I've told you?! After everything you *know*?!"

Luke lifted his hands, showing his palms. *Please don't hate me. There's a reason for this, I swear.* He gave her an imploring look. "Isla, listen . . ."

"*Don't you tell me to listen!*" she yelled, and rightfully so. Luke had known the consequences of dialing Skye's number. It had been a betrayal of the highest order, one he had no idea how he would have handled were the tables turned. What if it had been Isla placing the call? What if Luke had experienced trauma at the hands of a parent, and Isla had disregarded his pain and brought that person to their home? He would have been both heartbroken and furious, not to mention feeling cheated and dismissed. But what the hell was he supposed to do, just let her fall apart? Stand back and watch her deteriorate without ever knowing exactly why? They had kids, for Christ's sake, and those kids needed their mom. Skye had been his last, most desperate hope, and now, after what she'd told him, Luke was glad he'd called her.

Isla had been gone for three days.

It was something his wife had never mentioned because she *didn't know.*

"Isla." Skye was brave enough to speak. "I know you want nothing to do with me, but you're in dan—"

"Shut up!" Isla fumed, her face a mask of unforgiving anger. "Shut the *fuck* up!"

Luke tensed at his wife's profanity. It was unlike her, on the edge of something else entirely.

"Get off of my porch," Isla demanded. "Get the fuck off my property. Right *now!*"

"Isla," Skye tried again, her own hands held up in an *I mean no harm* sort of way. "I understand—"

"You don't understand a goddamn thing," Isla hissed, stepping forward, closing the distance between herself and her mother so quickly, Luke was certain Isla was going to pull her arm back and throw a punch. Either that or shove her down the steps. He stared at the two women as Isla came within inches of her mother's face.

And then something changed. It was as though Isla shut down, like someone slammed her power switch. One second, she was coming at Skye, ready to fight; the next, she was standing frozen in place, simply staring at her mother as though unable to identify her face.

" . . . Isla?" Luke hesitated, unsure whether he should reach out to his wife or give her a wide berth. Her sudden silence, her motionlessness . . . it couldn't have been more than a couple of seconds before Skye was looking to Luke, her expression a mix of startled bewilderment and tentative alarm.

"This is it," Skye croaked out. "Oh boy."

Isla continued to stand there, unmoving, stuck in one of her fugues.

"This is exactly why I had to make her leave. It's how she was when she came b—"

Isla's arms shot out, her hands grabbed hold of the sides of Skye's skull, and she began to press her thumbs into the soft tissue of her mother's eyes.

Skye jerked backward. Her bracelets jangled as a terrified yelp escaped her. But Isla's grip was steadfast, and the longer she held Skye captive, the more Luke began to panic.

He bolted forward and grabbed Isla by both her wrists. *"Stop it!"* he yelled into his wife's face, but Isla didn't flinch. He yanked on her hands, but they didn't budge. It was as though they were cemented in place.

Skye was screaming now, her own hands frantically pawing at her daughter's fingers.

"Jesus!" Luke yelled. "Jesus, *Isla! Let go!"*

He continued to fight her despite his own disbelief. Was this really taking place? The constant, frantic jangle of Skye's collection of bracelets assured him that yes, he was in fact awake. But before he could figure out what the next steps would be, there was commotion inside the house. One of the girls was shrieking. Was one of his daughters crying out in alarm because Skye was howling in pain? Were they seeing this shit? Their mother's hands clamped against the sides of a stranger's head, trying to crack it like an egg?

Luke could only halfway glance to Willow as she stumbled onto the front porch, her face shifting from afraid to mortified. *"Mom?!"* Juxtaposed over his mother-in-law's wailing, Willow's fearful timbre made Luke want to scream for it all to stop.

This can't be real. It can't be. No fucking way.

But as soon as Willow cried out, Luke felt Isla relax, and abruptly her arms fell to her sides. There was a beat of breathlessness, of wondering whether she would rebound and rush back at Skye, who was now clutching her hands over her injured face. But rather than attacking a second time, Isla blinked once, turned to Willow, and stood there as though nothing had happened, like she hadn't just tried to force Skye's eyes back into their sockets, Little Jack Horner sticking his thumb into a pie.

Isla remained silent, her eyes fixed on Willow.

"What is it?" Luke finally asked her. "What's wrong?"

"Sophie's gone," Willow wept. "I can't find her anywhere."

Isla said nothing.

"What do you mean? Where have you looked?" Luke demanded.

"Everywhere!" Willow insisted. "I swear, she's not anywhere!"

Isla suddenly pushed past Willow and darted up the stairs.

Knocking hard into Eden's shoulder as she ran past, Willow went in the opposite direction, rushing deeper into the living room, as if hoping her baby sister was playing a prank, hiding beneath the coffee table or behind the far side of the couch. "Sophie?!"

"Jesus, what's going on?" Eden asked, bewildered. Olive matched her expression as she appeared in the foyer behind her.

"Who's screaming?" Olive asked. "Was that Mom?"

Meanwhile, Skye was stumbling down the porch steps, her broomstick skirt swishing around her ankles. She paused beside her RV, the door to the vehicle held open by a hand. Luke could see his mother-in-law vacillate between staying and getting the hell out of there, never to return.

"Dad!" Eden made wide eyes at him. "What's happening?"

"We can't find your little sister," Luke told her, but he was distracted by what Skye had told him.

This is how she was when she came back.

"What . . . ?" Eden shot back, because how could that be? "Mom?" She darted inside, leaving Luke and Olive on the front porch.

Luke held up a hand to Skye. *Please, just wait.* He was tempted to rush down the steps, to beg her not to go. He'd called her because he needed help, and now he needed it more than ever. Because holy shit, what had he just witnessed? What the fuck *was* that? And missing for three days?

This is how she was when she came back.

"Skye," he began, taking a forward step to meet her out in the yard. But he didn't make it far, nearly jumping when the house phone rang. The sound of an actual wired telephone; it was the landline Luke refused to get rid of because Sophie, Willow, and Olive didn't have their own phones yet.

Turning back to the house, he watched Olive move toward the wall-mounted relic just shy of the foyer. That thing hardly ever rang, the ringer set so loud it just about shook the windows in their frames. For a second, Luke wondered if she'd even know how to answer the damn thing. Of course she did. She reached out, lifted the receiver from the cradle, and held it to her ear.

"Hello?"

Olive's voice was faint from inside the house, but something about the whole situation had Luke frozen in place. Seconds later, he watched the color drain from her face.

"No, he isn't. I—yes. No, Mrs. Rodriguez, I don't think—" She paused. "Hello? Mrs. Rodriguez, are you there? Hello . . . ?" Pulling the receiver away from her face, she peered at it as though suddenly bewildered by what it was.

"What?" Luke asked. "What's going on with Mrs. Rodriguez?"

Olive met her father's eyes. "I don't get it," she confessed. "She can't find Sebastian. She says he's missing, too."

39

WILLOW

Willow couldn't say it out loud, but deep down she was glad Sebastian was missing. It meant both he and Sophie may have been together. Maybe, having made some super confusing plan, those two decided to run away from home together. It was weird, but she supposed anything was possible.

Except that didn't make a whole lot of sense. Sophie was the last kid on earth who would have run away. At five years old, Willow's baby sister continued to be surprisingly helpless. Dad still brushed her teeth for her, and sometimes she got her arms pinned inside her T-shirts while getting dressed. She couldn't fall asleep without a bunch of white noise and spinning stars lighting up the room like a nighttime carnival. She'd only started tying her shoes a few months ago, and now she was on the run? *No way*, Willow thought. *Not even if Sebastian asked her to. Not even if she was scared of Mom.* Because what the heck had that been out on the porch, anyway? Willow had only caught a glimpse of her mother's hands around Grandma's head, but man, did it remind her of what Rowan had done to Sophie the morning her hearing had miraculously returned. *Maybe that's it*, she thought. *Maybe Sophie ran away because of Rowan.* But that was also unlikely. After all, the kid could hardly manage a peanut butter and jelly sandwich on her own. That, and then there was the most important detail of all. Unicorny was on Sophie's bed, and if Sophie had planned on going anywhere, that Squishmallow would have been right with her.

But if Sophie didn't leave home willingly, then . . .

Willow's stomach churned. Then where had she gone, and with whom?

Making her way back up to the second floor after yet another search of the house, Willow stopped mid-step while climbing the stairs. She'd been up and down those risers numerous times that morning, checking all the closets and bathrooms, looking under every bed twice. She'd even pawed through the dirty clothes hamper in Gus's room, which had been disgusting. She had no idea *why* her sister would have been hiding in there, but she'd checked regardless. And she'd come up empty.

Now it seemed as though there was nowhere else to look, and no one to brainstorm with. Willow was practically alone in the house; Mom and Dad had jumped into the car to search at the Rodriguez place. Olive was running around outside yelling Sophie's name, and Eden was on the front porch with their mother's laptop, calling everyone in Mom's contact list. Right then, with the house startlingly quiet, the fleeting thought of an intruder left Willow breathless and dizzy.

Her mind spun back to the day before, to when she'd seen a figure dash behind the barn. She thought she'd seen someone run across the rooftop as well, but finally decided it had simply been a trick of the light, especially when Gus had shown up a minute later, decked out in his typical black clothes. It had made more sense to assume the person she'd seen on their property had been her brother, not some stranger looking for trouble. But now her head was spinning . . . because what if?

"Oh no," Willow said softly, her heart thudding loud enough to make her ears ring. *"Oh no."* If it *had* been an intruder, her little sister's disappearance would be partly Willow's fault. She hadn't pushed Dad hard enough to investigate further. Gus had shown up, and everyone had immediately moved on, the incident forgotten. She had kept thinking about it, the whole thing not sitting right, but she'd convinced herself it was nothing, had told herself, *You're making it more of a big deal than it is. It was Gus.* She'd let it go. God, she'd *let it go.* And now Sophie may have been kidnapped.

How could Willow have been so stupid? There were all those bill-boards around town, all the missing kids from across the state. Had Willow pushed harder, maybe Dad would have gone outside and caught the culprit. Sophie would still be home. Safe. Where she belonged. But Willow couldn't think that way.

There was still one more possibility, however slim.

The woods.

Pivoting on the staircase, Willow did an about-face and jogged back down to the foyer. She stopped next to the front door, eavesdropping as Eden spoke to someone on the phone.

"Yes, we've called the police. . . . No, they're not making us wait."

With her stomach twisted in knots, Willow considered her options. She could ask her big sister for help and risk Eden vetoing the plan, or she could just go by herself. Somehow Willow knew Eden would prohibit a trip into the woods, especially with the explanation of why she wanted to look there.

That meant Willow was on her own. No matter how scared she was, she had to go into the trees behind her mother's garden. She had to follow her gut this time, which told her that Sophie was out there.

She had to be.

40

ISLA

Isla couldn't think straight. Her pulse was hammering against the curve of her skull. Mid-panic, she started to feel the onset of a migraine, the glimmer of auras that would leave her half-blind for hours. The pressure inside her head was intense, the ringing in her ears making it that much more unbearable.

But there was something else, confusing and ghastly, in the way Luke was looking at her. He had said all of three words since they'd climbed into the car, but she could feel him peering at her every few seconds, as if . . . waiting for *her* to speak.

His sideways glances were getting under her skin, irritating, because if anything, it should have been the direct opposite. She looked out the window, the thought of him calling her mother—her *mother!*—igniting anger deep inside her gut. But there wasn't time to argue about that now, was there? Or to ask him what he'd said to Skye after Isla had gone upstairs. Isla had glanced out the window just in time to catch Luke standing with Skye next to her RV, Luke's hand on her shoulder. *Sorry, Isla is crazy,* he'd probably told her. *Yeah, she's just absolutely nuts.*

Skye's hands had been pressed against her face as though in a fit of tears, which had turned Isla's stomach. Oh the histrionics. *She's never loved me!* Skye had likely wailed. *I'm her mother! Where's the compassion? Where's the respect?*

At least, that's how Isla imagined the exchange. But there wasn't time to demand answers now, to ask how Luke could not only invite that woman to their house, but go out there and comfort that traitor, that toxic monster, while Isla was upstairs losing her mind over not being able to find their youngest child.

They passed a billboard, and Isla's heart sputtered to a stop. For a split second, she swore it had been Sophie's face plastered up there. Sophie, with her blond pigtails and wide grin. Isla tore her eyes away from the image. Meanwhile, she could still feel Luke stealing glances at her, as though trying to figure something out.

Isla suddenly realized that she was in the same position she'd been in at sixteen, only Ruby Mae was replaced by Sophie, and her mother was replaced by Luke. This time, Luke shooting suspicious glances her way as though Isla was somehow behind this entire nightmare.

"What do you want?" she finally asked, unable to help herself. If he kept looking at her that way, she was going to pull open the door and jump out onto the road. Or better yet, grab the steering wheel and veer them into another ravine. Did he really think she was responsible for Sophie's disappearance? Would he say this was her fault?

"What do you mean, what do I want?" Luke asked.

She clenched her jaw at his tone.

When she looked away from him in stony silence, he exhaled an oddly shaky breath.

"Jesus, Isla, you could have put her in the hospital," he told her. "What's the matter with you?"

What? What was he talking about? Was it the way she'd grabbed Olive by the arm to get her attention just before she and Luke ran out to the car? *Check outside! Check everywhere! Find your sister!* Or the way she'd shoved her laptop against Eden's chest on the way out the door? She'd been a little rough with the girls, but she'd been in a blind panic. Was Luke really going to hold that against her? And surely her actions hadn't been anything close to putting anyone in the—

"Your mother!" Luke said sharply. "Why are you acting like you don't know what I'm talking about?!" He glared at her, both annoyed and confused. "Jesus, Isla, what the fuck?!"

Isla stared back at him, her chest suddenly tight, that uncomfortable feeling of reoccurrence throwing off her equilibrium despite her sitting down. She pressed a hand to her forehead, trying to wait out the vertigo.

"What do you mean, nearly put her in the hospital?" she asked, attempting to keep her tone even, daring to peek at him only to see his expression become that much more incredulous. She turned to watch the trees fly past, hoping to God another one of those billboards didn't cross her line of sight. If it did, she was convinced she'd bash her head against the window.

There was a long, uncomfortable silence. Finally, Luke spoke again: "You don't remember what happened? How is that possible?"

Isla shifted her weight, trying to appear as though she was simply restless in the passenger seat when, in reality, she was desperate to cover her mouth with a hand. She didn't want him to see her quake with emotion, desperate to hide the dread she was certain was plastered across her face.

Because she'd been here before, in this very same place.

How can you not remember?! her mom had yelled, convinced that the louder her inquiry, the more Isla's memory would be jogged.

Ruby Mae is gone, Isla, and you were with her! What happened?! Where is she?! How can you not know?!

"You grabbed your mother by her head," Luke said, dragging Isla back into the conversation. "By the *head*, Isla. One second you were cursing her out, telling her to get off our porch and out of our lives. The next, you were trying to gouge her eyes out with your thumbs. I couldn't get you off her. You only let go when you heard Willow yelling from inside the house."

Leaning back against the passenger seat, Isla tightened her hands into fists. She had been trying to ignore the warning signs, had tried to tell herself it wasn't real, but this was proof. She was losing time again.

Things had begun to slip after Adam had died. It had happened with the five other babies before him too, starting with the one she'd been carrying the night her mother had kicked her out of the house. She'd go to bed feeling fine but would wake up blood-soaked and hollow. Afterward, she'd spend months feeling off, only half herself. It was easy to blame it on postpartum depression and grief. What she hadn't done was accept that after each baby had vanished, the shadows became more frequent. What she had refused to put together until just then was, over the past twenty-some-odd years, the figures didn't just appear *after* she lost a child, but before as well. Long before. As though waiting for what they knew would come. They'd show up more and more often, almost as though playing a game: How many appearances would it take to convince Isla they were real?

But she never believed.

Instead, she blamed her mother.

She passed down the crazy.

And then, as if to hammer home that very likely possibility, she'd start to lose time; she'd zone out. Go to bed like normal and wake up on the living room couch, or in one of the kids' bedrooms, or at the kitchen table, just sitting there in a stiff-backed chair. She'd hop in the shower to clear her mind, and a second later, Luke would be checking to see if she was okay because nearly an hour had passed and the water was freezing cold. Every time those blips in time started to arise, she'd book an appointment with her doctor. If there *was* something going on with her, it was the responsible thing to do. That's when the doctor would order a battery of tests, and lo and behold, she'd be pregnant. And so the hallucinations would be chalked up to nothing more than pregnancy hormones. The lost time? Exhaustion and fatigue. The waking up in random rooms? Maybe sleepwalking. Who knew? Who cared? She and Luke were having a baby. Celebrate. Start planning the nursery. Forget the past. Never *ever* remember the past.

And she *would* forget the past, at least for a little while; at least until the shadows came back, lingering in her peripheral vision, daring her to look their way. *Hormones,* she told herself over and over. *Hormones, it's just the hormones.* But every baby that made her wild with those hormones? Every single one had been lost, as though her body had issued a warning, waving a red flag: *You can't have this one. This one isn't yours to keep.*

"Isla."

Luke's voice shook her. She shuddered but kept her eyes focused on the trees.

"What?" she whispered, the inquiry hardly audible past the growing buzz in her ears.

"Your mom, she said something weird," Luke noted. "It was about Ruby Mae, about when she went missing."

"Why did you call her?" Isla asked, not wanting to hear about Ruby Mae—not with Sophie missing, the sense of déjà vu pressing down on her like a million-pound weight. Talking about Ruby Mae would send her over the edge because, and perhaps Luke had forgotten, Ruby Mae never came home. She was *still* missing, a Golden Colorado cold case. They hadn't found a body. And now Sophie was . . .

No. Isla needed to shift the narrative. *Don't think that! Don't go there. Just don't . . .*

"I've told you so much about how she hurt me, about how she abandoned me," Isla said.

"I know, I just—"

"I was homeless because of her," Isla reminded him. "She put me out on the street, Luke. I was only around Eden's age, for God's sake. You know all that. But you called her anyway. We already tried to reconcile when August was born. I *tried*, but she just never . . ." Never seemed like she wanted to be part of Isla's life. Like she still expected Isla to make things right after Ruby Mae somehow; Isla, still guilty despite not having done anything wrong. "You *invited* her," Isla accused. "How could you bring her to our home?"

Luke looked straight ahead, his face drifting between sadness, worry, and regret. She could tell he hadn't wanted to call her, but he'd done it anyway, and now . . .

"What are we going to do?" she asked, turning her eyes back to the pines. "There aren't enough billboards in the world for them all. How will we find one for Sophie? What are we going to do?"

"She said you disappeared too," Luke cut in, his tone softer now. "It hadn't just been Ruby Mae."

Every muscle in Isla's body tensed, and without warning she was outside herself. She felt herself smile, felt herself shake her head just the slightest amount, felt herself about to lurch forward, grab the wheel, send the car careening off the road and into a tree. All involuntarily. All of it like puppetry, tugged by invisible strings. Something twisted inside her abdomen—a vicious cramp trying to fold her in half. The noise in her head was suddenly intolerable, a new bloom of pain forming deep inside her right ear canal. She clamped her hand over it, doubled over and let out a whine.

"God, what?" Luke asked.

Isla sensed the car slowing down.

Behind her closed eyes, she could see Ruby Mae out there on the prairie, far below those massive clouds, descending, apocalyptic.

"Isla?"

She could see the light: a deep red splintering across the sky.

There's something up there!

A shadow, round and flat.

Do you see it?

"Yes," she whimpered, "I see it."

"Isla . . . ?" Luke's voice sounded so far away. "See what?"

But before she could answer, it all overtook her. The twisting pain of her stomach. The needling inside her head. The sudden flash of light. The shadows leaning in, leaning over, staring down at her.

What?

She didn't know what she was seeing, didn't know who they were. But she was sure it was a memory.

Not imagined.

This time, she was sure it had been real.

41

OLIVE

Her mother told her to find Sophie, so Olive was frantically searching the property. But she also recognized the act for what it was: futile. The fact of the matter was if Sophie had run off, she could have been anywhere by now.

Their property was only a few acres, but property lines made no difference when there were no fences to mark them. When they had first moved to the farmhouse, Olive had been about Sophie's age. They had come from a nice house in the suburbs. Their old neighborhood had flat sidewalks, perfect for riding bikes. It had fancy lampposts that clicked on at dusk. But Mom wanted to live out in the country, so they had packed up their stuff and moved here, where things were more relaxed. Olive didn't have to get up to catch the school bus anymore. She could pick wildflowers and sit in the sun as long as she wanted. She remembered going on walks with her dad, Gus, and Eden. They'd lace up their hiking boots and traipse out the door, straight into the woods that butted up to their property. Mom called it "nature school." Olive called it fun. She remembered spending entire days in those trees, eating bologna and cheese sandwiches, scavenging for walking sticks. There were streams to cross, hills to climb. They studied moss and tadpoles and mushrooms and animal tracks. Olive had no idea how wide the forest beyond their homestead was, but it appeared to go in every direction.

Meanwhile, on the opposite side of the house, the highway unspooled like a ribbon. If Sophie crossed the road at the end of their driveway, she'd find herself in a millet field. They'd studied out there, too. If Sophie ran through it all the way, there was another grove of trees with a railroad track beyond. Follow the track, and who knew where you'd end up. Denver, maybe. Or Oz's Winkie Country, ruled by the Wicked Witch of the West.

Olive had her fingers crossed that Sophie was at the Rodriguez place, that both she and Sebastian were together, messing around, and that Mrs. Rodriguez had simply missed them somewhere out among her cottonwood trees. But even as she talked herself into that possibility, her logical brain persuaded her that it was unfeasible. The Rodriguez place was too far away. How did a five-year-old get miles down the road on her own? It was impossible, right? Preposterous, as her favorite books would have said. Audacious, if Sophie really did run away on purpose.

"Ludicrous," Olive murmured beneath her breath. "Nonsensical," she continued, allowing the vocabulary of Jane Austen and Louisa May Alcott to soothe her nerves.

She was supposed to be searching, but she was doing a terrible job. The sun was blinding. The heat was starting to beat down on her shoulders in a brutal sort of way. She could feel it through her sleep shirt, burning the part of her neck that wasn't protected by her thick braid of hair. She reached back to yank the elastic off the end of her ponytail, then unraveled the plait as she winced against the glare.

"Sophie?" she called out, then squinted at the figure spied just beyond her mother's garden. "Shit," she said quietly, because there. Right *there*. Sophie was standing just shy of the trees. If she ducked into the thicket, it could lead to another hour or two of hide-and-seek.

"Sophie?!"

Sophie didn't answer, didn't even look her way.

"God, what the hell?" Olive huffed, then fell into a full-on sprint.

Her long hair flew out behind her. By the time she reached the garden fence, she was winded and sweating.

"Sophie!" she yelled again, but rather than it being her youngest sister—

Willow spun around, wide-eyed, spooked and insistent.

"Damn it, Willow—I thought you were Sophie!" Olive exclaimed, then peered at the back of her sister's head. "Why didn't you answer me when I—"

"Shhh!" Willow hissed. "I'm trying to listen."

"Listen for what?" Olive asked, yanking the glasses off her face and wiping the sweat from the bridge of her nose.

Willow didn't respond for a few beats, creeping closer to the tree line. It almost looked as though she was stalking an animal. Almost, because there was nothing there.

"Crap, Willow, what are you doing?" Olive asked, annoyed that her sister was screwing around out here rather than helping her search. "Sophie could be anywhere, and you're standing around doing what?" She readjusted her glasses and gave her younger sister an aggravated sort of look.

"Trying to listen," Willow loud-whispered through her teeth, then shot Olive an annoyed look of her own. "But I guess that's over and done with now that *you're* here."

"Listen for *what*? Did you see her out there?"

God, she hoped not. The forest was thick. It was what Dad called dark woods, where the canopy blocked out the sun. The Hansen Nature School had taken place long before Sophie could participate in their foraging and hikes. If Sophie had wandered in there, they'd have to organize a search party. Cops and dogs. The whole community would have to come out to sweep the trees like on those documentaries Eden liked so much. Unless . . . *oh no.* Unless they were too busy searching for all the other kids. What if there was no one left to look for her? What if, when they called for help, the authorities told them, *Sorry, folks. We don't have the resources for that. Maybe find your own kid?*

"Please tell me you didn't see her out there," Olive said, instantly on the verge of tears.

"No, but I think she might be out there anyway."

"Why there? If she came out here, she could have gone in any direction, right?"

Willow frowned at that idea. "I guess," she said.

"Sophie's a scaredy cat," Olive reminded them both, desperate to convince herself that the woods weren't a possibility, that Sophie would never ever choose to go out there alone. "Why would she go into the forest by herself?" Heck, why would she leave the house? She couldn't even ride a bike without training wheels. Where did she think she'd end up, anyway?

"Why do you assume she went in by herself?" Willow asked, dumbfounded, as if confused as to why Olive wasn't putting the puzzle together. "Has everyone gone nuts? Why isn't anyone freaking out that maybe someone came and *took* her?"

"What? *Took her?*" Olive asked, flabbergasted. "Who would come in and take her while everyone was home?" That made as much sense as Sophie taking off on her own.

"The billboards, Olive," Willow said. "Duh."

"No." Olive refused to entertain the idea. "We have a security system. It didn't go off, which means nobody was in the house, right? Nobody beyond us. That's how security systems work, Willow."

Willow said nothing. She looked away from Olive, turned back to the woods, and crossed her arms over her chest in a protective sort of stance.

"Dad forgets to set the alarm sometimes," she remarked in a low voice. "You know that. Mom gets mad when he does it, but every now and again—"

"But he sets it like ninety percent of the time, right?" Olive asked, cutting in. "So, like, someone being able to sneak into the house during the ten percent when it's not on . . . those are crazy odds. Like, they'd have to be mind readers or something. Or, like, have already been inside the house to begin with."

It was then that Willow turned to look directly at her sister. Her expression was stern, making her appear far older. *Do you get it yet?*

"Rowan showed up right here," she said, pointing to her feet. "Just, *poof,* out of nowhere. And yeah, the official people looked and couldn't find anything, but kids don't just survive out in the woods on their own,

Olive. How come a bunch of kids are missing, but Rowan shows up like that? How does that make sense?"

"What does that have to do with the woods?" Olive asked, not liking where her sister was taking the conversation.

"What it has to do with the woods is, no matter if anyone can find them or not, Rowan has a family. *Everyone* has a mom and a dad, otherwise they wouldn't exist. That means they're out there somewhere," she said, pointing into the trees. "And maybe nobody was looking for Rowan when he showed up because that was the plan all along. Maybe he never had a billboard because his family knew exactly where he was this whole time. What if this is all just a big trick?"

A shudder ran down Olive's back.

"A trick?"

"Yeah, you know, like a setup. What if they knew we'd take him in?"

"You mean, they sent Rowan so he'd get inside the house? Like a double agent?"

Willow rolled her eyes. "Whatever. You make it sound so stupid."

Olive was suddenly nauseous, her train of thought hitching inside her head. Yes, it was improbable, but she was convinced Rowan had something to do with every weird thing that had happened to their family since he arrived. And then there was the time she saw him in the kitchen—how he'd appeared in the doorway, then vanished and shown up at the top of the stairs. There was no way he could move that fast unless there was someone there to help him. So, what if there *was* someone? Could someone be hiding in their house without them knowing?

Or maybe Willow was right. Maybe it was all a big lie, and Rowan was faking all of it. Maybe he *could* be fast, maybe—

"Crap." Olive squinted at Willow. "Where *is* Rowan, anyway?" She'd assumed Eden was keeping an eye on him, but Eden was outside with their mother's laptop, making phone calls. Their parents hadn't taken Rowan with them, either. Dad had yelled at them to watch him, but Mom had squawked for everyone to look for Sophie. It had been confusing.

Chaotic. But if Eden was on the porch, and both she and Willow were out near the woods . . .

Slowly both girls turned their attention back to the house.

"Olive . . . who's home?" Willow asked.

"Just . . . just Eden, I think?" Olive asked, uncertain of her answer.

There was silence between them, then the two girls looked back at each other before booking it away from the garden and across the wild grass.

Olive angled herself toward the back door, the closest port of entry, but Willow yelled between heaving breaths, "She's on the front porch!"

Olive followed her little sister, who was remarkably fast. But when they rounded the corner, the front porch was vacant. Eden had gone inside. The two girls burst into the house, but the place was as quiet as a casket buried deep beneath the earth, an altogether different sort of silence than Olive was used to. This was all-encompassing, like walking into a sensory deprivation chamber. As odd as it was, the quiet was overpowering, so loud it made her head hurt. She winced when Willow called out, her voice booming through the soundlessness of the rooms.

"Eden!"

They waited, holding their breaths, listening for footsteps overhead, for the creak of floorboards or the familiar groan of pipes. But there was nothing. Suddenly, rather than looking for Sophie, both Olive and Willow were splitting up, looking for Eden. Willow continued to call out to their big sister while Olive dashed up the stairs, then quickly scrambled to a stop at the sight of the empty upstairs hallway.

Once again, that ominous silence drifted across the curve of her right ear. It perched on her shoulder. She could feel it, heavy, soundlessly vibrating with an unseen sort of energy, and the air in the hallway also struck her as unsettling. Breathing it in made Olive's chest tight. It smelled both fresh and oddly metallic. It smelled like rain.

Olive stood motionless for a long while, quaking as she looked ahead toward Eden's room.

"Eden?" she said softly, the atmosphere thick as a blanket. Olive was reminded of the quiet that settled over everything after a thick snowfall. The weight of it assured her that her voice hadn't traveled more than a few inches past her lips before falling to her feet like a stone.

Tears sprang to her eyes as she forced herself to move. The hallway seemed to stretch out before her, longer, longer still, promising that no matter how many steps she took, she'd never reach Eden's room at the end.

She tried to push on, telling herself that this uncanny tension, this weird energy, was all in her head. It was fear. Anxiety. The peculiarity of the past few days was finally coming down on her. But if she just kept moving, she'd reach Eden's room. Of course she would. That's how reality worked.

But her nerves brought her to a standstill. Her fingers curled up, her hands forming fists. She only realized she was clenching her teeth when her jaw began to ache and only understood where exactly in the hall she'd stopped when she slowly turned her head to the right.

Rowan's room.

The longer she stared at that door, the more she swore something was shifting before her very eyes. At first it looked like a shimmer, but no . . . it was less of a flicker and more of a soundless vibration. The door was pulsating.

Check your glasses, she told herself, automatically yanking the lenses from her face. There was something wrong with her glasses, right? There had to be. *Yes, of course. Yes, it has to be.* She stood there, quaking, her teeth suddenly chattering against themselves. But despite her body telling her otherwise, she forced herself to believe that what she was seeing was not, could not, *would* not be real.

"Olive!" Willow bellowed from the first floor.

Olive jumped. She nearly squealed. Her glasses fell to her feet, and she scrambled to grab them, shoving them back onto her face. She gave Rowan's door one final look before pivoting in place and rushing down the hall, taking the stairs two at a time. She found Willow standing on the front porch, framed in the open doorway. At first, it appeared as though she was out there alone, but as Olive got closer, she noted that Willow was looking at something to her right.

"What is it?" Olive asked, her voice quaking.

No answer.

" . . . God, what—" Olive stepped onto the porch, finally laying eyes upon what had Willow so spooked.

There, sitting on the porch as though she'd been there the whole time, was Eden.

"No," Olive said. "That can't be."

Except it wasn't the Eden they knew. She was sitting in one of the rocking chairs, motionless. Blank-faced. Staring. Olive was tempted to reach out and touch her big sister, to check and see if she was still warm, still breathing. The only thing that kept her from doing so was the sudden, single blink of Eden's eyes. The only movement beyond that was Eden's hair blowing gently across her face.

"We would have seen her," Olive said, her tone strained. "She wasn't here, Willow. We would have *seen* her." She took a backward step and turned toward her little sister, opening her mouth to protest yet again— *this is nonsense, this can't be, I know what I saw*—but her indignance was lost in the summer breeze. Because there, on the opposite side of the door occupying their mother's rocker . . . was Rowan.

And he hadn't been there before, either.

Of that, she was a hundred percent certain.

42

LUKE

Luke had his hand on Isla's back, trying to comfort her as she groaned into her lap. Had the circumstances been different, he wouldn't have thought twice about flooring it to the emergency room, but things weren't that simple anymore. Not with Sophie missing. Not with time working against them.

"Isla," he said, afraid to speak beyond a whisper. Isla was clutching at her ears as though something was exploding within her skull. It wasn't clear if she could hear him from behind her palms, and she *had* to hear him right now. "What do you want me to do?" he asked, louder this time. "Do you want to go to the hospital? Should I—"

"No!" Isla jerked her head up from its bow. She gave him a desperate sort of look. He half expected her to ask him why they were driving around and not at home.

"Find Sophie!" she wailed, her face red from whatever awful ache was boring into her ear canal. Despite Isla's desperate plea, relief flooded over him. Because at least she remembered what they were doing out on the highway. At least she remembered their youngest daughter's name.

"Okay," he said, pushing himself back into the driver's seat. "Just tell me if you need anything, all right?"

"Go," Isla said, then looked away from him with a grimace. Luke shoved the sedan into drive and pressed his foot against the gas, easing into an eighty-mile-per-hour sprint down a highway marked fifty-five, praying that nothing like a rabbit or a deer dashed out into the road. At that speed, he knew it would be over. But if they didn't find Sophie, it was over anyway.

When they arrived at the Rodriguez place, Clara Rodriguez's property was full of cars and pickup trucks. Luke jumped out of the sedan as soon as it was in park, leaving his door open in case Isla called out to him. Strangers turned their heads to look his way—some of the men wore cowboy hats; all of them wore cowboy boots. They were talking fast, their dark eyes squinting at the stranger coming up the driveway.

"¿Quién es este?" he heard one ask another.

Luke lifted a hand. "I'm Clara's neighbor," he explained. "My daughter, Sophie . . . she's missing."

"Missing," one of the cowboys repeated, his Mexican accent thick as molasses. "Like Sebastian?"

"Like everyone!" one of the men exclaimed, throwing his hands into the air.

"They might be together," Luke told them. "I don't know. I . . ." Suddenly he found himself at a loss, the terror of his daughter actually being lost finally sinking in. "Jesus," he said, trying to wrap his mind around it while simultaneously rejecting the idea. No, Sophie wasn't gone—they just didn't know where she was. This wasn't like those other billboard kids. No way. They just had to look harder, be more efficient.

"¿Dónde está la policía?" one of the older men asked the group. Someone muttered that they didn't know. Another grabbed his phone out of his pocket and started to dial a number. Luke scanned their faces. They all had a slight resemblance to one another, to Clara Rodriguez. Family, no doubt. With expressions heavy with concern, their faces grew that much more startled when a wail came from inside the house.

Luke pivoted from where he stood, convinced that it was Isla despite the sound coming from the opposite direction. Nothing made sense to him right now, so why should this? Except it wasn't Isla. It was Clara, bursting out of the house and running toward the group of men. They rushed toward her as she wept, everyone speaking rapidly and frantically in Spanish, so quick and clipped Luke could no longer guess what they were saying.

Luke looked back to the car, wondering if he should check on his wife or proceed forward. Would the group even allow him to get any closer with Clara in such a state? He shoved his hands into his hair, not knowing what to do, the sun beating down on his face with an offensive relentlessness. The world was falling apart, but it was still hotter than hell outside.

"Luke!"

He jumped at his name being called. Clara stumbled forward, her steps an unsettling, perpetual reeling.

"Did you find her?!" Clara asked, her face puffy from crying, her expression pleading as she waited for good news. "Did you find Sophie?!" But Luke had no good news to offer. He shook his head, mute and diverting his eyes, not wanting to voice his failure in case it sealed some sort of fate. He didn't want to see Clara's face when he admitted no progress had been made.

"Oh God," Clara wept. "Oh Jesus, what is happening? Where are my babies?"

Luke's focus jumped to Clara's face, witnessing her anguish in full. "What did you say?" he asked, positive that he'd misheard her. He swore she'd said *babies*, plural.

"They're gone!" Clara cried. "All of them! Sebastian. Then Maya just an hour ago. I put Claudia in her crib to look for Maya, but I just went in her nursery and . . ." She faltered, reality choking her words. "Oh God," she whispered.

Luke gaped at her, dumbfounded. He only realized his mouth had fallen open when Clara reached for him, her hands tight on his forearms.

"What's going on?" she asked him, her eyes wide, imploring. "How is this possible, Luke? Who would take our children? Who would do this? Who?"

That word rang out like a sorrowful church bell inside his head. *Who?* The idea of Sophie being one of the missing seized him by the chest, forcing the air from his lungs. He looked down to the tips of his old Vans and began counting backward from ten. If he counted slowly, maybe all this madness would sort itself out by the time he got to one.

His phone rang when he reached four, and he lost count. Scrambling for the device, he pulled it from his pocket, and there on his screen was Eden's baby picture. His kids were calling him. A flare of hope ignited deep within his chest. This was it, then. The counting had worked. Sophie was found.

"Hello?" he asked, his voice strangely hoarse, as though he'd been screaming out loud instead of just inside his head.

"Dad?"

The sound of Olive's voice should have been a comfort. He expected a wave of relief, but the opposite came. Olive was using Eden's phone—a device that never left his eldest daughter's side. That, and Olive's tone wasn't one of celebration. If they'd found Sophie, he would have known the split second he'd answered the call. Olive would have been laughing, overjoyed. *We found her! Everyone can stop worrying! The world isn't ending! We found her, Dad. She's safe. She's home!*

"Olive?" His throat was suddenly as parched as the dirt beneath his feet. When the hell was the last time they had gotten any rain? Two months ago? Three?

"Dad, can you come home?" Olive asked, her voice unsteady.

"What's happening?" he questioned, suddenly picturing the worst. Maybe they *had* found Sophie, but it was contrary to a happy discovery. What if they'd found her in the woods and uncovered something awful?

Panic seized him all over again.

"Jesus, Olive. What?!" He gripped his phone so hard he could practically hear his knuckles crack. "Did you find her?"

There was a long, excruciating pause, then: "No. It's Eden. There's something wrong with her, Dad. There's something really, really wrong. Please hurry. Come home as soon as you can."

43

WILLOW

Willow stood on the front porch, peering past the glare of the sun toward the highway running along the front of their property line. She'd been waiting to see Dad's car come flying down the road but found herself distracted by the big bus-like thing that was now parked along the road, just down the way.

She'd overheard Eden. *Grandma.* Willow supposed the bus was hers.

What exactly had gone on between her mother and "Grandma" that morning wasn't something Willow was able to piece together on her own. She'd heard yelling from the front porch, had noticed the curious vehicle parked in front of their house from the bedroom window. Willow hadn't wanted Sophie eavesdropping on whatever was going on outside, so she'd wandered off to find her baby sister . . . and discovered Sophie gone. By the time Willow had started to panic, unable to find Sophie anywhere, the yelling outside had turned into a garbled scream, like someone had been hurt. And when she had run out onto the front porch to tell her parents Sophie was nowhere to be found, she'd caught a glimpse of Mom's hands wrapped around the unknown woman's head. *Grandma.* It had reminded her of the way Rowan had pressed his hands against Sophie's face the morning before, and for a moment she'd been positive it was *exactly* the same action—an attempt to crush a skull, to dig fingers into a brain. The news of Sophie's disappearance had tumbled out of her as a sort of impulsive verbal tic. As soon as it had, her mom's arms had dropped to her sides, like a robot powering down. It had been so bizarre the way Mom had just looked at her while Willow had cried about not being able to find Sophie. It had been confusing how Mom had simply gone inside, as if she hadn't heard the news, or hadn't wanted to hear it, or simply wasn't interested at all. And then there was the mysterious driver stumbling down the front steps—"Grandma"—frightened, hands pressed over her eyes.

Suddenly the dumbest, simplest idea struck her.

"Oh crap." Willow spun around to look at Olive. "That bus!"

Olive was kneeling next to Eden's rocking chair, clasping their eldest sister's hands in her own. Rowan had slunk back inside. Not surprising, as Willow had given him a vicious look. *What did you do to Eden? Where's Sophie, you stupid freak?* She had thought the words but hadn't had the guts to shout them. Like it mattered, anyway. What was Rowan going to do, suddenly understand her?

But now Olive squinted as if to say she didn't get it. "The bus?" she asked.

"*That* thing," Willow said, pointing to the big vehicle parked along the highway just shy of their house. "Olive, Sophie's probably in there!"

Olive stared at her for a beat, then snorted, as if flabbergasted that she hadn't thought of it first. "Oh my God." She nearly laughed the words. "Yes . . ."

Willow bounced up and down, waiting for Olive to say the word.

"Yes, go!" Olive urged her.

Willow bolted down the steps, booking it across the property toward the vehicle, feeling the grass and weeds whip across her calves and ankles, stinging like nettles, leaving thin scratches along her legs that would burn for days. But she kept running, her ballet flats pounding the earth until she hit the highway. She stopped on the cracked asphalt, wincing as she lifted her hand to shield her face from the blinding glare the RV's massive windshield threw across her eyes. And it was then, as soon as she reached the road, that she noticed something peculiar. It was quiet. Too quiet. There was no buzz or chirp of insects. As a matter of fact, she could no longer feel the hot breeze blowing across her cheeks, or the heat of the sun burning against the back of her neck.

She looked up. The sun was still there.

She then leveled her gaze again only to gasp, because the vehicle, which had been steps away a split second ago, was gone.

Willow spun around to look back at the house, but neither Olive nor Eden were on the front porch. *Where did they go?* But what dropped her stomach were the clouds in the distance, so black and ominous she was sure they couldn't be real. It was something she'd only seen in pictures—massive tornadoes forming above the Kansas plains, giant walls of dust rolling across dry Arizona deserts. Within those clouds beyond her house, lightning flashed in such quick succession, the clouds appeared to glow from within. Transfixed by the storm before her, that's when she saw it high overhead—trails of vibrant red streaking the sky like veins, leaving a faint green haze behind as they disappeared. The otherworldly crimson phenomenon was both beautiful and terrifying, each flash illuminating the sky like a red, beating heart. She stood staring, transfixed, conflicted about whether to stay where she was or run and warn Olive and Eden of the oncoming gale.

But what about Sophie?

Willow spun around to look behind her, half expecting the RV to be back where it had been. But there was nothing but an empty stretch of road.

How?

She hesitated, not knowing what to do. Hesitated until another flash of red lit up the sky, reminding her that while the RV was gone, the farmhouse was still there.

Yes, she *had* to warn her sisters. They had to get down to the basement. If the looming tempest was half as bad as it looked, it would likely tear the house from its foundation and take them with it, up like birds, like angels, like Dorothy spinning out of reality and into Oz.

She forced her weight forward—a runner preparing to leave the block—when the air shifted. Suddenly she could smell ozone. Her mouth went metallic, the same kind of steely taste she'd get after accidentally biting the inside of her cheek.

The clouds were rolling in fast.

The lightning was a strobe.

The sky was turning a dangerous shade of carmine.

You have to warn them, she reminded herself. *You have to get to the house. Now.*

Pushing through her trepidation, Willow began to run. She pumped her arms and legs as fast as she could, ignoring the uneven dirt, risking catching a divot and snapping one of her ankles in two. But just as she began to reach full speed, the scent of petrichor intensified. So did the tinny taste on her tongue. It felt like her feet were leaving the ground, as though she was flying. Scared that she'd fall head over feet, she stopped, crouching down to regain her equilibrium. It was then, in her brief stillness, that the atmosphere became electric. The hairs on her arms stood on end. The braided crown atop her head began to lift, bobby pins tugging upward as if attracted by some invisible magnet overhead. Willow's eyes went wide, and right then she was overcome with the urge to look up.

Do you see it?

Above her, the sky was gone. No storm. No red lightning. There was only a black disc, completely silent, so massive it likely covered the entire acreage of their property, reaching far into Rowan's woods.

Gripped by fear, Willow was left breathless. A cry began to bubble up from her belly. Tears streaked her cheeks as she continued to crane her neck, unable to look away, unable to close her eyes even when a blinding column of light hit her from above. She tried to fight against it as her back arched, but her arms and legs were limp. The cracking of vertebrae popped loud in her ears.

Willow tried to scream as she started to rise, but she couldn't find sound, couldn't even wonder whether she'd see her family again. All the thoughts inside her head—her terror, her need to escape—evaporated, and all at once she had no family.

She couldn't remember their faces.

Couldn't recall their names.

Couldn't remember a single thing about her life. No core memories. Not even how old she was, her favorite color, the book she'd been reading. It all vanished. And when it did, there was nothing left of her.

Nothing but the light.

44

OLIVE

Olive watched Willow do a full sprint across the property to the road, but she'd come to an oddly abrupt stop upon reaching the highway. Olive had called out to her: "Willow? Everything okay?" But Willow hadn't replied. She'd started walking, albeit slowly, across the road, and that was the last Olive had seen of her sister.

It had been a good ten minutes now, and Olive was starting to get worried. How long did it take to check if Sophie was inside an RV? She frowned at the vehicle parked along the road, recalling the way her grandmother had smelled, how her bracelets had jangled. She remembered her father's expression—anxious and worried, a man trying to hide a visitor after the visitor had rung the doorbell. It wasn't hard to figure out that he'd invited Grandma Skye to the house without Mom knowing, like unwittingly inviting a vampire inside. What *was* hard to figure out was why. Olive knew Mom didn't associate with Grandma. Of course Dad knew that too. No, he didn't just know it. He knew *better*. But he'd called Grandma Skye to the house anyway. And now Willow . . . and maybe Sophie, they were out there, inside that woman's RV, and who knew what kind of a person "Grandma" really was? Who knew what she was capable of?

Only their mother, a terrifying thought.

Olive shot a look to Eden.

"Eden," she said softly, "If you can hear me, I could really use your help right now."

Of course Eden didn't respond. She continued to sit statuesque, her eyes glazed over.

Olive didn't know if she could stand there doing nothing much longer. Every bone in her body was telling her to head out to the RV, to check on Willow, to see if Sophie was in there herself. But she was afraid to leave Eden alone, scared that if she did, Rowan would creep out from inside house and . . . what? She didn't know *what.* All she was certain of was that she was suddenly scared to find out.

God, Mom, Dad, where are you?

As if hearing Olive's question, Dad's sedan careened onto the gravel driveway, coming in so fast she worried that, instead of stopping, the car would come barreling through the front of the house. Grabbing Eden by the arm, she wondered how she'd be able to pull her sister to safety if the Honda kept coming. The car was kicking up a cloud of dust as tall as the house, eventually skidding to a stop. Dad seemed to exit the car before it had stopped rolling. Mom remained in the vehicle, staring ahead with a vacant look.

"Olive?!" He ran to her and Eden on the porch, his eyes wide and imploring, his face stricken with a kind of panic she'd never seen before. "Christ—Eden, what's wrong?" His hands caught Eden's biceps. He dropped to his knees, staring up into her face. Olive stepped back, her hand over her mouth.

And then, as casual as could be, Eden blinked her eyes and gave their father a troubled sort of look.

"Dad . . . ?" she asked, canting her head as if seeing their father for the first time. "What's wrong? Did you find Sophie? Is she all right?"

Dad's eyes fixed on Olive, and for a split second she saw it—a look that demanded answers. Olive had pressured him to come back home *now*, sent him into a frenzy. But it looked like Eden was . . . fine? *But how . . . ?*

A moment later, however, Olive watched Dad's anger shift to something entirely different. Their eyes met, and she understood the fear on his face. Eden *looked* okay, but she hadn't been a minute ago, which was exactly what had happened to Mom. *Episodes,* Dad had called them. *She has episodes.*

And now Eden was having them too.

45

LUKE

Eden becoming like Isla rattled Luke more than he'd ever admit. He'd spent about two decades watching his wife slip into zombie-like trances, and those episodes still terrified him. The fact of the matter was there had always been something wrong with Isla, which he could never figure out, and now, whatever that something was may have been slithering beyond her and settling onto the shoulders of their children.

When Luke and Isla first met, those episodes had been few and far between, maybe one every six months, short and quick and something that would scare the hell out of him but soon fade to a dust-and-scratches memory . . . until it happened again. But then he and Isla had started trying for a baby, and that's when her fugues had gotten more intense. Every time Isla got pregnant, the trances would amp up. At first it would be every month, then every two weeks, eventually down to a week and sometimes every few days. *Hormones,* Isla would insist. *The doctor just says it's hormones, Luke.* And he would accept that answer because he didn't know a damn thing. Who was he to tell his wife that "just hormones" was the wrong answer, no matter what the doctor said? Not him. And yet he had to wonder, what kind of hormones made a person sit on the couch looking toward nothing? Or face an empty corner with their back to the room? Of course, Isla didn't remember doing any of those things. Luke would relay the incidents, and she'd touch his arm and offer him a soft smile. *Calm down, it's fine.* But it wasn't fine. Because those fugues? Sometimes they'd increase in frequency and severity until, ultimately, the pregnancy would end in loss. Six times it had come to pass now. Repeatedly, on an endless goddamn loop.

At first, he hadn't noticed the pattern. Even the second miscarriage hadn't helped him connect the dots. It was by the third that he found himself triggered when Isla slipped into a stupor. He had put enough of the puzzle together to understand that the more episodes there were, the less likely the baby would survive. Isla *said* she couldn't remember, but he was certain that at least some part of her did, because it wasn't just trances. She'd get jumpy, as though invisible phantoms were leaping out at her from every corner of the house. *Just hormones.* She'd try to laugh it off when he caught her in those instances, but he could tell it scared the hell out of her, too. Her eyes were always big and glassy, always darting from one side of the room to the other. *Nothing to worry about.* Eventually, Luke began to suspect hallucinations. He started to worry about mental disorders. After all, Isla had made her mother, Skye, sound beyond imbalanced. Perhaps it was genetic. Maybe that was the missing link?

And now Eden was—

"Dad."

Luke snapped back to reality. He could see it in Olive's expression— here he was musing about trancelike states, and he had gone away somewhere, lost in his thoughts, in memories he hadn't considered in quite some time.

"Sorry," he said, then looked back to Eden.

Eden was watching both Luke and Olive with a disconcerting sort of fascination, as though she wasn't clear on what was happening. Like, *Why am I on the porch? Why is everyone so worried? Where have I been and how long have I been there?* He turned away, pained. It was too close to the look Isla wore after she came out of her own episodes of disassociation. An expression of *Who am I?* Of *Who are you?* He had learned to handle it with Isla, but seeing it on Eden's face . . . ?

"Dad, we didn't check there." Olive pointed to Skye's RV. "Willow went to see if Sophie had gone over . . ."

Luke straightened, looking to the recreational vehicle parked along the road. The morning had been such a whirlwind of panic he had practically forgotten Skye was still here. He now glanced toward the RV, honestly surprised to see it there after what Isla had done to her mother—another one of her blackouts, this time coupled with frightening physicality.

"She hasn't come back," Olive said.

His attention bounced back to his daughter. "What?"

"Willow. She's still out there. I was going to go check myself, but I didn't want to leave Eden here alone. I'm worried. I think you should maybe—"

He didn't give Olive the chance to finish her sentence. He was off the porch before the suggestion could be made, marching fast toward the highway. He bristled at the idea of Willow being inside that vehicle by herself. In a fit of fearing regret, Isla had allowed Skye back into her life after Gus had been born, but the reconciliation had lasted less than a week or two. Skye had acted beyond erratic when she had come to meet her grandson. Luke had picked up on a weird sort of apprehension immediately—the way she avoided eye contact with Isla, how she had declined to hold Gus in her arms. After she'd left, Isla had cried for hours. *You see?* she'd said. *She hates me. She can't even find it in her to love my baby.* Luke had agreed then that it would be best for Skye to not have a relationship with their child, with any of their future children. Not after how much trauma she continued to impart onto his wife. Not when the potential of dangerous mental instability loomed large.

And now Willow was in that RV with her. Maybe Sophie, too.

Falling into a jog, Luke reached the RV and banged on the door, calling out into the blistering heat. "Skye? It's Luke. Is Willow with you?"

When no response came, he banged on the door again, this time harder, his knuckles stinging as they rapped against the RV's exterior shell.

"Willow? Sophie?"

Nothing.

Luke's already thrumming pulse increased. He didn't like the silence, hated the fact that he was being met with an unyielding amount of it. Even the breeze seemed to calm, as if not wanting to give away any clues. Was Skye even in there? Jesus, was she okay after what Isla had done?

Luke looked to the seemingly endless grain field across the road, a good five feet tall this time of year. There was a possibility both Sophie and Willow had wandered into those crops, but it was something Luke wasn't ready to consider. He spun back to the RV and banged on the door again, then tried the handle. It was almost shocking when the door popped open. Luke stared at the interior steps, then leaned in, calling out again.

"Skye . . . ?"

No one replied, and Luke was suddenly consumed with an inescapable unease. The RV was Skye's home, her mode of transportation. Had she gone for a walk? No, no way. Not after what she'd gone through that morning. That, and the heat was intense and it was only getting hotter. But what if she'd wandered away from the RV in search of help, walked down the highway in the wrong direction, thinking she was headed toward the house, unaware of her mistake because she'd gone blind after Isla's attack? That idea lingered in his head for a moment—Skye, maybe a mile down the road, passed out and lying on the asphalt, just waiting for some inattentive motorist to come rolling down the tarmac. Luke had run over a rabbit at eighty miles per hour once. . . .

"Oh Jesus," he said, then hefted himself up inside the vehicle. He spotted her immediately, slumped over the tiny table across from the kitchenette. For a few seconds, he was convinced she was sleeping. Her arms were folded beneath her head, in the exact way the teacher told them to do in school. *Heads down.*

Yes, she was asleep. Resting. Except . . . Luke had banged on the RV door three times, and he hadn't been shy about it. Could someone sleep through that? Doubtful. She'd been distraught when she'd left the house, weeping with her hands over her face. She'd told him she was okay when he'd gone out to speak with her, but still, a noontime nap didn't track. Maybe a noontime drink . . .

"Skye . . . ?" He approached slowly, tentatively, scanning the RV's interior for signs of his two missing children. When he arrived at her elbow, her reached out, allowing his fingertips to brush her arm. Still, she didn't move.

He couldn't see her face beneath the wild curls of silver hair, but he didn't need to. All signs pointed to nothing good. He winced as he slid a hand between the table and her chest, lifting her backward out of her slump. The weight of her was proof that this was no joke. The morning had been stressful, disturbing. It could have been a heart attack, a stroke. Hell, after what had gone down with Isla, even blackout drunk would have been in the cards.

"Skye?" He pulled his arm out from beneath her, slid onto the bench seat across from where she sat, and grabbed both her shoulders. Then he pushed.

Skye Berkley flopped backward, her head lolling to one side. Luke gasped at the delicate trails of blood coming from her nose, from one corner of her mouth. But it was her eyes that burned into his brain. They were open wide, stained crimson. The red started at the tear ducts and worked across the sclera. The bleeding stopped just beyond her irises, leaving enough white at the outer edge of each eye to make whatever injury she'd sustained that much more gruesome. Luke leaned as far back in his seat as he could, stunned.

As he breathed out, two words escaped him. "Oh shit."

He didn't know her—not really, anyway—but it didn't change the fact that this was his mother-in-law. That, and he'd never seen a dead body before. To top it off, this wasn't just *died in their sleep* dead. This was something different. Something fucked up. Like out of one of Eden's homicidal podcasts.

Despite himself, he leaned forward to get a closer look, noticing the pinprick-like spots just shy of each of Skye's tear ducts. The tiny marks were ringed in faint purple, as though the tissue around each spot was bruised. The injuries looked as though they were starting to fester. But so quickly? Surely she didn't have those spots a few hours ago. Was it some sort of an allergic reaction? But Jesus, to what?

Backing out of the bench seat, he suddenly needed to get the hell out of there. Those marks were making him think terrible things. Visions of asylum patients strapped to tables and impossibly long probes and malicious-looking hammers skirted his thoughts. And here he was, the guy who had abandoned his own wife at an inpatient facility. . . .

"Christ almighty," he murmured.

But before he could stumble down the steps and back into the relentless sunshine, something beneath Skye's hand caught his attention. It was the corner of a piece of paper. When he slid it out from beneath her palm, his eyes settled upon a small note with a retro-looking roadside motel insignia at the top. Beneath it, strikingly elegant script.

Isla went missing with Ruby. They were gone three days before Isla returned. When she came back, she was different. Her eyes were empty. She wasn't my daughter anymore. When she had her blackouts, she became no one. She became violent. I was afraid, so I pushed her away. I'm so sorry, Isla. I was just so afraid.

At the bottom of the page, she'd written a list of names.

John Larusso. Abigail Steeple. Mary Martins. Steven S

The *S* of the last name was a slash across the page, as though she'd been startled, or perhaps something had jerked her wrist away midstroke. Luke read the note three times, the idea that Isla had once been a missing person turning his stomach all over again. He still couldn't process it, still couldn't bring himself to believe it was true. And who were these people Skye had noted? Isla's old friends? Folks related to Ruby Mae? Police officers who worked on the case? People to contact for help?

Luke's focus drifted to Skye once more. What the hell had happened here? Nothing was out of place inside the RV; it didn't appear as if she'd been attacked. It certainly wasn't suicide, and the pinpoints just shy of her eyes? They were far too accurate for self-mutilation. Too small to have been done by Skye's own hand.

Her eyes were empty.

Isla had gone for her mother's eyes only about an hour ago. Now someone or something else had finished the job.

She wasn't my daughter anymore.

He'd seen it with Eden only minutes before. That empty gaze. That weird smile.

He'd seen it with Isla when his wife had grabbed Skye without warning. He'd watched, too dumbstruck to react, gaping at a woman he didn't know. A stranger. An assailant. An invader. A shell.

She became no one. She became violent.

Except Isla hadn't done this to Skye. She'd either been in the house or with Luke after Skye had stumbled down their porch steps. For all Luke knew, Isla was still in his car, clutching her hands over her ears. And yet, somehow, he was certain Isla was part of all this. She was the key. It was the same feeling he'd had about Rowan. The boy could never be directly linked to any of the eerie events over the past few days, yet Luke was positive he was responsible.

"Oh *shit.*"

Rowan.

Shoving Skye's note into his pocket, he gave the woman a final look. "Thank you," he told her, because despite her own demise, she'd driven out to see him from who knew where and briefly helped him, at least with some answers. It was as if she knew she wouldn't see him again, scribbling that note.

Someone had obviously hurt her, but Luke didn't have time to play detective. Not yet. The number one priority was to find his girls. Before he lost his goddamn mind.

46

EDEN

Eden sat motionless on the couch, her eyes fixed on the blank television screen. She wasn't sure why Olive was so freaked out and staying close, or why Dad had given her a startled look before bounding off the front porch toward the road. Then again, she couldn't think straight about anything. Nausea was churning hard inside her. Vision was spotty, dotted with bright, glowing auras that always came before a blinding migraine. Cramps were starting to claw at the front of her hips. It was a deep, familiar ache; the inevitable onset of a heavy period even though her cycle wasn't supposed to start for another two weeks. That, and her ears were ringing like crazy. It reminded her of the time she had gone to a rave outside of Pueblo—risky, because her parents would have flipped had they found out. Eden had stood in front of the stacked speakers and let the bass rattle her from the inside out. Her ears had rung for three days after, but even then the sensation hadn't been as intense as it was now.

"Are you okay?" Olive asked quietly, pressed against her, their thighs touching. Eden nodded, but Olive didn't look convinced. Olive squinted at her, scowling as she spoke. "You look weird."

"Weird how?" Eden asked. She leaned forward, resting her elbows on her knees, her face hidden by her hands.

"Like, green weird. I don't know. You look sick," Olive concluded. "Puke sick. I'll get you some water."

It could have been the way the couch cushions shifted when Olive got up, or just a coincidence, but as soon as Olive rose, Eden experienced an intense, shooting pain in her abdomen like nothing she'd ever felt before. These were no regular menstrual cramps. It was a needling type of agony, hot like fire. It bent her in half, her knees suddenly grafted to her chest. As she squeezed her eyes shut against the pain, those auras were now fireworks, bursting into full bloom. She was unable to stop the whimper that escaped her lips.

"Eden . . . ?" Olive sank to her knees, her hands on Eden's shoulders. "Hey—what can I do?"

Eden couldn't catch her breath to speak. She was too busy bracing herself against the next wave of anguish. The sensation of her stomach corkscrewing within her body made her swoon with vertigo.

"Dad?! Mom?!"

Eden took in the sound of Olive's panic, and yet, even amid her misery, she managed to snort when her little sister called for their mother's help. Mom had gone upstairs after Dad had run across the front yard toward the highway. Her eyes had been glazed over. She hadn't said a word to either of the girls. Eden couldn't remember the last time Mom acted like a parent. She had gone through the motions: put food on the table, kept the house clean. But when it came to advice, to an actual emotional connection? Eden hadn't had a maternal figure for as long as she could remember. And she was certain it was worse for her sisters, them being younger. Yet Olive called for Mom anyway, simply because there was no one else, called out despite their mother not caring for the living, only pining for the dead, for the kids she'd lost. The children who existed were but a reminder of what she couldn't have. Walking memento mori. The living dead.

"I'm okay," Eden said weakly, lifting a hand to grab Olive's wrist. "It's just a cramp." But no way was it just that. It was a type of physical distress that would have warranted a visit to the emergency room. But there was no time for that, not with everything going on. Eden breathed through the torture, then tried to straighten her body. "Water, please," she said.

"Yeah, okay." A second later, Olive was running to the kitchen.

With Olive gone, Eden glanced up despite her hunch, and there they were: Mom and Rowan at the top of the stairs. Standing next to the balustrade, looking down through the foyer and into the living room. They stood side by side, hand in hand, staring dead on at Eden with blank faces and vacant eyes.

When Olive rushed back with water sloshing across her fingers, Eden whispered as she took the glass, "Look. Look up there."

Olive spun around, freezing in place when she saw them.

Dad chose right then to burst into the house, appearing as though he'd seen the devil himself. Olive turned to face their father, her expression so stern it could have been funny any other time.

"Dad . . ." she said, not asking why he'd taken so long or whether he'd found either Willow or Sophie. His expression gave promise that he'd certainly found something, but it wasn't their two little sisters. Not even close.

"I need you to stop and listen," Olive said. "Okay?"

Dad appeared both dazed and defeated, but he eventually nodded and croaked out an "okay."

"You ran off before I could explain," she told him. "I was out looking for Sophie. So was Willow. And then we realized we'd left Eden at the house alone with Rowan. When we got back, Eden was . . ." She glowered, either unwilling to describe it or unable to find the words.

Eden frowned as she stared down at her hands. She didn't remember much, only that one minute she was on the phone, calling friends and neighbors about Sophie, and then Rowan was at her elbow, so close it had made her reel away. After that, Dad was rushing up the steps and Olive was pale as a ghost with Eden's cell phone clasped tight in her hand.

"It's him, Dad" Olive said. "It has to be him."

Eden looked up at her sister, trying to decipher what exactly she meant. Surely she was talking about Rowan, but what about? *What* had to be him? She looked back to the top of the stairs.

Mom and Rowan were gone.

"You need to get Rowan out of here," Olive continued. "Dad, please. Get him *out*. Just take him back to that kids place and if things don't get better, then I'll admit that I'm wrong and you can go back and get him. But *please*," she implored, her expression strained, insistent. "Please, Dad. Take him away, *right now*, and let's see what happens, okay?"

She paused, clasped her hands together, suddenly looking so much like their mother it was disorienting.

"We have to get him out," Olive said. "I don't think Sophie or Willow will come back if he's still here. We have to get him *out*, Daddy, or we'll never see them again."

47

ISLA

Isla sat at the edge of the bed, her eyes fixed on the boy beside her. It was truly remarkable, being simultaneously repulsed by and drawn to someone, but that's exactly how it felt—a push and pull, an attraction paired with the desire to run the other way.

The longer she sat there, the more she realized this odd blend of emotions was nothing new. She'd spent most of her life both missing and resenting her mother, needing to be with her while never wanting to see her again. It felt a little bit like that now, with Rowan . . . because she knew there was something fundamentally wrong with him, yet she couldn't help but reach out to him like a moth flitting against a bulb.

Rowan sat motionless as he always did, watching her with eyes that appeared to have grown larger since he'd come to live with them. Though maybe that was Isla's own eyes playing tricks on her. She hadn't been sleeping, hadn't eaten in as long as she could remember, mimicking Rowan in what had struck her as a perpetual hunger strike. She perceived the past few days as having grown exponentially longer, giving Isla the sensation of being awake but not existing. There had been the constant undulation of shadows just out of sight, something always lingering, a sensation of being observed. And then there was what Luke had confirmed: the episode with her mother and Isla's sudden, brutal attack, the fact that Isla couldn't remember any of it. The trances were back. She was losing time, moving involuntarily through that lost space. Except it had gotten worse. Now she was trying to hurt people.

Isla could understand her subconscious urging her to lash out at Skye, but what if the next time it occurred, she attacked one of her children? What then?

And yet, the instant she considered confessing to Luke that, yes, she *was* having second thoughts about Rowan's presence, a deafening screech inside her head would derail her thoughts and render her helpless. She knew that noise. It had been the sound Rowan had made when Buster and Maize had rushed him that first day, a horrible, impossible racket. In those moments, when her thoughts shifted to the notion of letting Rowan go, the shriek inside her head became too much to bear; all she wanted was to make the pain stop, to save herself from the agony. Those fleeting impulses of getting rid of Rowan would vanish, and he'd be safe to stay another day.

Before that morning, Isla had kept close to him because she could feel Adam in his presence; she could sense Ruby Mae. Now Sophie was missing, and Isla was somehow certain Rowan knew where she was. She could feel it when she was next to him, could feel *her*, as though Sophie was communicating through Rowan's vibrations. It was the new reason as to why she was refusing to leave his side. Not only did Isla recover somewhat when she was close—the squeal inside her head silenced—but she could actually experience her youngest daughter reaching out like a phantom. It was the same kind of hippie bullshit she'd resented her mother for believing in: auras and chakras and crystals and third eyes. But here was Isla, deep in it herself. It was another anomaly of the mind. She knew all of it was ridiculous yet believed more than ever that it was true.

She held a hand up to Rowan, her palm facing out, and shut her eyes. The closer she moved in, the more she could sense a wavelength. It tickled her fingers and made the hairs on her arms stand up. She swore she could make out the tiniest spark of static. But mostly she could feel Ruby Mae's hand in her own as they stood in the prairie grass, gaping at the approaching storm. She could smell the oncoming rain, could feel the galvanized current as lightning bisected the sky. The closer the storm came, the more she wanted to run. She tugged at Ruby Mae's hand. *Ruby, let's go!* But Ruby didn't budge, her summer dress whipped at her calves as she peered upward, transfixed by a sky that was turning a frightening, inexplicable shade of red.

That's when Isla would pull out of the memory. An awfulness was coming, and Isla wanted nothing to do with that terrible thing. But now, with her hand reaching for Rowan and her eyes pinched tight, she swore she could hear Sophie yelling from within those same roiling clouds.

Mommy!

Sophie's voice went through her like a jolt.

Mommy, can you see it?!

"Sophie," Isla said with a gasp. "I'm here, baby. I'm here, where you should be."

I want to go home! I don't want to be here anymore!

"Where's here?" Isla asked the room, forcing her eyes to remain shut.

It was then, in Isla's mind's eye, that Ruby Mae turned to look at her. Her expression was blank. Her face a mask of dead-eyed detachment.

Here, she said, flat-voiced and robotic.

And then, as if on cue, the sky sparked like a firework. Veins of electric red sizzled through the air. Isla's attention bounded heavenward, her eyes like saucers as she finally saw what had been hiding in those clouds the entire time. And as Isla grappled with the reality of what she was looking at, Ruby Mae threw her head back. Her spine arched. Her arms and legs went limp. The toes of her sneakers only brushed the ground. Isla didn't move despite wanting to escape. She forced herself to stay on the prairie and watch Ruby Mae with horror-stricken awe. Because it was beyond unimaginable.

Ruby Mae was levitating.

Lifting off the ground.

Isla's eyes shot open. Her hand jerked back. She watched Rowan through heaving, gasping breaths. What the hell had she just seen? What had he just shown her? Ruby had vanished over twenty years ago. Meanwhile, Rowan was what, six, possibly seven years old? How could he—a child—exhibit what had happened to Ruby Mae if he hadn't been there, if he had yet to be born?

Because he's not a child, her inner voice concluded. *But you've always known that, haven't you? In your heart of hearts? You've always known he's the connection, Ruby Mae's answer, the "where."*

God's plan, remember? God is working through Rowan. Rowan is here because he's supposed to be.

But no. All of that was making infinitely less sense to her. She had clung to that possibility because it had been the only answer she could think of, the only feasible hypothesis. But now, gaping at the boy before her, Isla was no longer able to entertain her deranged theory. This wasn't about God. But she also refused to believe that what she'd seen in her head was what had really happened, because it was pure nonsense. Complete science fiction. The kind of thing her mom had whispered about before things had gone off the rails. *They're among us. They've always been. I've seen them.*

No.

"Bullshit," she said to herself, practically inaudible. "She's crazy. . . ."

But it was then, amid convincing herself of endless impossibilities, that she saw it in a solitary blink of Rowan's eyes.

Not one set of eyelids, but two.

Almost reptilian.

Isla cried out. She jumped off the bed and skittered back. Somehow she'd been blinded to how monstrous he truly was, but now the shock suddenly rendered her vision clear. All this time, she'd considered him to be helpless, abandoned, a sorry wretch of a being in need of saving. But now, standing across the room from him, she perceived nothing but horror.

Just what exactly had she invited into their home?

What in God's name had she done?

How could she have been so blind . . . ?

"Where's Sophie?!" she shrieked at him, a wave of vertigo rocking her off-balance. She reached out to grab the bedroom wall and knocked a few

framed baby photos askew. Ruby Mae's expressionless face flashed across the backs of her eyelids, and then Isla recalled it all so vividly it nearly made her sick.

The arching back. The way the tips of Ruby's sneakers just barely brushed across the grass. Isla running toward her cousin rather than away, screaming her name. *Ruby! Ruby!* And then the light. Blinding. Isla's body going numb. Not being able to scream anymore.

"Where's Sophie?" Isla asked, her voice a croak of terror. Rowan only watched her, his head canting in that unnerving way of his. Those massive eyes, so empty. His expression nothing but a mask of indifference. That apathy was what convinced Isla that her worst fear was upon her. Rowan didn't really care where Sophie was, how her disappearance made Isla seize with despair. It made no difference to him if Sophie *ever* came back, whether or not her vanishing would destroy their family. He didn't give a damn even if Isla lived, or if she died of an anguished, broken heart.

Rowan was indifferent because those things weren't any of his concern.

It was as if the artifice had suddenly been ripped away, a truth bomb dropping through heavy cloud cover, detonating across Isla's soul.

A voice from her past rang out inside her head.

You're pregnant.

Sixteen and hauled off to the emergency room, Isla had found herself standing in the back alley of a Safeway, caught in a downpour. And while she couldn't remember a damn thing about what had happened to her before the bag boy found her naked in the storm, every fiber of her being promised Isla that her condition was impossible. Because she'd been a virgin back then. She'd never been with a boy. And yet the doctor had insisted. The test didn't lie. And when Isla had arrived back home hours later—by way of the police because Skye had insisted she couldn't come—her mother had looked at her the way Isla imagined she was looking at Rowan now.

Who are you?

What are you?

Where the hell did you come from and what do you want?

She'd lost that first baby, same as the others. It was the first to have been torn from her womb. Vanished. Stolen.

"Oh my God," she whispered, her back pressed against the wall.

And hadn't she questioned the timing of a few of her pregnancies in the past? *So many times. So many . . .* She'd rolled her eyes before buying a test at the Walgreens in town less than a year before. *Honestly, what are the odds, Isla? You're hardly having sex.* And yet . . .

The blackouts. The missing time.

My babies . . .

Those two words tripped over themselves within her head.

My babies . . .

Something about that thought didn't feel right, like losing the meaning of a word after saying it one too many times.

My babies . . .

She'd been sixteen. Just a kid. Seeing the shadows for a while then, but afterward, oh, afterward . . .

"Oh my God."

Rowan had come into their lives only a handful of weeks ago; he'd come into their home three days before. But he'd been with Isla for decades, hadn't he? That's why, upon first seeing him beyond the garden fence, she had sworn she'd known him.

It was because he'd been with her all this time.

"What the hell are you?"

Voicing that question only made her that much more afraid. Because this creature, this *shadow* that had been plaguing her nearly all her life . . . this was the root of her misery, wasn't it? Rowan was the source of so much pain.

She twisted her body away from him, overwhelmed by the thought of it, disgusted by the idea, horrified that somehow, in some inconceivable way, she'd been taken and used. She'd been taken.

Taken.

Just like Ruby Mae.

She couldn't help herself. Despite her terror, a sob wrenched itself from deep within her. Because what the hell was he? And why was he doing this? After all these years, why now?

There was a bang against the door. Startled, Isla yelped when Luke threw it open and rushed inside. He stopped, gave Isla a wild-eyed sort of look, and then turned to Rowan. Upon Luke's abrupt arrival, Rowan jumped up with unearthly speed and was stood on top of the mattress, all angles and elbows, looking feral and on edge.

"*You!* You're coming with me," Luke snarled. He darted forward, grabbing Rowan by one of his scrawny, twisted arms.

"Stop, you're hurting him!" Isla heard herself protest, but the words were involuntary. The words weren't *hers.*

Rowan screeched in terror. He twisted against Luke's grasp, trying to get away. Luke didn't give him an inch. Isla threw herself over Rowan's crooked limbs. Turning to face her husband, she opened her mouth and roared, *"Get away from him!"*

Her voice. Not her words.

Luke stumbled back, his face a mask of stunned surprise.

"Don't you touch him," she sneered, feeling all control slip away. Inside, she was screaming for her husband to grab him, to force Rowan from her grasp. But outside, she'd turned into a seething atrocity—a woman choosing something she knew was malignant, vile, and dangerous over the sanctity of her own family.

Luke began to back out of the room. She wanted to call out *No! No, Luke! I'm sorry! Don't leave me here with him! Please, help me! Can't you see I don't want this?! I don't WANT this! I DON'T WANT—*

But Luke left as quickly as he came in, slamming the door behind him, and Isla found herself cradling the creature that left her aghast beneath the protective curve of her spine. This thing, the source of Sophie's disappearance. This thing, the reason Ruby Mae was gone. And her lost children, her babies . . .

No, she told herself. *They were never my babies. . . .*

Nothing had really been hers in decades, had it? Not since it had all started: the shadows, the fugues, the blood on the sheets.

Nothing really belonged to her.

Quite the opposite, actually.

All this time, she belonged to them.

48

LUKE

Luke glowered at the master bedroom door as Isla's face twisted into a fierce snarl inside his head, an image now burned there forever.

It had been stupid of him to think getting Rowan out of the house would be so easy. Clearly, grabbing him and shoving him in the car wasn't going to work. Besides, even if he could wrangle the kid into his sedan, there was no car seat in there, no way to keep him from crawling out the windows or, hell, into the front and clawing Luke's eyes out while he drove. And then there was that awful screech. Piercing. Deafening. Ear-shatteringly terrible when Buster and Maize had charged the sedan days before, Maize falling onto her side and convulsing, as though seized by Rowan's incomprehensible shriek. All it would take was for Rowan to open his mouth, and Luke would be veering the car off the road in no time, just like Isla.

Except his wife was protecting the kid now, so there was that. He didn't know why he'd expected any different. He supposed that somewhere, deep within his heart, with Sophie missing, Isla would have finally come to her senses. But no such luck. If Luke was to stand even the slightest chance of getting that kid gone, he needed Rowan away from Isla. But for that, he also needed help.

Moving toward the stairs, he shoved his hands into his pockets, his frustration mounting. He should have just told Isla to back the hell off. The girls had disappeared, for Christ's sake! Except Isla didn't know about Willow, did she? How in the hell was Luke supposed to tell her that not one but *two* of their children had vanished into thin air?

Just as he was about to pivot back toward the bedroom—too fucking bad, Rowan was coming with him whether she liked it or not—his fingers brushed something inside his right pocket: Skye's note.

All at once, he realized that Willow's disappearance wasn't all Isla wasn't aware of. Skye was still out there, the RV long past its preheating stage, baking in the late morning sun. Olive said Willow had gone out to the RV to look for Sophie, but she hadn't come back. Where the hell would she have gone, into the field across the street? She'd never wander off out there, unless . . .

She would . . . if she thought she'd seen Sophie.

He pinched the bridge of his nose, the entire scenario an impossible nightmare. Had it only been Sophie, he would have found himself paralyzed with panic. But because it was now *two* of his children, the unlikelihood of it all kept him moving. If he fell into stasis, his mind would seize this moment of inactivity, and that would be the end of him. He'd slip into madness.

This is all some weird fucked-up dream. That's the truth—if I'm lucky. But something told him that luck wouldn't be coming into play today.

Looking down to Skye's note, he read it a few times, searching for an answer in her careful script. *John Larusso. Abigail Steeple. Mary Martins. Steven S.* The names meant nothing to him, but if so, Skye wouldn't have bothered writing them down.

Luke rushed down the stairs and paused, seeing that Eden and Olive were waiting in the living room. Their faces said it all. They'd heard Isla's outburst. *Don't touch him!* They'd already put it together for themselves.

Olive watched him with such troubled worry, he could hardly stand to hold her gaze. No thirteen-year-old should have been capable of that sort of unease, especially his own little girl.

"It's okay," he told them both, hoping his response wouldn't distress them more. They wanted the truth, but he couldn't give that to them. At least not yet. *Soon,* he hoped. *I just need to do this one thing. . . .*

His fingers tightened around the note in his palm. He turned away from his daughters and pushed open the home office French doors. Circling around the front of Isla's modular IKEA desk, he popped open her laptop, smoothed out Skye's note atop the blotter, and ran Google Search.

The keys clacked in the quiet.

John Larusso

A host of links came back. There was a lawyer by that name out in Chicago. A fire chief in a small Wisconsin town. A guy named James Larusso in a California state prison. Another James had a posted obituary, dead eight years ago at the age of ninety-three. No . . . none of these felt relevant.

Luke thought for a few seconds, then said in a low voice, "How about . . ."

John Larusso missing

Boom. A missing person poster. John Larusso, age six, missing from Golden, Colorado. July 1995.

Luke's heart somersaulted inside his chest. Golden was a Denver suburb. That was *Isla's* suburb, the place she'd grown up until her childhood was cut short.

He typed *Abigail Steeple missing*

Another missing person poster, this time of a young girl smiling wide, pigtails framing her round face and gap-toothed grin. Abigail Steeple, age seven, missing from Golden, Colorado. July 1995.

With his heart thrumming in his ears, he entered another name: *Mary Martins missing*. This time, no poster, but there was a local newspaper article instead: "Golden Local Takes in Mystery Boy."

He clicked on the article link. The piece was short, straightforward, but enough to make Luke feel like the ground was shifting beneath him, that the earth was suddenly spinning faster than before:

Golden local Mary Martins has opened her home to Colorado's own Mystery Boy after finding him stranded on Chimney

Gulch Trail. Despite their best efforts, local authorities have not been able to pinpoint where they boy came from, nor are they able to locate any of his family. The child cannot offer any clues, as he is nonverbal. He has been in the care of Child Protective Services while awaiting a permanent home, which Mrs. Martins was able to provide after months of red tape. . . .

"What the *fuck*," Luke hissed through his teeth. He scrolled to the top of the page, searching for a publication date. When he found it, he leaned away from the laptop, repelled.

July 1995.

Luke's attention paused on Skye's note again. There was one more person on the list, this one without a last name. *Steven S.* He tried to search it anyway, typing in: *Steven S, missing Golden, July 1995*, and there it was: another poster.

Steven Schneider. Fifteen years old. Vanished without a trace.

Fifteen. This one not a little kid, but older, like Gus.

Who hadn't been seen since . . . when?

Yesterday.

Luke sat motionless for what seemed like minutes, his eyes fixed on the laptop screen, his heart suddenly still, a frenzied noose cinching around his neck. And as he sat there, two words ran through his brain like a broken record.

No way.

No way.

No way.

No way it was Gus.

No way that one missing kid had suddenly turned into three.

There was no way.

Right . . . ?

No fucking way.

Couldn't be. COULDN'T FUCKING *BE—*

Jerking into motion, he fumbled his phone out of his pocket and speed-dialed his eldest. It went straight to voicemail. Frantic, he searched his contacts, eventually finding Noah's name. He waited for Gus's best friend to pick up.

"Hello? Mr. Hansen?" Noah asked, clearly surprised to be receiving a call from a friend's father.

"Hey, Noah. Real quick—is Gus with you?" Luke asked. No time for bullshit.

"Um, no, he isn't," Noah said. "I heard about Sophie—"

"Do you know where he is?" Luke asked, cutting him off. "I need to know where he is, Noah. Like, right now. Don't you guys have some way to track each other?" He immediately hated himself for tuning his kids out whenever they talked. He swore he'd heard either Gus or Eden mention apps that let friends find one another. Some sort of geo locator or friend tracker. Jesus, who the hell knew? Noah, that was who. If Gus had something like that installed on his phone, Noah would no doubt be using it with him in tandem.

His eyes flicked up from Isla's desk. Olive was hovering near the door, listening, fingers tugging at her bottom lip.

"Uh, yeah, yeah we've got—" Noah paused on the line, as if thinking better of trying to explain how it all worked to a forty-something-year-old. "Hang on. Let me pull it up," he said, then: "Mr. Hansen, I only brought Sophie up because people are freaking out."

"Freaking out," Luke repeated. He looked away from Olive, waiting for Noah to explain what he meant.

"Yeah, um, there's a kid that's down the street. Aiden Parker. His parents came to our door like an hour ago. They can't find him."

Every muscle in Luke's body tensed.

"One of his friends, too, I guess? Except that kid lives, like, clear across town."

Luke blankly stared at the glow of Isla's laptop screen.

Can't be . . .

"Dad?" Olive said softly, unable to help but to interrupt. "What's wrong?"

"I don't know," Noah continued, sounding less like a teen and more like an adult confounded by the goings-on of his neighborhood, like a taxpaying citizen weirded out by the creepy new mail carrier or a grown man confused by the newspaper he'd never ordered and didn't pay for showing up on his doorstep every Sunday. "There's also some siblings over by where you are," Noah said. "I think they're just down the road a few miles from where you guys live."

Luke said nothing, trying to fend off a scream. He didn't look up at Olive, afraid of what she might see written across his face.

"It's just really weird," Noah continued. "Anyway, here, the app?"

"Th-the app," Luke stammered.

"Yeah, the tracking thing? It just pinged Gus ten minutes ago."

Luke pushed his fingers against his eyes. "Jesus, Noah, what does that mean?"

He could feel Olive creeping closer. Part of him was relieved he wasn't alone; the weight of the moment was too much to bear by himself. Another part of him wanted to wave his arm at her to get out, to go. He didn't want her hearing any of this, didn't want her seeing him on the verge of hysterics.

"It means the app found him ten minutes ago," Noah clarified. "It checks your location every so often and updates it automatically."

Luke let his hand drop to Isla's desktop. The slap of his palm on the surface paused Olive's approach.

"And where was he ten minutes ago?" he asked, his throat clicking dryly, snagging on his words.

"Um . . ." Noah hesitated. Luke could practically smell the kid's hesitation on the line.

"Noah, my God, *where*?!" Luke insisted, losing his patience.

"It says he's home, Mr. Hansen."

"Home."

"Yeah. Um . . . I don't know. It says he's been there for the past twenty-four hours. Last time he moved, he was at my house . . . but that was yesterday."

Yesterday—when August shoved his way out of Luke's car and marched down the street toward Noah's house. Yesterday—when Luke grilled him relentlessly about what the hell had transpired in the barn. Gus hadn't come home that night, and neither he nor Isla had given Eden's worries about that fact any thought. Luke had been distracted by Skye saying she was coming over. Isla had been too busy, obsessing over Rowan. It wasn't as though Gus hadn't spent the night at Noah's before, so Luke had just assumed his son was hanging out with his best friend. He certainly hadn't wanted to be at home, that was for damn sure. But now that he thought back, Gus hadn't called, hadn't texted, not a word, and that wasn't like him. Eden had told them that, but they hadn't fucking listened. Despite all his hard-headed eccentricities, Gus had always been sensible enough to let his parents know where he was.

Until last night.

"Mr. Hansen?"

"Dad . . . ?" Olive said, uncertain.

Luke shuddered at the sound of both his names.

"Is Gus all right?" Noah asked.

"Is everything okay?" Olive asked.

Luke couldn't bring himself to answer either question. Or think about it long enough to know where to even begin. So, rather than replying, Luke ended the call, cutting Noah off and dropping his cell phone onto the desktop.

His mind was reeling, his head spinning, his heart beating its way straight out of his chest.

Skye's final note.

The revelation of Isla vanishing along with Ruby Mae.

All those missing people in Golden at once nearly thirty years before.

The "mystery boy."

Suddenly shoving himself away from the desk, Luke prepared to rush across the room and bolt up the stairs. If this was happening—if it was really, *truly* happening—it meant Ruby Mae had to have gone missing as well in July 1995. He had to ask Isla, had to confirm—

But he stopped dead in his tracks, because there was something standing behind Olive, far past her in the depths of the living room. It was an impossibly tall silhouette, its thin limbs all harsh angles, its head massive atop its frame.

Luke's jaw went slack as the air in the room thickened.

Is that what I think it is?

He found himself struggling for breath, because it matched the folklore. All the stories he'd heard, all the movies he'd watched . . .

Olive confirmed his terrified expression when she croaked out a panicky "Daddy . . . ?"

But before he could think to grab Olive or to stumble backward in an instant of selfish self-preservation, the thing darted away, as though startled by having been seen. For the briefest blink of time, Luke was overwhelmed with relief, because at least it was gone. Then his relief shifted back to terror, because where had it gone *to*? Upstairs to Rowan and Isla? Somewhere downstairs, where Eden was?

"Where's your sister?" he asked Olive, his words breathless, tripping over themselves.

"She's in the living room. Dad," Olive said. "What is *going on*?"

"In the—"

. . . the living room . . .

There was another shift in atmosphere, perfectly timed, as if orchestrated to keep him rooted in place. It was like nothing Luke had ever experienced, electric and pulsating, as though the entire house had suddenly turned into a live wire. That sensation was accompanied by a smell—ozone, the scent just before a heavy rain. And somehow, he felt *lighter*.

Furrowing his brow, he stared down at his hands, holding them out palm down as if the gesture would somehow help him test the gravity that should have been there but now struck him as all wrong. Worse yet, when he looked up to meet Olive's eyes, he could see she was experiencing all the same things.

"What—" she whispered, her open-ended question hovering between them.

Luke said nothing as he watched loose strands of his daughter's long hair slowly rising, drifting on a breath of air the way a jellyfish's tentacles dance upon an ocean current. Olive's eyes jumped left, then right, though her head didn't move. She stood frozen in place, her mouth forming a distinct O of alarm.

He couldn't recall the last time he had been so helpless. It was as though his brain was misfiring. All he could do was stand there, statuesque, gaping, hesitant about his next move. Here it was, his most epic failure come to pass, his inability to protect his family, to be a good father, to be *anything* but that hapless husband he was so afraid of becoming. He reached out in an almost involuntary motion, his fingers spreading out toward Olive across the electric current that had enveloped them both. He wanted nothing more than to touch her, to remember how it had felt to hold her hand when she'd once been so small.

Something twisted inside his chest, and he was suddenly overwhelmed by it all. Finding Skye in her RV, the idea that Sophie and Willow might be gone, that August may have vanished right along with them. He heard Isla's scream inside his head for him to get away, to leave her with Rowan. At least, he *thought* it had been inside his head. But that illusion was shattered when Olive's body tensed, and she reflexively turned toward the sound.

"Mom?!"

Before Olive could look back to Luke for reassurance, they were both slapping their hands over their ears.

The house came alive.

Every piece of electronics that could make a sound began to beep and blip and blare a furious alarm. Every speaker blasted at full volume, each one playing something different—country music, talk radio, a car dealership commercial. There was a cacophony from Sophie's playroom, her toys screaming like a legion of demons trying to summon her back from wherever she'd gone. Luke's cell phone vibrated erratically atop Isla's desk, the screen flickering, the ring tones cycling through sounds he had never heard before. The ceiling over his head shivered with a deep, rumbling bass—Luke was standing directly beneath Gus's room. Above him, he could make out Johnny Cash singing about God cutting people down. But was this God? Was this the test Isla was so convinced of? No, this was something altogether different. This was that shadow figure. The boy upstairs. Isla, screaming. Isla, screaming. *Isla . . .*

. . . screaming overhead.

"Get your sister!" Luke yelled. *"Get out of the house, now!"*

Olive gasped, startled. She shook her head, frantic. *I'm not going outside without you,* her expression read. All at once, she wasn't the independent thirteen-year-old he knew. Instead, she was the little girl refusing to do something scary unless Mom or Dad held her hand.

"Olive!" he said, grabbing her by the shoulders, "You have to!"

"But *Mom!*" Olive shrieked, looking back up the stairs.

"I'm going to get Mom," he replied. "But you and Eden get out *now,* understand?!" When she didn't respond, he gave her shoulders a shake, stern enough to rattle her glasses. "Okay?!" He searched her face, imploring her to fall into the role she'd always taken on so naturally. Olive was the caretaker. This was her chance. He needed her help, needed to lean on her before he himself completely fell apart.

"Okay," she finally said. "Okay, Dad." Then she turned away from him and ran toward the living room.

Now alone and surrounded by ceaseless deafening chaos, Luke breathed deep, then released the air in a tortured yell. It wasn't lost on him that he couldn't hear it—nobody could—and in his own foreboding terror, nobody could spare him. This was all on Luke Hansen now.

Whatever would unfold when he got upstairs remained to be seen, but it was better than what would happen if he refused to go.

The same thing that had plagued other families back in 1995.

Just like Isla before he ever knew her, before she was in his life.

49

OLIVE

Despite the riotous noise and their mother's screams, Olive found Eden exactly where she'd left her: on the couch, looking straight ahead at the television screen. But rather than the screen being blank, it was now cycling through endless channels, the sound so loud Olive could feel it in her teeth. Seeing her sister motionless amid that insane nightmare forced Olive to pause despite the clamor. It was just like Mom zoning out, as if far away. Or Rowan standing dead-eyed and motionless, a thought that made her skin feel infested—ten thousand tiny spiders skittering up her spine. Her mind blipped to something dark and forbidden. Olive wondered what would happen if she simply left Eden, ran out of the house by herself. Would anyone stop her? Would anyone even know?

Still able to hear her heart whooshing in her ears despite the deafening roar of a house gone mad, Olive couldn't help but cast a glance to the front door.

Just go, a little voice told her. *Get out. Just like Dad said. There's already something wrong with Eden. Next, it'll be the same with* you.

Olive's chest tightened at the thought, but that was silly. It wasn't as though Eden had caught their mother's tendency to go catatonic and glassy-eyed. That sort of thing wasn't contagious, was it? If Olive reached out and grabbed Eden by the wrist, she wouldn't suddenly find *herself* trapped in a frozen stupor . . . would she?

Olive's bottom lip began to tremble, her moral obligation pulling her in one direction while fear pushed her in another. Was she supposed to do what Dad asked and be a good sister, or was this one of those moments she'd read about in so many books, where a survivor has to stand alone?

"Shit," she said beneath her breath.

"*Olive!*"

She jumped at her name, surprised that she could even hear it. Reeling around, she found her father staring at her from the bottom of the stairs. His expression was strained, stretched thin in a mask of his own terror. It was enough to assure her that she had to do what was right. Dad was about to climb those stairs and discover God only knew what; Olive could see it was the last thing he wanted to do. And so, if he was going to push through *his* fear, she had to push through hers, too.

Turning away from her dad, Olive took three brisk steps toward the couch, caught Eden by her forearm, and gave her a quick forward pull. Eden's eyes jumped to Olive's face.

"*Get up!*" Olive yelled, hoping her sister could hear her through the pandemonium. "*We have to get out!*"

Eden gave Olive a curious look, not understanding, but there wasn't time to spell it out. Olive gave her sister another yank away from the couch, then issued an imploring look. *Let's go!* She was about to pull on Eden's arm for a third time when the glassiness of Eden's eyes vanished, the muscles in her face rearranging themselves ever so slightly, as though relaxing for the first time in forever. All at once, Eden seemed like Eden again, returned from who knows where.

Then, a half second later, Eden tore her arm out of Olive's grip. Her hands pressed against her ears as Olive realized, *She couldn't hear it until now. She'd gone deaf, like Sophie. . . .*

The thought of it only made the urge to run away even greater, but she resisted the temptation and yelled again: "Dad said to get out of the house!"

Grabbing Eden's elbow, she forced her sister to her feet; but once Eden was up, it was as though instinct kicked in. Instead of Olive tugging her toward the front door, Eden was grabbing Olive's hand firmly in her own and bolting for the foyer.

Both girls flew down the front porch steps, but rather than heading toward the highway—which is where Olive wanted to go—Eden pulled her around the house and into the backyard.

"Why are we going back here?" Olive complained in gasping breaths, her words clipped and warbling as her feet pounded the wild grass beneath her sneakers. They should have been running toward the highway, toward where a motorist might have seen them and stopped to help.

Eden didn't reply. She only kept running. Eventually, their hands separated, and Eden began to run faster, her arms pumping in tandem with her legs, her long hair whipping behind her. Olive wanted to yell for her to stop, but she was too out of breath and too afraid to lose her, so she bore down and kept on racing, desperate to stay on her big sister's heels.

They ran across the full length of the backyard, past their mother's neglected garden and picket fence. The tree line wasn't far off, maybe a dozen yards or so—the beginning of those "dark woods" they'd spent so much time in with their father. Olive chased Eden into the trees and farther into the forest, dodging branches and jumping over fallen logs.

They went for what seemed like a mile, but Olive knew that wasn't possible. She would have never been able to keep up for that long. As a matter of fact, Olive began to trail behind, hardly able to catch her breath anymore. Eden continued to run, and for a horrifying instant Olive was certain she'd lose her in the woods. But the trees opened up, and Eden stopped when she reached a clearing.

Olive slowed to a standstill, her body folding forward with her hands pressed against her knees. The sun played off Eden's flaxen hair like white-hot fire. Meanwhile, Olive's chest burned enough to make her wheeze.

"God." Olive winced. "My lungs are gonna explode." She cringed against the pain, then shot an upward glance at her sister.

Eden was standing stock-still, her face turned up to the sky.

"What are you doing?" Olive asked, hardly able to speak without coming up for gulps of air.

"Do you see it?" Eden asked, her gaze fixed skyward.

"See what?" Olive asked, moving closer. She hummed against the sting of her chest but managed to straighten her back, then looked up. Squinting behind her glasses, she tried to make out what Eden was talking about.

"There," Eden said, pointing. "In the clouds."

Olive hadn't noticed the clouds until just then, because hadn't it been sunny just a second ago? When Willow had run out to the RV checking for Sophie, the sun had beaten down hard on her neck. The sunshine lit up Eden's hair a second before. And yet there was sudden darkness, like a murmuration of starlings blotting out the sun. The just-materialized clouds were so thick they looked dangerous. So dark they made Olive think of tornadoes. Of Kansas. Of Dorothy. Of Oz.

"Do you see it?" Eden asked again. As if responding to her, a bolt of lightning bisected the sky. Except . . .

This was a deep, ominous red. An artery brimming with blood.

" . . . what the . . . what was that?!" Olive gave her sister a startled look, all at once overwhelmed by a paralyzing sense of dread. "Eden, what *was* that?" she asked again, feeling herself falter. "Eden?!"

But Eden either wasn't listening or couldn't hear her again. She was nothing if not frozen in place, speaking more to herself now than to Olive.

"Do you see it?" she repeated. "Up there, look. Up there, do you see?"

Another thread of electric red darted across the sky. Then another, setting off an uncanny sort of static charge that made Olive's skin tingle and buzz.

"Look," Eden said, and so Olive did.

She looked. . . .

The light that struck her face was so bright it numbed her.

Olive's pupils constricted, and she could no longer see.

But she could hear, and next to her Eden exhaled a startled "oh!"

And then Eden was yelling her name. "Olive! Olive!" Each repetition growing fainter, as though Eden was fading somehow. "Olive!"

Distracted by her own name, she didn't even feel her feet leave the ground.

50

ISLA

When Luke shut the bedroom door, Isla coiled her body into Rowan. To an onlooker, it would have appeared to be the protective embrace of a doting mother, but that was the last thing Isla intended. If anything, her slouched back and hunched shoulders was a final line of defense, a desperate plea for her own safety. Though she knew it was futile.

They were coming for her. She understood that now. They'd been coming since she had been sixteen years old, maybe even before then. Now there was nothing left to do but wait.

She could feel it in the way the air sizzled with static, sparking against her skin. She could smell it. The room, which had been perfumed by faint traces of lilac candle and stale sheets, now reeked of a metallic sort of electricity. It was a scent she knew, triggering a memory that was only coming clearer as her time grew short.

Unbidden, Isla's recollection of Ruby Mae in the field behind her aunt's house was no longer unreliable. The girls had been out there together well into dusk, having wandered farther away from Aunt Sunny's place than they had ever gone before. Isla could still see the faint yellow glow of the kitchen window from where they were, but it was little more than a speck in the slow-growing dark. The sunset had been too spectacular to ignore that night, which was what had kept the girls out so late, so far away. Rather than its typical melon pinks and deep blues, the sky had shifted to a gorgeous shade of lavender—Ruby Mae's favorite color.

She had been mesmerized by its resplendence, her eyes fixed heavenward like a believer. But the deeper the lavender became, the more anxious Isla had been.

Ruby, it's getting late, she'd complained. *Ruby, we should head back.*

But by the time Isla had become insistent, Ruby Mae hadn't been able to hear her. Isla had grabbed for her hand, had tried to pull her in the opposite direction. Her efforts had been temporarily curtailed when she'd noticed the distant storm.

And now, with her body coiled around Rowan, Isla recalled a detail she'd forgotten, that she'd suppressed deep within her until that moment.

Finally, for the first time, she remembered her own panic. Her fear.

When young Isla's eyes had settled on that bank of clouds, dread had dropped her stomach like a lead balloon. As veins of red slithered outward across the sky, her instinct was to run like hell. But that would have meant leaving Ruby behind, and Isla couldn't bring herself to do it. Not her best friend, the closest person she'd ever have to a sister. So she'd grabbed her cousin's hand, pulling and screaming.

Ruby, please! Ruby, let's go!

But Ruby Mae was cemented in place, her eyes never leaving the horizon, her chin tipped upward, an eerie look of stunned awe stretched across her pretty face. Isla recalled only now that it hadn't been as much an expression of fascination as something akin to a trance. No matter how much Isla had yanked at her hand or cried for her to move her feet, Ruby Mae hadn't heard a single, pleading word.

Because she couldn't hear me, Isla suddenly realized. *Oh my God, SHE COULDN'T HEAR ME. . . .*

Sophie's strange, sudden affliction. Sophie hadn't been the first.

All of this has happened before. Oh dear God, please help me.

Except, now, her silent pleading struck her as senseless. It had been ridiculous to put this on God; this was all a test, remember? Rowan was supposed to be heaven-sent. A gift. An apology for all the children she had been so hopeful for but had never been able to hold. Now she knew better. A gift? *A nightmare come to life.* A test? *A curse.* An apology? As though the creature against her chest could even fathom what penance was.

All at once, Isla's nostrils flared against a peculiar scent. It was coming off Rowan, smelling slightly sulfuric and sharp, like a chemistry lab. That, and he was suddenly cold to the touch. Clammy. Like a dead baby in her arms.

The harder she focused, the more certain she was that she couldn't feel any body heat radiating off the thing in her embrace. What she *could* make out was a muffled clicking coming from deep within its throat; an insect-like chittering. It reminded her of cicadas. Of grasshoppers rubbing their legs against their wings in summer fields.

She'd heard that sound before, and not just once, but many times. It was a sound that, vibrating within the canals of her ears, made her heart jump into her mouth. All she wanted was to get as far away from that thing as she could, even if it meant crab-walking across the carpet to the farthest corner of the room, straight out the window, to a reward of a broken neck among the rhododendrons.

Her muscles tensed.

She tried to move.

It was then that she realized she couldn't.

Like Ruby Mae frozen on the prairie, Isla found herself struggling to free herself from her huddle. She was a home, and within her, that creature stirred. She could feel it moving beneath her, her stomach lurching with the memory of her babies rolling and kicking and growing within the hollow of her womb.

That core memory of motherhood thrust her back into that awful, breathless understanding. *My babies.* The ones that had been there one second but were missing the next. Every time she'd miscarried, Luke would report fugue after fugue. He'd take on a look of perpetual anxiety, of a dread he couldn't shake. Isla, on the other hand, remembered nothing. And then she'd go to bed. She'd smell blood. She'd see light. She'd hear . . .

The noise coming from "Rowan" ceased, as though he somehow knew he'd triggered a dark memory, a dangerous awareness. It was then,

in that brief lapse of the creature's concentration, that Isla finally regained control.

She jerked away from it with a scream.

Scrambling backward, she pushed it away as the thing uncoiled itself
from its ball-like posture. It looked at her, glowering with a face trans-
formed. While Rowan had always looked bizarre, the thing that glared
at her now wasn't human. It was as though, while curled over him in
that protective embrace, she'd incubated a metamorphosis. The creature
that emerged from such a nurturing chrysalis was nothing short of monstrous. Its face was skeletal, its cheekbones sharp and chin elongated to a
point. The nose was gone, replaced by two slanted, oblong holes. Those
holes mimicked the shape and angle of the monster's eyes, so massive
now they reminded her of a praying mantis's rawboned face. The thing
that used to be Rowan blinked at her as she choked for breath, a transparent scrim sliding vertically across both its eyes. Then the monster stood
to its full height. Seven feet? It had to be, at least. It was startlingly thin,
its joints grossly misshapen, arms and legs splaying out in an insect-like
stance. Seeing it fully now, she found herself drowning in an overwhelming sense of awareness. It wasn't just that it wasn't human—it's that it
wasn't friendly.

This was not a good-natured visit.

This was a hostile takeover.

A gasp filled her lungs, ready to explode out of her diaphragm in an
earsplitting wail. *Perhaps this is all just a terrible dream. Maybe I'm back
at the hospital. Maybe I've finally fallen too far from reality.* But before
she could spend another second convincing herself that none of this was
truly happening, that she had simply lost her mind, those thoughts were
stolen. An eruption of noise so all-encompassing had her instinctively
rocking forward, the heels of her hands pressed hard against her ears.
Isla could feel the cacophony within her, as though some piece of her
was vibrating in tune with the sound. With her thoughts scrambled, she
fought through the fog, reminding herself that she had to move, had to
get out of that room. She had to find her family and get out of the house.

The invasive thought drifted across the shell of her ear: *And go where? And do what?*

Where could she go where they wouldn't find her? They'd been with her for her entire life. She'd be a fool to imagine they'd simply leave her alone after all this time.

She suddenly looked up, a mother's instinct promising her that if she fought, if she didn't let them take her, they'd settle for her children instead. And while she armed herself with a newfound bravery, she couldn't help but shriek when, rather than only seeing "Rowan," she found herself face-to-face with four creatures instead of one. They stood in a loose sort of line, blocking her exit, all of them swaying just slightly, their nostrils flaring at the sound of her cry.

No, this wasn't her mind playing tricks on her.

She could smell them. She could *hear* them.

Run! the voice inside her demanded. *Don't just sit there—get the hell out!* But by the time her brain sent her feet the signal to move, it was too late.

Isla gaped at her useless legs, wide-eyed and disbelieving. An instant later, her arms were as heavy as stone at her sides. Not having anyplace else to look but back to the living terror that stood before her, her eyes flicked upward in a panic. It was then that those things descended upon her, their motions eerily smooth and calculated. She tried to shout, but it was no use. She couldn't breathe, choking on an invisible bite of food. Had she been able to lift her arms, her hands would have been clawing at her neck.

One of the creatures stepped in front of the others, leaning in until it was close enough for Isla to catch her own terrified reflection in the convex lenses of its inhuman eyes. It lifted a hand, its fingers gruesomely long, thin as a spider's legs. It pointed a single digit at Isla as if to acknowledge her. *You,* the action said. *We know you. We always have.* And whether it was Isla's hysteria forcing hallucinations upon her, or whether she really was seeing it, the pointing digit appeared to elongate toward her—lengthening, sharpening into a vicious, unforgiving point.

Paralyzed, all she could do was watch as the needle-like appendage aimed for the tear duct of her right eye. She couldn't move, couldn't scream, couldn't even look away as she heard a pop inside her head, certain that the organic probe had punctured through some soft oculus membrane. She was fully aware when her body began to convulse. She could feel her hands and feet banging against the bedroom floor. She even understood that the light blooming behind her open eyes wasn't the pathway to heaven, but another piece of critical memory being restored.

Harsh white light.

Faint shadows along the fringes.

Cold metal at her back. A sensation of nakedness, of paralysis, same as she had now.

And beneath the shadows and light, she could hear a faint but distinct clicking sound. It was them. They were communicating. Though she couldn't make out whether it was part of her memory, or whether they were chittering as her convulsions began to still, as the bright light began to fade and her lungs began to collapse, as her brain began to die.

The room grew dark, but Ruby Mae's comforting smile appeared as a blur against the growing blackness. In Isla's mind, Ruby reached for her hand, looked up to the sky, and posed the question Isla had replayed inside her head a hundred thousand times throughout her life.

There's something up there. Do you see it?

But rather than seeing something in the sky, Isla saw something else.

As if her brain was sending out a final spark, she remembered herself and Ruby Mae only days before her cousin had disappeared. They were both giggling at the local art market in downtown Golden, Isla holding a locket in the palm of her hand. A woman smiled at her, a name screenprinted across her forest-green T-shirt: MARY MARTINS TRINKETS.

Isla's focus drifted over the woman's shoulder as Mary described how she'd made the piece in her home studio. And as Mary spoke, Isla noticed a small, uncanny boy standing a few yards shy of the market tent. It was a peculiar boy, one with hair as red as flame. That had been so long ago, the summer of '95.

Isla remembered, *finally* understanding why Rowan had seemed so familiar, why he had given her a perpetual sense of déjà vu.

Because he *was* familiar. She'd seen him before.

He'd been there at the beginning.

And now, here he was, at the very end.

51

LUKE

Luke expected resistance. So when the master bedroom door swung open freely, he stumbled headlong into the room. He was startled by the lack of opposition, startled by the emptiness of the bedroom before him. But what exactly was it that he thought he'd see? Shadow people? Rowan crawling up the walls like something out of *The Exorcist*? Perhaps the kid would be perched atop Isla's chest while she was splayed out across the bed, unresponsive—like something out of a gothic horror painting hanging on a wall of the Louvre.

Luke didn't find any of that here. As a matter of fact, for a flash of a second he was convinced Isla had gathered Rowan up and left the house while Luke had been googling the names from Skye's note. No one would have heard her, that's for damn sure. The house was still shuddering with noise, its walls having come alive. For a few heart-sickening seconds, he wondered how he would explain to his children that their mother had abandoned them in favor of a young stranger. And yet, in that very same instance, he wondered if Isla leaving would really be that awful of a thing. The tension between them, the way she'd started to ignore the kids, and now this shit with Rowan . . . it had gotten to be too much. So perhaps her walking into the trees, hand in hand with a demon from the woods, would bring the family some sort of furtive relief. But that was the thing about demons, wasn't it? Free will didn't play into it. Demons took what demons wanted.

But he's not a fucking demon, Luke reminded himself. *And your children are missing.*

His heart tripped over *that* grim reminder, his windpipe suddenly tight with newfound alarm. Because what the hell was he supposed to do if he found Isla missing as well?

He shoved his hands into his hair, his breath hitching before he called out, "Isla?!" Not that she'd be able to hear him over the fucking wail of this lunatic asylum. He could hardly hear himself.

His focus drifted to the bathroom, wanting to believe that it was the only place she could be. The door was ajar, and they had a large walk-in closet in there. She'd hidden there before after one of her miscarriages, crying among his button-down shirts. The noise had likely pushed her back into the same place, and she was waiting for Luke to come find her. The possibility forced him forward, his steps across the carpet slow but deliberate.

Slow, until they came to a full stop.

Because there, just beyond the corner of the bed, was one of Isla's bare feet. He hadn't been able to see it before, but it was clear as day now. Motionless. Turned inward.

Part of his brain screamed to not take another step.

You don't want to see that.

You don't.

You don't.

You don't.

But the frenzied, irrational side won out. It threw him into a forward motion until shock gave him a stern backward shove. Luke stumbled a few steps, his eyes wide at what he found before him.

Isla was slumped against the wall between the nightstand and bed. The legs of her linen lounge pants were shoved up to her knees, as though she'd kicked them up during a struggle. Luke gasped and looked away from her face, which was frozen in what could only be seen as a terrified shriek. A moment later, he forced himself to look back to her. God, her eyes. They were wide open. And the whites? Tinged with blood.

Something tightened within the cage of his chest, a hydraulic press crushing his heart, draining it of every drop of precious blood. The room spun once, twice, then came to a dead stop as if to let Luke get a good long look at his wife.

No, he thought. *Bullshit. This isn't real!* After all, the longer he stared at her, the more he was convinced that her chest was rising and falling, an almost imperceptible motion, but he could *see it*.

She's alive, he told himself. *None of this is real. She's alive. She's screwing with me.*

But then he remembered Skye, dead in her RV.

Isla's eyes. They were the same.

Fuck. They were the same.

Luke started to rush toward her, then stopped himself. That awful expression on her face kept him at a distance. Her twisted grimace was a dark promise that something wicked had been here, that something wicked might still be lurking.

Backing away, he thought of his kids. His heart was breaking into a million pieces, but there wasn't time for a breakdown. Not now.

But Isla . . .

He played this awful game of tug-of-war for a good minute, inching toward his wife, turning away and looking to the door, sometimes allowing his eyes to dart around the room, afraid of what he might see. If someone—something—wanted to sneak up on him, he'd be helpless to stop it.

His mind was spiraling.

The house continued to roar.

He was on the verge of screaming.

And then, all at once, the overwhelming noise just . . . stopped.

Click.

Luke froze, the sudden silence so all-encompassing it left him disoriented. His ears whooshed against the quiet, unhappy with the abrupt lack of feedback. He looked back to Isla, and for a breath of an instant he was positive he'd see her get up and laugh—*Got you.* He studied her with bated breath, waiting, praying to be the butt of an awful joke. But she didn't move. Meanwhile, the silence was an ominous hush, one heavy with the promise of something bad if he didn't leave.

He gave Isla a final pleading look.

Please get up, hon.

But of course she didn't. Luke cringed as he turned away from her, physical pain accompanying a move that struck him as a betrayal.

As he fled the bedroom, he promised her he'd be back.

I'll come and get you. I won't forget you're here. Hang on, Isla.

He just had to find Sophie. And Willow. And August. Jesus, *August.*

He trusted that both Olive and Eden had gotten out of the house, understood that neither Sophie nor Willow were on the property, so looking again would only be a waste of time. But August. Where the *fuck* was August? Luke didn't know where the hell to focus. His mind was being pulled in all directions.

Find Gus, he decided. *Find Gus, then find the girls.*

Stumbling down the stairs and out the front door, he reached into his pocket for his phone, but it wasn't there. He stopped, tried to remember where he'd left it. He'd had it when using the laptop. Before he could trip down the front porch steps, he ran back inside and into the home office, snatched his cell off Isla's desk, and finally ran out to his car.

Once inside the Honda, he tried to bring up Gus's number, but his phone was fried from the demented event inside the house, having lit up, vibrated, played through dozens of ringtones.

"Shit," he hissed, then threw the phone onto the passenger's seat. He dug his car key out of his pocket and shoved it into the ignition.

Luke's heart stuttered to a standstill.

The car refused to start.

He tried again.

Nothing.

"Oh no, oh no, fuck me, you've got to be fucking *kidding me!*" he roared. The ridiculousness of the situation wasn't lost on him. This was a cheap shot, a way for the bad guy to get the good guy in the end.

This?! Of all things, this is how I'm going to die?!

Except it made sense, didn't it? He had felt the static, had smelled the electric current in the air. He'd gaped as Olive's hair had stood on end, as though she'd put her hands on top of an electrostatic plasma ball. All the electronics had gone haywire, and what was a modern car if not a veritable robot? But Luke's car wasn't quite as new as it should have been. He had a soft spot for his old Honda, technology be damned.

He tried again.

Come on, baby, come on. . . .

Once more—still no dice.

Exhaling a frustrated, desperate sigh, he shut his eyes tight. Last shot. "Come on!" he growled. "Come on, you piece of *shit!*"

He cranked the ignition.

The starter clicked.

The engine caught.

Luke laughed, the catastrophe of it all briefly forgotten in a surge of triumph. *Fuck you!* he wanted to scream out, though he didn't know at who. The Honda was proof that not all was lost. Even now there was still hope, whether he understood what was happening or not.

Swinging the sedan around, he was jolted back to reality by the sight of Isla's damaged van. He was mentally transported to the side of the road, recalling how Isla had looked at him when he crawled into the car seat next to her. She'd been confused. Afraid. His heart lurched again, threatening to spill over with grief.

He felt the house drawing him in. *Go back. Figure out how to prevent all this.* He wanted to return to the morning Isla had found Rowan standing just beyond the garden. Perhaps, if he knew then what he knew now, he would rather have gouged out his wife's eyes than allowed her to have ever seen him.

You mean same as how she tried to blind her own mother?

He shook away the thought. Those were all wishes of the past. Impossibilities. He had to concentrate on what he could do now, in the present. He had to find his kids.

Luke didn't know where he was going, only that he had to go somewhere. He'd searched for Sophie. He'd searched for Willow. He knew

Olive and Eden were safe together, somewhere outside. Gus. That's who was calling to him now.

Pointing the car toward town, Luke began to drive to Noah's place. He'd check there first. If he didn't find Gus, it was time to go to the police. Except how the hell was he supposed to explain everything that had happened? Luke's kids were missing. His wife and mother-in-law were dead. Luke, on the other hand, was fine. Unscathed. A-okay, how about that? Was he going to tell them that their forty-pound foster kid was to blame? The one who didn't speak and could hardly walk on his own?

And where is your foster son now, Mr. Hansen?

Or maybe he'd let them know he saw a shadow figure in his house right before the place had gone berserk. That would definitely convince them of his innocence, of his sanity, of everything—

"*Shit,*" he said, his hands gripping the wheel hard enough to make his fingers hurt. "Oh shit. Oh God. Oh *fuck.*" He couldn't breathe past that newfound spike of anxiety but stepped on the gas anyway.

And what about Eden's beloved podcasts? How many of those had he heard? At least half a dozen. And what did those all have in common, what was the binding thread?

The husband always did it.

The speedometer needle climbed from forty to fifty, from fifty-five to seventy.

Luke couldn't remember ever going down that highway faster than eighty, but the Honda now crossed that mark without a flinch, climbing to ninety before leveling off.

His mind reeled.

I'll be arrested.

If his kids were out there—

They'll think I'm a murderer.

There was no way he could prove his innocence.

It's over.

No way he could.

Over.

None.

He wouldn't have noticed the approaching storm had it not been for the red streak that flashed across the sky. It was bizarre enough to momentarily startle him out of his dismay. He blinked hard, as if to clear his vision. Beyond a missing person billboard, another flash of red bisected the cloud bank.

"What the—"

He leaned forward, his chest flush against the steering wheel as he tried to get a better view.

Lights. There were *lights* up there, arranged in concentric circles. Hovering, unmoving, pulsing like a heartbeat.

All at once, he realized he was transfixed. Realized that he couldn't look away.

His foot was still on the gas.

Had he been transported out of the car to take in the scene, Luke would have witnessed the Honda hauling ass down a lonely road. No obstructions. Nothing on the asphalt. No animals waiting in the wings to jump out at the wrong time. No fresh roadkill being picked apart by a vulture's wake. Nothing but a straight line of track that should have taken him toward what felt like inevitable fate.

But less than a mile from the farmhouse, the front of the car struck something invisible. The shock wave was instantaneous. It traveled from the front bumper down the hood of the vehicle and rippled the metal of the car, as though turning it to silk. Pistons still firing at full capacity, the Honda's engine exploded through the back of the compartment, severing both of Luke's legs at the knees. He didn't feel it. It was too quick. He was too distracted by the sensation of lifting, of turning, of flying. Too startled by the airbag punching him hard in the chest, a choking, sulfuric stink suddenly stopping up his throat.

He watched the sky turn from the gray of storm clouds to the gray of concrete. Performing a graceful pirouette, the car remained airborne for what seemed like an eternity, then skidded to a stop—the sound akin to a shrill, mechanical scream, one rather close to what had come out of Rowan the first afternoon they'd brought him home.

Finally at a standstill, Luke dangled limply, upside down, held aloft by the seat belt he always wore. He stared through an exploded window toward the horizon, where storm clouds continued to snarl, where red lightning flashed in continuous warning.

He didn't know what dying felt like, only that what he was experiencing had to be the end. He waited for it to come while involuntary groans escaped him. A river of blood was pouring from where his legs had once been, sending a torrential cascade onto the roof beneath his head, the red spreading like a sunset above him, like a crimson sky.

He waited to gain some clarity, some magic revelation that would answer every question he'd had for the past few days, months, years: the entire time he'd suspected that something he could never understand had been plaguing his wife. It was then, as if able to discern his final wish, that a throaty click sounded from beyond the car.

Luke didn't need to see him to know it was Rowan. And how had all this transpired? How the hell had an outlandish, orphaned kid from the woods been able to cause all this chaos? How had any of it come to be?

His thoughts began to run together as the sky started to darken, his vision beginning to blur. But just before it all faded to black, a silhouette stepped into view. Towering over him, it extended its arms, the thing reaching toward him, Luke's mouth gaping, his nearly blind eyes wider than the world. And finally, Luke knew.

However impossible. Improbable. Illogical. In those last few seconds, he finally knew.

EPILOGUE

THREE DAYS LATER

EDEN

It was raining when Eden opened her eyes and peered past the hair plastered to her face.

There was no moonlight.

No lightning.

No sound save for the roar of a mid-summer downpour, the rain coming in sheets.

Eden stumbled to her feet. She pushed away from a cottonwood tree, her legs weak beneath her. They felt like foreign objects attached to her body, as though the muscles had fallen asleep and were failing to wake. She paused at a picnic table, pressing palms flat against the wood. It was only when she noticed the ice cream stand at the far end of the park that she realized where she was.

The park looked different in the darkness.

She was in town, but how she'd arrived there was anyone's guess.

Squinting into the torrent, she lifted a hand to wipe at her face, but it was no use. The deluge was unrelenting, as though attempting to drown her, trying to save her from some unforeseen circumstance. Or even better, shielding her from being able to see with any sense of clarity at all. The world looked coated in TV static, a movie deteriorating on an old VHS tape.

Her head hurt, and even though the rain thundered against every surface, she could still hear the high-pitched whine deep within her ear canal. It made the inside of her skull itch, as if something had crawled inside her head and made a home. She tugged at her right earlobe as she slunk away from the table, her legs as wobbly as a colt's.

Why am I here? She mouthed the words silently as she moved. *Why am I here?*

Who had brought her to the park, and why would they have left her?

How long had she been there, and why did she feel as though she hadn't walked for days?

Halfway to the ice cream stand, she had to stop. Crouching in the flooded grass, she found herself staring at her bare feet. A second later she realized her legs were just as naked. Up, up, up crawled her awareness until it settled on her waist, her midriff, her chest.

Her arms spasmed, pretzeling across her body. It was a feeble attempt to shield herself from no one and everyone all at once. A tremor racked her from the inside out, a sudden rush of cold, an overwhelming sense of alarm. She was alone out here, naked in the rain, but someone was watching. Someone *had* to be watching, because how else had she gotten out here? Someone had left her. Or maybe . . .

She thought of her mother, recalled the way her face had looked over the past few days. That vacant stare. That empty expression. There'd always been something wrong with Mom, of that Eden was sure. It had become beyond apparent over the past few weeks, painfully obvious over the past few days.

And now, deep within her gut, Eden was certain that fractured mental state wasn't something unique only to Mom . . . at least not anymore. Out in the park in the dead of night, drenched, with no clue as to how she'd gotten here, Eden knew there was something wrong with her, too. Because why didn't she remember? How could she *not* remember? How the hell had she gotten here? What the fuck was going on?

Looking up from the sodden grass beneath her, her attention settled on the billboard across the street. It was dark, unlit, half-obscured by trees. Practically forgotten.

HAVE YOU SEEN ME?

Sophie. Oh God.

Had they found her yet?

She had to get home.

Eden tried to straighten, but her back ached. Like her legs, the vertebrae of her spine felt like they had fused together, as though she hadn't moved in a week. She hobbled a few yards to the right, every joint in her body screaming against the exertion, but she made it to a trash can despite the pain. She pulled off the plastic push-door top and tossed the lid aside. The bag was so heavy—full of sticky debris, used napkins and ice cream cups. Everything was wet. Her fingers, the bag, all of it slick with rain. She couldn't get a good grip. Twisting the plastic around her palm, she braced herself against the concrete trash receptacle, and a small scream of exertion burst from between her lips as she gave the bag a sturdy pull. It suddenly came free, as though having been caught on something. Eden stumbled backward, her bare feet skidding on the sopping grass. She fell hard, crying out as a fresh bolt of pain bloomed within her abdomen the instant she hit the ground.

That zing of misery made her stomach lurch. It was all she needed—an affirmation of her deepest fear. Someone had left her naked in the park, and whoever that someone was had done whatever they had wanted.

The irony wasn't lost on her.

All those podcasts. The hundreds if not thousands of hours she'd spent eavesdropping on other people's tragedies, all in the name of entertainment. Her fingers skimmed her stomach, her palm pressing against the small hollow she knew existed within her. *Oh God.* No truer a crime. An atom bomb made up of all the dark shit Eden loved, now ironically dropped into her own once comfortable reality. *Boom.*

She shielded her eyes from the pelting downpour, the torrent continuing without pause. It was ice-cold, an odd rain for summer. She turned her focus to the half-torn garbage bag next to her, grabbed it by the bottom corners, and spread the contents across the grass. Paper napkins melted into the surge. A few ice cream bowls floated down the slight slope of the lawn, then paused to bob in a rainwater lake. She tore a hole in the bottom of the bag, then tore two more on each side before wrinkling her nose in disgust. It smelled bad, but she had no choice. Pulling the fouled plastic over her head, she slipped her arms through the holes she'd made. The bag only reached a quarter of the way down her thighs, but it was a hell of a lot better than nothing. At least now, when she found help, they'd stop to listen rather than averting their eyes.

That was, if she could make it out of the park at all.

Eden stood again, her legs slightly more stable. But now the pain in her abdomen bloomed fast and hot, enough to double her over as soon as she got to her feet. She cried out but could hardly hear herself over the squall, over the incessant buzzing in her ears.

"Hello?!" she shouted into the night. Perhaps there was someone down the street, sitting in their car, parked along the curb, waiting out the rain.

Maybe it's the same person who left me here in the first place. Maybe they're coming back for me. Maybe they're not done.

She got to her feet again, wincing against the ache within her but refusing to let it win. She had to get home, back to her family. She needed to find out what had happened to Sophie, needed to talk to Gus.

God, let him be back by now.

Something about this whole situation convinced her that, somehow, for some inexplicable reason, he of all people would understand what had gone on here; because something had happened to him, too, out there in the barn.

This was that same something, wasn't it?

Wasn't it?

Eden shuddered at the memory of her brother facing the corner, whimpered against the recollection of his stricken face.

She began to limp, her arms crisscrossed tight across her stomach, the trash bag crinkling with each step. The rain against the plastic was twice as loud as it should have been, but she ignored it. She just had to get to the road; then she'd find some help. If she got to the street, someone would eventually drive by. They'd stop. They'd take her to the hospital. The people there would call her parents. They'd make sure she was fine.

Because I am fine. I am.

Everything would be okay.

The world was cruel, but kindness could save it.

And yet that ominous thought remained rooted at the base of her skull.

Maybe they're coming back for me.

All at once, that thought anchored her in place as she looked forward, her eyes wide and focused on a copse of cottonwood trees. It was hard to see through the torrent. The whole world appeared like a fuzzy photograph, but she could see them regardless.

There was someone hiding behind a gnarled tree trunk. Watching her.

Because they're not done.

Her body begged for her to run in the opposite direction, to sprint as far and fast as she could. *Run!* she thought, the same way she had with Olive, their hair whipping behind them as they'd bolted away from the house and into the woods.

Yet Eden stood motionless, her heart hammering with a sick, nauseating intensity against the curve of her ribs.

The figure began to move, not into hiding, but out in the open, and the more it revealed itself, the more a scream clamored up her windpipe. But no sound came.

Even when the figure stepped fully into view—bone thin and inhumanly tall, its arms and legs held at peculiar, sharp angles—no sound escaped her.

She willed herself to make a noise, *any* noise. She begged herself to find strength.

Move your feet! You have to go!

But she did nothing but stand there, her face a mask of horrified disbelief. Because the thing was moving toward her, slinking through the cloudburst. Its movements simultaneously smooth and awkward, and the closer it approached, the weaker Eden became.

Her legs buckled.

Her knees gave out.

She crumpled into the puddle beneath her.

The closer it came, the louder her ears buzzed.

The closer it came, the more she could feel an undeniable sensation within her gut.

Something was inside her, slowly twisting like a worm.

The movement within her took her breath away. She curled into herself, writhing against the grass. With her face turned and her eyes diverted, she waited for whatever that thing was to grab her, to tear her limb from limb.

But instead, the rain stopped.

Click.

Like a shutoff valve had been flipped.

She breathed hard into the grass, gathering the courage to peek out from beneath her arm. When she finally looked, Eden found herself alone, yet not alone at all.

Rolling onto her back, she blinked up at the sky. Concentric circles of lights hung overhead. She'd seen them before but just couldn't remember where.

And it was then, with the lights' sudden pulsing, that the thing inside her began to writhe.

Squirming.

As if excited to go home.

ABOUT THE AUTHOR

Ania Ahlborn is the bestselling author of the horror works *Brother, The Devil Crept In, Within These Walls, The Bird Eater, The Shuddering, The Neighbors, Seed, If You See Her, Good and Joyful Things*, the novella collection *Apart in the Dark*, the thriller *Dark Across the Bay*, and the novellas *The Pretty Ones, I Call Upon Thee*, and *Palmetto*. Born in Ciechanow, Poland, she now lives with her family in North Carolina. Visit her at AniaAhlborn.com or follow the author on Facebook and Instagram.